City of Darkness

City of Mystery, Book 1

By Kim Wright

To the Brinker's Writing Group:
Ed, Paul, Shontelle, Laura, Leigh, Mark, and Alan.
You read every line, every paragraph, every draft.

PROLOGUE
August 7, 1888
2:25 AM

She saw the coins first. She always did. A palm filled with silver and copper, extended from the shadows, held by a man dressed in dark broadcloth. A man whose hands were clean.

This was a lucky turn, for Martha had not secured a single gentleman all evening. She'd been roaming the pale gray streets of Whitechapel since ten, looking for a last-minute sailor – even a drunken or aged one, perhaps, for who could afford to be choosy with the hour so late and the stomach so empty? She'd smiled hopefully at each man she'd passed, and now, just as she'd been on the verge of turning back, her persistence had finally been rewarded.

She took the arm he offered her with dignity, as if she were being led to the center of a ballroom. Martha suggested the lodgings she shared with a half-dozen other girls, for they weren't far away, but the stranger declined, steering her instead toward one of the innumerable alleys which flanked the waterfront. A gentleman, yes, but apparently a gentleman in a hurry. The men who wore black broadcloth were often in a hurry, Martha had noticed. They never seemed to need much preamble, rarely expected her to open the front of her dress, didn't request a name or a kiss. All the better. She'd be at the pub within minutes, money in hand.

The man breathed something into her ear and extended an arm around her waist. Liked taking it from the back, he did, as was often the case with men who could afford wives and carriages and Mayfair homes and perhaps even a bit of a conscience, the greatest middle-class luxury of all. This was doubtless why they turned the faces of the whores away from their own, why they arched their backs and concluded the matter so fast. Martha didn't mind. She'd always figured that whatever a gentleman pictured when he closed his eyes was no business of hers. She let the man turn her. She pressed both hands against the chipped brick wall and bent forward obligingly, giving him access to what he'd paid for, her mind on the coins and what they would buy. Beer and bread and stew, enough to fill her and perhaps a friend, because Martha Tabram was a generous sort, never able to enjoy her own supper while another went hungry, quick enough to give an extra twist or a moan if the man had clearly gone lacking for a while. We're all in this dark world together, she figured. None of us saints.

But the man did not lift her skirts. Instead, he murmured some words that Martha didn't quite catch, and then she felt a strange tug at her throat. He had begun to laugh, a low uneven chuckle.

Something was wrong.

She tried to scream, but all that came out was a gurgle and, looking down, she saw the front of her gown turning dark. Her lungs ached for a breath that was not there, and the weight of her own body began to feel impossibly heavy. She raised her hand to her throat and felt blood spurting out, running through her fingers like water from a pump. Red, warm, and sticky.

He released her. She fell at his feet. A light flared from above – was he striking a match? - and dimly illuminated the cracks of the cobblestones. The pools of blood grew larger and blacker around her until she could no longer see, but the other senses were still with her and she could smell, yes, the sulfur of the stranger's match and the rich warm earthiness of his tobacco. It was the smell of her father and if Martha could speak she would have said "Papa?" She would have asked her father to pick her up and carry her away from this place, carry her like a child. There was a sound, the clink of metal against stone. Once, then again and again. Silver coins rained down into the street and the last emotion Martha Tabram felt was surprise.

He was paying her.

CHAPTER ONE
September 9, 1888
2:14 PM

"Grandfather certainly picked an inconvenient time to die,"
Cecil muttered, gazing out the carriage window into the
shimmering heat of late summer. "The Wentworths are having
their ball on Friday and I – "

"Will be home well before then," William said sharply.
"How long can it take to read a will? It won't be like last week
with the funeral arrangements and all those bloody scientists
coming in from all over the continent. This is just the family."

Ah yes, just the family, Tom Bainbridge thought, glancing
from one of his brothers to the other. Just the blessed family.
Cecil and William had been dreaming of this day for years. The
one when William would at long last inherit, and although
they'd been on the road to his grandfather's estate for more than
an hour, William's hands still gripped his cane with palpable
tension. Tom's mother and his sister Leanna sat across from the
three men, their faces obscured by their mourning veils. Tom
suspected there were many unspoken advantages to being
female, and one of them was the privilege of hiding one's
thoughts behind a curtain of lace. Leanna had been weeping for
a week, and she now sat slumped silently against the shabby blue
velvet of the carriage wall, as if she no longer had the strength to
even cry.

"Do you think you could manage to show a little more
respect?" their mother asked icily. She was the calmest of the
lot, perhaps because Leonard Bainbridge had been a father-in-
law and not a father, but more likely because the events of her
life had taught Gwynette the virtue of patience. She was the
only one in the carriage who was traveling to Rosemoral with

neither grief nor hope.   "Those scientists were Leonard's colleagues and they'd come from great distance, at great inconvenience I would imagine, to pay tribute to what he had done with his life."

"Gad, mother, what was that?" Cecil said, hitting Leanna's knee as he shook a fly off his top hat. "Taking an estate like Rosemoral and turning it into some sort of ridiculous laboratory with ape skeletons lying about the place?   The last time I was there he had a full scale model of the….the digestive tract of a pig sitting on the French tea cart the Prince of Wales gave Grandmama."

"It was his tea cart, not yours," Tom snapped.   "And if that's truly the last thing you remember, it only shows how rarely you visited him. He hasn't done digestive experiments for years."

The carriage gave a sudden lurch. It had been some time since the family had been able to afford a matched team, so for this long and heavy journey to Rosemoral, a short-legged pony had been yoked to an aging horse, resulting in a remarkably uneven ride. Just one more indignity in a series of indignities, Cecil thought, shifting towards his younger brother, who'd nearly been unseated by this most recent bounce. "Naturally, you and Leanna would defend anything Grandfather chose to do in his dotage, even if it did involve displaying the remains of farm animals on priceless antiques."

"This is neither the time nor place for this discussion," Gwynette said, pulling aside her veil to reveal eyes of such a supernaturally pale blue that they never failed to elicit comments from anyone meeting her for the first time. Gwynette had been a beautiful woman when she married Dale Bainbridge – the portrait in the upper hall attested to that – but thirty subsequent years of struggle had left their mark. Her beauty was not the kind to age well, and, since her husband had finally drunk himself to death five years earlier, her eyes had seemed to get

6

lighter and lighter, giving Tom the uneasy impression that his mother was fading away. "I won't have this squabbling," she said. "Especially now, when we're coming to the end." Whether she meant the end of the family's genteel poverty or merely the end this particularly unpleasant carriage ride wasn't clear, but none of her children requested further illumination, and for a moment the group fell into silence.

"A lovely speech, Mother," Cecil finally said, yawning and stretching out his legs. He was the only one who looked at all like her, the only one to have inherited her unusual eyes. "But cast a glance around. Bainbridge blood in every vein and yet here we sit in a broken down carriage I'd be ashamed to haul hay in. It's being pulled by a borrowed pony and a horse that should have been shot a decade ago, and all this time we've struggled, Grandfather has lived in an estate fit for a duke. You can't honestly say you aren't relieved that the day is finally here when William is going to inherit."

"We've managed to support ourselves at Winter Garden well enough."

"Managed to hold on, isn't that more like it? Creditors are at the door every week and they'd have closed in by now if they hadn't known that grandfather would surely oblige us all by dying sooner or later."

"Enough, Cecil," Tom said. "Leanna's here. Have you taken leave of your senses?" The whole family turned their chins slightly toward the silent figure in black, but the girl still didn't move. She was normally the family chatterbox, so her refusal to speak had the odd effect of dominating the conversation.

Her grief is so damn ostentatious, William thought, as Tom and Cecil fell into another pointless debate. Of course, she loved Grandfather and probably spent more time at Rosemoral than any of us, but all the same... Ever since the telegram had come announcing that Leonard Bainbridge's heart had at long last given way, William had indulged a private fear. Was it possible his grandfather would have ignored primogeniture and divided the estate among them all? Such a stunt wouldn't have been unprecedented in Bainbridge family history, for Leonard's own father had settled a startling amount on his daughter Geraldine. Not just enough to allow the girl to marry well, which was prudent, but enough to allow her to not marry at all, which was lunacy. The woman had spent her life tearing about the world from India to Chile, throwing family money into any number of crackpot causes, and Leonard – far from being upset that his own inheritance was diluted – had always seemed amused by his sister's exploits. William knew his grandfather would leave Leanna money, and undoubtedly funds would be set aside for shrewd baby Tom, who had paid the old man the ultimate compliment of following his footsteps straight to medical school. A share for Cecil on general principle, enough for his mother to make the much-needed repairs to Winter Garden....

But he wasn't liberal enough to cut the estate into quarters, was he? The question had been tormenting William for the past eight days. Estates passed to first born males for a logical reason, to hold family fortunes intact rather than allow them to be frittered away across generations, and on one hand, Leonard Bainbridge had been nothing if not logical. He respected the traditions that had preserved Rosemoral for centuries, ever since it had been granted to a Lancaster loyalist during the War of the Roses, and he would not likely make any decisions that would put it into jeopardy now. William loved the property too, and was prepared to devote his life to being a fit custodian for the land. He and he alone understood the smell of the dirt, the calm of the trees, the silence of the upper rooms, the patina on the leather chairs in the library. Leonard must have known that

William was the one who would protect Rosemoral with his last breath.

But, on the other hand - and this is what had kept William from a week of good sleep - Leonard had occasionally looked up from his scientific experiments to express interest in the same sort of political causes that consumed his sister. Socialism. Decolonization. Even women's rights, a subject William held to be on an equal par with experiments on the digestive tracks of farm animals. William stared at the limp form of his sister. Surely Leonard would not have left her a full share, knowing that a twenty-year-old girl would likely take any inheritance into a marriage and thus out of the family. Leanna or Rosemoral? His grandfather loved them both. Which was he thinking of at the end?

"Besides," Tom was saying to Cecil, his voice rising to a pitch that pulled William from his thoughts. "You could have sought some sort of profession other than the social circuit. And what of William? He's twenty-eight and hasn't turned his hand to anything."

"Professions aren't for eldest sons," William said, relaxing his grip on his cane, and feeling suddenly sure of himself. "Professions are for youngest sons, like yourself."

Tom wasn't going to let it go. "Grandfather was an eldest son, and an heir, and he still did something useful with his life."

"Please, dear Tom, we've spent a week hearing Grandfather eulogized to the skies," Cecil said. "No further accolades are necessary, or we'll have to send to Rome posthaste to have the man canonized. It's certainly bloody hot in here, isn't it?"

Leanna jerked a gloved hand from the folds of her skirt and pushed open the carriage window. Cooler air rushed in, bringing the road dust and flies with it, but the rest of the carriage occupants didn't protest. They merely sat staring at Leanna as she settled back into her motionless state.

"So if elder sons inherit and younger sons find professions, what happens to middle sons?" Tom asked.

"They marry well," Cecil said promptly. "What about it, William? Hours from now when you're firmly in the money, will you remember me? Enough at least for a new suit of clothes and a decent carriage so I can win the hand of Hannah Wentworth? So far I've been able to offer her nothing but charm, which I luckily have in abundant supply, but we all know that if I actually propose marriage, her father is going to expect to see more than a winning smile. I overheard him at the track saying I was all blue but no green."

"Meaning exactly what?" Gynnette asked testily. At one time gossip had obsessed her and she still maintained a certain reflexive interest in the social standing of her family, even if she was powerless to stop its slow decline. The remarks she had overheard during the last few years were rarely pleasant, but she catalogued every snicker and sarcastic comment, rolling them over in her mind the way a tongue compulsively prods a sore tooth.

"Meaning we're all of the right class, hence the blue blood, but we haven't any cash, hence the deplorable absence of green," Cecil said. "Meaning, to be a bit more blunt, that we're acceptable enough to ask to tea but not suitable to marry the daughter of the house. Is that clear enough?"

"Yes," she said shortly, and dropped her veil back over her face.

"But now," Cecil said, "I have the next best thing to money, which is a brother with money. So William, you've never answered. Can I count on you for enough cash to court Miss Wentworth and reassure her father?"

"Of course," said William. "It would be a smart move to align with the Wentworths, even though I can't see why you're so determined to marry that girl. She has a face like that horse you keep threatening to shoot."

"True enough," Cecil said agreeably. "But second sons have to take care of themselves. "

"Not like this," Gynnette said. "As long as we still have that blue blood you find so amusing, I won't have you sully the family name by chasing wealth." Her hand fluttered nervously to the opal and diamond brooch on her chest. It was the only thing left from the early years with her husband, the good years, and with the mention of the Wentworth fortune, her mood must have shifted, because Gwynette tended to fiddle with the brooch whenever she was anxious. It's her talisman, Tom thought, something she touches whenever she needs to bring back a bit of her old power. "I remember when Silas Wentworth was nothing more than a dairy farmer. And why do you insist on going to that racetrack? It's what killed your father."

"Is it my imagination," Cecil said, "or is this an exceptionally tedious conversation?" He settled back into the cushions and closed his eyes.

Tom leaned back too and wondered if it would be possible to sleep, to clear his mind for the ordeal ahead. Cecil, for all his crudity, was quite right. Older sons inherit, second brothers marry well, and youngest brothers seek professions. William would be master of Rosemoral by sunset today and Tom only hoped that his grandfather had left an adequate allowance for his final years of medical school. Leonard had been proud that at least one of his grandchildren inherited his love of science and had been more than happy to pay Tom's tuition, just as he had paid for Leanna to continue at boarding school after their father was killed. Otherwise, Tom suspected Leanna would have been shipped back to Winter Garden the minute their mother had grasped the true enormity of her late husband's debts.

Leonard Bainbridge had always made it clear that Tom and Leanna were his favorites and had been extraordinarily generous with them both. But a single term at Cambridge had taught Tom that academic men were often disastrous judges of human character, unable to accept that not everyone was similarly ruled by logic. Tom knew his grandfather's motives were pure, but he only prayed that provisions for him and Leanna had been spelled out specifically in the will and that their grandfather hadn't left them dependent upon William's unsteady sense of justice. Grandfather wasn't a fool, Tom thought, as he began to drowse. He would have left Leanna a significant dowry, certainly, probably enough to help her form a good alliance when the time came. Otherwise, it would fall to her brothers to arrange her marriage, and Tom cringed at the thought of what William and Cecil might consider a suitable match for their sister.

3:26 PM

Within another hour they were at the gates of Rosemoral, and as Leanna peered out at the familiar entrance, her spirits lifted. Her mother had pushed aside her veil too, but seemed oblivious to the beauty. Leonard, who'd dabbled in botany as well as zoology, had taken pride in the fact his gardens had color from April through November, a not insignificant accomplishment for England. Leanna turned in her seat, leaning her face out of the window and relaxing for the first time in days. There had been so many times in the past she had impatiently ridden past these gates, had bounded from the carriage and run squealing through the foyer and into her grandfather's study, certain of the welcome she would find there.

"Your hair," Gwynette murmured, smoothing back her own. Although they both were blonde, Leanna did not have the delicate beauty of her mother, but rather the rosy, vibrant coloring of the Bainbridges. Normally it would have been difficult for her to sit still during a two-hour carriage ride, but behind the wall of her veil she had realized that invisibility granted a certain freedom; since they couldn't see her face, her family had quite bizarrely seemed to conclude that she didn't exist, or at least that she gone deaf. They had talked about subjects she was normally not privy to hearing, and Leanna had held herself immobile, pretending to sleep, but really mulling over the implications of the conversations, and the deeper implications of her brothers' anger.

This is what Tom has been trying to warn me about, she thought, when he says the money is passing into less benevolent hands. The power will go straight to William's head, that's a given. And things appear to be far worse than Mother knows. Cecil's been gambling – daily and probably heavily, and probably with that man they call Edmund Solmes. He's been cornered enough to consider marriage to a woman he doesn't love, and Tom's terrified too, frightened that William won't see him through medical school. But the biggest shock of all had been the realization that William simply wasn't as smart as the rest of them. He seemed to think every problem in the world could be solved with money, an opinion Leanna knew was only held by the most foolish of men.

As a child she had always looked up to her eldest brother. They had wandered the halls of Rosemoral together and she had let him press her into service in any number of tasks. She'd been his lieutenant in arms, a princess in a tower, his nurse, his valet, his pupil, his adversary in a duel fought with willow branches. Leanna had played whatever role William had wished her to play, happily, and with pride that he would notice a younger sister, that he would single her out – even if he was singling her out to die an ignoble death in their grandfather's flower gardens.

But a new and uncomfortable truth was beginning to dawn. William may not be the quickest in wit, but, due to the fluke of birth order, he would shortly be lord of them all. Cecil would try to weedle, Tom would try to argue, and her mother would pretend they were the Bainbridges of fifty years ago and not sad remnants of an unraveling family cloth. And meanwhile she, Leanna, was both young and female and thus the most vulnerable of all. Once her grandfather had taken her out on horseback and they had ridden the perimeters of the estate. He'd talked about how the house and grounds were large, and how it took a great deal of money to sustain them. Looking back, she supposed it was Leonard's attempt to explain the difference between genteel wealth and cash in hand. She had been no more than fourteen. She had not grasped the full implications of his lecture.

Now she did. Rosemoral, while impressive to the eye, did not necessarily provide the sort of endless income that an outsider might imagine. Leonard had been trying to explain why the estate could not be cut up as easily as a pie at dinner, why he had not bailed his own son out from his debts, why William might not be able to rescue Cecil, why what seemed like family coldness was sometimes family survival.

Her grandfather had been warning her that, appearances aside, there might not be enough to go around.

An elderly man was waiting for them under the portico of the south wing and as the carriage rolled to a stop, he stepped forward, peering up with an anxious squint. Leanna recognized him as Charles Galloway, her grandfather's barrister, and she smiled as he lifted a shaky hand to help her down the steps.

"Mr. Galloway, I'm so glad you're here. I was afraid you'd send one of your aides."

"For the reading of Leonard Bainbridge's will? You wound me, child. Your grandfather was my dearest friend. Tom, William, it's a fine thing to see you both again. I wish it could be under better circumstances, of course, and last week at the funeral I tried to… Ah, and you of course are…." As the rest of the family climbed out of the carriage, the barrister fumbled for a moment, despite the fact he must have prepared for this meeting. Tom finished the introductions. Galloway had obviously never met Cecil, proof of how rarely Leonard's middle grandson had visited Rosemoral, and he seemed utterly flummoxed by Gwynette who, even in mourning, could still stop a man in his tracks.

William brushed by the old man, as if determined to be the first to enter the house. He and Galloway would have regular dealings from now on, Tom thought. Presuming, of course, William had no plans for throwing Leonard's best friend aside in favor of a barrister his own age.

"Um, yes, yes, let's step in," Galloway said, following William into the main hall where a young maid collected the canes, hats, and gloves. "Tillie here can bring tea to Leonard's study and I thought that afterwards – "

"We can hear the will now, in my opinion," Cecil said. "We only brought bags for one evening and our plan is to be underway early tomorrow morning. I have pressing social engagements and I don't think any of us see the point in dragging things out."

"Ah yes," said Galloway. "Yes, we must send a boy for your things. The rooms have been prepared, of course, but I thought perhaps…" He broke off, as if he were unaccountably disappointed they wouldn't be staying longer, and nervously fingered the leather portfolio in his hand.

Leanna reached over to grab the maid's arm as she sped by. "Tillie," she whispered. "If it's no trouble, can I have the pink room with the French doors?"

"Of course, Miss, just as it's planned. Mr. Leonard always called that 'Miss Leanna's room.'" She bobbed an uncertain curtsey and it occurred to Leanna that this must be hard for the staff as well, the death of a much-loved master and an abrupt change of the guard. William watched this exchange silently, then turned to Galloway.

"I agree with my brother," he said. "Let's get on with it. I can't imagine it's a particularly complex document."

"No," Galloway said evenly, pushing open the double doors of Leonard's study. "Mr. Bainbridge had only one child, who predeceased him, so the people in this room represent his entire issue. Are you sure you won't take tea?"

"It's almost four," William said, a slow flush of anger beginning at his neck. How dare the man offer him tea in his own house? "I presume some sort of dinner has been arranged, so we'll be eating soon enough. We've had an exhausting journey, and just as Cecil said, we'll be going home tomorrow to begin the arrangements."

"Arrangements?" questioned Galloway.

"Arrangements to move," said Cecil.

"Move?"

"Move from Winter Garden to Rosemoral," William said, in complete exasperation, thinking he'd send this old fool packing as soon as he could. "As you said, the eldest son of the only son is in this room."

"I believe I said the issue – "

"Quite. So let's begin. As you can see, my mother is exhausted."

Gwynette had already settled into a chair and she looked anything but exhausted. When she turned her gaze on

Galloway, he flinched, thinking that her eyes were so light that the blue looked eerie, otherworldy. He wondered why only minutes ago he had thought of her as beautiful.

"I believe I would like tea," Gwynette said, and Tillie went scrambling toward the door.

Galloway took his position behind the desk. Leanna was hit with a painful wave of nostalgia, remembering how many times she had seen her grandfather in that very chair, pouring over his journals. No, she thought, pressing her eyes closed, I won't cry again. She was relieved when Tillie promptly returned with the tea tray and they were all able to busy themselves with the familiar rituals of napkins and cups. She was not the only one upset, she saw, for Tom's hand trembled as he took a saucer and, for once in his life, William refused food.

"There's a good deal of talk in the opening about sound mind and all that," Galloway began. "And I can assure you Leonard was of sound mind. The will was witnessed by four barristers and one of his doctors who had just performed a most thorough examination." Galloway grunted and picked up his spectacles. "He begins by leaving bequests to his household staff and to his alma mater, Cambridge. He also leaves the university his scientific papers and any proceeds which might be realized from the publication of these papers. I could spell out the particulars, if you – "

"Spare us," William said. "The dons can come tomorrow and cart out every skeleton and test tube in the place for all I care. Tell them to do so, in fact. Anything that's left when we move in will go directly to the trash heap."

"Indeed" said Galloway, thinking that genetics was a funny business. Neither Leonard's son nor his two eldest grandsons had shared his love of learning. The peculiarities of the will were now beginning to make more sense. He'd tried to dissuade Leonard from the arrangement himself, fearing the terms would be contested, but Leonard had gone to great lengths to render the document unbreakable. Now, looking at the solemn faces of Tom and Leanna, Galloway understood for the first time why his friend had been so tenacious.

"Indeed," he said again, turning back to the papers and beginning to read aloud. "I leave a thousand pounds in trust for the medical school expenses of my grandson Thomas. If my grandsons William and Cecil should decide to attend university in view of obtaining professional status in any field, a like amount shall be drawn from the general coffers and put in trust for them." William and Cecil both frowned, but remained silent and after a pause, Galloway continued. "Four hundred pounds a year will be transferred from the general coffers into a fund for the maintenance of Rosemoral. This will allow all presently employed servants to keep their positions, whether or not the house is occupied."

That's odd, Leanna thought, looking up from her tea. Occupied or not? She tried to catch Tom's eye but he was slumped his armchair, hand to his mouth, deep in thought.

"To my daughter-in-law, Gwynette Bainbridge, and to each of my three grandsons, William, Cecil, and Thomas, I leave a monthly allowance of fifty pounds, also to be drawn from the general coffers..."

Everyone was frowning now.

It isn't what he's saying, it's what he isn't saying, Tom thought. Where does Leanna come into all this?

"The Bainbridge family emeralds and the Gainsborough portrait of our mother, I entrust to my beloved sister Geraldine," Galloway droned on. "Since she benefited from our father's estate, I leave her no other funds and believe she will understand my reasoning ..."

Suddenly an idea began to dawn in Tom's head and he glanced quickly around the seated circle, trying to gauge if the same thought had occurred to anyone else. The reminder that his own father had left money to a daughter, the reminder of a family tradition of heiresses, Tom thought, his heart beginning to beat faster. The confident look had left William's eyes and Cecil was bent forward, staring at a single flower on the Oriental rug.

"The estate of Rosemoral and all surrounding properties," Galloway was reading, "along with the stocks, bonds, and monies on deposit at the Leeds Trust which constitute the general coffers...."

Galloway had everyone's attention now. A clock struck in a distant hall and Tom jumped. One. Two. Three. Four. The chimes reverberated, trembling in the air. It's four o'clock, Tom thought. Four o'clock and the end of the world.

"...I leave to my granddaughter, Leanna Bainbridge."

In the weeks and months to come, Tom would lie in his dormitory room at Cambridge and try to reconstruct that moment, wondering whose face had borne the most appalled expression. Most nights he would decide it had been Leanna's. She went absolutely white, as pale as the paper in Galloway's hand, and beside her, both Cecil and William sat literally open-mouthed. Gywnette, a master at hiding her emotions after years of practice, gazed down into her tea cup as if she were trying to divine the future. Galloway rushed on to the last sentence of the document, nearly stammering as he read.

"My grandson Thomas is named executor of the estate."

That said, he looked up, and wiped his brow. This final statement seemed to have stunned the listeners fully as much as the announcement of primary heir, for it was at least thirty seconds – measured by the tormenting beat of the clock – before William rose shakily to his feet.

"He was mad, obviously mad..."

Galloway gazed at the younger, stronger man with no expression. "He knew you would say as much, which is why he went to such pains to make sure the document is beyond reproach."

"Beyond reproach, my —"

"We'll fight it, you must know that," Cecil said, moving to stand beside William. "To leave a fortune of this size to an nineteen-year-old girl —"

"Twenty." The voice seemed to come from nowhere.

"I'm twenty," Leanna repeated slowly, also rising to her feet.

"Well, I beg your pardon," Cecil snapped. "That puts an entirely new face on everything. And naming this boy as the executor is surely the final joke of a man gone mad from inhaling too much formaldehyde."

"I'm not a boy, and Grandfather named me executor for a reason," Tom said. "He knew I'd protect Leanna, that I wouldn't let you break the will..."

"Protect her?" Cecil flopped back into his seat with an ugly laugh. "Well I'm sure our sister will sleep better in her room tonight knowing that you're her designated guardian. Oh, but they're all your rooms now, aren't they, darling? Tell me, can mother and William and I stay the evening, or do you plan to put us in the barn with the livestock?"

"You must know that I never..." Leanna stopped and tried to take a breath, struggling to inhale against the tight ribcage of her corset.

"Leanna?" Tom said, extending an arm. She was very pale.

"Perhaps you should rest, Miss Bainbridge," Galloway said. "There's a couch — "

Tom was moving towards her, but he was too late. Leanna made one last attempt to speak and then the floor rose up and slapped her in the face.

CHAPTER TWO
September 9
4:05 PM

It may have been high tea in the more civilized neighborhoods of London, but there was little time for ceremony at Scotland Yard. As had been the case for days, the front lawn was overrun with reporters, eyewitnesses, whores, lunatics, preachers, and politicians, all demanding to know what the police were going to do about the East End murders.

Trevor Welles cut through the crowd with a speed which belied his size. He was of a body type often called portly, a term he detested, for he was proud of the fact his back and shoulders were dense with muscles. Besides, years on the force had taught him that a long low stride covered ground as well as a run, and there were few men in the Yard who could outdistance him when it mattered.

As he entered the building, a desk sergeant jerked a thumb to indicate he should take the stairs. Trevor bounded up three flights to the meeting room where at least two dozen plainclothes detectives sat waiting. At the front of the room stood a slate and a small table with several items littered about the surface. Trevor picked his way to the front row. Inspector Arthur Eatwell was sitting behind the table staring at the bare wall in front of him and he failed to acknowledge Trevor's greeting.

"You may smoke, gentlemen," the Inspector said, without moving, and all the detectives pulled out their pipes. There were a few coughs, a scraping of chairs, and then a variety of aromas, from cherry to leather, began to fill the air.

The door behind Eatwell opened and a small, gray haired man entered carrying a black leather bag. "Thank you for joining us, Dr. Phillips," Inspector Eatwell said, finally turning from the wall. "Gentlemen, I'm sure you'll all recognize our chief coroner. Begin anywhere you wish. "

The doctor nodded toward the men, and sat his bag on the table. "Then I'll start by saying to date Scotland Yard has completely bungled the investigation of these two murders."

A murmur swept through the room and Eatwell's ears reddened, although he kept his look of rapt attention.

"Don't you mean three murders, sir?" Trevor asked, raising one hand, and leafing through his journal with the other. "What about Martha Tabram, found August seventh?"

"And there have been other knifings of women in the East End this year," came a voice from the back. "Annie Millwood in February, Ada Wilson in March, Emma Smith in April…"

Trevor turned to see that this last speaker was Rayley Abrams, who was leaning against the far wall of the room. Abrams had come on the force a year before Trevor and his solemn demeanor, coupled with his almost ludicrously thick spectacles, had earned him the nickname "professor" around the Yard. But unlike Trevor, Abrams knew how to outthink his superiors without annoying them, how to make a suggestion without it sounding more like an accusation. Some predicted he'd make the rank of Chief Detective by the close of the year, at least if he managed to attach himself to a high profile case. And no case in the Yard was drawing more attention than this one.

The doctor glanced at Eatwell, as if looking for guidance.

"Tabrum was stabbed thirty-nine times," Trevor blurted out, aware that he was repeating information well known to everyone in the room, but still determined to make his point. "That indicates a killer in a frenzy, exactly the sort of man we're looking for."

22

"Our inquiry only concerns these two women," Eatwell said. "If we included every unfortunate in the East End we'd fill up the walls." He stood to flip over the slate. It read:

Mary Ann "Pretty Polly" Nichols
Age: 42
Killed August 31, Shoreditch

Anne "Dark Annie" Chapman
Age: 47
Killed September 8, Hanbury Street

"Now, Doctor," Eatwell said, "would you care to specify your findings?"

Phillips advanced to the podium. "My efforts were hampered by the fact the bobbies who originally found the bodies were rather, shall we say, overzealous. Nichols was moved to a workhouse mortuary, cleaned and washed before a doctor was even called in. Who can say how many vital clues were literally swept down the drain?" Eatwell looked at his fingernails with sudden interest as the coroner went on. "Things were not much better with Chapman. Her body was carried to a shed before it could be properly examined and again, by the time I arrived, a good bit of evidence had been destroyed. It's been said before but must be repeated. A body should not be lifted and moved."

In his seat, Trevor inwardly groaned. Despite the papers beginning to circulate on the importance of proper forensic procedure, the bobbies were notorious for trampling the evidence. Their casual manner toward bloodstains, fibers, and body position was not surprising, for even a few of the high-ranking inspectors had utterly failed to grasp the significance of physical clues. Eatwell, one of the worst offenders in Trevor's view, frowned at Phillips.

"You're suggesting we leave the body as we found it, lying in a public street with a crowd mulling around? Perhaps you somehow managed not to notice it as you arrived, Doctor, but we have a mob on the front lawn that's growing by the hour. The public is in a panic, and the sight of these bodies…let us just say it wasn't exactly death by natural causes."

You don't calm a panic by moving the bodies, you fool, Trevor thought. You rope off the area and move the crowd.

"What I'm suggesting," Phillips said calmly, "is that the best solution to public panic is bringing the killer to justice. And part of that task is to preserve every shred of evidence."

"I agree," Eatwell said, with such an audible sigh it was plain he did not. "Despite the difficulties, I assume you did learn some things?"

"Of course," Phillips said, glancing down at his papers. "We feel safe in saying the same person committed both crimes. The killer is most likely left-handed, for the wounds on both victims were made in a left to right pattern." He illustrated with a trembling diagonal slice of the air. "If not left-handed, then he's as skillful with the left as he is with the right. Both women had their throats slashed from ear to ear, as the papers so gleefully reported, and in Chapman's case the head was almost severed. These mutilations were deftly and skillfully performed on both victims." The doctor looked up, his aged eyes sharp and piercing.

"It is impossible to overstate the significance of this last point. It suggests a killer with anatomical knowledge. Chapman had her kidneys and ovaries removed and apparently taken. The murder weapon was a knife about four to six inches in length and extremely sharp. As sharp as a surgeon's scalpel."

A tickle of excitement began in Trevor's throat. "You're saying the killer could be a physician?"

Inspector Eatwell slapped a palm to the table in protest. "I hardly feel a beast such as this could be a man of medicine, nor a gentleman of any sort, for that matter."

"Educated at Cambridge!" scoffed a detective from the back of the room. The other men snickered.

Trevor scribbled in his journal: "Doctor?"

"Were they raped?" The voice came from the back. Abrams.

"No," Phillips said. "Whatever his game, that's not it." He looked directly at Trevor. "Earlier you said the killer had been in a frenzy, which I'll admit is a logical assumption, but one the facts don't support. Our killer is vicious, certainly, but methodical. The victims showed no signs of struggle and there was very little blood at the murder sites."

Trevor looked up from his journal. "But there were mutilations, even organs removed…. Why no blood?"

"There's very little bleeding after death, Detective. Once a heart stops beating, blood begins to gel in the veins and arteries of the body. Perhaps they were smothered or strangled first, or it's possible that the first wound was so well-placed the victims were dead by the time they hit the ground. In the Chapman case especially, there was far less blood that one might expect, so quite possibly the killer drained blood from the body."

"Drained blood from the body?" Rayley Abrams asked the question that everyone else in the room was thinking. "Wouldn't that take a rather long time?"

"Anywhere from twenty minutes to an hour," Phillips said. "Depending on his skill and experience level."

The room sat in silence while the detectives digested this information.

"Could the two women have been killed someplace else and their bodies dumped at the site where they were found?" Trevor finally asked. "Draining blood would take a certain kind of equipment wouldn't it? Something less portable than a knife?"

"I doubt even a madman would risk being seen dragging a dead body about the streets of London, Detective." Inspector Eatwell interjected coolly, as again snickers arose from the back.

"Tubes and hypodermics are really all that's required," said Phillips. "A bottle or pan to catch the blood, of course. It's more a matter of having the skill to tap the right vessels in the right places and the ability to find them quickly in the dark."

"So we are speaking of a doctor," Trevor said.

"It's a strong possibility, but one I present reluctantly," Phillips answered, his face suddenly looking old and tired. "It's hard to accept that such barbaric crimes could have been committed by someone who has undertaken the Hippocratic Oath."

"This line of thinking utterly circumvents the issue of motive," said one of the detectives in the front row, his voice sharp with protest. "People kill for a reason."

"Indeed," said the man seated beside him. "Jealousy, greed, lust, revenge…something logical that one can understand. But who could possibly benefit from these deaths? There has to be some way, beyond the obvious similarity of their profession, that these women were connected."

Not necessarily, Trevor thought. The strong have always preyed upon the weak, perhaps for no other reason than because they are weak. And there were few creatures in London more vulnerable than an aging East End prostitute.

"In this particular case," Phillips said, "I'd say that method trumps motive. Why these women died isn't as important as how."

An uneasy buzz ran through the crowded room. Trevor printed "method over motive" in large letters in his notebook, then glanced back at Abrams, who was still leaning against the wall. For the briefest of moments, the eyes of the two men met.

"Motive is quite naturally the beginning of all criminal inquiry," Eatwell said, ignoring the doctor and directing an adamant nod toward the detectives in the front row, like a professor congratulating a promising pupil. "It will narrow the list of suspects faster than rounding up every man in London who happens to have skill with a knife."

"I only know this," Phillips said, beginning to cram his notes back into his over-stuffed satchel. "Working at top speed it would have taken me forty-five minutes to drain a body and remove four organs. True, this fiend may not be a gentleman, but he does have knowledge of the surgery. Now, if there are no further questions, I'll be excused, for I do have other cases to contend with."

Eatwell watched him shuffle out with obvious relief and waited until the door was safely shut before he again addressed his detectives.

"Gentlemen, on the table before me, you will find the physical evidence gathered at the site of the Chapman murder," Eatwell said. Trevor scribbled down the meager inventory as his fellow detectives rose and milled around the table.

-Three pennies
-Two farthings
-Two brass rings
-Portion of bloodstained envelope bearing the name SUSSEX REGIMENT and postmarked August 28
-One leather apron

"Not exactly the purse of a duchess, was it?" Rayley Abrams said softly. "Poor wretch. What do you make of this Sussex Regiment post?"

"A client, perhaps," one of the men said. "Or a brother."

"More likely a son, given her age," said another.

"I can't see what the letter would have to do with the death," said a third. "Some bloke wrote her...lover, son, brother, what does it matter?"

"The significance is not that she happened to have a letter," Abrams said. "But the fact that most of that letter is missing. I'll see if any men with the last name Chapman are stationed with Sussex."

"And what of this?" one of the men asked, lifting the leather apron gingerly from the pile. "It's the kind they use in slaughterhouses to keep the blood from their clothes."

"There are at least two slaughterhouses in Whitechapel," said Abrams. "A butcher would have access to knives by the dozen."

"And the skill to dissect a human body?" Trevor asked, arching an eyebrow.

"At least a butcher would know how to drain blood," Abrams said.

"And would he be able to remove organs as skillfully as these were removed? Phillips as much as said it was too well done to point to an amateur."

"Phillips has a love for drama," one of the detectives said, leaning between Trevor and Abrams to idly flick a penny with his fingertip. "When you two have been with the Yard as long as the rest of us, you'll see that he can't resist throwing in some bizarre theory with each coroner's report." Most of the men were filing out by now and, after a pause, Abrams turned to join them, leaving Trevor to gaze thoughtfully at the items before him.

"Expecting to find his calling card, Welles?" Eatwell asked, as he was erasing the blackboard.

"It could very well be here, Sir, if we knew where to look."

"Hmmm, nice to know murder is so simple for our first-rank detectives. I'm sure you and Abrams will have our killer off the streets before tomorrow teatime."

Trevor stood hesitantly. He'd never known how to respond to Eatwell's sarcasm. "We'll try, Sir," he finally said, backing out of the room.

"Better do more than try," snapped Eatwell, and he beat his erasers until white dust flew across the table, slowly settling over the last worldly possessions of a woman named Anne Chapman.

CHAPTER THREE
September 9
4:10 PM

When Leanna opened her eyes, Tom was staring down at her with a half-curious, half-worried expression. Behind him, Galloway was pacing. Leanna struggled to raise her head.

"You're missing your cue," Tom said. "You're supposed to ask 'Where am I?'"

"I know where I am," Leanna said, pushing away the damp cloth someone had placed on her forehead. "Grandfather's study. Where's everyone else?"

"Mama and the big boys have retreated to the parlor to nurse their own shock," said Tom, letting a small smile slip. "Tell the truth, did you fake that faint? It was an admirably efficient means of clearing the room."

"Of course not," Leanna said. "You know I don't faint. At least I never have before, and I remember when Grandfather was trying to teach us how to dissect a rabbit that you were the one who.... How long was I unconscious?"

"Just a few minutes, but long enough to give me time to confer with Mr. Galloway. We have to talk fast. They'll be beating on the door any minute."

"It might be prudent," Galloway said, "for you to leave Rosemoral for a few weeks. Take a holiday of sorts while your family has the chance to get used to the idea."

"They'll never get used to the idea," Tom corrected him. "But at least until the paperwork is finalized."

"A holiday? I've never been anywhere alone in my whole life. Mama doesn't even let me ride into town without – "

"You wouldn't be alone, Leanna. Galloway thinks you should go to London and stay with Aunt Geraldine. She's settled in Mayfair and, more to the point, she knows the situation. Apparently she is the only one other than Galloway whom Grandfather included in his plan and she understands it, Leanna. All of it. She was the one who suggested you come to her home."

"I hardly know her," Leanna said, her mind jumping to a memory of a large, jolly woman with a booming voice and pockets full of candy.

"But I do," Tom said. "The first month I was in school she sent me a message inviting me to dinner at her home in London and ever since... You'll be happy there, Leanna."

"I don't follow any of this, Tom. Why didn't you tell me Aunt Geraldine was back in London, or that you'd been to see her? It makes no sense. She didn't even come to Grandfather's funeral."

"She was there," Tom said firmly. "In the back. Apparently in disguise, and apparently a good one because I didn't recognize her."

Leanna looked questioningly at Galloway.

"Leonard knew he was dying," Galloway said gently. "When he told Geraldine the terms of his will, they concocted this plan. Part of it is that your mother and the older boys shouldn't be aware that Geraldine was even back in the country. Otherwise, her home in London wouldn't be a very effective hiding place, would it? Tom knew of her presence but he was sworn to secrecy."

"Yes," said Tom. "But until today I didn't know why."

Leanna's head was swimming at the thought of her grandfather, Aunt Geraldine, and Galloway all scheming together, three elderly people going to such trouble to shield her from what would undoubtedly be a very rough time. "But to stay in hiding at her own brother's funeral..."

"Oh, I think she rather enjoyed that," said Galloway and Tom laughed. "Your aunt loves a challenge, Miss Bainbridge, and I can't think of anyone better suited to assist you through this rather unique social transition."

Leanna shook her head, at last fully alert, as if she had broken through layers of water to reach the surface. She inhaled sharply. "So everyone thinks I should run, is that it?"

"Not run, Miss Bainbridge, but, if you can take refuge for a month or two –"

"I'll be back in school in a few weeks," Tom said. "And then I'll come see you. In the meanwhile, Galloway can set up an account you can draw on by wire, so you'll have funds."

"Within the week," Galloway promised.

"But how do I get to London and what do I do for money in the meantime?"

"Heavens, Leanna, don't be such a dolt. You'll take the train and you'll be living with Aunt Gerry, who will hardly be charging you rent."

"I've brought funds for just that purpose," Galloway said, glancing at the door from which came the sounds of conversation, the low murmur of Gwynette's voice, the shrill yelps of William's indignation. Tom put a finger to his lips and slipped out the door to divert them.

"I can't accept your money," Leanna said.

"I expect my loan is secure," Galloway said, with a smile, and it hit Leanna for the first time that she was a wealthy woman. That while she had been in her swoon it was as if she had been transported, carried to a new country with different customs and a language she had yet to learn. The implications were too much to deal with at the present, though, so she let her mind drift to trivial things.

"I haven't any clothes with me. I only brought that one bag –"

"There are plenty of shops in London, my dear."

Leanna paused, thinking of the narrow-hipped jewel-colored dresses she'd seen in the pages of magazines, so different from the filmy pastel gowns her mother had made for her by the local seamstress. The idea of going shopping, alone, with her own money in her pocket...

The barrister laughed. "So I've finally hit on the argument that will sway you. The chance to buy new clothes in London is irresistible for any woman, even our stern little Leanna."

"I haven't been to London in years," she said, looking up as Tom reentered the room. "And never alone."

"Really, darling, try to focus," Tom said. "You won't be alone. I'll wire Aunt Gerry from the train station so she'll know to be there for you tomorrow morning."

"Tomorrow?" Leanna protested.

"It's the best way," Galloway said, as he pulled a pouch from his pocket and carefully began to count out pounds. "There's a train which departs Leeds station at five-"

"Five in the morning?"

"Yes, Leanna, businessmen take it to London for the day. Grandfather was always going in for the libraries and museums, don't you remember?"

"You've worked out every detail, haven't you?"

"We'll leave by carriage at four. They'll all be dead asleep at that hour and for several hours beyond, judging by the way they've made a run for the decanter," Tom said. "And they won't be able to chase you, because they'll think they have to stay here and fight for their interests. Galloway and I will see to that."

Leanna sank back against the couch. "I feel so strange - part excited and part frightened to the core. When I give in to the fear, the joy comes rushing in but when I try to feel joyous that little tickle of fear is there to distract me. I wonder what it is."

"Freedom."

Leanna gave her brother a sidelong look of doubt.

"No really Leanna, that's what freedom is like- a bit of excitement, a bit of fear. You'd better get used to the feeling."

"This is final proof of what I've been saying for years," William sputtered, setting an over-full wine glass on the mantle. "Grandfather was senile."

"You never called him senile when you thought you were his heir," Cecil drawled, swirling the brandy in his own glass. "And you're being awfully careless with the claret given your concern that Rosemoral be kept in such pristine condition."

"It's Leanna's estate now," William said thickly. "Let her hire more maids. You've been notably silent, Mother. What are you thinking? Are we doomed to spend the rest of our days in Winter Garden?"

Gwynette looked up. "You could follow the counsel of the will and take up a profession, I suppose."

"I can only assume that you're joking. And what of Cecil's marriage plans? We've all been left in the lurch by this appalling turn of events."

"Not necessarily," Cecil said. "We'll go home tomorrow and I'll call on Edmund Solmes. He must know a dozen barristers who could dance circles around Galloway."

"I don't know if you can afford to ask Solmes for any more favors," William mumbled, ignoring Cecil's warning glance as he clumsily reached for the wine bottle. "Especially now that your collateral is no longer in your possession."

"What?" Gwynette asked, looking from one son to the other.

"Cecil has run up gambling debts."

"He exaggerates, Mother. Edmund and I are friends. He doesn't intend to press me."

"What did you mean by collateral?"

"Leanna," William said brusquely. "Solmes has his eye on her and Cecil agreed to press for the match. He came to me and said when I was officially head of the family - "

Gwynette stood, eyes blazing, and focused the full force of her fury on Cecil, who although he remained casually sprawled, visibly tensed under her scrutiny. "Let me see if I understand," Gwynette said. "You intended to use your sister's virginity to pay off your debts from the horses?"

"A callous turn of phrase, Mother. It isn't as if Edmund wasn't prepared to marry her."

"Marry her? He's four times her age! He would be too old for me!"

"Granted, Mother, but Leanna doesn't have your fire -"

"Spare me your flattery. You've really gone too far this time, Cecil. Our family fortunes may have fallen, but I was not aware we were to the point you found it necessary to sell your sister. Especially not to that odious old man."

"That odious old wealthy man, Mama," added William, enjoying the rare sight of Cecil squirming.

"Wealthy indeed," said Gwynette. "And so doddering he would probably drool on her. Just how severe are these debts?"

Cecil hesitated. "No more than three hundred pounds."

Gwynette sighed. "If you'll admit to three hundred, it's more than likely twice that. You're just like your father, Cecil, and it pains me to admit the fact."

"Don't start on that again, Mother," William said. "I don't see why Cecil and I should suffer because of Father's sins and be cut out of what is rightfully ours. No one leaves that kind of money to a woman! No one!"

"Agreed," Cecil said, relieved for the chance to change the subject. "Every wolf and fortune hunter in the countryside will be after her now."

"I scarcely see how she could do any worse than what the two of you had planned for her," Gwynette said. "And Cecil, for you to call anyone else a fortune hunter is quite unendurable."

"They're in there plotting, you know," William said darkly. "Even as we speak, Tom and that corpse of a barrister are strategizing their next move."

"Oh, I have no doubt what they'll do," Gwynette said. "There's really only one logical option. They'll hide her with your Aunt Geraldine in Mayfair."

Her sons turned to her with puzzled faces.

"I thought I saw her at the funeral in a rather ridiculous disguise," Gwynette said. "Now I suppose I understand why."

"Given her eccentric nature I scarcely see how you could distinguish a disguise from her everyday clothing," Cecil said. "Remember, William, she's a huge ogre of a woman, spouting feathers on her head and indigestible political beliefs…"

"Which is precisely what happens when a woman doesn't marry," William said.

"Yes, without question, that's their plan," Gwynette went on, her brow creased in thought. "Leanna will be spirited away to London."

Cecil rubbed his temples vigorously, but the headache from his hastily gulped brandy refused to be erased. "Then we must stop her."

"I'm not sure we can," Gwynette said. "And besides, it might be best for everyone if some time passes before Leanna takes up residence in Rosemoral."

"As far as I'm concerned she can stay in London forever," William muttered. "The longer I can go without facing the boys at the pub, the better."

"Why you're right, both of you," Cecil said with some surprise, for he considered it his duty within the family to think of things first. "No one outside our small circle knows of this, do they? The assumption will naturally be that William is the heir and as long as our little sister is tucked away in Mayfair, we have a pocket of time, enough for me to…" Cecil sprang unsteadily to his feet, his spirits quite restored. "Yes, bravo to you both, that's quite the plan. We will proceed to the Wentworth ball next week and no one will be rude enough to ask. They will see us there, laughing and gay, as if it has all gone precisely as expected."

"When I first met Geraldine I was just a bride," Gwynette murmured, gazing toward the open window and the blazing colors of Leonard's autumnal garden. "And she seemed to me almost as if she'd come from a different species. I'd never known a woman who was free to marry as she pleased, and if she chose not to marry at all, I suppose there are worse fates. I can still recall the day my father summoned me to the library and told me I that I was going to be escorted to the dance that evening by a boy named Dale Bainbridge…"

"Perhaps I should even get something new for the ball, something brightly colored," Cecil mused. "Gloves, do you think? Perhaps an ascot?"

William looked at Gwynette with a play of emotions on his face, something between a child's indignation and a man's sadness. "You surprise me, Mother. You've always claimed you and Father were a love match."

"Oh we were, in a way, at least in the sense he was the youngest and most attractive of the options my father offered. But I was sixteen and hardly knew what I was doing. Then, years later, after you children were born, I saw I should have chosen a different sort of man. It's the way Hannah will feel if you persuade her to marry you, Cecil. There will come the day, a normal seeming sort of day, and she will look across the breakfast table…"

"I won't hear this," Cecil said. "It's almost as if you're suggesting that a child like Leanna would know better what she needs than her own brothers. Solmes may be older than her but he is settled, prosperous…"

"Forget it, Cecil," William said, pushing himself from the settee and walking toward the open window. "She isn't ours anymore."

"No, she isn't, is she," Gwynette said, her voice almost as low as a whisper. "Your grandfather hasn't just handed her an estate, he's cut her quite loose from the earth. I feel she's up somewhere floating high above us, not bound by the same rules anymore. Someday you'll both understand that this was the true purpose of Leonard's will. Not to punish the two of you, but to allow Leanna to be a different sort of woman."

"Like Aunt Geraldine?" William said. "If so, he's cut her loose but I'm not sure it was a kindness."

"Perhaps she was his last experiment," Gwynette said tiredly. "The last species he attempted to evolve. The independent woman. But you're right, I'm not sure it was a kindness."

CHAPTER FOUR
5:35 PM

"It's a bit early in the investigation for us to be literally running down blind alleys, wouldn't you say?"

Trevor turned to see Rayley Abrams standing behind him. "This is where they found Martha Tabram in the early morning of August 7," he said.

"I know where we are, Welles. But Tabram isn't part of our inquiry."

"She should be. Throat sliced ear to ear and then stabbed thirty-nine times, for God's sake, not three weeks before the Nichols murder. Are you so sure she shouldn't be under consideration?"

Abrams shook his head. "Not sure at all, but you heard Eatwell. We can't investigate every woman who comes to a bad end in Whitechapel. And perhaps he's right. Prostitution is not just the world's oldest profession, but also the most dangerous. They're statistically more likely to be killed in the line of duty than we are."

Trevor shot him a skeptical look.

"It's true," Abrams said, "and, even more to the point, thirty-nine stabs point to a different sort of mentality. Not surgical. Not precise. You said it yourself, a multiplicity of wounds implies a frenzy of anger, as if the killer knew the victim personally. The last two are more....as if you are taking something meant to heal, a surgical scalpel, and very deliberately turning it a different way. Do you see what I mean?"

"It's just as the doctor said. The how will tell us more than the why."

"Precisely," Abrams said, removing his glasses and blowing on the lenses.

Trevor looked down at the overgrown grass and bits of broken windowpane where Martha Tabram had drawn her last breaths and a slow shudder came over him. "Our normal means of deduction are quite useless here. Our killer didn't necessarily have any prior relationship to our victim."

"Quite right again," Abrams said. "Which is why the hour I spent tracing the Sussex postmark turned out to be a blind alley too. Chapman was taking some sort of pills and the box that held them broke. So she tore a piece off an envelope she found in the rubbish at her boarding house and folded the pills into it. Wasn't even her letter. It makes you long for the good old days, doesn't it? When criminals were decent enough to only murder people they knew?"

The men turned, as if by silent agreement, and began walking back toward the street. Trevor had spent his own afternoon combing the East End, moving back and forth between the slaughterhouses and the bars. He had seen a dozen aprons of the kind Phillips had displayed in the conference room and had observed several people holding a pencil, cigarette, or whiskey bottle in their left hands. He had taken note of everyone in the area, even women, and wouldn't Eatwell have a laugh at that? But a midwife or nurse might have enough medical knowledge to effectively wield a scalpel, and Trevor would not allow himself to leave any stone unturned.

"It's a daunting task, is it not?" Abrams said, as if reading his mind. "Within the confines of Whitechapel there are 233 lodging houses with over 8000 occupants, an estimated 1,200 of them making their living as prostitutes."

"Over a thousand women?" Trevor said with surprise. He wouldn't have guessed as third as many. "Abrams, you're a marvel. Wherever do you get all your statistics?"

"Home Secretary report, Welles. Released last week."

Trevor stopped on the sidewalk, so abruptly that the man behind him bumped into him with a low curse, and dug his journal from his pocket. "233 lodging houses?"

"Sixty-two of them established brothels. I say, Welles, you're a marvel in your own right. You don't go anywhere without that little notebook of yours, do you?"

"Where do you keep your reports?"

Abrams tapped his temple lightly.

"Bully," Trevor said stiffly. "But I want to make sure I don't forget anything and a case like this has so many – where are we going, by the way?"

"I'm visiting the mortuary to have a look at Annie Chapman," Abrams said. "And since you're walking with me, it would appear that you're headed there too. She's set to be buried tomorrow morning, and seeing them off is a bit of a ritual with me, I suppose. There's nothing to be done with it, of course, but I can't seem to resist paying my final call."

"You've never worked with a partner, have you, Abrams?"

"Never saw the need. He travels fastest who travels alone, as they say. And you?"

"Never saw the need either."

"I suppose your little notebook is your partner."

"Scoff if you will, but if there are over a thousand prostitutes in Whitechapel, each with a hefty number of clients, how many interviews do you think we'll have to conduct before this matter is brought to an end? Look at the sheer amount of people on this street, the number of possible victims, the number of possible suspects. How are we to determine where a random killer will turn his sights next?"

"I don't know," Abrams said, his shoulders drooping a little. "I suppose if a man's a hunter, any bird in the sky will do. Ah, here we are."

Trevor and Abrams entered a plain gray stone building beside the graveyard and followed the dull sound of hammering to the back of the hall. "What can I do for you?" asked a voice slightly muffled by the pounding.

"Abrams and Welles of Scotland Yard," said Abrams. "Here to see the remains of Anne Chapman."

"Remains is right, Detective" said the man, stepping out from behind his work bench and gesturing with his hammer toward a doorway. "Poor Dark Annie was butchered sure enough. She's in the pine box in the back."

Trevor walked into the second room where a man he supposed to be one of the coroner's assistants was bent over a coffin. Why they had done their examinations here, in this ramshackle mortuary, and not at Scotland Yard was a mystery to Trevor and he wondered if the case was truly receiving the attention it deserved. The assistant seemed to recognize Abrams and Welles as detectives, or perhaps he had overheard the conversation in the hall, for he stepped back from the body smartly, in an almost military manner.

Trevor walked over to the humble coffin and paused for a moment. He gave a nod of credit to the assistant, who was now setting up a camera on a tripod, for the expression on the ashen face was peaceful and Annie Chapman was neatly dressed, her body giving little evidence of the violations of two nights before. Her eyes were shut and her arms had been neatly crossed over her chest.

"Where would you drain blood from a body?" he asked the assistant.

The young man turned clumsily from the camera, startled at having been addressed. "In the mortuary at Scotland Yard, Sir."

"No. No, I mean what parts of the body?"

"Throat, wrists, behind the ear."

"Then I regret I must spoil your admirable work," Trevor said, reaching into the coffin and seizing one of the woman's waxy white hands. He turned it over and there, just as he predicted, was a tiny aperture in her wrist.

"See this, Abrams, unmistakably a hypodermic needle," he said, forcing himself to shrug, although he was so excited it took all of his control not to tremble. "Now we just have to find the bastard who drained her blood."

"It was me, Sirs," said the mortuary assistant.

Trevor looked up.

"When we embalmed her, Sirs."

Abrams gave a soft laugh and Trevor felt himself flush.

"And did you happen to notice," he said, in what he hoped was a cool and level voice, "if there were any such apertures when you began?"

"Doctor Phillips reported she was very nearly drained when they found her," Abrams said, by way of explanation, but the young man still seemed confused.

"When doing your embalmations, your... your preparations for the coffin, you didn't stop to wonder at the absence of blood?" Trevor asked, his voice revealing more exasperation than he intended.

"The incision in her throat, Sir, six to eight inches long and three deep –"

"Quite," said Abrams, shooting Trevor a warning look. A case could be made that the woman's near-decapitation, followed by a bumpy cross-town transit in a cart, was a reasonable enough explanation for the fact she'd arrived to the mortuary almost bloodless. Besides, they wouldn't aid the investigation or win any friends by snapping at the assistants of powerful men.

Trevor sighed, looked down at the pale hand in his own. Phillips had scolded Eatwell for not better training the bobbies and yet it appeared he also chose his own assistants more on the basis of their silent efficiency than for their curious minds. But he supposed it wasn't this boy's task to look for needle marks on a corpse, any more than the bobbies could be blamed for the manner in which they swarmed the crime scenes. The men on top liked their underlings physically strong and mentally deferential, quick to do whatever task they're ordered but unlikely to ask troubling questions along the way. No one knew that better than him.

"But see here," Trevor said, still staring down at the woman's hand. "There is something. Under the fingernail."

Abrams handed Trevor a pencil and all three men held their breath as he carefully used its tip to remove a raveled red fiber. Trevor held the thin piece up to the light to examine it better and slowly, carefully untangled a red thread about an inch long.

"From the clothes of the killer, perhaps," Trevor said. "There may have been a struggle and she grabbed at him. Tore at a shirt or scarf." He removed the journal once again from his breast pocket and carefully laid the red thread between two pages, then reached back over Annie to get a better look at her other hand.

"I assure you, Detective, you will not find a pulse," came a familiar voice from the doorway.

"Doctor Phillips," Abrams said, extending a hand. "We got here just in time to see you photograph the retinas." The two men chuckled and, noting Trevor's uncertain expression, Abrams explained. "This morning The Star ran an article suggesting the police photograph the dead women's eyes. Apparently there's a theory floating around that the last image one sees before death is forever seared into the retina."

"Would that it were that easy," said the doctor. He motioned to his assistant, who was waiting with the camera. "Go ahead, Severin, take your picture. Eyes closed, of course, the detective was just having his little joke. What were you doing with her hands, Welles?"

"In the morning meeting you said the victims may have been strangled or smothered first, which allowed for so little blood."

Phillips nodded.

"If I was being choked, I would at least try to lash back at the assailant. I would grab or scratch at anything I could reach, just out of desperation. A simple reflex, wouldn't you say?"

"And your point?"

"Just this. Did you examine the hands of both victims? Did you noticed if these women had anything under their nails indicating they fought back? Was there blood, or hair, or skin found? Could they have scratched or wounded the attacker? Anything?"

The pop of the camera made them all jump and Phillips blinked, perhaps in anger or perhaps just because of the flash. "Young man, are you seriously questioning my ability to do an autopsy?"

"He found a thread," Abrams said, both his expression and voice utterly devoid of emotion. He was once again leaned against the wall, arms crossed over his chest and head tilted in an absurd parody of the dead woman's position. Isn't he the cool one, Welles thought. Slight in build and with those thick eyeglasses he truly does look more like a scholar than a detective - but a bit of a dandy too, his shirtsleeves always clean and his tie knotted just so. Never puts himself on the line with a theory, at least not when a superior is in earshot. And yet he's always there, observing everything.

"A thread?" Phillips asked. "And you think you can follow it all the way to our killer? The men who found the body tried to lift it, Detective, then thought the better of it and wrapped her in a blanket. By the time I got to that shed she was covered head to toe in fibers and there is nothing to suggest that any of them came from the killer."

"But this one was under her fingernail, Sir. Not just lying on her chest like it came from a blanket used to move her but dug in, as if she'd grabbed something and held on." Trevor opened his notebook and removed the fiber, holding it delicately between two fingers, but the doctor shook his head.

"Even if she did manage to grab the clothes of her assailant, that would tell us nothing. A red thread. A man with a red scarf or coat."

"But Nichols and even Martha Tabram, Sir, meaning no disrespect, but did you check their hands? If something similar –
"

"Enough, Welles. Tabram and Nichols are in the ground and this poor woman will follow them there in the morning. Take advice from someone who has been dealing in police affairs for forty years. Do not make waves or go over the heads of your superiors. Follow procedure, or you will find yourself walking the streets again as a bobby."

"But Sir, I feel I owe – "

"Of course you do," Phillips said, his expression softening. "You haven't seen as many dead bodies as I have. Of course you feel you owe them something. Some sort of justice or redemption. But if you carry these feelings too far they will draw you from your true purpose, which is the protection of the living, not vengeance for the dead." The doctor took a final look at Annie Chapman's face as his assistant lowered the lid of the coffin, moving so slowly and carefully that it closed with only the softest of sighs. "And if it provides you any consolation, Chapman would have been dead within the year. From the condition of her liver, I'd say she liked her drink."

"Who is claiming the body for burial, Doctor?" Abrams asked. "Do you know?"

"Her children, Detective. A son and a daughter, both grown. Yes, they have families, these women," Phillips said more sharply, as if Trevor or Abrams had contradicted him. "Everyone has a family, even them."

Trevor and Abrams said their goodbyes and returned to the street. They walked a couple of blocks without speaking and Trevor, his face still red from the lecture Phillips had given him, was aware that he taking such large strides that the far shorter Abrams was almost trotting to keep up with him. "Procedure!" he finally said. "You'd think the doctor, of all people, would understand. All those bobbies who bungled the case to begin with were only following procedure. Bloody idiots! And why did they examine the body in that dismal shack, rather than taking her to Scotland Yard? Why didn't the man who embalmed her take note of any other needle marks? Did you see the way he looked at me when I asked a simple question?"

"I imagine the bobbies took her to the nearest police mortuary," Abrams said, struggling for breath. "And the assistant was Polish or Czech or somesort, judging by his accent. He may not have even understood what you were asking. You've got to…"

"Be more politic?"

"It wouldn't hurt. Let me buy you a drink, Welles."

"I don't need a drink."

"I think you do," Abrams said. "And don't make an enemy of Phillips. He's one of the good ones. He caught your meaning, even if he pretended not to. Next time he'll take special note of the hands."

Trevor slowed down and looked Abrams right in the face. "You're that sure there will be another?"

"Without question. I'm afraid our boy is just getting warmed up, that it took him two or three tries before he figured out how to make things interesting. And now that he has our attention, he won't want to lose it. Phillips thinks so too, for what it's worth, that's why he told us to keep our focus to the living."

"Oh God," Trevor said. "Look at all these people. That man has a red scarf, and that one too, a red collar on his jacket. Don't you laugh at me, Abrams, but look. They're all wearing red. Every person on this street."

"Not all of them, Welles, and believe me, I'm not laughing. Come on. We both could use that drink."

CHAPTER FIVE
September 10
7:40 AM

The train lurched away from one more small station and
Leanna settled back into her window seat. It had been over two
hours since she'd waved goodbye to Tom but she'd been unable
to nap. Her mind was swirling with thoughts of everything that
had happened - the loss of her grandfather, the sudden
inheritance, the jealousy and anger of her family. Any of these
events by themselves would have been a shock, but it was nearly
incapacitating to face so many changes so rapidly. Not to
mention she was now on a train by herself, entirely free and
unescorted. Her only previous trips to London had been with
her governess or her grandfather, for purposes of education, but
she had glimpsed enough from carriage windows to know there
was life beyond the museums. The shops, theatres, and carriages,
the streets teeming with people from all over the world, the cafes
where ladies sipped brightly-colored cordials and whispered their
secrets.

As the train gained speed and the car began to gently rock to
and fro, Leanna's eye fell on a newspaper that someone had left
on the seat across from her, with the headline shrieking KILLER
STILL AT LARGE! It was crumpled but readable, and,
glancing around, Leanna grabbed it. Everyone in the
countryside was avidly following the story of the East End
slayings and, in fact, just a few days ago her brothers had been
discussing it over the breakfast table. The description in that
morning's article had been confusing to everyone but Tom, so
he'd asked her to help illustrate.

Tom had Leanna stand up and he'd crept behind her,
slipped an arm around her waist, and used his butter knife to

indicate where the cuts must have been made. William and Cecil, their attention fully fixed on their younger siblings for once in their lives, had sat rapt by the reenactment, complete with dramatic sound simulations by Tom and a bit of squeals and thrashing by Leanna. Cecil had asked how Tom knew the killer had attacked his victims from behind.

"It's all that makes sense considering where the wounds are," Tom had said, reaching for Leanna and tracing the pattern all over again. "One, two, three, just so. But the angle's awkward."

"Perhaps he's left-handed," Leanna had said. "Try it with the knife in your other hand." But just then their mother had swept into the room and interrupted what was probably the most stimulating breakfast conversation the family had enjoyed for years. Cecil and William had returned to their eggs and Tom, frowning thoughtfully, replaced the butter knife on its tray. Gwynette had glanced at the paper and then quite pointedly launched into a discussion of what Leanna might have worn had they only been invited to Wentworth family's latest tea.

She made them stop talking because of me, Leanna thought. Boys can hear about all sorts of interesting and bloody things, while girls talk about tea parties. But there was no one to stop her from reading now. She pulled out one of the cheese buns that Tillie had packed in her valise, burrowed deeper into the seat, and squinted down at the blurry print.

The knife, which must have been a large and sharp one, was jabbed into the lower part of the abdomen and then drawn upwards, not once but twice. The first cut veered to the right, slitting up the groin, and passing over the left hip, but the second cut went straight upward, along the center of the body, and reaching to the breastbone. Such horrible work could only be the deed of a maniac!

Suddenly a dark reflection in the window cast a shadow on the paper and Leanna jerked upright to find someone standing in the aisle. Startled, she asked "May I help you?"

Looking down on her was a dark-suited man with a flat-topped hat. "Are you comfortable, Miss?" he asked.

"Very much so," she replied, easing a bit.

He remained standing and staring at her until she said "Is there something you want?"

"Your fare, please."

"Oh, yes, yes of course. I beg your pardon," she stammered, searching her satchel for the money Galloway had given her. "One moment please, I have it here somewhere."

But the blue silk purse where she'd put the money must have sank to the bottom of the satchel as it seems whatever's needed always does, because she couldn't manage to lay her hand on it. The conductor gave a gentle cough and shifted his weight with a sigh. It was clear he perceived her as a country bumpkin, or at least had correctly concluded he was dealing with a woman who had never been alone on a train before.

As she began nervously pulling things from her cloth bag, Leanna felt the presence of someone else, someone taller, standing beside the conductor. "Might I be of some assistance?" a voice asked.

Leanna's cheeks flushed as she looked up at the face of a strikingly handsome man whose dark hair and mustache stood out boldly from his pale skin. "I appreciate your kindness, but my fare is in this bag somewhere," she mumbled, pulling at the side pocket of her valise. Finally her fingers found the silk of the purse, but when she looked up the conductor had already turned his attention to the lady behind her.

"Excuse me Sir," she said, "I have the money."

The conductor glanced in her direction. "The gentleman took care of it, miss."

"Oh….oh yes. Yes, thank you," Leanna said, turning to where the man had stood but all she caught was a glimpse of his cape flowing behind him as he exited the car. Leanna knelt to the dusty train floor to replace the items which had rolled from her bag and her eyes suddenly fell on the worn patches of her skirt. She'd been wearing the same ill-fitting black dress since her grandfather's funeral. He probably mistook me for a beggar, she thought, irritated at the idea that such an elegant man had been drawn to her out of charity. Not much of a way to begin her great adventure.

Her restless night back at Rosemoral was finally beginning to catch up with her, and Leanna tilted her head against the window. Not to worry that he's gone, she thought, as the rolling of the car took her into the first shallows of sleep. London would be full of men like that.

10:20 AM

Not remembering exactly what Aunt Geraldine looked like and unsure where she was to meet her, Leanna stepped down from the railway car and began to study the women in the station. No one seemed to be looking for anyone, so Leanna walked over to a bench and dropped her satchel. People were always commenting on how much she resembled Tom, so perhaps if she stood here long enough her aunt would recognize her.

The activity of the station was all-consuming. The babble of voices formed a non-language and a faintly acrid smell filled the waiting area, some combination of cinnamon, coal dust, human sweat, and rotting apples. Men pushing carts, women pushing prams, boys selling papers, girls selling fruit. A group of people with yellow skin and doll-like slanted eyes walked by Leanna, swathed in vibrant yellow and green silks. She tried to keep from staring until she realized that in the easy familiarity of the crowded station, staring was acceptable.

Suddenly, a loud noise, a woman's scream, came echoing through the hall, and this universal sound of fury seemed to catch the attention of almost everyone. Leanna could not see what had caused the commotion, and she wondered desperately if Aunt Geraldine could be waiting outside in a coach. Groaning as she lifted the satchel, Leanna began shuffling slowly toward the front of the building, and as she walked, the voice became clearer.

"Who is responsible for this outrage? Who is in charge here?" demanded the woman. "Stop right there!" she said, as a single file line of a dozen dark-skinned men wearing white turbans came abruptly to a halt. Leanna strained to look over the gathered heads to see whose voice was so unrelenting, but the only thing in her line of vision was another dark-skinned man, this one in a red turban, who was standing with an air of offended dignity and an oversized umbrella pointed at his nose.

"My lady, we are in the employ of Sir Randolph Walterbury," replied the porter in a sing-song voice.

"And where might I find this coward?"

"I am Sir Randolph, Madame," answered a bald gentleman breaking through the crowd. "Rahaj, why aren't these men loading the transports outside?"

As the people had made way for Sir Randolph, Leanna had been able to slip close enough to catch a glimpse of a tall, broad-chested woman dressed in lavender with a matching hat and an umbrella she used with skill. The umbrella was no longer at the nose of the porter, but was now pointed at the face of Sir

Randolph himself. The man in the red turban signaled to the others to continue with the cargo.

"You stop right there!" shrieked the lady, moving to block the progress of the workers with surprising agility, considering her age and her size. "I have counted eighteen elephant tusks, four tiger pelts, two water buffalo heads, and heaven knows what else. What could possess a person of your stature in society to butcher these innocent animals? They were put on this earth for all of mankind to study and appreciate, not just for the wealthy to destroy and display in their drawing rooms. Well, what do you have to say for yourself?"

"These beasts are trophies of sport, taken on a safari in East India," answered the man, glaring down. "So if you'll let us pass, Madame-"

"Sport? Safari? Why is it every time an Englishman goes out to prove his manhood, it involves killing? Safari indeed! You take every creature comfort you can from London with you, to be carried by these men for miles in the hot sun, trampling the jungle as you go. No doubt you paid them peanuts for their labor. And sport! You call it sport to hire a hundred porters to chase a poor, defenseless animal in front of your rifle sights to be slaughtered? Perhaps if the tigers had been given guns too it would count as fair contest, but were they? I think not!" By now the crowd was murmuring and, at least among a few of the listeners, sympathy seemed to be switching to the side of the woman.

"What I think Madame, is that this is all none of your business! I'll not delay another minute listening to this nonsense." Sir Randolph turned and barked to his men, who were scrambling to carry the rest of the crates onto the transport.

"If you wish to prove your strength, Sir Randolph, then why don't you do something that will improve England? Start a factory and create more jobs! Help the poor!" the woman shouted at his retreating back. A smattering of applause broke from the crowd.

Suddenly the woman glanced back toward her audience and her eyes fell directly upon Leanna. "Darling!" she cried, as the heads of the onlookers turned. "I'd recognize that Bainbridge profile anywhere." Leanna drew back, startled by the shift in the crowd's attention, as the woman bustled toward her, both arms outstretched. "I am your Aunt Gerry! Welcome to London!"

CHAPTER SIX
Autumn, 1872

His father had taught him to hunt.

The man had taken the boy, when he was no more than nine, into the oak woods outside their home. Had given him a gun, one of the sandwiches they had wrapped the night before, and had taught him how to find a place to hide. Not deep in the brambles, as one might imagine. If the hunter sought too much coverage or buried too deep, his father explained, then the slightest move would give his position away.

The father illustrated. He climbed into a nest of broken branches and covered himself entirely. Then he made a great, loud sneeze and the entire pile had shaken, puffing stray leaves into the air. The boy had laughed.

Far better, the man explained, crawling out and brushing the debris from his jacket, to hide in an open area. Perhaps "hide" was not even the proper word. It was more a matter of blending in, of being unobtrusive, of becoming so much a part of the landscape that the birds knew you were there, but did not register your presence as alarming. Ducks, pheasants, and quail were dumb creatures, dumb and plentiful, and if one sat still long enough they would come of their own accord into your sights. The victim would choose himself, would practically beg to be shot.

The boy nodded. He'd always had the gift of grasping concepts quickly, of understanding certain things before his childhood vocabulary gave him the ability to explain them, even to himself. He may not have known the word "contradiction" but he understood his father's message well enough. The key to survival was to be special, smarter than the other creatures around you, yet still to blend in.

The blending, of course, is the challenge. Most who are special cannot seem to stop themselves from announcing the fact, despite the dangers that come with being different from the rest of your species. If you tie a red string around a wren's leg, the others in the flock will peck it to death.

CHAPTER SEVEN
September 25
8:20 AM

"I'm still not certain that it's proper to wear a purple dress in mourning," Leanna fretted, as she pushed a slice of pear around her plate. "Grandfather has only been buried for three weeks."

"You loved Leonard, we all know that," Geraldine said, looking up from her copy of the morning paper. "The important thing is that you and Tom were a comfort to him while he lived, not some barbaric custom you choose to observe after he is dead. Besides, your new gown looks lovely on you."

Leanna ducked her head a bit guiltily, knowing what Aunt Gerry said was true. In the two weeks since her arrival, Leanna had roamed the streets of London daily with Gerry's maid Emma in tow. She had indulged herself in several gowns but the purple one, delivered just the evening before, was her favorite. It brought out the grey in her eyes and she had never worn a color quite so deep and striking. Gwynette had been more of the opinion that maiden girls should wear shades of pink, robin's egg blue, and yellow – colors which suited neither Leanna's temperament nor her coloring.

Ever since Aunt Gerry had mentioned having a dinner in her honor, Leanna had been so carried away with excitement that she'd forgotten to be homesick. Had practically forgotten she was in mourning. But Gerry was right, her grandfather had never been one to stand on ceremony and if he were here he would most certainly tell her to wear what she pleased. Leanna resolutely broke off a bit of bread and smeared it with jam. She wouldn't worry. This was a new life and the old rules did not apply.

Emma entered the room with a fresh pot of tea and, after a rapid glance at the table to make sure all the serving dishes were full, sat down across from Gerry. At first Leanna had been stunned by the casual manner in which Gerry ran her household. She had never seen a home where servants dined within arm's length of their employers and were in fact frequently sought for counsel or companionship.

It was hard to peg Emma's exact social position, but Leanna had to admit that, thanks largely to Emma, what the home lacked in formality it compensated for in efficiency. Emma ordered the food, managed Gerry's daunting social calendar, and supervised the cleaning efforts of the pregnant girls who came in twice a week. Gerry was a patron of a home for unwed mothers and liked to offer these young women the chance to earn a pound or two. The first morning after her arrival, Leanna thought she had gone mad when she bounded down the staircase only to find four big-bellied, child-eyed girls on bended knee polishing the entry floor. Her shock had been magnified when a half-hour later Emma rang that breakfast was ready and they all trooped in to join them at the table, wolfing down massive portions of oatmeal and hot buns. It was all she could do to maintain her composure from cracking into a fit of giggles at the sight of seven women - four of them pregnant and one older woman wrapped from head to foot in an orange silk kimono- sitting in a circle waiting for their tea.

It was at that moment the door to the kitchen opened and she had first spied Gage, the sole male member of Gerry's household. Heaven knows from what charity Geraldine had acquired Gage, but he served as a combination cook and butler and was quite timid. Gerry had informed her on the first night of her visit that Gage had prepared a special welcoming supper but lacked the nerve to serve it to her himself. The ensuing meal had been delicious - a standing rib roast and a delicate apple tart for dessert - and Leanna had begged Gerry to have Gage come out and take his bows. But now that she was actually seeing him she nearly cried out with surprise. Gage had an enormous goiter which obscured the majority of his throat and gave him the appearance of a bullfrog. Other than the large pouch and his eerie silence, he was a model butler, attired in a white linen serving suit even at dawn, and a superlative cook. Leanna couldn't blame the pregnant girls for stuffing extra almond buns into their pockets. If she'd had pockets, she'd have been tempted to steal a few herself.

It was Emma who provided order amid all this chaos, who proved to be the still island around which the flotsam of Gerry's wild life drifted. Leanna wondered why Tom had never mentioned the girl, for she was an enigma to Leanna. Emma could scarcely be any older than herself, yet she was so calm and assured, not only in the brownstone of Mayfair but also in the shops and streets of London. And she spoke in beautiful tones, saying words Leanna had never known a servant to use. She had the look of the Irish, with her gingery hair and milk-white skin, and Leanna was surprised Tom had not found her intriguing. But then he had never mentioned Gage either and Gage was certainly a fascinating specimen of humanity.

"Oh heavens, darling, read this," Aunt Gerry said, dragging Leanna's thoughts back to the present. "Aloud, so Emma and Gage can hear."

Leanna swallowed, and reached for the front page of the Star. "Last night," she read, "the following letter was delivered to the Central News Agency of Fleet Street."

Dear Boss:

I keep on hearing that the police have caught me. But they won't fix me yet...I am down on certain types of women and I won't stop ripping them until I do get buckled.

Grand job, that last one was. I gave the lady no time to squeal. I love my work and want to start again. You will soon hear from me, with my funny little game.

I saved some of the proper red stuff in a ginger beer bottle after my last job to write with but it went thick like glue and I can't use it. Red ink is fit enough, I hope. Ha, ha!

Next time I shall clip the ears off and send them to the police just for jolly.

Jack the Ripper

"Hmmm..." Leanna finished, letting the paper drop, "It's been a few days since they've reported on the killings. Jack the Ripper, he calls himself? It's very fitting."

"It's absolutely ghastly!" said Gerry, "and whatever does he mean 'I'm down on certain kinds of women?'"

"Prostitutes," Emma said shortly. "He hates prostitutes." Gage rose and silently left the table.

"Well he has certainly given Scotland Yard fair warning that he plans to try again," Leanna said. "It's a schoolboy taunt, is it not? Like he's rubbing their noses in the fact they haven't been able to catch him. Oh, look, farther down, they quote one of the detectives. 'Trevor Welles...'" she began.

"Trevor Welles!" Emma and Gerry cried in unison.

"He's a dear friend of mine," Gerry said, "and he'll be your dinner partner on Sunday. Trevor being quoted, imagine that. I knew him when he was just a bobby." Emma gave a little snicker. "Well go on, Leanna," Gerry insisted, "What does he say?"

"He says Scotland Yard has every intention of apprehending the Ripper," Leanna said, dropping the paper again. "He's certainly a talkative sort, isn't he?"

"Tell Leanna how you and Trevor met," Emma said innocently.

"He arrested me," Gerry said.

Leanna raised her eyebrows.

"No, truly, some time back Tess and I and several of the other women in the suffragette movement were protesting the fact women weren't allowed to row on the Thames -"

"Row on the Thames?" Leanna asked skeptically.

"Yes, can you believe it? Any fool or drunk of a man can take a pleasure craft into the water but no woman can steer a boat on the Thames. So we went to Hyde Park and we chained ourselves to trees and we said we would not leave until Parliament -"

"Aunt Gerry," said Leanna, half amused and half impressed. "You chained yourself to a tree outdoors in the elements without food or water or any...facilities? However did you manage?"

"Oh I doubt we were there more than ten minutes," Gerry went on, so absorbed in her story she was oblivious to Emma's muffled giggles. "They sent out the bobbies and Trevor was the one who arrested me. Quite the gentleman he was, and as he was loading me into the wagon he said 'Stick to your guns, ma'am,' rather low under his breath. I'll never forget that. He gave me a bit of courage just as I needed it."

"They seriously took you to the prison?"

"To Newgate, worst in the city."

"Gage and I had to go down and post her bond," Emma said dryly. "She wasn't in a cell. Mr. Welles had taken her and the others into a private room and even fetched them a spot of refreshment."

"I was incarcerated, nonetheless," Gerry said, pulling herself up with great dignity.

"And now he's a detective on the Ripper case," Leanna mused. "This is going to be quite a party."

"Oh dear," Gerry said, peering at her grandniece. "I have two young men coming, but it has suddenly struck me that the others are my age or more. We'll probably seem to be hopeless fuddie-duddies to a girl like you. I do hope you won't be disappointed."

Leanna grinned. "I doubt very seriously I'll consider your friends to be fuddie-duddies," she said, "But are you certain about the purple dress? I wouldn't want to make a false step…"

Emma excused herself and left the table, several plates stacked deftly in the crook of one arm. Gage had cleaned the kitchen, leaving her only the last dishes to do and she lowered them into the warm water of the basin and began to swish them about slowly. The fact that the Ripper promised to kill more prostitutes plagued her mind, and the silly story of Gerry's arrest had not distracted her as thoroughly as it usually did.

It had been four years since Emma had seen her older sister Mary, but she thought of her daily and all the publicity about this madman, this Ripper, was turning her concern into an obsession. Mary - pretty, saucy, and outgoing as she was - had been the idol of her shy, bookish younger sister. Their childhood in Dorchester with their brother Adam, their gentle mother and their schoolmaster father had been idyllic, or at least, Emma thought grimly to herself as she pushed her hair back with one damp palm, it seemed that way in retrospect. Their father had earned a respectable-enough living. Their mother was the angel of the county, so compassionate and skilled a nurse that people called her in to deliver their babies and comfort their dying.

Then came the tuberculosis epidemic seven years ago, which closed the school for three whole terms, leaving her father without the only kind of trade he knew, and which ended with bodies piled high in the local cemetery and few men strong enough to bury them. Emma still dreamed sometimes of the piles of shrouded corpses, stacked as neatly as firewood. Her mother, worn down from incessant nursing, was the first to join them. Her father died four months later, leaving behind three children ranging in age from twelve to nineteen, a heavily-mortgaged home, and boxes crammed full of books.

But if the schoolmaster and his wife had not managed to live to the age of forty, their children shared a strong instinct to survive and a ruthless lack of sentimentality. Within weeks Mary and Adam had stripped the house of every saleable item, divided the paltry lot, and begun to make plans to cope with an uncertain future. Adam had a chance to go the States - a former schoolmate had settled in Seattle and written that there was opportunity for a lad who was young and strong and fearless. It would take everything he had to get there, but he lit out nonetheless, promising to write and send money when he'd made his fortune.

Mary had an idea she could become a governess, so she packed up Emma and the two headed for London. If nothing else, their father had left them a level of education rare in girls, and Mary quickly found work in the home of a prosperous tailor. Grudgingly, he and his wife agreed Emma could stay on too and the girls shared cramped space in the attic, with Emma running errands and doing chores for the humorless housekeeper while Mary drilled Latin into the unwilling heads of the tailor's three sons.

She hated her life. Emma knew it, could sense it, felt the desperation behind Mary's quick smile. Many women on their own with a younger sister to support had done far worse, but she was nineteen years old and the days droned on like the beat of a metronome with no prospects of becoming richer, or fuller, or leading her out of the attic. Emma was powerless to help her sister and now, looking back, Emma could only marvel that Mary had been able to stick it out for two years, so ill-suited was she for the position of governess. One day, shortly after Emma had turned fifteen, Mary had simply disappeared, leaving a note and every pound she had managed to save tied in a scarf on the flat little cot. Emma leafed through the money, unable to blame her sister and too frightened to be angry at this latest desertion.

The note had suggested Emma could stay on as the household governess - a final effort, Emma supposed, for Mary to assuage her conscience. The thought was not altogether ridiculous, for Emma was in fact a better student than Mary had ever been and had continued her studies, in secret, in the evenings. But she was only a year older than the tailor's eldest son and slight for her age. The tailor had roared in fury and deposited her posthaste in the hands of his local sexton with instructions to escort her to the nearest workhouse. Emma sat quietly, politely, as the two discussed her fate. No matter where the sexton took her she had already determined that she would not stay. She had a good mind and thirty pounds tied in a scarf; surely London held something better than a workhouse for her.

It was then that, after years of lucklessness, Emma's life suddenly took a turn for the better. The sexton was a friend of Geraldine Bainbridge, and he mentioned Emma's plight to her. Within hours Emma was delivered not to the squalor of the Knights Home for Indigent Youth, but to an elegant house in Mayfair, where it was at times her job to cook and clean but generally just her job to be sane. To impose discipline and order on an undisciplined and disorderedly household. It was a task for which she was uniquely well-equipped.

She had not minded taking care of Gerry, Emma reflected, as she gave the last plate a cursory flick with a towel, nor had she balked at the string of misfits and ne'er-do-wells Geraldine routinely took into her home. Emma was acutely conscious in every pale face that there, but for the grace of God, went she, and she ladled out soup and sympathy with a sure hand. But this girl, this Leanna, was a different matter. She had talked quite freely with Geraldine about the money she'd inherited and her family's reaction and Emma had for the first time felt the sickening thud of jealousy. Not even the fact that she realized Leanna had been raised in a venomous household instead of the happy normalcy she'd known for twelve years, could abate Emma's envy. Dear thoughtless Gerry had prattled on about the many pleasures London afforded an heiress until Emma could stand to listen no longer and had excused herself.

Leanna, to her credit, at least had enough conscience to seem uncomfortable about the magnitude of her wealth. She had pleaded with Gerry not to introduce her as an heiress, but simply as her grandniece, as her ward, and Gerry had reluctantly agreed.

"It's too new to me," Leanna had said. "I can't get used to the money or the power it represents and I'm afraid people will look at me strangely because of it."

"I inherited money and people don't look at me strangely," Gerry had protested.

Leanna had burst into giggles. "Oh but Aunt Gerry, they do."

Then Geraldine had laughed herself. "You're right, darling, but they don't look at me strangely because of the money. Quite the opposite. A little wealth gives you the right to be as queer as you wish yet remain socially acceptable."

"Well, at least don't mention it around any young men," Leanna had said firmly. "If I should attract suitors I don't want to worry about if they're only interested in my estate. Oh, Aunt Gerry, have I told you? I met the most attractive man on the train. He thought I was destitute and he paid my fare..."

And so she had launched into the same story she had told a half-dozen times since her arrival and Emma finally escaped into the kitchen. If she should attract any suitors? The girl was mad.

With her beauty and breeding she would attract suitors immediately, and Emma had never so acutely felt what Mary must have endured in that attic years ago. She was now the same age Mary had been – almost twenty - and she could feel her youth and womanhood as if they were a palpable ache in her chest. Gerry had offered her a home and a purpose and, like Mary before her, she had kept her mind on her work for a full five years. But she was young, and while she did not have Leanna's long-limbed grace, Emma knew she was pretty. Men looked at her on the streets when she passed. But however was she going to meet any of them? The only man she saw on a regular basis was Gage.

Geraldine had mentioned soup for lunch, but they were out of carrots. Emma reached for her cloak so that she might dash out to the greengrocer. She was glad for the excuse to take a brisk walk. The day was clear with a bite of autumn in the air and the morning fog had burned off to reveal a crystal blue sky. Emma automatically strode the familiar route to the corner grocery, barely noticing what she passed, for her mind had drifted again to her sister. With all the news of the Ripper it was impossible not to think of Mary, for Emma was not being entirely truthful when she told herself that she had not seen her for five years. One winter day, the past December, she had gone with Gerry to deliver toys to an orphanage, ironically one attached to the very same workhouse she had herself so barely avoided. In the dark, dank evening, as they made their trips to and from the carriage with loaded arms, Emma had become aware that someone was watching her. She'd turned to see a solitary figure standing on the sidewalk across the street and although the woman was draped in a lacy red shawl from her nose to her waist, there was something familiar in her stance. Emma stood stock still, unable to look away from the form of her sister, and finally the figure raised one hand, in a kind of greeting, then turned away and disappeared.

She had been quiet for the rest of the evening, unable to enjoy the squeals of the children as they tore into their gaily wrapped gifts, scarcely able to make polite conversation with the nuns who ran the orphanage. When Gerry had inquired why she was so silent, Emma had muttered something about taking a chill. But a mystery of sorts had been solved. Adam had never written the promised letters from Seattle. For all she knew, he had sailed off the edge of the map as the navigators in the old days had threatened, and for years she had thought Mary must have fallen off the earth somehow as well. But now she knew. There was only one reason a woman alone would walk the streets of the East End in a red shawl, and the Ripper had stated to the world that he didn't like that kind of woman. Emma handed the grocer her shopping list with an automatic smile, which stayed plastered on her face as the elderly man flirted and teased her, just as he always did. But her mind was in Whitechapel, which may as well have been a thousand miles away.

CHAPTER EIGHT
September 29, 1888
7:10 PM

Aunt Gerry had been right when she told her not to worry
about the purple dress. Compared to Madame Renata in her
shapeless sari and Tess Arborton in her multicolored plumes,
Leanna would surely be the most conservatively attired woman
in the room. She paused uncertainly on the landing, biting her
lip as she considered the scene below. This was hardly like the
country parties at home, or the scientific conferences
Grandfather had sponsored at Rosemoral, and it wasn't as if she
could expect an escort to be waiting at the bottom of the
staircase.

Besides Tess and Madame Renata, who had stuffed
themselves companionably into the smallest divan, there was an
elderly gentleman in what appeared to be an ancient admiral's
uniform. He was crouched in an absurd, twisted manner,
bending over Tiny Alex, a midget who had traveled the
continent with Barnum before retiring to become the darling of
the London social circuit. Tiny Alex's appeal was not
immediately apparent to Leanna, for the man, who had the
disconcerting manner of a five year old with a beard, seemed far
more interested in Gage's canapés than the swirl of
conversation. Gerry herself, looking flushed and breathless, was
engaged in what appeared to be a debate with a man in grey
broadcloth, a man whose neat shoulders and long, slender torso
seemed somehow familiar to Leanna. This was hardly a group
to be concerned about a young woman who wore purple instead
of the usual black of mourning and Emma, who was circulating
among the group bearing a tray of champagne glasses, noticed
her and gave a nod.

Emma's hair was pulled back in a neat bun and in her stiffly starched maid's uniform she looked like a very bastion of propriety. Silently she paused at the banister and handed up a full glass of champagne. Leanna downed it in one fast gulp and shakily gave the glass back to Emma, who raised her biscuit-colored eyebrows. Leanna didn't care. The champagne was cool and tart and gave her a fast burst of courage. There was surely time for her to drink a magnum; no one below had noticed her arrival.

Tess suddenly stood in a quite agitated manner. "Forty years?" she said incredulously to Madame Renata, who sat still and implacable. "You must have made some dreadful miscalculation. Geraldine, this woman has said there won't be suffrage for forty years."

"Most likely forty thousand," said the tall man in the military uniform, but no one appeared to be listening to him.

"That is what I see," Madame Renata said, folding her arms over her ample abdomen. "It will be the 1920s at the earliest."

"Then your glass ball must be all cloudy or you've read the wrong tea leaves," Tess said, two high spots of color in her cheeks. "I know the women in this movement and they think - "

"Balderdash, they don't think," sputtered the man Leanna had come to think of as The Admiral. "What of that woman who threw herself under the policeman's horse at the front of Westminster Abbey? Damn near unseated him."

Leanna had never heard a man swear in the presence of women, but no one else seemed surprised by the Admiral's choice of words.

"You don't think that shows the depth of her commitment??" Tess demanded.

"Shows the depth of her stupidity. You're confusing hysteria with courage, my dear Tessy."

"I'm not your dear anything and it does show courage. She was willing to risk her life to bring attention to her cause and I –
"

"Balderdash!"

"Hush, Fleanders," Aunt Gerry said. "I know you're all salt and vinegar but the others – "

"He's saying women haven't any courage," Tess said, her chin bobbing furiously.

"Courage, what do women know of courage? Were women in Crimea?"

"Florence Nightingale was," Gerry pointed out. "She spoke to our ladies auxiliary to raise funds for a hospital in-"

"A simple nurse!"

"You're an old fool," Tess said judiciously, accepting another glass from Emma's tray.

"Don't ask me, ask this young man, he looks as if he knows something of women. Tell us all, and speak up, have you ever known a woman to exhibit a real courage, to act as if she had the necessary constitution…"

The gray-backed young man spoke quietly, so quietly that Leanna had to stretch over the railing to hear him. "You'll never convince me women have no courage, Sir. I am an obstetrician. I have watched them fight their own wars on a daily basis."

With this he turned, and Leanna let out a long low gasp of shock.

It was the man on the train. Even though no one had looked at her - and, given the intensity of the discussion, no one was apt to - she sank to her knees and tried to conceal herself behind the railing. She had the sudden foolish feeling that all her thoughts had been laid bare, and that anyone glancing up at the stairwell could have read her emotions in a single look. What manner of coincidence was this, that the man who paid the fare to bring her to London would emerge here as a friend of Geraldine's? And that he would be a doctor?

"You see, Fleanders, that's what happens why you try to circumvent a proper introduction," said Gerry. "This is John Harrowman, the doctor I've been telling you all about, the one who plans to open an East End clinic."

"Really?" said Tess, all smiles now. "When Gerry told me you planned to put a clinic there I was quite swept away."

"I'm afraid saying I plan to do this is a bit premature," said John, emerging from the shadows of the entry and stroking his dark mustache. In the stronger light, he suddenly looked younger, more hesitant, and unaccustomed to such attention. "I haven't the funds yet, so I suppose it should be rightly introduced as more of a dream than a plan."

"What sort of clinic?" asked Fleanders, removing his spectacles to reveal enormous watery eyes.

"An obstetrics clinic."

"Whatever for?"

John paused. "To... deliver babies."

"I repeat, whatever for? They've gotten along all right down there for generations breeding like rabbits without any sort of clinic..."

"A poor woman is as likely to experience a difficult delivery as is a woman of the middle classes."

"Balderdash, there's some sort of difference in the pelvis, isn't there? Ladies have narrow hipbones and their children have large craniums but in contrast those East End women, I suppose you could call them, have large pelvises..."

Leanna remained rigid, her hands gripping the banisters. She had never overheard such a discussion as this in her whole life, but no one in Gerry's parlor seemed to think it at all odd. In fact, Madame Renata was doddering on the edge of a nap, and the midget seemed only concerned with how many clams he could balance in one chubby palm. John, however, stood nearly as still as Leanna, his dark eyes intent on the Admiral.

"I assure you, there's no difference in pelvic size among the classes, nor in cranial size."

"Perhaps you should go back to anatomy class, young man. How else do you describe the ease with which they drop their young?"

A slow flush was beginning along John's cheeks but he took another sip from his glass and when he spoke his voice was low and controlled.

"They don't all drop them so easily, Sir. Both the maternal and the infant mortality rate in the East End is three times that of Mayfair, which is why they need a clinic."

"The young doctor is very forward thinking" said Tess. "You could learn a lesson, Fleanders. This isn't the Dark Ages."

"When it comes to breeding," Fleanders said decisively, "they're animals."

"When it comes to breeding," John said, just as decisively, "we all are."

Just at this moment Madame Renata let go of her crystal ball and it rolled down the valley of her legs and onto the floor with a thump as she settled back with a soft snore.

"See there?" Gerry said. "You've bored my guests with all this dreary talk of pelvises. And where is Leanna? This is her party and - - why, here she is. Come along, darling, everyone is wild for the chance to meet you."

Leanna blushed and stood up quickly as six pairs of eyes rose to the landing. "I'm sorry, I know it looks as if I were eavesdropping…"

"Glad someone found the conversation so enthralling," snorted Fleanders. "Come down and let me have a look of you. Why, you're the image of your grandfather. See here, John, Leanna's grandfather was a physician too."

Leanna supposed that in the nebulous world of Gerry's parties this qualified as an introduction, and she stole a cautious glance at John. Would he remember her as the pauper on the train? But evidently he did not, because he was advancing toward the stairwell smiling and holding out a hand. "Miss Bainbridge, I'm delighted."

Leanna descended one step and suddenly her palm was inside his. She took a deep breath and tried to steady herself as he leaned forward in a confidential manner. "I must apologize, I had no idea a young lady was in a position of overhearing."

"Oh no," she said quickly. Too quickly. "Just as the gentleman said, my grandfather was a physician so I believe I can withstand a discussion of anatomy. My very first memory is when I was three and he let me hold a monkey's head. Or skull, I should say. I held a monkey's skull." Why was she running on like this? She must sound like a lunatic. Fortunately, in this particular room it was unlikely anyone would notice.

"Good heavens John, don't monopolize the child," Tess ordered. "Bring her down here into the light so we can all meet her." John offered his arm and Leanna moved into the circle of scrutiny.

"Fleanders, you're mad," Tess snorted. "This girl is a beauty and Leonard Bainbridge had a jaw like a bull terrier. Tell me, Leanna, what do you think of our position in India? Did you read the editorial in today's Star?"

An hour later Leanna found herself seated on the divan with the still-snoring Madame Renata. After her initial nervousness had passed she had begun to enjoy the party enormously and had found herself becoming quite animated, even venturing into discussion of Darwin with Fleanders, who had proven to be not a retired admiral but a retired major-general. Still, the flow of conversation had been exhausting and she was happy to take a moment's refuge with a second glass of champagne and the slumbering mystic. The divan also offered her a perfect place to observe John Harrowman.

He had not appeared to recognize her at all, which was a tremendous relief… and a slight disappointment. At what point had all her feelings become so muddled? Leanna could remember a time when she felt clearly and strongly about every subject, when she was not dogged by second thoughts and strange random intuitions, but ever since that evening she had fainted in Grandfather's study she had awakened to a different, blurry world.

"I say, Geraldine, do you intend to starve us?" Fleanders suddenly roared. "It's well past eight and there's no sign of a meal."

"One of the guests has sent a message he's been detained, so I suggest you have another clam," Gerry said. "I won't announce dinner until Trevor Welles is here."

"Trevor's coming? Marvelous," squealed Tess. "Do you think he'll know something new about the Whitechapel murders? I'm sure they don't put all the facts in the paper. Geraldine, you're a sly fox to nab such a celebrity. I do hope you've seated him beside me."

"Balderdash, the young man wouldn't want to hear your prattle. Geraldine has the judgment to seat him beside me."

Leanna frowned. Trevor Welles must be quite the paragon to have won the approval of both Fleanders and Tess. She could see Emma gesturing frantically from the doorway and, since Aunt Gerry was too engrossed to remember her hostess duties. Leanna got to her feet and slipped into the hall.

"What's wrong?"

"If Geraldine doesn't decide to serve soon I won't be responsible for this lamb. I've basted it and basted it but it'll dry out if we wait much longer. Gage is completely in a state."

"She says Trevor Welles has been detained."

"Well, she'll hold dinner even if he doesn't appear until midnight, that's for sure. She adores him and with all this publicity about the Ripper -"

"Emma, are all her parties like this?"

"Not quite. They're keeping this one sedate, in your honor."

Leanna sunk back against the wall suddenly feeling overcome with the heaviness of the dress and the unaccustomed champagne. "I suppose you know who is to be seated on my other side as well?"

"Aren't you the very lucky one? It's Doctor John."

Leanna bit her lip again. John made her so nervous she was afraid she would either babble or go mute. She could only hope Trevor Welles proved as fascinating a conversationalist as everyone believed he would be and would keep the talk flowing without much help from her. "Your aunt wanted you between the two eligible men," Emma said. "Those were the only seating instructions she gave, except for the fact that of course she'd be beside Fleanders."

"Why do you say 'of course'?"

"He's Geraldine's beau."

Leanna stared at Emma. "Balderdash."

Emma laughed. "So are you pleased to have the doctor at your side?"

"Better than dining with Madame Renata, I suppose. Wait. Is that the door knocker?"

"It had better be the elusive Mr. Welles. For heaven's sake, eat a few of those clams. You're pale as a ghost."

Emma dashed off, smoothing her apron. Leanna gazed after her, wondering if they would ever become true friends, if indeed it were possible for an heiress to become friends with a maid. She had always regretted her lack of sisters and although she loved her mother, she had never quite broken through Gwynette's reserve. Leanna glanced at her reflection in the mirror and was not displeased. The wine-colored dress, the dress which would never have been allowed in Rosemoral but which seemed almost stuffy for Mayfair, made her look like a woman of the world. She gave the bodice one last nervous yank. The excited murmur in the parlor had confirmed the arrival of Trevor Welles.

Welles was a compact, energetic man and as he shucked his overcoat and handed it to Emma, Leanna noticed the pull of the muscles barely concealed beneath his tweed jacket. He and John were a picture in contrasts with Trevor being blond, ruddy, and giving the sense of a barely contained power - a marked juxtaposition to John's languid dark eyes and long, elegant form.

"Welles," said Fleanders, "Bloody decent of you to make time for us in the middle of all that's happening. Geraldine says she was certain you'd become an inspector from the very first time she laid eyes on you."

"Really, Fleanders, he was just a young copper then. When was that, Trevor, a year ago?"

"Two," Trevor said, his voice deep and a little gravelly. "And I'm afraid I'm a detective, not an inspector."

"And yet they've put you on the Whitechapel case," Fleanders persisted. "That must be quite exciting for all you boys at the Yard. I can't remember a time when everyone in London was so obsessed with the same thing, not even when there was that scandal with the Duke of Clarence and the horsewhip -"

"Emma's going mad," Gerry cut in. "I hope you won't think us abrupt, Trevor, but we've held dinner as long as we can..."

"No, no, I never dreamed you'd hold it at all. Please, let's sit down before we keel over from hunger." He stepped out of the circle of admirers and paused, his eyes lighting on Leanna. "I take it this is our guest of honor?"

"My grandniece," Gerry said promptly, "Leanna Bainbridge. Darling, I have no doubt you know who this is."

"I read the article this morning that quoted you," Leanna said. "And I've been following everything Scotland Yard is doing, even on the train coming in from Leeds." Would this jog John's memory? But apparently not, for he was still twirling his champagne in a meditative fashion. "That article," Leanna told Trevor, "was my first impression of London."

"And you came on anyway? Brave girl."

She laughed, finding him easy to talk to, as easy as Tom, and she let him escort her into the dining room and pull out her chair. Emma, grim faced, was already circulating with the bowls of soup and everyone scurried to their seats like school children.

"Gad, Geraldine, this soup is pink," muttered Fleanders.

"It's borscht, dear. Beet soup and they eat it daily in Russia. Full of iron and good for the blood."

Fleanders dubiously lifted his spoon, not waiting for the ladies. "So tell us everything, Inspector Welles. Give us the sort of gory details they don't put in the papers."

"Yes, do," Tess murmured.

"Please, I'm a detective and not an inspector yet," Trevor protested. "And I'm not in charge of the Whitechapel case, as dearly as I'd love the opportunity."

"You will be before this is over," Gerry said confidently, "and I'll brag to all my friends I was important enough to be hauled in by the Chief Inspector of Scotland Yard."

"Geraldine," Trevor laughed, tasting the borscht with enthusiasm. "If everyone had as much confidence in me as you do, I would be a happy man. You should summon your carriage and take all your friends to the Yard at a gallop to demand I be named head of the case."

"But you should be, darling, and then I'll be able to mention the romantic story of how we met. I can say you arrested me when you were still in your salad days."

"Salad?" trilled Madame Renata. "Did you say we were having salad? Tell the girl to bring it on, I can't bear much more of this horrid soup."

"What's the feeling at the Yard?" John asked, leaning around Leanna and eyeing Trevor in a sympathetic manner. "Do you suspect you're being stuck with an impossible case?"

"Oh, we never say a case is impossible, any more than a doctor would use those words. But it's a difficult one. It was mucked up terribly at first."

"With the first killing they couldn't have known what they were dealing with," John said. "I've done a bit of work on the East End myself, and I know that the women who live there do not necessarily enjoy long lives."

Trevor raised his bushy brows. "You work there?"

"I'm an obstetrician."

"Indeed? You must be the Dr. Harrowman I've heard so much about. Some of the women we've interviewed in connection with the case have mentioned your name. Saint John, I believe they call you and I must say your plan of a clinic is commend-"

"Blast that clinic," Fleanders snorted, drops of borscht in his white beard. "Tell us what you know."

"Not much," Trevor said bluntly. "The doctor is right, with the first case they had no idea they were dealing with a serial killer – "

"Serial?" Geraldine asked, frowning.

"Serial, as in a series. Multiple killings at the hand of one person, with the victims chosen apparently at random. It's a new term, there's no reason you should have heard it." Trevor turned back to John. "The body was moved and washed before we could even inspect it. The whole area was hosed down, wiped clean by the local coppers..."

"Well of course they wouldn't leave the mess for their superiors," Madame Renata said.

"Actually Madame, they left us a bigger mess. Any evidence that may have been in the area was washed away. There's no respect in the force for forensic detail, they just rush in topsy-turvy and mop up the crime scene as if it were a ballroom after a party. So there's no way of knowing what we might have missed. For example, perhaps there were footprints in the blood which would have given us some indication of the killer's shoe size."

"Frustrating for you, I can imagine." John said.

"Maddening," Trevor confirmed. "And the second case was handled nearly as badly. But this time I think the killer wished to leave us a bit more of a clue."

"A clue? What do you mean?" said Leanna.

"It's odd, but it seems we're being teased a bit. The second unfortunate woman- I'm almost finished with the soup, yes, thank you, Emma..." Leanna looked up, surprised Trevor knew Emma by name. "The second woman had been worked on a bit more thoroughly than the first."

"Do tell, tell us everything," Tess said. "Good heavens, this is exciting and the papers are so incomplete in their descriptions. When will there ever be another story like this one in London?"

Trevor nodded vigorously. "I agree. It's the case of the century, in my humble opinion. In the second woman, Annie Chapman , both the ovaries and her kidneys were missing..."

"Dear lord," gasped Gerry. "We're dealing with a madman."

"No, no, not totally," Trevor said. "That's the interesting part. The organs were removed with great skill, with very little trauma to the outer tissues, as if the person doing the job was a professional of some sort. There was a washed leather apron found nearby, quite devoid of evidence, unfortunately, but it was an apron of the type used by people who work in slaughterhouses. And there are two in the area."

"Ah, I see, so you think the killer may work in one of them," said Gerry. "A butcher would have some anatomical knowledge."

"That was our first thought, yes," Trevor said, leaning back to allow Emma to take his soup dish and replace it was a steaming plate of lamb.

"But that seems almost too obvious, doesn't it?" Leanna said, so absorbed in the story that her shyness had disappeared. "To leave a slaughterhouse apron is almost like a joke."

Trevor turned to her, his eyes piercing. "Yes, yes, Miss Bainbridge, that's precisely as I see it. I believe he meant us to think of the slaughterhouse, just as you say, as a type of nasty joke, but I don't believe the killer would leave an apron in sight if he actually worked there. My superiors cling to the idea and in fact the papers originally called the killer Leather Apron, before he himself provided us the far more memorable moniker Jack the Ripper. But just as you say, Miss Bainbridge, I think the apron is a planted clue. Meant to throw us off the true scent." Trevor sighed. "And the killer had more than just some anatomical knowledge. To remove four bodily organs so quickly…"

"….would take a surgeon," John finished. A brief silence fell on the party as they all sat absorbed in their private thoughts.

"I think so too, as does the police physician who did the autopsy on the body," Trevor said. "A bit of his report was printed in the paper."

"But a doctor wouldn't be in those streets and wouldn't commit such savageries," protested Fleanders. "It's almost as if you're saying you think the Ripper is...a gentleman."

Trevor laughed. "Well he was hardly a gentleman, was he? But I think it's possible he could be of the upper classes, could be an educated man."

"Balderdash," roared Fleanders.

"Yes, that's pretty much what my superiors say," Trevor conceded. "Geraldine, this rack of lamb is a marvel." Everyone else looked down at their untouched plates.

"Yes," Leanna said hollowly, picking up her fork. "Tell Gage it looks wonderful."

"But if you're saying that the Ripper is an educated man," Tess protested, "I must say that for once I'm in agreement with Fleanders."

"I'm only repeating what the autopsy revealed," Trevor said with equanimity. "A body couldn't be drained of blood that quickly unless -"

"Drained of blood?" everyone howled in unison. Even Tiny Alex, perched precariously on a stack of books, looked appalled.

"Yes, that's the oddest thing of all," Trevor said. "Both bodies had been nearly completely drained of blood. There were few bloodstains around them, but very little when you consider the severity of the wounds."

"They were killed somewhere else and moved," Leanna ventured.

"You think like me, Miss Bainbridge," Trevor said, clearly paying her what he considered to be the ultimate compliment. "But there were no trails of blood, no stains anywhere else."

86

"If they were strangled before the butchering began," John said thoughtfully, "that would have reduced the bloodflow when the throats were cut."

"Exactly as Dr. Phillips saw it."

Leanna slumped down, dismayed. John and Trevor were literally talking over her head.

"But the spill would still have been significant," John went on. "Unless Leanna is right and the body was moved, I don't see how it could have been drained on the spot without leaving behind bloodstains."

"A madman," Gerry repeated. "A maniac."

"He'll never be found," Madame Renata intoned. Everyone paused and stared at her.

"This Jack the Ripper," she said. "He will never be apprehended."

"I'm set to prove you wrong, ma'am," Trevor said.

"Oh don't be dismayed by her, Inspector," Tess said. "An hour or two ago, she told me women wouldn't receive the vote until the 1920's. She's not so gifted a clairvoyant as she thinks."

"It's not the purpose of my gift to just tell people what they wish to hear," Madame Renata said, delicately picking at her rice pilaf.

"And I'm not an inspector." Trevor said, more to himself than anyone else.

"With so much attention is there any chance Jack will simply move on?" John asked. "He has to be aware he's the priority of Scotland Yard."

"All the more reason we think he won't stop," Trevor said. "He enjoys the stage he's built for himself." Trevor was aware that the "we" he referred to was not the whole of the Yard but rather just himself and Abrams, but he nodded with confidence as he spoke. "There was a definite sense of escalating violence between the murders, even though they were only a week apart.

In the first case, Nichols, the throat was merely cut. In the second, not only did Chapman lose several body organs but the initial slash was so deep that her head was nearly severed from her body…"

Leanna lunged for her water glass, feeling light headed and queasy. Even Tess had paled a bit in this last description and Trevor looked around the table, suddenly embarrassed. "I'm sorry. I have such a mania for this case that when I begin talking I must confess I lose all reason. I've forgotten the ladies."

"Hmmm," said Fleanders, looking none too hale himself. "Let's talk of Jenny Lind."

"Indeed," John said, lifting his wine glass. "Let's talk of Jenny Lind. Did you hear Barnum is asking sixty pounds for a ticket to hear her sing at the Palladium? Did you command those fees on your tour, Alex? That's a crime of robbery, wouldn't you say?"

Leanna took another gulp of water and looked around the room. The group had grown subdued and Trevor was looking down with reddened cheeks, cutting into his lamb with – there was no other way to say it - the concentration of a surgeon.

Later, in the kitchen, Emma stood scraping bones into a pail while Gage busied himself with the tea. Despite the delay in serving, Emma thought dinner had gone well. She was so preoccupied with her chores that it was a minute before she heard the rapping. Wiping her hands, she walked over and squinted out into the darkness but the small glass plate in the center of the door revealed no one. She cautiously unbolted the door to find a young boy, cowering in the darkness and compulsively wiping his nose on a raggedy sleeve.

"He's heard of Geraldine's charity," Emma thought, prepared to bring him in and warm up a plate. "All the stray dogs of London know about Geraldine." But before she could speak the child blurted out, "Is Saint John 'ere?"

"I beg your pardon?"

"Saint John, ma'am, 'is cook said he's come 'ere. Me Mum, she's awful bad with a baby…" He broke off, wild-eyed, and Emma took his arm and drew him inside.

"Yes, just take a breath. Dr. Harrowman is here and I'm sure he'll come with you. Gage?" But the butler had already disappeared into the dining room, returning in a matter of seconds with John.

"It's me Mum, Saint John," the child stammered, bursting into tears of relief. "She said I was to find you."

"So the baby's come calling a little early, um, Bobby?" John said, pulling on this black cape and tying a red scarf loosely around his throat. "We'll find a cab and be across town in an instant." He put an arm around the boy's thin shoulders and handed him a handkerchief, as they stepped out into the night.

"Thank you Emma, Gage," John called back. "Lovely dinner. Please give my apologies to Miss Bainbridge and Geraldine." Emma stood in the doorway, watching the two until their backs were obscured by the mist, occasionally catching scraps of John's voice gently saying "Hush, Bobby, your mum's come through this sort of business before." Emma's chest tightened as she remembered how frantically she and Adam had gone from house to house seeking the county doctor when her mother had begun her own death rattle. But there had been no doctor, no carriage, no hope.

I suppose it's true, she thought to herself, staring after the dark man in the dark cape disappearing into the dark night. He really is a saint.

CHAPTER NINE
Winter, 1872

The snows came, and it was time to go back to school. The boy was a good pupil and most days he had finished the problem while his classmates were still struggling over their slates. Sometimes he even caught his teacher in small mistakes, although he was careful to never let this awareness show on his face.

One Sunday he protested a sore throat so that he would not be required to walk to the village church with the rest of his family. He wanted to take his father's gun and go hunting by himself. He sat at the foot of an oak for an hour, neither moving nor hiding and, just as his father had promised, the birds soon ceased to register his presence at all. He watched as a covey of quail trotted no more than a meter before him, one of them straggling behind. Was it his imagination that the bird looked willing, that it seemed to somehow self-select? He sent it a silent message in his mind. Slow down. Even more. Yes, that's it. Separate yourself a bit farther from the group.

A snapping twig. His awareness snapped too, back to the broader world of the clearing and when he looked up he saw to his horror that a wolf was standing opposite him, wary and crouched at the top of the bank. It was a huge and hulking beast, dark, its mouth stretched into a horrible parody of a human smile. How long it had been there or what had kept it from springing he could not say. He scrambled to his feet, fumbled with the gun, shot wildly into the air. The wolf disappeared into the underbrush and the boy fell trembling to his knees.

How quickly the hunter can become the hunted. How quickly the hungry can become the meal. It was a lesson he would never forget.

He spent three Sundays searching before he found it. When he did, he opened fire and heard a long low bellow of pain when the bullets found their mark. Followed the bloody stagger until the beast dropped, and then ran across the field to its body. Its final expression was a grimace of surprise. So this is death, the wolf's face seemed to say. Not at all as I'd imagined.

Should he bring it home, mount its head or clean its pelt? No, there was no way to explain this to his parents, who had forbidden him to go into the deepest parts of the forest, had forbidden him to take the gun, who were growing suspicious of this fever than only seemed to befall him on holy days. And besides, now that he was observing the wolf up close, he was disappointed. It was not the great rival he'd pictured. In fact it was a shaggy, malnourished creature, with clotted hair and protruding ribs, not even a proper trophy. He looked down at it sadly. Everything seems smaller when it's dead.

The bullet marks seemed a violation of the wolf's flesh and he knelt, impelled by something he did not fully understand, and pulled his knife from the pocket of his jacket. Its dull blade made ragged progress across the animal's belly, but the rising blood briefly delineated the cut, creating a perfect and elegant line before it began to spill. He said something aloud. A word he would not later remember. He felt the heat emanating from the wound, felt the promise of something more profound beneath the mottled skin. Felt himself being called, like a priest to the altar or a sailor to the sea.

Throughout the long winter, while the other pupils read the lesson, their brows furrowed and their lips moving, the boy would practice sitting completely still. Monitoring his breathing to the point of silence. Controlling the many small impulses the flesh is prey to – the desire to scratch, to yawn, to blink. The clock on the wall ticked away the seconds, measured the times between blinks, between exhalations, between the movements and fidgets that would betray lesser men. He understood. He saw it all. His family was poor, nondescript. Their limited funds would go to educate his oldest brother, to provide his sister with a dowry. The village they lived in was dying. Anyone with any wit left as soon as he could, headed for the city where the newborn factories and mills offered a sort of brutal hope.

If he was to attend the University, to become a physician, it was up to him. If he was to have a life, he must author it himself.

By the time spring came, the boy could go ninety-four seconds between blinks.

CHAPTER TEN
September 30
12:36 AM

It was well after midnight, but Leanna wasn't sleepy. She'd been wearing both her hair and her corsets looser since she'd come to London, so she'd been able to undress herself without Emma's assistance and she now lay sprawled across the puffed pink bedspread in her camisole and bloomers, with her hair tousled down around her shoulders.

Emma rapped twice on the door and, not waiting for a response, entered. She was exhausted herself and Leanna's languor was an irritating reminder that she still had plenty picking up from the party to do. Leanna rolled over and propped herself up on her elbows. "It was a wonderful evening, wasn't it, Emma?"

"Seemed to be."

"I'm just sorry John couldn't stay to the end."

"Poor girl. Left with only one adoring male and not a matched set." Emma signaled for Leanna to stand and pulled the corset over her head, a little more roughly than usual. "It was a child who came for John, scared out of his wits because he thought his mother was dying in childbed. If you could have seen the gratitude which swept him when John walked into that kitchen you wouldn't be so sorry that you lost an escort."

Leanna sat down and began to unlace her slippers, face flaming. At home, it would have been inconceivable for a maid to speak to her in such a tone, but things in London were not so clearly delineated. Gerry introduced Emma as her companion, surely one of the most conveniently vague words in the English language, and Emma most often dined with the family. But not tonight, not on the more formal occasion of Leanna's launch into society. Tonight she had served them, had fastened the innumerable hooks of Leanna's plum silk and then gone to button up her own black cotton, had watched John and Trevor contend to pull out Leanna's chair while she gulped down a few bites in the kitchen with Gage, had carried plates and serving trays rather than gay conversation. No wonder that the girl sometimes showed temper.

"Besides," Emma went on, her voice softening almost as if she had read Leanna's thoughts, "it wasn't as if Trevor didn't remain to dance attendance."

"You like him, don't you?" Leanna asked, not raising her eyes. "He comes here more often than you and Aunt Gerry said."

"He's a fine man," Emma said shortly. "Easy to talk to."

"Exactly my thoughts, and I found him quite fascinating. In a different way from John, of course. But Trevor speaks to me..." Leanna paused, "As if I were a human being."

"And how does John speak to you?"

"As if I were a lady."

Emma shook out the plum gown. "I didn't realize the two were mutually exclusive."

Leanna watched Emma adjust her dress on the hanger and thought back to the day they had bought it, how differently the shopkeeper had treated the two girls. He had approached her with – well, she supposed the word was "respect" but it didn't feel like respect, it had felt like a refusal to speak directly to her at all. But Emma he had treated like an equal. Men categorized women very quickly, that was clear, but what was the basis of the sorting?

"You know," Leanna said "John didn't recall meeting me on the train."

"Um?"

"John. He didn't recall meeting me in the train."

"He was the man who paid your fare? How bizarre."

"Apparently I failed to make much of an impression."

Emma shrugged. "You were different then. I remember how you looked standing on the doorstep a few weeks ago. Lost, frightened, practically swimming that black mourning dress. Tonight ....it's not so surprising he didn't remember. A woman isn't like a man. She can change and become anything she wants to appear to be, based on her clothes and her way of walking and talking."

"Odd," Leanna said. "But you're right. Men don't look us in the eyes. They take in the clothes and the bearing and they adjust their behavior accordingly."

"Trevor Welles looks women in the eyes," Emma said quietly.

"Yes," said Leanna. "He would be a hard man to fool."

"Now in my opinion, that is the odd remark," Emma said, turning to leave.

"Emma?"

"Yes?"

"Do you have any sisters?"

"No."

"Neither do I."

"How unfortunate for you," said Emma, closing the door behind her.

"Auugh," sighed Leanna, rising from the bed. Of all the things she had struggled to understand since coming to London, Emma might have been the hardest. Leanna went to the dressing table and began to brush her hair so hard that tears came to her eyes.

1:24 AM

At the entryway to the George Yard stables, Trevor stood looking down at the lifeless form of a woman. An hour earlier a man had been trying to lead a workhorse into the courtyard when the creature had shied and refused to enter. He'd summoned a bobby making rounds and the boy had quickly found the trouble: a white-stockinged leg sticking out from a gate. Trevor breathed a silent prayer of relief that the bobby - although young and obviously terrified - had exhibited enough presence of mind to rope off the area and leave the body unmoved. Now Eatwell and a few others milled around, awaiting the arrival of Dr. Phillips and trying to keep the throng of onlookers at bay. Although the night was warm, Trevor trembled violently.

"Isn't typical, is it Sir?" he ventured, as Eatwell paced by.

"What do you mean?" Eatwell asked distractedly.

"Her throat is cut, left to right like the others, but there aren't any mutilations."

"You sound disappointed," Eatwell said. "Ah, Abrams, what do you make of this?" Trevor looked up to see that Rayley Abrams had joined their circle. While the other detectives looked as if they'd been summoned from their beds – as indeed he himself had been – Abrams was as neatly groomed as ever. He stared soberly down at the woman.

"Surprising that he'd change his method, Sir."

"I agree," said Trevor. "Just a few days ago in the paper he bragged that he would –" Trevor stopped, a sudden revelation sweeping with nauseating certainty. "He didn't finish."

"She's finished plain enough," Eatwell said but Abrams looked at Trevor and gave a slow, almost imperceptible nod.

"We need to scour the area, Sir," Trevor said, his heart beginning to pound. "Something – probably the man with the horse – interrupted the killer before he could leave his usual calling cards. And that would have made him furious."

"Perhaps," said Eatwell. "But why should we care if he's furious?"

Because people kill when they're furious, you imbecile, Trevor thought. Struggling to control his voice he said, "Perhaps a patrol of the area is in order, Sir, or at least an alarm with the whistles. If Jack's still about, we'll flush him."

"This many coppers in the area and you think he's still about?" Eatwell said. "In my experience, killers flee once the deed is done and this deed is most assuredly done. Sir Warren himself is on the way here and I want the whole contingent at the ready."

"I believe that's Phillips now, isn't it?" Abrams said quietly, directing Eatwell's attention toward the street as a carriage rattled up to the front of the stable. The inspector turned to greet its occupant.

"See here," Trevor said, using the diversion to step back from the circle and whisper to the bobby who'd found the body. "What's your name, lad?"

"Davy Madley, Sir."

"Look round the area."

The boy nodded and slipped off without questions. Trevor hung back, watching Phillips' assistant all but lift him from his carriage and lead him over to the body. "Good God," said the old man. "Another one."

"But she doesn't fit the pattern..." Trevor said.

"No, by all appearances this one gave him a bit of a fight," Phillips said, crouching and gingerly turning over the long, lean body of the prostitute. "Look, even now you can see bruises forming..."

"Check her nails," Trevor insisted. "Women fight with their fingernails." Phillips ventured a grim smile.

"What are you, mad for fingernails? Very well..."

Just then three sharp blasts of a whistle pierced the night and the men clustered around the body all jumped. Davy Madley was running toward them, his face chalk-white and his breathing ragged. "Come, come, it's just as you said, Sir. There's another and he – he had plenty of time for this one, Sir."

Trevor turned to the bobby and shouted "Get back there, and keep the crowds away. Keep the police away." Davy spun and ran back into the darkness as if he were being chased by the devil himself.

"Don't let them touch her," Trevor cried after the boy's retreating form. "Don't let them move her. For the love of the Virgin, don't let anyone near that body."

2:22 AM

At his home in Brixton, a half-hour on foot from the house of Geraldine Bainbridge and an equal half-hour from the streets of Whitechapel, John Harrowman stood at his wash basin. Slowly, methodically, almost dreamily, he washed the last vestiges of blood from his hands. His favorite scalpel, the one he'd performed his very first surgery with and the one which still felt most at home in his hand, lay disinfected on a folded white towel and a bundle of bloodied clothes had been stuffed in his hassock. He'd been up for twenty hours, but John was not tired. Instead, as he scrubbed and the water blushed from pale pink to red, he was conscious that he was humming, that he was happy. He found a sense of exhilaration and power in his work.

No matter how late the hour, he always returned from the streets of the East End feeling right within himself.

Still humming, he turned from the washstand and walked over to his window. His working class neighborhood was sleeping, and John's thoughts drifted back to the girl, Leanna. He had been absorbed in his medical practice for years, perhaps too many, and meeting her had reminded him there was another life out there, a life beyond the women of the East End. He caught a glimpse of himself in the window-glass and softly cursed. It had been a rough one; even his undershirt was splattered with dried drops of blood, and he thought for a moment of removing it and adding it to the pile of laundry. But he crawled in his bed instead, letting out a deep sigh, willing sleep to come and stop this strange pounding in his chest. He hugged his own arms, the memory of the night comforting him and in truth - for he was a doctor to the core - even the faint smell of blood was a pleasure.

CHAPTER ELEVEN
2:22 AM

"There, Sir!" Davy held up his light and pointed to a heap lying on some overturned garbage, then involuntarily averted his face from the overwhelming, slightly metallic smell of freshly spilled blood. Trevor rushed by Davy and held up his light also, gasping as it showed the extent of the carnage which lay at his feet. Davy, who had seen far enough already, dipped his own lamp and stepped back.

Trevor took Davy's lantern and laid it on the ground beside the body, then placed his own on the other side, allowing the flickering oil light to spill over what was left of the woman's face. He pushed his palm firmly against his mouth, willing back the wave of nausea which had quickly overtaken him, while poor Davy huddled against one of the cold alley walls, fighting a losing battle with his own stomach.

"Sorry, Sir," he gasped, wiping away tears with the back of his hand. "Isn't like me, Sir."

"It's alright, son," Trevor muttered, wondering if he would be joining the boy in another minute. "Pull yourself together when you can and keep those people back in the street."

Davy nodded, then squared his slight shoulders and headed back toward the mouth of the alley. The size of the crowd moving toward him made him pause and almost turn back, but Detective Welles was already on his knees beside the victim and Davy would rather have been ripped to shreds than to once again appear weak before a superior.

Davy stretched out his arms and gave several firm blasts of his whistle, but nonetheless people pushed forward. Finally, a few feet short of Welles, the crowd stopped and gasps circulated throughout as each onlooker caught sight of the body. There was a second of silence, then a woman screamed, "Why 'tis Cathy! Catherine Eddowes! And 'e's lopped off her ears like 'e said in the Times!"

"Damn it," Trevor hissed over his shoulder at Davy. "Get that woman out of here this instant! All of you, go home to where you belong." The crowd stood still, more from shock than defiance, until, using his cape somewhat in the manner of a matador, Davy began to shoo them out of the alley. The rest of the officers had at long last arrived and were standing uncertainly in the street.

"You two," Davy shouted, too distraught to care that he was yelling at men who outranked him, "push this mob back. And someone take a cloak and shield that body until the doctor arrives."

"T'would be my pleasure, Sir," one of the men muttered, while the other, with a snort, began to disperse the crowd. The bobby became decidedly less flippant when he saw Catherine Eddowes and he swayed a bit on his feet as he unclasped his cloak.

"Steady, man," said Trevor, who had been following a thin trail of blood from the body. "I need you to follow this line to its end."

"I...I, Sir..."

"Here, dear God, are you going to faint? Just stand and hold up that cape, just so, like a wall. Davy, lad, you take up the trail of blood. And be careful," he shouted as the boy faded into the fog.

"You were right," a voice said, with a tight and barely controlled anger. Without turning, Trevor knew it was Rayley Abrams and he was relieved to have the man at his side. "The blood's plentiful and fresh," Abrams said. "Damn it to hell, this time we could have stopped him...." Abrams spat, the vehemence of the gesture surprising Trevor, and then, without further comment, the two men began to use their lights to look behind barrels and crates. Their minds were running in the same direction, but there was no murder weapon to be found.

"Worth a try," Abrams said. "The bastard's so sure of himself I wouldn't put it past him to leave the knife in plain view." They could hear huffing and puffing coming from the direction of the street, and two figures were approaching with lanterns, the smaller carrying a satchel. "Is that you, Inspector? And is the Doctor with you?"

"Yes, and yes." Eatwell said shortly. The brisk walk from George Yard had obviously not agreed with him.

Trevor led the two men back to the garbage pile, as Abrams, with a gesture he found impossible to interpret, slipped from the alley and back into the street. "Before you look," Trevor said to Phillips and Eatwell, "I warn you to expect a most gruesome sight. The absolute worst yet."

"Really, Welles, you missed your calling on the stage," Eatwell muttered as he pushed aside the young copper who had been holding up the cape. "Mother of God!" he gasped, as he quickly turned and stepped away, his face dissolving into an expression Trevor would have enjoyed under different circumstances.

Without a word, Phillips signaled to the men standing behind him. His chief assistant, Severin, stepped forward to clasp the doctor under the arms and slowly lower him to his knees. The other moved in with two more lanterns, which he placed at the feet of the body and the additional light illuminated the enormity of the task before them. The woman had been disemboweled with at least an arm's length of her intestines carefully draped about her shoulders, as if they were a shawl. The eyes, nose, lips, and cheeks were all gouged and sliced, giving her face the appearance of a discarded doll, lying in the street but staring up at the heavens. As promised, her ears had been neatly severed. Phillips did not look up at Trevor as he closely investigated the woman's fingernails, but apparently Catherine Eddowes had not been given time to strike back at her assailant, for her hands were unmarked. Nor did it appear she had been drained or moved because the alley was awash in blood, so much so that when Phillips finally stood, again with assistance from his companions, his pants were brown and dripping. "Very recent," he said quietly. "No more than a half hour at most."

"Detective Welles! Come quick!" shouted Davy from farther down the street and, giving Eatwell perhaps a bit more of a shove than was necessary, Trevor raced toward the young man's cries. He found Davy and Abrams staring at a stone wall chalked with letters.

"Read this." Abrams said quietly, holding his light up to the wall.

THE JUWES ARE NOT THE MEN THAT WILL BE BLAMED FOR NOTHING

Trevor frowned. "What does it mean?"

Abrams shook his head. "It could mean anything. I presume he's referring to Jews, although if he's the educated sort we thought he was, the misspelling makes no sense. And the double negative. It could mean we shouldn't blame the Jews. It could mean that if we do blame the Jews we would be justified in doing so. It may not be related to these bodies at all. For all we know, those words may have been written a week ago by some random person with a grudge against the Hebrew faith."

"Oh no Sirs, begging your pardon, Sirs," said Davy. "This street is on my regular rounds and there was nothing on this wall when I passed it earlier tonight. These words were written in the last hour, I'll vouch for that."

106

"Dear God, what now?" Eatwell gasped, rounding the corner. He stopped and considered the wall in silence, then let out a long low curse.

"Wipe that wall," he said.

"Inspector," Abrams said, "We have reason to believe this message –"

"Is an abomination and should be wiped off immediately," Eatwell snapped, staring at the wall with the same expression he had turned toward the mutilated face of Catherine Eddowes. Then he motioned to Trevor and said, between clenched teeth, "You've wanted your chance, you made that plain enough. Alright then, I drop the whole bloody mess in your lap. From this point on you're chief coordinator of the Whitechapel investigation."

Trevor stared at him in the flickering gaslight, incredulous. "It's mine?"

"It's yours, damn you, it's yours."

Trevor turned blindly toward Abrams but the man wasn't there. Instead, he was walking the length of the wall, moving his lantern slowly back and forth. It should be his case, Trevor thought. I want it and I'll take it, but by all rights, he's the better man for the job.

Abrams turned toward him with a soiled cloth in his hands. "A woman's apron," he said quietly, so quietly that Trevor had to strain to hear. "Most likely belonging to one of the women and the beast must have wiped his hands on it before leaving. "

"This isn't right, Abrams –"

"Mark it. Fiber evidence."

Trevor started to say something else but was interrupted by the sound of approaching footsteps. "Davy," he called down the street. "I said keep those blasted people back in the courtyard!"

"I am Police Commissioner Sir Charles Warren," came a deep voice form the mist. "I take it you're in charge here, Detective?"

"Excuse me, Sir," Trevor stammered. In seven years of police work he had never even seen Sir Warren, who directed activities from his office and was reputed to be a criminal genius. "Yes, I am Detective Trevor Welles."

"Before the newspaper people start nagging at me in a few hours, I'd like to know if there is anything to report besides two more butchered whores."

"Well Sir, we found this bloodstained apron and these writings on this wall," answered Trevor, holding up a light so the Commissioner could read.

"Wash this blasphemy off this instant, Detective."

"But Sir, we're quite sure it was written by the killer. Shouldn't someone else have a look at it?"

"I don't care if it was put there by the Queen herself. Wash it off this instant, or we'll have every Jew in London murdered in a racial backlash. Things are bad enough as they stand and I have no wish to add some sort of religious purge to our problems. Do you, Detective Welles?"

"The papers don't have to know of this, Sir."

"Are you mad, Detective? Do you honestly think they'd leave a stone unturned in trying to report the case of the century? They lack all discretion when it comes to selling a paper and I won't have it on that wall a second longer. Am I quite clear?"

"Yes Sir."

"Then if you have nothing more to report, I'll leave you to your investigation." Sir Warren raised his lantern to his face, affording Trevor his first clear look at the legend, who in truth resembled any other white-haired, aging Londoner.

"Very good, Sir," said Trevor, his shoulders slumping with discouragement. Abrams seemed to have disappeared and Davy was already wiping off the wall. Trevor stared at the last faint chalk marks, frowning.

"You think this means he's Jewish, Sir? Or that he wants us to think he's Jewish? Maybe he just hates Jews the way he hates prostitutes, Sir?"

"Maybe so," Trevor said wearily. "I don't know what the deuce it means."

"Abrams is a Jewish name, isn't it, Sir?"

"Yes. Which is precisely why I was placed in charge instead of a more deserving man."

He walked slowly back toward the mouth of the alley where Phillips had finished his preliminary examinations and was overseeing the wrapping of the body in a standard Scotland Yard shroud. The Commissioner had also stopped to talk with Eatwell, who had obviously heard the tongue-lashing he had given Trevor and who now appraised him with an irritatingly self-satisfied expression.

"Do we know who she is yet?" the Commissioner was asking.

"A woman in the crowd identified her as Cathy Eddowes. We have a man taking her statement," Trevor said quickly, anxious to reestablish that it was he, and not Eatwell, who would be answering the questions. "We'll have the name of the first woman within the hour, Sir."

"I want a full report as soon as possible. See to it, Detective," said the Commissioner before he faded into the early morning.

Doctor Phillips had finished his notes and started putting his instruments back into his black bag. "I don't have to tell you that things are getting worse," he said to Trevor. "Perhaps I'll know more after I examine her in the laboratory, but..."

"I'll see you to your coach, Doctor," said Eatwell, stepping in and even grabbing the doctor's arm in his haste to keep thing moving. "And I want a copy of that report also, Detective Welles. You're head of one case, my boy, and that's all. You still answer to me."

"Of course, Sir."

"I'm leaving Severin to make sure the body gets to the proper morgue this time," Phillips called from the steps of his carriage. "No more of this shed-washing."

"You know me better than that, Doctor."

It was hard to tell in the fog but Trevor believed the doctor may have smiled as the disappeared into the dark confines of the carriage.

5:59 AM

The sun was rising, barely visible but there nonetheless, and Trevor stood alone in the street. Davy and Severin had loaded the two bodies on the cart and Trevor felt that, young as he was, Davy would competently oversee their delivery to the Yard.

As the rickety wagon passed by the gathered onlookers, a girl of no more than fourteen broke through the barrier. Although her form was that of a child, her low bodice revealing more bone than flesh, she was dressed in the colors and style of a Whitechapel working girl just back from an evening's labors. "Mother!" she shrieked, reaching toward the cart. "Oh, it can't be you!" A woman tried to restrain her as she fell upon the draped body and wept, and another woman, similarly dressed, emerged from the crowd and pulled the girl to her chest.

Trevor clutched the bloody apron tightly in his hands. The citizens of Whitechapel were roped back at one end of the street and yet again at the other, and Trevor stood between the two mobs, alone, turning in a slow circle. The girl gave one last anguished wail and then was gone, sucked back into the crowd as swiftly as she had sprung from it. Trevor wondered if he had imagined her.

CHAPTER TWELVE
October 1
9:45 AM

"I'm glad you could come out with me, Leanna," John said, holding the reins lightly in his hands as the two horses trotted toward Hyde Park. "I know I wasn't able to give you much notice."

"It's fine, really," Leanna said, smiling slightly as she recalled the mad flurry of activity John's letter had brought. She had read the invitation in one glance, squealed, and then breakfast was abandoned while Emma and Gerry helped her dress and put up her hair. There hadn't even been time for a roll, much less the morning papers, but Leanna had spent enough time with physicians to know that a woman must take their company whenever it is offered, even if an invitation comes at the unseemly hour of eight in the morning. She beamed up at John as her stomach grumbled.

"See there?" John said, gesturing with one leather-gloved hand. "Down that street a few blocks is where I hope to put my clinic. We're very near the East End, which I imagine is one part of London Geraldine hasn't taken you touring." He glanced down at Leanna and laughed at her odd expression. "Don't worry, I shan't take you that way either. There's a café on Bank Street just across from the commons and I thought we could stop there for a bit of breakfast."

Leanna pulled Gerry's green velvet cape a bit more tightly around her shoulders. The air held autumn for the first time and she was suddenly and unexpectedly hit with a wave of homesickness, for at Rosemoral the grounds would be awash with the brilliant colors of fallen leaves and here in London there was no mark of the change of season except a slight chill in the air and a brief hint of winter pallor.

"You seem far away," John commented, pulling his shoulder from hers.

"I was thinking of home."

"Leeds, isn't it? I was there not long ago myself on one of my jaunts to try to raise funds. Speaking to a ladies club, but I'm afraid they had limited sympathies for the medical problems of the women I treat. Now, if it were an orphanage..."

So that's what he was doing on the train, Leanna thought. "If they don't find it in their hearts to support your efforts," she said sharply, "they may find the orphanages more full than they can handle."

"Quite right," John said, surprised at the intensity of her tone.

"So that's how you're raising your money? Speaking to women's groups?"

"Mostly. I have my private practice, of course, Mayfair ladies who pay handsomely enough that I can afford to treat my East End patients for nothing."

"That's just as my grandfather worked," Leanna said. "The middle class paid him enough to tend some of the poorer farmers for nothing, or next to nothing. It seems I remember that they often had their pride, though, and he was always receiving a jar of gooseberries or a hen in payment." She looked at John archly. "So tell me, do your ladies of the East End offer you something in exchange for your services?"

John laughed. She really was a most extraordinary girl, he thought, clever and nearly the match of her aunt in sheer audaciousness. "No, I'm afraid these women have but one thing to barter and at the time I see them they're usually in no condition to offer even that. I must settle for their gratitude."

114

"Which is indeed excessive. I understand they have dubbed you 'Saint John.'"

He flushed. "I assure you, I did not request such a title."

Leanna was afraid she may have gone a bit too far and offended him and she cast about for a way to bring the conversation back to neutral ground. "Are you disappointed at the pace the fundraising is going?"

"Hmmm. How to answer, how to answer...There are some pounds so earmarked in my account, but not nearly enough for what I have planned. I visualize a small clinic, perhaps six or eight beds with a midwife constantly present and two doctors standing by on call. That's what's costly, the trained medical staff."

"Your family doesn't support your mission?"

"Regrettably, they're more of the mind of our friend Fleanders, and believe that ladies need obstetrical assistance and poor women do not. I'm the first physician in my family and the ignorance runs deep. And I'm a third son, Leanna, you may as well know that, if Geraldine has not already told you."

"Meaning what?" Leanna asked, although she knew well enough what it meant.

"Meaning I don't inherit. As a younger son it falls to me to seek a profession and -"

"To marry well?"

He looked at her out of the corner of his eye. "I don't intend to choose my wife for her dowry, if that's what you're implying."

Leanna clasped her hands over her ears. "I'm sorry, it's just that we've stumbled onto a rather sore subject for me. Oldest sons seem to have been dealt all the cards of any value, youngest sons struggle by with the remains, and women..."

"And women?"

"Are left with the Joker."

John laughed easily, and the horses slowed as they approached the more crowded streets flanking the park. "I sometimes wonder if I can challenge the lethargy of the medical establishment and here you seem posed to take on the entire social structure of England. I didn't mean to imply that I'm a pauper, Leanna. I have a home of my own and my practice. To follow your analogy to its end, it is now my duty to play the cards dealt me, not to wail that I wasn't sitting at the right place at the table when the shuffling began. I'll have my clinic in time, you shall see."

"You should have it now. It isn't fair."

"Nothing is fair."

Leanna turned away from John, afraid her feelings were too plainly written on her face. At that moment she wanted more than anything to confide to him the sudden stroke of fate which had changed how she viewed everything. Strange, she reflected, that when she had little power over her future she never worried about the injustices of life but that now she was steering her own craft she found herself angry at every turn, wondering how others could bear the constraints she herself had endured without complaint for years. Trevor struggling against his obviously inferior superiors, John forced to wait for the fruition of his dreams, and Emma…Leanna was certain there was some story behind how Emma had ended up with Gerry, but she felt too uncomfortable to ask.

"I'm sorry, my dear, if I've upset you," John said, misinterpreting her ducked head and silence. "I must say I admire the way you maintain total composure during a talk of blood and murder but grow shaken at the thought of social injustice. Quite a refreshing change from the ladies I know who pass by the factory children without a glance and then swoon at the spider on the wall. The right sort of things make you ill."

"An unusual compliment."

116

"But sincerely meant. Tell me, did we strike too close to a sensitive subject yet again? Is it an older brother who will arrange your marriage?"

"No, no, he has nothing to say in it."

"So your grandfather did leave you something?"

Leanna turned her head.

"I'm the one who is sorry now," John said quickly. "I realize how that sounded, but I was just concerned for you. So many women have no say in the matter."

"I'll be the one to choose my husband."

"I'm glad to hear it."

Leanna fiddled with the clasp of the green cape, more confused than ever. Was his interest in her freedom only altruistic, or did he have another reason for wondering who would be the one to grant her hand? His question about her dowry seemed odd in the wake of their discussion of his own financial problems. If only Tom were here to help her sort through it all...

"There's the café," John said, pulling up and handing the reins to a small Indian boy in a crisply tailored blue suit, before lightly leaping to the sidewalk. "Wonderful food. I'm sure you won't be disappointed." Then he put his hands on her waist and lifted her down from the carriage step. She stumbled a bit - her country sure -footedness was failing her in London - and bumped into him, letting his arms slip momentarily around her. His touch was appropriate. Firm enough to steady her, not so firm as to be taken as impropriety, and as she looked up into his pale aristocratic face, Leanna admitted that it was only sport for her to wonder what his motives were. For in truth she didn't care why he had called, only that he had. She was already half in love with him.

9:52 AM

In a café two blocks south of the one where Leanna and John were just beginning to dine, Trevor Welles sat with a newspaper and a cup of morning tea, enjoying neither. He had gotten home around six and tried to sleep for a few hours but his mind had been racing and he had finally acknowledged defeat, risen, splashed water on his face, and stepped out for some breakfast, hoping that the walk would clear his head. As he often did when preoccupied, Trevor had walked much farther than he had intended, and he had finally paused, bought a paper on the corner, and ordered tea in a café. Its courtyard offered a pleasant view of the park but, Trevor was too preoccupied to see the beauty of the morning. He opened his notebook and stared down at the single sentence.

THE JUWES ARE NOT THE MEN THAT WILL BE BLAMED FOR NOTHING

What the devil did it mean? Had the person who wrote the words actually meant "The Jews are not the men to be blamed for anything," hence that the Jews are innocent? Or did he rather mean that the anti-Semitism of London was justified, for the killer was Jewish? But if he were Jewish, why had he announced that fact in foot-high letters? And why would anyone, Jewish or not, misspell the word "Jews"? Sir Warren had - perhaps correctly - feared a wave of anti-Semitism if the words were circulated and Trevor had complied with his order that the message be kept a secret. The morning papers, while full of speculations, didn't have this. Trevor sighed. Well, he'd wanted the case and he'd gotten it, so there was no need to cry now.

118

His pocket watch informed him that he'd better start back if he would be on time for his appointment with Phillips and Eatwell. Trevor drained his cup and slumped in the thin iron café chair. Only a few moments before, his eyes had happened to fall on a young couple in a carriage, progressing slowly down the street, apparently rapt in conversation. He had remained very still until the carriage rolled past his table, uncertain why the sight of Leanna Bainbridge riding with John Harrowman should disturb him. He'd certainly found Leanna attractive the night before - although in truth, the dinner party seemed like a year ago to his rattled senses, and seeing her again had been just one more surrealistic scene in the tableau of the last twelve hours. Trevor had often teased Geraldine that if he'd been born earlier he would have surely set his cap for her, and he had always privately thought "Yes, if you were not only younger but a bit more sane..."

And then came the reality of Geraldine's grand-niece, undeniably younger and not only sane but very bright, and he had somehow missed his chance. For there she was, a mere circle of the watch face later, gazing up at John Harrowman, who had been gazing back with a far-from-saintly expression.

There was nothing to be done about it. Trevor knew he was at least four years away from a promotion to inspector - unless he managed to solve this Whitechapel mess, but no, he wouldn't think of that. Four years from a promotion meant four years until he would have the money and position to take on a wife, and until that time it was sheer folly to entertain any thoughts of the Bainbridge girl. If one had to count the years until one could court a woman, one was better off not counting at all, but rather making do with dinner party conversation and an occasional stroll to the East End. He fumbled for coins to pay his bill, thinking of the reasons why he knew the streets of Whitechapel so well, why he had known them well enough before the events of the last two months. It was nothing to be proud of, but nothing to be ashamed of either, although he had to admit he was ashamed, at least when in the presence of a woman he admired.

So Leanna was out with the good doctor and he had no right to be disturbed. No right and no time, for he was now chief investigator of the most important criminal case of the decade. Perhaps the century. He could not allow himself to be distracted by Leanna or anyone else. I won't think of her, he said to himself, and then, again, almost aloud this time, "I swear I just won't think of her." This determined, he sat off in a roundabout path back toward the Yard for he knew it would be easier to not to think of her if he could manage to not see her again.

10:48 AM

"You were right, John, that was wonderful," said Leanna, pushing back her plate with a contented sigh. "I'm sure you think I've never eaten before."

"Nonsense, I like to see a woman enjoy her food."

Leanna reached up impulsively and let one finger trace a faint scratch on John's face which began just at his temple and disappeared into the dark brush of his sideburns.

"Last night," John said, answering her questioning gaze. "A rough delivery and the mother fought me a bit." He reached across the table and took her hand. "Are you free this evening? There's a new play, you may have heard of it…"

"Hmmm?" murmured Leanna, distracted by the sight of her hand in his.

"A play," John repeated. "I'd be delighted if you could accompany me. It's by Robert Louis Stevenson, and quite the sensation. Have you heard of it?"

Leanna hadn't, but she nodded quickly, just the same. She was hardly able to believe her luck. She would see him in the day and again in the night.

"Excellent," said John. "I'll come at eight to pick you up. Years from now you'll be able to say you were among the first in London to see *Doctor Jekyll and Mr. Hyde.*"

CHAPTER THIRTEEN
10: 55 AM

"I want Abrams."

"That," Eatwell said, "is entirely out of the question."

"If he's been cast off the case because he's Jewish, I must tell you how unfair—"

"Listen to me, Welles, and don't make me regret my decision to give you this assignment. You keep your head in that notebook, and your focus serves you on some levels, I'll be the first to concede. But you often manage to miss the larger point. This case isn't about a single maniac, it's about the whole of London. What will become of this city if the panic goes any higher, if people begin to lose confidence in the Yard? And most specifically, the inevitable violence that will follow if the public decides a Jew is responsible." Eatwell looked steadily at Trevor over the top of his glasses. "You're not getting Abrams. For his sake as much as anyone's."

Trevor sighed. "Davy Mabrey, the young bobby who found the body – "

"Fine, fine, take him. The parade of witnesses will shortly commence and, even though the chances of someone saying something helpful are small, I want you to record every testimony. I won't have the papers saying we let something slip through. They're already starting to doubt us, Welles, and that's the one thing that cannot happen. I've had a visit from a Mister Lusk of the Whitechapel Vigilance Committee just this morning informing me of his concerns. A group of local tradesmen afraid that the blood running in the streets might be bad for business."

"The observations of the public can be relevant, Sir, if we –"

"Relevant?" Eatwell snapped. "Of course they're relevant, and that's why you'll interview every lout we drag off the streets. But the group Lusk heads is a vigilance committee, Welles. 'Vigilance' as in 'vigilante.' We can't have the citizens taking the law into their own hands, or London will be no better than one of those savage outposts in the American West. And that's why we - Ah, here's the doctor now."

Phillips entered the room, less steady on his feet than ever. Up all night just like me, Trevor thought, only he's thirty years older. This case will kill him before it's over. The doctor nodded curtly and took the chair beside Trevor.

"I was able to construct a most definite time line," Phillips said, shortcutting any pleasantries, if indeed any were to be offered. "Elizabeth Stride died first, just as we thought. Apparently put up a bit of a fight, I'd say, due to her bruising, which was not post-mortem. Nothing under her nails or in her hands, Welles, so save your breath. A single gash across the throat, about five inches long, left to right. Not nearly as deep as what we saw on Chapman or even Nichols. Enough to sever the carotid artery but not a cut to the spine like the first two women."

Eatwell frowned. "A different killer? A copycat?"

"I think not. Same narrow blade, same left to right motion, so likely the same man as the others. But this time something stopped him. The fact she fought back, perhaps, or he could have heard steps approaching. Either way, she was still warm when I arrived. So we must assume that he was interrupted before he could do his usual tricks of draining blood and dissecting organs."

"Approximate time of death?" Trevor asked, pencil poised above his notebook.

"Between 12:45 and 1:15."

"That's quite precise," Eatwell said.

"Mabrey made the first call at one," Trevor said.

Phillips nodded. "The bobby finds her at one, she's still warm at 1:45 when I arrive. Meaning she couldn't have been dead more than an hour, which would take us back to 12:45. So what we lack in clues we gain with a very tight time line."

Trevor scribbled in his notebook, excitement building. "And at about that same time, another aspect of the story was unfolding," he said. "Catherine Eddowes, the second victim, was being released from the Bishopsgate police station. She had been brought in about four hours earlier for public drunkenness. Some sort of nonsense about imitating the sound of a fire engine, raising a big ruckus and then refusing to give the arresting officer her name. But apparently they knew her on sight at Bishopsgate, as she'd been in before on various charges. She slept if off in a cell and they released her at —" Trevor reconfirmed his notes — "12:55."

"Damn tight," said Eatwell.

Trevor nodded, barely able to contain himself. They were finally getting somewhere. Warm bodies and police records were far more substantial than the paltry evidence collected from Chapman and Nichols.

"So here we have it," he said out loud, struggling to keep his voice professional and neutral. "Catherine Eddowes is walking out of the police station just as Elizabeth Stride is being killed. But our killer is interrupted in his task. So he hides and watches, possibly was still watching when Mabrey arrived on the scene."

"Indeed," said Phillips. "Stride killed just before one, found by Mabrey at one. Takes thirty to forty-five minutes for the three of us to all arrive at the murder scene, during which time our killer slips away and encounters Eddowes on her way home from the jailhouse."

"He knows we are close by, but he also knows we are distracted," Trevor said. "Time of death on Eddowes, doctor?"

"1:30-1:45. Warm when I examined her at two."

"Dear God," Trevor said, not caring that these facts were a slap in the face to Eatwell. "Do you see what this means? He truly was right there. We didn't see him, but he saw us."

"Yes, so again, there's no time to drain blood or risk moving a body. But he did have time enough to slash up the poor woman." Phillips looked down at his notes. "Clotted blood, indicating she fell when her throat was cut and died on the spot. The mutilations were post-mortem - thank whatever God we still have to thank. Abdomen sliced, intestines removed, cuts to the groin as if he planned to flay her, rather like a fish. Pancreas cut but not removed. One kidney taken out – miraculously neat job, considering the conditions and the darkness – and apparently removed from the scene. Cuts to the womb and of course the complete….the complete desecration of her face, which we all observed."

"Done within minutes," Trevor said bitterly. "While half of Scotland Yard is within shouting distance of the crime. How he taunts us."

CHAPTER FOURTEEN
7:10 PM

Leanna was ready for her theater engagement with John, but once again the entire household had been upended by the effort. Geraldine had offered the use of the Bainbridge family topazes, which Leanna had seized upon eagerly, but the necklace and earrings had looked as dull as brown glass against the blue satin gown she had planned to wear. Gerry had suggested her own russet silk would be perfect, but of course it was too large for Leanna and Emma had protested when Gerry had offered to baste the gown underneath to adapt it to Leanna's slender form.

"Those stitches will tear that silk, Geraldine, no matter how carefully you take them," Emma declared, "And actually I think black is the best choice with topaz jewelry."

"Black?" Leanna said skeptically, standing before Gerry's oval mirror in her chemise. "I look a fright in black."

"No you don't," Emma said. "Black is striking. Mature."

"Hmmm…" said Leanna, biting her lip as she always did when unsure. It would certainly be wonderful to appear striking and mature before John, whom she suspected sometimes viewed her as a giddy schoolgirl.

"Perhaps she's right," Gerry said. "Fetch that mourning gown you came in."

"But it's ghastly," Leanna wailed. "That dress was homemade in Leeds and the fit makes me all, how should I say, flat across here and flat in the back…"

"Just because a gown wasn't bought in London doesn't mean it can't be fashionable," Emma said stubbornly.

"But to go to the theatre in such a simple dress…" Leanna said, just as stubbornly.

"Simple is better with jewelry as elaborate as those topazes. At least try it on. If you don't like it, nothing is lost."

"Nothing except time," Leanna fretted, but she pulled on the gown, just the same. It looked precisely at it did the day she had worn it to the reading of the will - shapeless and drab - and she stood gazing grimly into the mirror until Emma slipped up behind her and began to snip away at the black netting which covered the bodice and throat.

"What are you doing?"

"There's a proper dress underneath all this somewhere," Emma said, carefully loosening each tiny thread. "You'll see. When we get this covering off, there will be a lovely, striking, plain black gown which will set off that necklace like a star against the night."

"Just as you say," Leanna mumbled, too keyed-up to protest further. The light supper of fruit and cheese Gage had sent up lay untouched on her dressing table and she felt slightly faint. To make her first London theater appearance in a homemade mourning gown? But a few seconds later, when she glanced up just in time to see the netting fall, she knew immediately that Emma had been right. Together they did up her hair in a simple, high bun and Geraldine, watching from the doorway, had to blink back tears.

"You look like my mother, in the portrait at Rosemoral," she said simply.

"No, no one will ever equal Great-grandmother Bainbridge," Leanna said, for legends of her beautiful ancestor had been handed down to her ever since she had been a gangly child. Just at that moment the door knocker sounded and Leanna jumped. "He's here. He's early."

"Gage will get the door," Emma said, still fumbling with the triple-clasp of the heavy necklace strand. "You don't have to run down the stairs." The women all fell silent, waiting for the

128

sound of John's voice in the entryway, but instead they heard unfamiliar high tones and then Gage's heavy tread up the staircase.

"Miss Leanna," he said, his throat creaky from rare use, "there are flowers for you."

"Wonderful," squealed Leanna, rushing past Gerry to take up the huge spray of red roses Gage proffered. "Good heavens, but they're heavy. This must be two dozen."

"Read the card," Emma called down after her.

Leanna fumbled for the attached card and, after one quick glance, sat down on the top stair with a thump, the roses scattering beside her.

"Whatever's wrong?" Gerry asked as Emma joined her in the hall.

"He isn't coming," Leanna answered flatly. "He's been called to a case and he's..." She picked up the note again. "Devastated."

"Darling I'm sorry," Gerry said. "But I'm sure he truly is devastated. You understand as well as anyone that a physician's hours are never his own."

"I know," Leanna said tonelessly, making no effort to halt the slow descent of the roses as they escaped her grasp and began to slide down the staircase. "I do know," she said, again, looking at the brilliant red puddle at her feet and this time speaking with more conviction. "Gage, get me some water and a vase, will you please? A big vase."

"That's the spirit, Leanna. The play will be running for months," Gerry said, putting an arm around Leanna's waist as they descended the stairs together.

"It isn't missing the theater that's so tragic," Emma thought, stooping to pick up the remaining black threads from the rug in Leanna's now-silent room. "She'll never look any lovelier than she does tonight."

Two hours later, as Leanna, still in the black dress and topazes, sat with Emma and Geraldine playing a dispirited three-handed game of bridge, the door knocker sounded again. "Perhaps it's John after all," Geraldine said hopefully. "Perhaps it was an easy delivery and he's stopped by to apologize in person."

But it was Tom Bainbridge who stepped into the parlor, shaking raindrops from his hair like a playful puppy.

"Tom," Leanna said, leaping up. "I've never been so happy to see anyone. Come in, we'll have tea, we can make up your room. How long will you be here?"

"Slow down," Tom laughed, as he reached out to hug his sister. "Good heavens, is this what you customarily wear for a family evening of cards?"

Leanna's hands flew to the strands of amber which encircled her throat. "I was supposed to go to the theatre, but my escort...he's a doctor, Tom, I've met the most wonderful doctor."

"Let me guess," Tom said. "He was called away by a patient, thus disappointing you and undoubtedly breaking his own heart in the process."

"I certainly hope so," Leanna said dryly.

"Oh, but I'm sure he is beyond consolation," Tom laughed. "You look wonderful and it's clear the city agrees with you. Hello, Emma."

"Hello," Emma said.

"Tom, Leanna is right, we must make up a room for you and not let you escape for weeks," Geraldine said.

"Thank you, Aunt Gerry, but this is a two-night visit. I'll be back in class the day after tomorrow and I just wanted to come by and see how Leanna is doing."

"So the business at home is completed?" Leanna asked.

Tom nodded.

"Oh please tell me what has happened," Leanna said nervously. "We have no secrets from Aunt Gerry or Emma or Gage."

"Nonsense, you need your privacy," Geraldine said. "Tom, help yourself to the sherry and we'll see about getting you some dinner." Geraldine paraded out with Emma and Gage in tow, leaving Tom and Leanna to sit a moment in silence.

"Well, it's good news," Tom finally said, rising and heading toward the liquor table. "Galloway was a rock, an absolute rock, and the will wasn't broken."

"But they tried, didn't they?" Leanna said. "Your letters were so maddeningly incomplete."

"Not on purpose, Leanna, we just couldn't say from day to day how things were developing. Cecil got an attorney recommended by Edmund Solmes..."

"Who? Oh yes...."

"One of Cecil's friends, or more accurately, one of his debtors," Tom said, ruefully thinking of how close Leanna had come to being made all-too-aware of Edmund Solmes. "Either way, they imported a barrister from London who made quite a squawk, but Galloway held firm. Turns out the problem wasn't William, not really. The problem was Cecil, and the amount of control he had over William. At least that's what Galloway claims, that Grandfather knew Cecil would manage to gamble away everything and William wouldn't have lifted a finger to stop him."

"Grandfather had watched Papa almost drag us all down and he wasn't going to let that happen again," Leanna said. "He said as much to me a dozen times although I never really grasped the implications."

Tom nodded. "We're younger, but he evidently saw us as stronger. With you as heir and me as executor, Rosemoral has a prayer of going forward."

"Natural selection," Leanna said thoughtfully. "Remember all those times he lectured us about Darwin? Remember that beagle that he called The Beagle even though hardly anyone understood his joke, or that box of finch bills he kept on his desk? I loved to play with them. Grandfather would line them up, smallest to largest, so that he and I could discuss which sort of bill would be most effective at cracking open seeds and getting to the meat inside. 'It's not the strongest or the swiftest who survive, Leanna,' he used to say. 'But the most adaptable. What do you think happens to those baby birds whose mothers have the wrong sort of bills?' Looking back, it seems a rather gruesome lesson for a child."

"I don't remember the box of bills," Tom said, "but I remember his moth wings under the microscope. He'd explain how the black-winged moths could hide better on a smoky wall so you saw more of them in the city, but the brown-winged ones blended in better on a tree trunk so they could thrive in the country. And we'd talk about how often survival came down to a simple ability to blend in with one's background." The memory of his grandfather's patient, gentle voice pained Tom, but he didn't want to indulge the melancholy, so instead he picked at the cloth of his sister's dress. "By the looks of it, I'd say you found your black city wings soon enough."

"Tom, you know I love Rosemoral and I would never turn my back on Grandfather's wishes..."

"Uh oh. What's coming?"

"But what if I decide to live in London?"

Tom swirled his sherry and laughed. "So the city agrees with you, does it? I'm not surprised. If you stay in London, you stay in London, and that's just grand. It's an inheritance, Leanna, not a prison sentence. We'll find an estate manager for Rosemoral. Many families maintain both a country and city home."

"But Mother and Cecil and William…" Leanna said.

"Have a perfectly adequate roof over their heads and a comfortable allowance. I'm sure right this moment Mother is gossiping and William is babbling about the soil quality in some garden, and Cecil is continuing his improbable pursuit of poor Hannah Wentworth, all as if nothing has changed. Don't let them make you believe they are destitute, Leanna, for that isn't the case. Granted they don't wear heirloom jewelry while lounging about the house…"

"Oh, you're ridiculous," Leanna giggled, letting one of the settee cushions fly at his head. "And I owe you everything."

"Remember that," he said, rising and calling toward the open door. "Aunt Gerry, you can stop eavesdropping in the hall and come back in now. See, I brought some iodine pills for Gage. I really think we can eradicate that goiter…" Leanna sat back in the chair, reflecting on how nice it was to have him there. Tom would know if John were really devastated about the cancelled evening. Tom would know if she had misread the situation.

Emma called from the hall. "The green room is ready, Mr. Bainbridge."

"Ye gods, 'Mr. Bainbridge' is so stuffy."

Emma entered, smiling slightly. "Should I have said 'Dr. Bainbridge'?"

Tom laughed and raised his glass to her. "You never let up on me, do you, Emma? How many times have I asked you to call me by my given name?"

"Quite a few," Emma admitted. "Perhaps on your birthday I shall do it."

"But today is my birthday," Tom said cheerfully.

"Isn't that what you said the last time you were here? And the time before that?"

Leanna was surprised at this easy banter. Neither Tom nor Emma had ever mentioned each other to her, yet they obviously were on a friendly basis. But why shouldn't they be? They were both young and single and things were done so differently here in London. Back in Leeds she would never had been allowed to go unchaperoned for a carriage ride with a gentleman caller but his morning Aunt Gerry had packed her off with scarcely a backward glance. Leanna hadn't seen enough of London to know if such casual conversation between the two sexes was allowed everywhere. Most likely this informality only existed in Geraldine's household.

But still...this new view of her younger brother was a revelation. The Tom of Winter Garden was dwarfed by Cecil and William, cursed by his birth order, alternately stammering and defiant. But the Tom of London appeared to be a different type of creature altogether – relaxed, laughing, confident. Leanna sat back in her chair, and watched her brother continue to spar with Emma. Freed from the burden of constantly trying to prove he was a man, it appeared Tom might actually become one.

Their conversation might have seemed casual to an observer like Leanna, but Emma was shaken by the exchange, just as she always was whenever Tom appeared. And he appeared so regularly - could it just be filial devotion to Geraldine, or was it something else which drew him to Mayfair on his free afternoons? Her hands were unsteady as she went about laying out the tea and cakes, and as she sloshed a bit over the lip of one of the cups Tom glanced up and winked at her, which promptly caused her to slosh even more over the lip of the next.

He was certainly different form the other men she knew, Emma thought, watching him from the corner of her eye as he leaned over in a near-prone position and resumed his conversation with his sister. Not that she had known so many men, but those dull ones who'd blush and nod at the grocer's or on the afternoon drives with Geraldine – they all lacked Tom's easy manner and quick laugh. They're like me, she thought. Grim and determined and always thinking of what's to be done next. It's the working class expression and I'm a fine one to say it isn't good enough. Nonetheless, an evening spent strolling with a young man who felt constantly weary and whose time was never his own would be quite different from an afternoon with Tom, who could take her to the theatre, for a ride, to the cafes.

"What am I thinking of?" Emma scolded herself, pulling her thoughts back to the reality of the present situation. She was no more likely to be invited out by Tom than she was to receive a summons to the palace. Flirting with the help in the confines of his aunt's home was one thing; taking a serving girl out on the town was something else again, and Emma knew that deep down Tom was far too prudent a man to risk censure by doing so. "I won't think of him," she said to herself. "It isn't going to be, so I won't think of him." Then she pulled off her apron and slipped up the back stairs to the privacy of her room where - just a few steps above the door of Tom's bedroom - she could have the uninterrupted luxury of plenty of time to think of him.

CHAPTER FIFTEEN
October 2
3:15 PM

Cecil lit his pipe and a wave of good feeling, as
unaccustomed as the autumn sunshine, washed over him. Ever
since the ball, he and Hannah were practically engaged, as
evidenced by the note which had come three days ago asking
Cecil, William, and their mother to attend the annual
Wentworth grouse hunt. Such invitations were scarce and much
to be valued, for the hunt was very nearly a private family affair.
His plan of pretending that William was the heir had succeeded
brilliantly. Edmund Solmes had danced an arthritic little jig
when Cecil had ridden over specifically to wave the invitation in
his face and had barked, "You're as good as in her bedchamber,
my boy!"

Yes, well every silver lining did have its cloud, Cecil
reflected, eyeing Hannah as she dismounted from her horse and
began the long walk across the brilliant jade lawn toward the
portico. She didn't look so bad from a distance, but he would
never be able to claim he'd married a beauty. The long features
and bushy brows which sat dashingly upon the father did not
look so charming on the daughter. But the man had sired no
sons, bless him, and Hannah would someday have this all.

Hannah and her husband, Cecil thought, leaping to his feet
as the girl neared. Winter Garden and even Rosemoral were
mere hovels in contrast with the Wentworth estate, which
boasted twenty bedchambers and a stable the size of most
universities. It would take some flowers, some candy, perhaps
the promise of a honeymoon in France...

"Cecil," Hannah greeted him calmly, her face flushed and
small beads of perspiration dotting her lip. "The ride was so

invigorating. I'm so sorry your back pain prevented you from coming with us."

"Ah, yes, polo injury," Cecil lied smoothly, for no force on earth would persuade him to mount one of the Wentworth Arabs. Mounting their daughter would prove challenge enough. Beyond Hannah's shoulder he could see William shakily lowering his huge frame from a gloriously white stallion and even his mother, who rode sidesaddle with a surprisingly sure hand, looked a bit off-balance as she was helped from a dark mare. "But the hunt was a success, I take it?"

"Very much so, although none of us eat grouse, of course. But the servants shall be happy tonight," answered Hannah, flopping down gracelessly in the chair beside him and indicating with one gloved hand that he was also free to sit. "It's a strange world we live in, is it not? We ride far out in the field and dismount, trekking through the muddy woods in search of grouse for the servants to eat. And all the while they remain here at the estate butchering lamb for our dinner."

"It's sport, darling. 'Tisn't meant to make sense."

"Daddy took in seven fowl himself."

"Daddy must have quite the steady aim. I shall remember that," Cecil said, smiling.

"You should," she answered, with no smile at all.

A young maid was circulating with refreshment for the riders and Cecil did not let his sedentary morning prevent him from trying a bit of trifle. The girl gave him a saucy smirk as she passed, not the first of the day, and Cecil returned the favor. It truly wouldn't be so bad, he thought. Once he managed to get Hannah with child a great deal of pressure should fall from his shoulders and he would be free to do as he pleased, either with this bold little wench or another. Hannah was of a social class to understand and perhaps even appreciate a man's need to sow freely, just so long as he was discreet and squired his wedded

138

wife about the county with proper respect. Cecil fully intended to play by the rules.

"I must bathe," said Hannah, not at all self-consciously, and the other ladies were also filing upstairs in giggling groups of two or three to change into day dresses. "Cousin Marguarite plans to play her violin in the south parlor for our amusement, and amusement is indeed the right term because she's dreadful. Should I expect you to wait for me?"

"Eternally," Cecil said fervently.

Hannah turned steady grey eyes upon him.

"Half an hour should be enough," she said, rising. He was certainly handsome, she thought fleetingly, and he said the right things, but did she really want to look at him across the breakfast table for the next forty years? Hannah sighed, dreading the moment she would have to exchange riding gear for the constrictions of a corset and stays. Dreading the moment she would have to trade girlhood for the constrictions of wifedom and motherhood. But the day was coming soon enough, for she was past twenty and she had faced the fact long ago that any man who married her would be doing so for her money. She was rich and she was plain and there was no reason to pretend otherwise. If not Cecil, it would be some other suitor, equally poor and handsome and eager, and her father made it clear that the one thing he expected from his cherished daughter was a brood of grandchildren. Perhaps Cecil would at least have the prudence to get her with child and then leave her alone. He seemed a sensible sort, beneath all that lace and velvet.

The remainder of the riders straggled off to change, the servants darting off behind them to provide basins, water, and towels. Cecil was left alone once again in the portico. He took up his sherry and looked around for the yellow-haired maid.

"Thought you was to marry Miss Hannah," whispered the girl, squirming a bit as Cecil worked his hands beneath the tight ribcage of her bodice.

"Who told you that?" he answered breathlessly, finally managing to pull her down beside him. These rosebushes clustered in back of the stables provided a safe hiding place. He would have to remember.

"Slow down and do it proper," said the girl, as arrogant as Hannah in her way. "You're going to rip it," she added primly, rising back to her knees and beginning to unhook the miniscule buttons with swift, sure hands. "There, we can loosen it up a bit, but I daren't take it all off here in the daylight. And everyone knows about you and Miss Hannah, even the deaf girl who does the mending."

"I don't care for her," Cecil said, watching the girl daintily lift up her black cotton skirt to expose two ivory garters. "It's a business arrangement, pure and simple."

"Who do you care for?"

"No one. You. I care for you. What did you say your name was?"

The girl giggled, letting him pull her back down on top of him. "I'm June," she said. "Remember that name when you're master of the house, won't you, love?"

Cecil mumbled something incoherent and then they both were silent. The heat of Indian summer mixed with the nearly overpowering scent of the roses and the surprising sureness of the girl was too much for him. She seemed to sense this.

"Lie back," she said throatily. "I'll take care of it."

Ah, yes, Cecil thought, letting his head roll to the grass with an inelegant thud. This is how it should be. The master of the house should lie back and let the serving girl take care of it.

140

"Hush," said the girl, her face suddenly frozen in fear.

"Hmm," murmured Cecil. He hadn't said anything.

"Hush," June whispered. "I hear someone. Bloody Bob, he works in the stable and he thinks he owns me."

Cecil froze too, for there were unmistakably the sound of footsteps approaching, soft in the grass but distinct.

"There," Silas Wentworth was saying. "These are the rosebushes I wanted you to see. We keep them out back where the sun is a bit better, but they are Hannah's pride, aren't they, darling?"

"Yes," answered the familiar voice, calm and self-assured.

"Oh God," Cecil thought, the blood suddenly deserting the lower limbs of his body and rushing back to his head with such veracity the thought it would explode. June was lying immobile beside him, her eyes and legs wide.

"My grandfather grew roses," William said. "He took several prizes, didn't he, mother?"

"Indeed," Gwynette said, although Leonard Bainbridge's horticulture experiments had never been quite such a social asset before. "You must come with us sometime to Rosemoral, Hannah, and gather cuttings for your own gardens..."

The voices faded and for a dizzying moment Cecil thought he was safe. Then he heard his brother - fat, wretched, stupid, hopeless William - say mildly "I do like that peach colored variety over there. I say, Miss Wentworth, is that one of your specialties?"

"The color is nothing compared to the scent," Silas Wentworth said proudly. "I shall pluck you a sample..."

And then the bushes parted as the gates of hell and four startled faces looked down at the couple sprawled beneath them. With a muffled shriek June leapt up and sprinted toward the stables, buttoning her dress as she ran, but Cecil could do little more than gape up at the expressions of his accusers.

Wentworth speechless with fury, his mother ashen with shock, William unaccountably amused, and finally Hannah. Her face, as always, was difficult to read and Cecil was in no condition to be perceptive.

Drat it all, Hannah was thinking. I shall have to go through this tedious courtship process yet again.

CHAPTER SIXTEEN
2:50 PM

Eager to inform Davy of his unofficial promotion, Trevor scoured the Yard for the lad and finally found him having a smoke with some other bobbies at the back entrance. Praise youth, Trevor thought wryly. Davy looked none the worse for his grisly early morning experience and he snapped to attention when Trevor motioned him over.

"Davy, I don't know if I expressed my gratitude adequately to you last night. Securing the area, keeping back the mob, the bit about the chalk message. It all adds up to good police work."

"Just my job, Sir."

"And now I have one more request. That you go to your flat this instant, change out of that uniform, and be back here in one hour in plainclothes. You've been assigned to me for the rest of the investigation."

Davy's face went from puzzled to shocked as he stammered for something to say. He lacked at least two years of being qualified to work in plainclothes and this would certainly make him the envy of all the other bobbies. "I hardly deserve it, Sir, it was just a matter of being in the right place at the right time..."

"And doing all the right things. Don't sell yourself short, Madley, there are plenty of people willing to do that chore for you."

"Thank you, Welles, I mean Sir. I...I..."

"Don't just stand there, boy, be off. Report to the interrogation room at four. We'll be questioning people the rest of the afternoon. Not suspects, mind you, just witnesses. God only knows how valid their observations are, but Eatwell wants them duly noted, every one. "

As Davy took off like a man possessed, Trevor was hit with a sudden wave of exhaustion. The two shallow hours of sleep he'd snatched at dawn wouldn't see him through this day, he suspected, and he wondered if he might grab a quick nap in his office before the interviews began. He glanced at the members of the press milling about the lawn and they looked back at him hungrily. The rule was they couldn't come within twenty feet of the doorways of the Yard, but there had been few details in the morning paper. With two murders, nice and fresh, they wanted more gore for the next day's editions. Trevor watched them with narrowed eyes and decided that yes, perhaps there was time for at least twenty minutes of a nap. The center square clock was striking three.

Forty-five minutes later, a red-faced Davy Madley was walking down the corridor in his Sunday best suit - his only suit for that matter - and manfully trying to ignore the shrill whistles of his fellow bobbies. Although his cheeks flamed, Davy took it all in good spirits because he too would have made fun if any of them had enjoyed such a dramatic twist of fortune. As he approached the interrogation room he noticed some of the witnesses had been assembled outside on a bench. It was a motley crew to be sure.

Trevor, mercifully, did not tease him at all, but simply pointed out his first desk. A regulation issued brown box, but Davy ascended to it as if it were a throne.

"Here are some blank reports and pencils, Davy. Just listen to what each has to say. If you feel it pertains even remotely to the facts in the case, then write the statement down and get their names, address, and where they work. Don't write down everything everyone says, for a good part of our job is the ability to distinguish the crackpots from those who look like crackpots but who have useful information. No matter how daft they seem, be polite."

"Aye, Sir. Be polite."

"My desk is in that corner, so I'm close at hand if anything unusual arises. Gad, what am I saying, it will all be unusual. I mean unusually unusual."

"Yes, Sir," said Davy and motioned to the sergeant stationed at the door to send in the first witness. She entered, clearly a lady of the evening who was translating none too well to full daylight. She smiled a slack-mouthed grin at Davy, and Trevor was pleased to see he greeted her in a professional manner.

Trevor's first interview was with a shabbily-dressed man with a pronounced limp and the smell of urine about him. Nevertheless, Trevor sat the poor, small creature down in the chair beside him with grave dignity, and leaned back as far as possible.

"I did it, Guv'ner! I did!" said the little man, grinning broadly and not bothering to wait for a question.

"You did what, my good man?"

"Killed 'em. Murdered each 'un in cold blood!"

"Who?" asked Trevor, his face still suitably serious although he doubted this man could hurt a flea.

"Why, 'ose bitches from Whitechapel, of course." he said, spraying Trevor's papers with spittle. "Did 'em all in. Two last night."

"And how, may I ask, did you kill the two last night? Excuse me, I didn't get your name."

"Why, Hoppy! Hoppy Darby, of course! Oh, it was bloody, Guv'ner, bloody indeed. The first one, I snuck up behind 'er and slit 'er throat 'fore she knew it. Then I stayed

and serenaded 'er on me mouth harp while she bleeded to
death. But she went too quick and that wasn't 'nough for me.
Hadn't finished me song. That' why I went for the other one."

"And how did this second poor girl go?"

"Pulled 'er arm off with me bare hands. Then I beat 'er over
the head with it til she passed out, I did."

"Indeed?" said Trevor. "Dreadful."

"Aye, dreadful," Hoppy said happily.

"And then, Hoppy, what did you do with the woman's
arm?"

A brief pause. A wrinkled brow.

"I took it home, cooked it up, and ate me fill, I did. I even
fed the bones to me dog. So Guv'ner, you'd better lock me up
and throw away the key. I'm no good at all, ye see?"

"Lock you up!" Trevor shouted, slapping a palm to his desk
and rising so forcefully that even Davy from across the room
drew back a bit. "Hoppy, you have been very naughty indeed!
We hang people for crimes like these, hang them as soon as
possible." Trevor started leafing through his calendar on his
desk.

"Hang me!" Hoppy gasped, clutching his throat in retreat.
"Who'll feed me dog? Why canna you just put the both of us
away for the rest of our born days?"

"I'm sorry Hoppy, for your crime it's hanging. Are you
ready? We can hang you and your dog this afternoon."

"Hang me mutt, too? Why, 'e's done nothing."

"You said it yourself, the dog ate the evidence. So we'll
string him up there alongside you. Where is this criminal canine
anyway?"

Hoppy got up from his chair and took a few shaky steps
backward. "I made it all up, Guv'nor, didn't kill anyone. Please
don't 'ang us. Didn't do it, was a story."

146

"And now you're saying you're a liar too? Hoppy, I'm so disappointed in you. Well you'd better be out of my sight or I'll hang you and that damn dog both, just for lying."

Hoppy could barely get the door open in his haste. Trevor followed and laughed as he watched the tattered figure jerking down the corridor. The people on the bench observed the exit with impassive eyes and once Hoppy was out of sight they turned back to Trevor, whose expression had changed from smiling to sternness again as he shouted, "Next!"

By the time Trevor had returned to his desk Davy was interviewing another witness, Robert Spicer, a constable Davy knew from the East End.

"Good day, Robert. We've all made our reports, so what brings you down to the Yard?" asked Davy, shaking Spicer's hand. Trevor was eager to observe Davy's interviewing skills but he didn't want to listen in too obviously and thus make the boy nervous, so he pretended to be absorbed in his nonexistent Hoppy notes.

"Well Davy, something occurred to me last night, but in all the excitement I neglected to put it in the report. It may be important to the case and it may not." answered Spicer, adjusting himself in the chair.

"In this case, we'll take all the information we can gather. What's it about?"

"Late in the evening yesterday I was making my rounds just off Commercial Street when I came upon Rosy Matters, one of the local girls, and she was sitting on a dustbin having a laugh with a gentleman. What I thought queer was he was really a gentleman. I mean, here was this well-dressed, well-bred sort just sitting in a dark alley, late at night, with old Rosy. I noticed Rosy had a few coins in her hand, and she was jostling them up and down in her palm, like..."

"Like she'd just been paid?" Davy prompted.

"Or like she was stating her fee. I asked them what they were doing in the alley, and Rosy told me to mind my own business. I could tell she was drunk and could easily have been taken advantage of. So for her safety, and with this trouble about, I asked the man in for questioning."

"Questioning about what?" Davy asked, surprised.

"Well it is a crime to solicit a streetwalker, albeit a crime that isn't much pressed."

"Indeed. Go on."

"I took the gentleman to the station house. He was very courteous for a man being arrested, did not even argue. He told Inspector Bradley he was a doctor, and he had given Rosy the two shillings so she wouldn't have to sleep outside for the night."

"What was this gentleman's name, Robert? Do you remember?"

"No, because the Inspector spoke with him in a private room. After a short while he released the man and said since he saw no reason to detain him."

"And you don't remember his name," Davy sighed, glancing toward Trevor. "Would your Inspector remember him? Was he entered into the jail registry as an arrest?"

"I would doubt it. He was there only briefly. I know I made no report on him."

"Where might we find your Inspector Bradley?" Trevor broke in.

"He's on duty at night, but most of the time you'll find him at the Boar's Head Tavern. He likes his whiskey."

"Thank you, Robert. We will definitely check the man out. And if there is any credence to the story, we'll make sure you get the credit," Davy said, offering his hand once more. "What do you think of it, Sir?" he asked, when Spicer was out the door. "Worth anything?"

"Possibly. I know a doctor who treats women in the East End without charge so I suppose these souls do exist. To think an inspector wouldn't have the presence of mind to take down every name at a time like this..."

Trevor's words were scarcely out of his mouth when the door flew open and in marched Rayley Abrams. He went straight to Trevor, whispered something in his ear and Trevor rose to his feet. "Davy, take your next witness. With such a late start we'll have to keep moving steadily if we're to get all the statements today."

"Of course, Sir," Davy said matter-of-factly as Trevor followed Abrams out the door. Trevor thought with some satisfaction that it was as if the boy had been doing the job for years.

Once away from the mob in the hallway, Abrams turned to Trevor. "Someone downstairs I thought you might want to see. Name Micha Banasik. A Pole, brought into Bishopsgate early this morning for roughing up a prostitute. And he works in a slaughterhouse."

"What time did they bring him in?"

"Between three and four, and he can't account for where he was before that. He says he was drinking at a pub, but doesn't remember where or for how long."

"I appreciate this, especially under the circumstances," Trevor said. But Abrams looked straight ahead as he walked and Trevor decided that to thank him more profusely might be taken as insult. The man had never been jovial, was accused of being too intent upon his work to have time for a joke with the other boys. But in truth the same criticism had often been made of Trevor.

The two men marched steadily down the stairs to where the prisoners were kept, descending deeper and deeper into the damp basement of Scotland Yard. The lighting was poor as they approached the holding cell where a virtual giant was circling steadily, not pacing as a man would, but rather moving in small, tight circles in the manner of a caged cat. Trevor stopped a few yards back from the cell and stood in the darkness, both to give his eyes time to adjust to the gloom but also because he wanted to watch the man for a minute or two. Banasik kept his huge hands clasped behind him. He was certainly strong enough and he seemed to have the temper.

"Is he what you pictured the Ripper to look like?" Abrams asked.

"I can't say I've ever been able to really form an image of the man. To me he's like a dark hole. Faceless."

Abrams nodded. "Part of his appeal, is it not?"

"His appeal?"

Abrams looked at Trevor curiously. "You don't feel it? I should think your obsession with the Ripper - a feeling I can sympathize with, by the way - would have grown out of some sort of identification with him. He's no man, he's every man. He's faceless, just as you say."

"It's part of his intrigue…"

"Precisely."

"But I wouldn't call it part of his appeal."

Abrams shrugged. "Have it your way, Welles. Would you like to talk to the Pole alone?" Trevor nodded and stepped out of the shadows. At the sound of his footfall, the man turned in alarm.

"Are you Micha Banasik?" Trevor asked, looking the man square in the eyes.

"Yes. Why you have 'rested me?"

"You know why you're here. Assault on a woman."

A bit of a smile played around the thick lips. "She tell me she not press charge."

"Perhaps she didn't, but that doesn't mean you're off the hook. You know that phrase, Micha, 'off the hook.' But of course you do, you're a butcher."

"If woman not press charge, you must let man go."

"It's not surprising you're familiar with the laws concerning assault. I see from your file this is the third time you've been brought in for just that reason. Broke a woman's wrist last spring, didn't you?"

"They trying to take too much money from me, because they think I don't know English."

"So you beat them?"

"Would you not if you being robbed?"

"No, Micha, I would not. Where were you last night at 1 am?"

"I no remember. Drinking."

"Drinking where?"

"I sometimes frequent the Pony Pub," he said, with sudden formality. "I may was there."

"And this is where you met the woman that you struck?"

"I no know. Why you ask?"

"Last night two women were butchered in the East End. Do you know of this crime?"

Again the dignity, the pulling back of the shoulders. "I not aware."

"Did you see those women too? Did they try to cheat you of your money? Did you get mad at them?"

"No! And I am not Ripper!"

Gad, even the sewage in the street knew the name. Trevor looked around for Abrams, but the other detective remained in the shadows, leaving the questioning to the man who, rightly or wrongly, was the official head of the case. "Well Micha, we must detain you until we can check your alibi at the Pony Pub," Trevor said. Surely such a large and brutal-looking man would stand out in someone's memory if he had indeed been there.

"Make it fast, I not afford to lose job."

Trevor and Abrams turned away and started for the stairwell.

"What do you think, Welles?"

"We'll need to check out the pub before we think anything. People should remember his accent and his size. We have a good time line, thanks to Phillips. If someone at this Pony Pub can alibi him for the period between 12:30 and two, we'll have to let him go."

"Ninety minutes? Now, that is something." Abrams paused at the top of the stairs and jerked his head in the direction of the cells below. "What's your instinct?"

"Not our man."

"I don't think so either, but there was something ...worth interrupting you, I hope."

"Oh absolutely. Good form, Abrams." Trevor dreaded the next question, but felt he should ask it. "Where have they put you now?"

"Spitalfields," Abrams said shortly. It was the Jewish ghetto, an area known for tailor's shops, kosher butchers, and virtually no crime. "I'm keeping the peace in Petticoat Lane."

"If Barasik does by chance lead to something, I'll see you get credit," Trevor said.

"Credit? I don't care if it's the Queen herself that finds him, I just want this bastard caught and hanged," Abrams said, pulling on his coat. "Speaking of which, I suppose you've heard the latest rumor?"

"Which one? Oh, let me guess. The Duke of Clarence."

Abrams nodded. The Duke, known to the family as Eddy, was not only Queen Victoria's grandson, but the eldest son of her eldest son and thus in direct line of succession. A less compelling case of the future of the monarchy could hardly be found – the young man was in his twenties and a great dandy about town but rumored to be slow-witted, bisexual, partially deaf, and riddled with syphilis. His escapades were gossiped about in the best parlors of the city and even the papers made thinly-veiled references to the various scandals in which Eddy had been embroiled. Never naming him, of course, just referring to him as "Collar and Cuffs," a nickname that Trevor could only hope was meant to mock the Duke's penchant for ostentatious clothing.

"He's an easy enough target, I suppose," Trevor said. "Been accused of everything short of stealing the crown jewels."

"Known to frequent the East End," Abrams said amiably. "In search of certain pleasures."

"Are you suggesting he could really - ?"

Abrams held up a palm. "No, no, not suggesting anything of the sort. Besides, I already checked and he has alibis. Infallible ones. In training with his cavalry unit for the first two, with his formidable Grandmama for the second two. I just wanted to make sure you understand how frenzied the speculation is becoming."

"You requested an alibi for a member of the Royal family?" Trevor said, stunned but more than a little impressed. "However did you manage?"

"By checking the whereabouts of all bloody forty-seven of them," Abrams said, pushing open the door. "And pretending it was a matter of their personal security. City in a panic, you know, that sort of thing. Don't worry Welles, the Queen's private guard thanked me for it, said it showed great thoroughness on the part of the Yard. No feathers ruffled."

"Good man," Trevor said softly, as Abrams stepped out in the street.

Davy was on his ninth interview and was developing a bit of a rhythm. Trevor came in with another witness but he seated her at Davy's desk, not his, then sat down in his own chair, pulled out his notebook and began scribbling notes. Davy looked over for some sort of sign from Trevor about the surprise visit from Abrams, but Trevor gave none. So Davy turned his attention back to this new witness, figuring that Trevor would fill him in later.

"Now you say you saw a man last night with Elizabeth Stride?" Davy asked the old woman seated beside him.

"Yes I did. A looker he was. A handsome dark moustache, a real respectable appearance. I looked him over as I passed Lizzy and him on the corner of Turnbull Street."

"Could you describe him?"

"About twenty-eight, five feet eight inches tall, with a dark complexion. A foreigner maybe."

Davy sat back in surprise. Most of the previous witnesses had been able to give only sketchy descriptions at best of men who had been seen with Catherine or Liz, but this woman was very sure of herself. "Why would you say foreign? Did he have an accent?"

"I couldn't hear what he was saying, but he sure made Lizzy giggle. But dark skin, you know, like a Turk or a Greek."

"What was he wearing?"

"He had on a hard felt hat and a black coat. Pretty he was."

"Was he carrying anything in his hands? A parcel?"

"Couldn't see his hands. But he might have had something under his coat. It was big. Poor Lizzy, she was such a sweet girl too."

154

Only a woman as old and used up as this one would call the gap-toothed Elizabeth Stride a girl, Davy thought. Of course, on the streets, he supposed beauty and youth were relative.

Trevor rose, pushed back his chair, and went to the door to call a new witness for himself, a fact that deflated Davy a bit. He'd appeared to be listening in at first, but evidently Trevor had decided the woman's testimony wasn't relevant after all.

"I thank you for coming in" Davy said. "You've been a big help."

"My pleasure, dearie. If you ever need some warmth or comfort you can usually find me on Elm Street," she said with a smile.

Dear God, was their no retirement age for this particular profession, Davy wondered, opening the door for her to leave. He looked out in the hall and saw one final witness, this one lying on the bench, snoring. But before he would bring the person in, he decided he had better take full notes of the description the last witness had given. As he turned back toward his desk, Trevor signaled him over to his own desk so he could listen to what the person he was interviewing had to say.

"I think it's Mad Maudy who's been murdering them poor girls in the East End," the young woman seated at Trevor's desk was sobbing. With a quite dramatic flair, she pulled a handkerchief out of her bodice and vigorously blew her nose before stuffing it back in. "She's as mean as a drunken sailor."

"Who is this Mad Maudy?"

"Why everyone's heard of Maudy," the girl said, surprised. In another place and time she might have been quite pretty and her diction suggested she may have once known better times. But her face was marred by pox scars and the riotous orange of her hair rinse did nothing to flatter her pale coloring. "Maudy Minford, a midwife in the East End. More like a butcher though. Killed as many girls as she's helped."

155

"Killed?"

"She isn't...very good at her work."

"There are any number of midwifes in the area. A few doctors are available too," Trevor said. "Why would the girls keep going to someone with such a bad record?"

The girl fingered her dangling ear hoops, but said nothing. Trevor sighed.

"Where can we find her?"

"Ask anyone in the East End. They'll point you in her way. You can't miss her, she's as ugly and as foul as a stablehand. But she's always there, Sir, always seems to be around the spot where the girls get offed. I saw her in the alley last night when they were taking poor Cathy out. And she was there when they carted off Dark Annie too. Always there, just looking."

"Don't worry," Trevor said. "We'll talk with this Mad Maudy."

"Thank you, Sir," the woman said, standing to leave. "She took my sister, you know Sir."

"Took her?"

"Took her home, Sir. To the angels."

The girl left and Trevor sat back, rumpling his hair. "Good God, what a day. Are there any more people outside, Davy?"

"One."

"Finish it up and then we'll discuss the reports over a beer at the Boar's Head."

"Very good," answered Davy promptly, although he was surprised. A beer already? But a quick look down at his pocket watch showed that it was well past eight. His first afternoon in plainclothes had gone fast.

The person on the bench outside was hard to rouse. It took Davy a minute to ascertain if the lump was male or female, but he finally decided that the hat which had fallen to one side indicated another woman.

"Excuse me Ma'am, are you here to make a statement?" asked Davy, shaking her shoulder. "Ma'am?"

"Ma'am?" the woman slowly sat up and threw back her shabby cloak to reveal bare shoulders and a ruby gown. "Oh Davy, don't be so formal. Don't you recognize me? It's Frilly. Frilly Withers." She struggled to a sitting position, the gown dipping more precariously than ever and her breath strong with the smell of hard whiskey.

"Here, girl," said Davy, for her face was indeed familiar from his days of patrolling the East End. "Hold 'round my waist and try to get to your feet." She lurched against him, giggling and pawing and he felt his face go red again as he fervently prayed that none of the other officers would happened own the hall and witness his predicament.

"Right this way, Frilly," he said, kicking open the Interrogation Room door. "Here, have a seat."

She plopped herself down with scarcely a glance at Trevor, reached into her bag to retrieve a pint bottle, half full, and took a gulp. She then offered Davy a drink, but he violently shook his head.

"Why are you drinking so early in the evening, Frilly?"

"It's dark as midnight out there," she answered. "He struck down two last night and you go and ask me that? If that demon gets ahold of me I don't want to know about it."

"Why are you here?"

"Aren't you coppers supposed to pay for information?" she asked with a sly grin. "Come on Davy, it be right good information I bring."

"I'm sorry, but we can't pay you."

"A quid. Only a quid, Davy. It's definitely worth a quid," she asked again, leaning across the desk so that her breasts nearly slipped from her gown. "I don't much want to work tonight, you know what I mean. Just a quid for my supper." Davy glanced at Trevor.

"If it's important, maybe a quid," Trevor said. The Yard didn't make a habit of paying informants but it bothered him to think of this girl on the streets in her condition. Perhaps a little money would buy her the chance to sleep it off in safety.

"Oh, it's important, alright. I danced beside the Devil himself. Last night, I seen the Ripper with Catherine Eddowes, only thirty minutes before he carved her up." Frilly paused and reached into her bag once more for another taste of the flask.

"Here's a pound, Frilly," interrupted Trevor, putting the note in her hand. "What else can you tell us?"

"Why thank you Guv! See Davy, I told you it was good information. I saw old Cathy Eddowes, late last night."

"How late?" Trevor interrupted.

"Church just struck one bell."

"And where was she?"

"Coming down Market Street."

Trevor nodded slowly. The time was right and the part of town was right, just a few blocks from the jail where Eddowes had been released at 12:45.

Frilly smiled with satisfaction at his reaction and continued. "She was in the company of a man about thirty years old. Medium tall, medium build, with a mustache, but formally dressed, a gentleman."

"What was he wearing?"

"He wore a dark cape and…and…"

"And what?"

"A red neckerchief. Yes, a red neckerchief, loose around his collar."

"Was he carrying anything?"

"Yes, he had something in his left hand, tucked under his cape, but I couldn't see what. But the man made me go all queer, you know, as if my senses knew he was a bad 'un. You get the instinct after you've been on the streets for awhile. I got cold chills up and down me backside, as I passed them."

"Anything else? Did you hear him say anything?"

"No, he seemed to be whispering to Cathy and she was giggling, pleased as punch." The woman stopped and raised her eyebrows reflectively. "Guess the old gal never did develop the instinct, did she?"

"I guess not," Trevor said. "Use that money to get some food in you, Frilly, and a warm place to sleep tonight."

"Thanks again, Guv'ner. Davy, if you come over to Market Street, look me up. It's been a long time, you know," she said with a wink as she left the room.

"Detective Welles," Davy said, springing to his feet the second the door was closed. "Earlier another person gave a very similar description of a man seen with Elizabeth Stride."

"Let me read the statement."

Davy handed him the report. "See, Sir? A dark man, medium, well-dressed, a moustache and a full cape or coat. Full enough to hide something – something like a doctor's bag, Sir? Seen once with Eddowes and once with Stride and that's unlikely chance, wouldn't you say?"

"I think we have a real lead here, Davy. And the red neckerchief relates back to something I earlier found, a red fiber under Anne Chapman's fingernail. Well, we certainly have no lack of suspects, do we? Midwives and foreigners and dark men in capes."

Davy nodded. "I have sheets of notes here. Everyone in London seemed to see Liz or Catherine last night with a man or two or three. Given the professional calling of the ladies they didn't seem to lack for men about."

"You seem to know a few of the ladies yourself, Mabrey."

Davy flushed. "The East End was my beat, Sir, has been for months – "

Trevor laughed and stood up, stretching. "Relax, boy. I don't think there's a man on the force who's prepared to cast that particular stone at your head. Now get your hat and coat. I'd like to have a pint and look over each other's notes to bring us up to date. Damn it."

For in putting on his own coat, Trevor had dropped a pack of tobacco to the floor. As he bent over to collect it he noticed something lying under the door, a gray envelope with 'DETECTIVE' neatly printed on the outside. Trevor tore open the seal and pulled out a single sheet of writing paper. Aloud he read:

DETECITVE WELLES, I SAW YOU THERE
I CROUCHED AND WATCHED FROM MY LAIR
I WITNESSED YOU SICKEN AT THE SIGHT
OF POOR OLD CATHY, IN THE ALLEY LAST
NIGHT

YOUR BOBB IES, HOW THEY SEARCHED FOR ME
BUT IN THE DARK THEY COULD NOT SEE
I DID NOT BLINK AS THEY DREW NEAR
I SAT AND CHEWED ON CATHERINE'S EAR

I SEND THIS NOTE, TO LET YOU KNOW
I'LL RETURN TO STRIKE A BLOW
AT SOME OLD WHORE STILL WALKING ROUND
HER TIME FOR LIVING, I WILL COUNT DOWN

I'LL LAY HER OPEN, SEE HER SPOUT
WHO KNOWS WHAT ORGANS I'LL TAKE OUT
SO REST DETECTIVE, I'LL SAY GOODNIGHT

BUT I WILL RETURN FOR MORE DELIGHT

JACK THE RIPPER

"You think it's real, Sir?" Davy asked. "You think he's been here, in Scotland Yard?"

"Probably not," Trevor said, although the note in his hands was trembling slightly. "Most of these things are hoaxes."

"Hope so, Sir. I mean, how many people could even know you're head of the case now? It's only been a few hours. Hasn't been in the papers, has it, Sir? But yet Jack called you out by name."

"Yes," Trevor said shortly. "Yes, he certainly did."

CHAPTER SEVENTEEN
11:29 PM

A human kidney is a beautiful thing. It has an almost pearlized pink sheen, especially when it has been as carefully cleaned and trimmed as the one he now holds in his hand. It has a womanly shape, a graceful undulation, and he regrets that he must sacrifice such perfection to this jar of alcohol before him. But he has waited as long as he dares. This kidney is – he pauses to do the math – forty-six hours departed from its owner and although he knows the alcohol will dull its glow and begin to nibble at the sharp outline of the severed veins, he also knows that if he wishes to keep this memento at all, he must take steps to preserve it.

He opens the jar, drops the kidney inside, and watches it descend through the clear liquid to the glass bottom. He puts the jar on his table before his candle, cocks his head, and stares with absorption.

Blood is the great equalizer.

There are a few others who also acknowledge this truth, who share with him in this brotherhood of blood. The world sets the royal above the common, the male above female, white above black, Christian above Jew, the first born above his younger brother - and yet in the end the blood is all the same. Forget ashes. Forget dust. We begin in blood and end in blood, a fact the vast majority of society strives steadily to ignore.

Despite what the papers say, he knows he is not a beast. He believes in God. Actually, he believes in two gods. The god of order, of law, the god of the mind and of science. The one he worships as he eats his breakfast, as he listens to violins, as he walks the morning streets looking at the girls in their soft blue dresses. The girls he knows he is supposed to want, the ones he sometimes does.

But he is no hypocrite. No, still not quite a hypocrite despite the steady and methodical manner in which life has attempted to make him so. He acknowledges this god of daylight and also the deeper, angrier god, the leveling god of sex and death, the one that watches over this kidney, the one who roams the streets at night and who cries out into the darkness like a wounded wolf.

There is nothing unnatural in this, is there? We are all enslaved to the same cycles and there is no reason to feel shame. He walks in light, he walks in darkness, and yet sometimes he wonders: Which one is real, and which is the dream?

CHAPTER EIGHTEEN
October 3
4:40 PM

Despite his best intentions of getting some rest, Trevor found himself once again standing at the door of Geraldine Bainbridge's house. In the days when he was a new detective and one who approached every case with an inordinate degree of seriousness, Trevor had adopted the habit of turning to Geraldine whenever he was fitful or depressed. The Mayfair home may have been unorthodox but it was a haven, perhaps the only true haven he knew in London.

Or so he told himself. But he also knew that it was probably the presence of Leanna which now drove his feet up these familiar steps. This was insanity. With his schedule, he should be seizing these brief hours to sleep, not to mention that only the previous morning he had vowed to avoid her entirely. But he had come back to this door nonetheless, to soak in the warmth of the fire, the tea, Emma's quiet sympathy, Geraldine's comforting habit of taking on his troubles as her own. And yes, perhaps, to see the girl.

Leanna and Tom had been playing chess when he arrived, and they rose rapidly as introductions were made all around. Trevor had often heard Geraldine speak proudly of her nephew but he had never actually met the boy and it was a bit startling to see him standing there so vibrant and blond, the male version of Leanna. Tom grasped Trevor's outreached hand in both of his and urged him to tell every detail of the Ripper case. The morning papers, as well as the afternoon and perhaps, judging from the size of the heap, those of the day before, lay on the divan and Tom impatiently pushed them aside, settled in beside Trevor, and demanded a recounting of the story. Trevor was careful not to divulge sensitive information, but he still enjoyed getting a fresh perspective on the case and within minutes Leanna, Emma, Gage and Gerry also pulled up chairs, allowing Trevor the pleasant sensation of being on stage.

"My fondest hope," he confided to Tom, "is to someday have a forensics laboratory like the one in Paris. Our present methods are quite hit-or-miss and it's appalling to think an institution like Scotland Yard has allowed itself to fall so far behind on the times."

"I can't imagine there could be resistance to such a laboratory," Tom said. "Is it purely a matter of money?"

"Would that it were. More money always helps, of course, and there is a bright side to this Ripper business. Since the Yard is enjoying so much publicity, Parliament has held a special session and granted us more funds. But that money is going to beefing up the staff with more bobbies, not a laboratory." Trevor mustered a small, tight smile. "But even funding is an easy task compared to the problem of changing attitudes. Scotland Yard likes to deduce. To talk to people, interview witnesses, and draw motives. Nothing wrong with that in itself, but interviews can prove misleading and contrary."

"While facts don't lie," Tom prompted.

"Generally they don't. The Yard has simply failed to recognize the importance of actual physical evidence, of establishing proof and not just motive or opportunity. Deduction is all well and good in those sort of drawing room mysteries the ladies like to read," – here Trevor turned toward Gerry with an elaborate head bow which made her snort in mock indignation - "the kind where there are only ten suspects and four of those conveniently die before the fifth chapter. But in a city which holds hundreds of potential Rippers..."

"Indeed," said Tom "Are the French truly that far ahead of us forensically? I know they've made some recent medical strides we just can't match though my professors are loath to admit it."

"Ah, it drives me nearly mad," said Trevor. "They've developed something called the Bertillion System, although I'm probably pronouncing it wrong. Impossible language, you know. But the idea is that there are certain physical measurements – around the cranium specifically, but also the fingers and toes – that are particular to each person and these measurements don't change throughout life."

"I don't understand," Leanna said. "How do bone measurements help you find a killer?"

"I'm not sure," Trevor admitted. "I think the methodology should be more useful in indentifying if the person in question is the right one, or, conversely, in eliminating someone as a suspect. This Bertillion chap has apparently measured every inmate in a certain Parisian prison, created a file of their particulars, and was later able to identify 241 multiple offenders. Multiple offenders - you know, a person who commits the same type of crime over and over, like our friend the Ripper. 241. An amazing number of cases to for a single man to retire, but I don't know how Bertillion did it."

"Would the Parisian police share this information?" Tom asked.

"Oh, almost certainly, if I could go there and study…" Trevor laughed ruefully. "A pipe dream."

Leanna sat frowning into the fire as the talk swirled around her. She was pleased to see Trevor and Tom becoming such fast friends, but it was annoying to be summarily dismissed, especially when she considered that a mere two days earlier Trevor had seemed to seek her opinion. But then she remembered that even on that night, she'd felt pushed aside once he and John had began talking. Perhaps Trevor was one of those men who spoke to women as equals only when there were no other males present.

"What are you thinking, Leanna?" Trevor broke in, smiling as he smoothed down his sideburns with a fingertip.

"I was wondering if the women fought back," she lied smoothly. "The killer may be walking around with bruises or scratches."

"Yes indeed, Liz Stride scratched him. Very astute of you to think of it. She was the only one to get in much of a blow at all, I'm afraid, since it would appear he strangles first and strangles from behind."

"They must be terrified."

"Hmmm?"

"The women of Whitechapel," Leanna repeated. "They must be terrified."

"I rode through the East End on my way here last night," Tom said dryly. "Business hadn't seemed to fall off much."

"They don't have a choice," Leanna said. "It's how they earn their living, feed their children."

"Hard to think of prostitutes having children," Tom mused.

"You should talk to John," Leanna said irritably. "They have them, more than anyone. Which is why they need his clinic...."

With this, she picked up her needlepoint and began to jab at the circle of daisies with shaky little punches of her needle. Tom filled the silence with an amusing story about one of his anatomy classes and Trevor sat looking at Leanna with heavy-lidded eyes. How could she have guessed of Catherine Eddowes' daughter? Or of Frilly's terror? Obviously she did not know any women in their line of work, but her remarks were close enough to the truth. Leanna had the gift of empathy, of sensing what life must be like for others without ever having directly experienced such trouble herself. In a society which forced women to be either ignorant or jaded, with no levels in between, Leanna's imagination made her a rare specimen.

Rare and beyond his reach. She had already begun to mouth John's opinions as her own.

5:40 PM

Mary Kelly looked into the cracked mirror and smiled back at herself, pleased. The new lip rouge was quite becoming and she had pulled her russet curls up in a new manner this evening, a style which would have been too severe for most women but which was fetching on one who possessed, as did Mary, a perfectly proportioned profile.

She commanded a top price and could afford to be a bit choosy in her selection. She liked them young and relatively clean - the fishmongers and slaughterhouse workers weren't for her, thank you - and if business was slow on a particular night and she was forced to temporarily lower her standards, then the price went up. As high as two pounds. Her pretty face and her ability to drive a hard bargain had earned her this room of her own off Hanover Street. It wasn't much of a home, and Mary knew it, but it was her own nonetheless, and returning to it each evening gave her a sense of privacy and dignity. She didn't have to share a bed-let with a gaggle of other working girls or, worse, resort to knee-tremblers in the alleyway. She could have a fire and a wash basin and even a spot of tea between trade. The bookcase with its titles of Milton and Smollett and Chaucer would have struck her customers as quite odd should any of them have paused to look, but the gentlemen were not in the habit of staying long and Mary did not encourage even the slightest gesture of familiarity once the job was done.

The other girls were abuzz about the killings but such thoughts did not overly distress Mary Kelly. The Ripper seemed to favor a very different sort of woman – older, unsteady, desperate, weakened by alcohol and too many years in the life. The sort of woman who would still be on the streets at one or two in the morning, who would be willing to risk following a stranger into an alley. Her father had read her the works of Charles Darwin, and – although she doubted her father would have agreed with this particular interpretation – Mary considered The Ripper an agent of natural selection. He did little more than hasten the inevitable for the poor wretches he took, and he'd never shown a proclivity for a woman like her. Someone who was young and strong and sober, who had her wits about her, someone with a steady enough clientele that she was usually back in her own bed alone before midnight.

On this particular night Mary pulled her favorite red stole over her bare shoulders and headed out in the direction of the Fox and Hound. Although the streets were dark she strode confidently through them, her empty purse slapping her thigh with each wide step. The purse would not remain empty for long.

Nor, God willing, would her stomach. There was generally a gent or two at the tavern who would buy her a pint and a bit of supper in exchange for the pleasure of her company, and perhaps as a prelude to other pleasures. Mary had the reputation, rare among her rivals, of being charming company even when upright.

As she turned east on Merchant Street, Mary stopped. A man, very still and well-dressed, stood in the fog wearing a tall hat and red muffler. Mary smiled slightly. Perhaps the walk to the tavern would not be necessary tonight.

"Evening, Sir," she said, proud that her voice carried not the slightest trace of a cockney accent.

The man turned halfway, his face so concealed by the hat brim and muffler that only his dark eyes were visible. Such concealment was not unusual for the East End where a certain class of man might be hesitant to be recognized, and Mary had even known a couple who'd adopted a full disguise. A little more subterfuge than the situation called for, at least in her opinion, but perhaps the costuming had been part of their naughty game. No matter. It was scarcely her job to wonder at the motives of men.

"Evening," the man said.

"Frightful weather, is it not?" she asked, a particularly inane remark for London where the weather was always frightful, but one had to begin somewhere. The man made no reply and only stared at her with narrowed eyes.

"Are you out for dinner?" Mary continued, a bit uneasily now, for it had crossed her mind he might be a copper trying to draw a working girl into his lair. She would have to choose her words carefully. "I'm on my way for a bite myself, you see, and I…"

"I dine alone."

"Yes, yes, of course," she said, stammering, for she had evidently misjudged the situation badly. She backed up, nearly stumbling as her foot left the curb and offering the gentleman a tremulous smile in parting. He did not look at her and as she stared off into the mist she found herself, to her own surprise, running. For a moment she felt disoriented as if she had not walked these streets a thousand times in the last five years.

"Fair Mary, where ye goin'?" lisped a familiar voice from the curb and she stopped, gasping against the constraints of her corset and looking into the face of Georgy McDale, a regular customer at the local bars and - for the time being, at least - somewhat of a friend.

"The strangest man," she gasped, unable to go on.

"Aye, girl are ye mad? Roamin' the streets with the Ripper around? It's no time to be findin' new customers, I can tell ye that. 'Tis a time to be seein' old friends who ye know," he smiled at her, holding out one arm and displaying brown, uneven teeth.

Mary raised her chin. "I'm hungry. I want some stew."

"Aye, well enough."

"And don't think my price has gone down, just because these are hard times."

Georgy laughed, "I wouldn' be takin' advantage of ye, Mary. There's a tavern here across the way." Mary nodded, taking the extended arm and wondering if Georgy was right. The gentleman on the corner had done nothing, not really, but he had frightened her nonetheless. Perhaps fear were a palpable thing in the air, floating above London and mingled with the fog, and they would all breathe it in eventually, even the young and the clever and the strong. Perhaps it was truly better to stick with old friends, even if they did have bad teeth. Even if it did mean coming down a bit on her price.

6:10 PM

"Whoever can that be?" Geraldine murmured, heading for the front door since both Gage and Emma were involved in a raucous game of charades. She pulled hard on the oaken door, which tended to stick a bit, and swung it open to reveal the thin, elegant frame of John Harrowman, swathed from head to foot in his black broadcloth cape.

"Darling," Geraldine exclaimed. "Do come in. We've having a sort of impromptu party and Leanna will be so delighted to see you."

"I'm forgiven for canceling our theatre plans, then?" John asked, his voice attractively husky from the night air.

"Yes, of course. The girl isn't that petty," Geraldine said, showing him toward the parlor.

"I have it, I have it," Leanna was saying. "It's 'Bird in a Gilded Cage.'"

"At last," Emma said, sinking to the couch. "I thought none of you would ever guess and I would be forced to attempt to act out the word 'gilded.' Why, hello doctor," she added, looking at the door with surprise.

"Hello, Emma, Leanna, Welles, Gage," John said, advancing into the room and shirking his cape.

"Do you know my nephew, Tom?" Geraldine asked.

"Thomas Bainbridge. Your reputation precedes you."

"As does yours," Tom said, extending a hand. "I take it you're John Harrowman." Leanna glanced at her brother nervously, hoping no teasing was forthcoming, but Tom stopped there. "At the risk of stating the obvious, we're playing a game or two, hoping to take poor Trevor's mind off his troubles."

"And his promotion as well," John said, turning to Trevor. "I was, of course, reading the evening edition of the papers intently, as was all of London, and was gratified to learn you've been named chief coordinator. Congratulations."

"Thank you," Trevor said stiffly. "But I'm afraid Tom's right. My promotion has led to my troubles and I've run here to Geraldine's home for comfort. I'll be leaving in a second, though. It's the evening shift for me from now on."

"Of course, crimes of the night," John said, and his eyes fell on Leanna for the first time. He raised his brows questioningly.

"Care to play charades, with us, Doctor John?" Emma asked. "And we have a custard about to come out of the oven."

"I would be a fool to leave such stimulating company," John answered. "Yes, by all means let's play and speak of nothing important."

"Come, John, be on our team," Leanna said quickly "and help even things up. Aunt Geraldine has the concentration of an infant and so far the men are trouncing the ladies most thoroughly."

"Well we can't have that, now, can we?" John said.

6:50 PM

Forty minutes later, warmed by the custard and the steady flow of conversation, Trevor found himself seated across from John Harrowman at the chess board, while Tom lay stretched across an armchair smoking. The ladies had ventured off and the room was silent save for the occasional crackle of the fire and Tom's enthusiastic inhalations on the pipe, a ritual he performed with such gusto that Trevor suspected he was a beginner at smoking.

Trevor glanced at his pocket watch. He had told Davy he would meet him at seven-thirty to begin rounds and it was nearly seven. He should have left some time ago, not let himself be drawn into a game of chess, and in fact he was not even sure if the game was going well or not. John was an enigma; he made his moves quickly and with little apparent forethought, while Trevor was in the habit of lengthy consideration. Trevor had taken the first three pieces, a setback John bore with such cheerful equanimity that Trevor suspected these minimal early losses were part of some overall strategy. Or perhaps he didn't care about the outcome of the game at all, a thought which gave

Trevor pause. He had always viewed chess as a type of mental war and was incapable of playing a casual game.

"Mind if I ask you something?" he inquired. He had waited until the women were out of earshot.

"Feel free to ask anything," John said.

"Have you heard of a woman named Maud Mitford?"

John raised his chin, all the complacency out of his face. "How the devil would you know Mad Maudy?"

"One of the women we interviewed mentioned her. I take it she's an East End midwife?"

"Midwife?" John said with a sharp exhalation. "It's stretching matters a bit to refer to Maud Milford as a midwife. She performs abortions."

"Oh," Trevor said. He was shocked but he tried not to show it. John made a careless move, exposing his bishop, and Tom put down his pipe and sat up a little straighter.

"Mind you, my objections aren't moralistic," John said. "The vast majority of those babies are better off never being born, although perhaps I shouldn't express such a belief to a man of the law. My complaint with Maud is that she is untrained, stubbornly ignorant, and refuses to observe even the most rudimentary rules of sanitation. Half of the desperate women who come to her don't live to see another day, killed either by her scalpel or by the nearly inevitable infections which follow. Of course, women who are determined to have an abortion know the risks, but they haven't much place else to go. Certainly no reputable midwife or doctor would attempt one."

Trevor took John's bishop.

"And it isn't just the working women of Whitechapel," John went on distractedly. "I've always suspected Maud's knife was behind the death of a young debutante last year, a girl from the very best of families, who found herself in need of Maud's rather unique specialty. By the time she arrived at a proper hospital the gangrene was too advanced to treat." John shook his head, trying to clear the memory. "A spectacularly horrible way for a sixteen year old girl to die."

Tom stood up, frowning, then went to pour himself another brandy.

"Seems like the sort of mistake that would put her out of business for good," Trevor said with surprise, for he couldn't recall the case making its way to Scotland Yard. "The girl's family took no interest in who might have done this to their daughter?"

"Not likely to pursue the story too far, were they?" John said, and his mouth twisted in disgust. "The socially accepted story is that the girl died of consumption and Mad Maudy goes free to turn her scalpel on her next victim… My God," John said, looking up from the board as comprehension finally dawned. "Are you suggesting she's a suspect in this Ripper business?"

Trevor shrugged. "She was seen in the vicinity of two of the killings. From what I gather, she is large-framed enough to pass as a man with the right clothing a bit of a fake facial hair added."

"She wouldn't have to add much," John said. "She has half a mustache as it is."

"Yes, I get the impression she's rather masculine."

"Hardly begins to describe it. I've always felt she hated her own sex, that there was a deliberate cruelty behind her carelessness. I've offered her some of my instruments, some training…if she's going to ply her trade she should at least have that much. But each time I've been rebuffed. Evidently the high mortality rate of her practice does not distress her." John looked down and made another bad move.

"Hates her own sex?" Tom repeated, entranced. "Do you mean she hates them for being feminine, for having obviously

176

attracted a man, which she could not? Or do you rather mean she's a puritan of sorts who hates them for being pregnant and uses her tools to punish them for their sins?"

"More of the latter," John said, impassively watching Trevor take another of his pawns. "It sounds ridiculous to say she's an abortionist who hates women who have abortions, but -"

"No, not ridiculous at all," Trevor cut in. "When you remember the sort of psychology we're dealing with. I must make it a point to call on this Maud."

"Have a drink first," John advised. "But there's another thing, something which makes me doubt she's your Ripper. You've stressed how skillfully the dissections were done and I doubt poor Maud could take out an ovary cleanly if you offered her diamonds. And the Ripper writes rather elaborate messages while I'd imagine Maud's literacy is limited at best." He casually moved a knight and Trevor stared down at the board, thinking of the letter which had come to the Yard, with its poetic meter and neat penmanship.

"Both good points, but I'll visit her nonetheless. Witnesses say she seems to always be near the trouble. It's a shame you're going back to school so soon, Tom. I know Gage means well but he's elderly and, let's be frank , a bit odd. I'd feel better if there were a young man in the house with Geraldine and the girls."

"You don't honestly feel upper class women are in danger?" Tom asked. "I mean, here in Mayfair…"

"No, no, you're right, such a thing is unlikely," Trevor said, moving his rook. "Paranoia is a natural outgrowth of my job. You're confronted with the very worst society has to offer and you see it hour after hour, day after day. After a while, the whole world begins to look dangerous to you. Everyone's suspect."

"I've had the same problem with medical school," Tom said cheerfully. "I've developed the symptoms of half of the conditions described in my textbooks already. Rashes and tremors and headaches, the lot. Did that ever happen to you, John?"

"Hypochondria and paranoia are diseases of the educated mind," John said, taking Trevor's rook. "At least that's what I tell myself for comfort, since I'm rather prone to both. It takes a certain level of imagination to concoct dangers where none exist. Or perhaps Trevor's right and this is all just the natural outcome of the professions we've chosen. When you work with the diseased and the criminal all day, they become your reality. You begin to look for those same traits in yourself."

"I think I want to be a doctor..." Tom said slowly, looking up at the ceiling, "but there are days when I wonder if I'm more like grandfather, destined for the laboratory. The thing is, I'm not sure I could bear losing a patient. Even if someone were old and sick, perhaps I would torment myself, always thinking there must have been something else I could have done. I suppose you get used to death, though, do you not?"

"Don't turn death into the enemy, Tom," John said, looking at the chess board. "If you do, you will lose every game you play."

"But as a doctor, surely you –"

"As a doctor I can do no more than forestall the inevitable conclusion of a rigged contest. Death is the end we all march toward.... rich and poor, old and young, the healthy and the infirm. All I can do is keep it at bay for a year or a decade, more if the patient is lucky. But death isn't such a bad thing."

Tom frowned at the ceiling. "I should think it's the worst thing."

"Ah...but if we were immortal, how cruel would we be?" John asked, as Trevor confidently advanced his queen. "Fear of death, and what comes after, is all that keeps most men from even deeper depths of depravity than those we currently navigate. If we all lived forever, we would have no fear of God. Perhaps no need of God at all. Immortal men would become their own gods, and I suspect that, given such power, we would be neither just nor merciful. Do you agree, Trevor?"

"A month ago I might not have," Trevor said. "But given the events of late I too am beginning to wonder if there's such a thing as innate human decency. And next month at this time I may be more cynical yet again."

"I take it you aren't predicting a rapid conclusion to the investigation," Tom said, turning to look directly at Trevor.

"Well we've got it narrowed down to a butcher, an abortionist, the Duke of Clarence, doctors, sailors, the Poles, the Turks, the Greeks, the Jews, Mad Maudy, and a man of medium height who's wearing a hat. So, no, I think it's safe to say I don't predict a rapid conclusion to the investigation." Trevor slumped back in his chair and rubbed his eyes. "You'll have to forgive my tone. I'm exhausted and it's all just beginning. I shouldn't have come here today, I should have gone home to rest. But I can't seem to sleep."

It was true. Trevor had been up before six that morning to brief the bobbies beginning their rounds, and then there was a whole new gaggle of suspects in the cells to interview. Well, to call them suspects was stretching the point. Everyone on the force, no matter what their ranking, was so determined to find the Ripper that the jails were full of vagrants, drunkards, prostitutes and their customers, and men whose only offense was the imprecise crime of "looking suspicious." He and Davy had gone through them one by one, filling more sheets of papers with their endless notes, and then broken off about three. Trevor had urged the boy to go home for a few hours rest before they took up again at nightfall. But he had found himself unable to take that same advice himself.

"I could give you something to help you sleep," John said quietly, staring at the board.

At that moment the door opened and Emma entered, carrying three brandies on a tray. The men fell silent as they each took a glass from Emma and thanked her.

"Will you be back next weekend, Tom?" John asked casually. Trevor had taken his other bishop.

"I wasn't planning on it," Tom said. "I'm dreadfully behind at school, all these problems with the settling of my grandfather's estate." He caught himself just in time, remembering how Leanna had pleaded with him to let neither Trevor nor John know of her inheritance. "I have two missed papers to present, but if you think I should -"

"No, nonsense. Your priority is your studies," Trevor said sharply, with a glance at Emma.

But her personal safety was the last worry on Emma's mind. The thought of Tom leaving tomorrow felt like a knife to the heart. This was no sort of life for her, she thought, hanging on from visit to visit for the pleasure of just watching him, feeding him, perhaps exchanging a few friendly words with him. And with each departure the ache grew stronger until the weekdays were becoming nearly unbearable.

Stop it, she thought to herself. He comes and he goes and if you haven't figured that out by now, you are a proper dunce. All this moaning is more like the thoughts of a wronged romantic heroine. More like Leanna. Aloud she said, a bit saucily, "May the ladies venture back into this smoke-filled den? You've banished us for nearly an hour."

"Banished you?" Tom protested. "I could have sworn you had banished us. Yes indeed, the ladies must all come back in, I'm bored to death of this masculine conversation."

"We've been in the doldrums without you," John laughed. "Checkmate," he added, glancing at Trevor as he pushed himself back from the table.

CHAPTER NINETEEN
October 4
3:20 AM

After their largely uneventful rounds had been completed, Trevor and Davy had stopped off at the Pony Pub, the place Micha Barasik had claimed to be the night of the double murders. Trevor's choice of a place to drink was not accidental. Barasik's alibi had been confirmed earlier in the day, so the giant had been released, but something about the situation still niggled at Trevor's mind. He had offered to buy Davy a beer but the young officer had, quite sensibly, opted instead to go home for a few hours sleep.

"Not likely much will happen on a Tuesday anyway, Sir," he'd said. "The Ripper strikes on weekends, doesn't he, Sir? If we rule Martha Tabram out, the other four were on a Friday or Saturday. Maybe a working man, turns in early through the week but cats around on the weekend."

"Quite right, Davy," Trevor had said, ashamed he hadn't thought of that himself. "Get some rest and I'll see you at the Yard tomorrow."

The boy had a profound gift for the obvious, Trevor reflected, idly wondering if the barmaid sliding him his pint was the same girl who had provided an alibi for Micha. That bit about the murders occurring on weekends was so basic that everyone else on the case had somehow managed to miss it. For the hundredth time in the last two days Trevor blessed he series of coincidences that had brought Davy Mabrey to his attention.

Eatwell had said he could take more men and Trevor had initially been tempted to do so. But perhaps, he reflected as he gazed at the exhausted girl struggling to lift a tray laden with glasses, it was better if just he and Davy did the interrogations and let the other men handle the patrols. It was hard for him to remember, in the dawning light of this new day, what he had hoped to accomplish by walking the streets of Whitechapel. There were plenty of bobbies to do that, nearly twice the number assigned to an area on a typical Tuesday night. Davy had not questioned his judgment directly, but he was right. They needed to spend their time following up leads, not mindlessly roaming the serpentine streets of the East End. Perhaps on the weekend, but not through the week.

Trevor drained his pint in three long gulps and looked around. Despite the fact it was nearly four in the morning there were still a surprising number of people clustered around the Pony Pub. It's not just me, Trevor thought. No one in London can sleep. We have become a city of insomniacs. The barmaid turned an inquiring face and he nodded. Yes, another. Why not?

"I wish you would listen," the girl said, sliding a beer toward Trevor, but talking to a man several seats down the bar. "We should go to my sister's house, that's what I think. London's not a fit place for the decent, but she said she'd take us in..."

"Excuse me," Trevor said. "Miss —"

"Name's Lucy," the girl said, turning her attention promptly back to Trevor.

"Pleased to meet you. I was going to ask about a man named Micha —"

"Oh yes, Micha, right as rain," the girl said. "A copper bloke came in asking if he could be the Ripper, can you picture? But I told him he'd been here the whole night. His usual charming gentleman of a self, right as rain." She laughed, showing a row of teeth that were surprisingly white and even considering this was the East End, and Trevor found himself laughing back. Perhaps it was his disheveled appearance or

184

perhaps the fact he was drinking at four in the morning, but for some reason the girl taken him as a friend of the brute.

"Not likely to forget a face like that, are you?" Trevor asked and the girl shook her head vigorously, glancing down the bar as she did so. Trevor couldn't see the man sitting at the end, but he was likely the jealous sort from the nervous little titters that erupted from the girl whenever she looked in his direction. He had undoubtedly seduced Lucy at some point and didn't like it when she showed another man attention. We're all of us beasts in a way, Trevor thought. The man at the end of the bar probably had her easy enough, cares for her not a whit, and even without looking him in the face I'd bet the crown jewels he hasn't the slightest notion of taking this poor little simpleton to her sister.

"Not likely to forget that ugly devil" the girl agreed with a giggle. "He pays for it, or he has it not at all, that's our Micha."

She had picked up English phrases and diction well enough, but but her accent, especially on certain words like "ugly," revealed that she was Polish. Like Micha, and probably half of the people in the Pony Pub. The bar catered to the squadrons of people escaping Eastern Europe for what they imagined to be a more humane and civilized life in London and the tightness of these communities was one reason that Trevor conducted his interviews with skepticism. The Poles vouched for the Poles, the Jews for the Jews, the sailors for the sailors, and, farther to the west, the Royals vouched for the Royals. Trevor had often argued that the natural human impulse to protect your own kind rendered most alibis useless, but the Yard continued to put a great deal of faith in them, still behaved as if investigating even the most heinous crimes was a gentleman's game. Yes, guv, I'd slit a woman's throat ear to ear but I certainly wouldn't lie about it.

The girl continued to chatter as she wiped the bar, saying that she was frightened, which was undoubtedly true. Saying she wanted to go to her sister, who was in Jersey, somewhere rural and green and safe, at least to this girl's mind. Half the men in this bar have mustaches, Trevor drily noted, and most of them dark hair. The physical descriptions provided by the witnesses, he was rapidly beginning to see, were as pointless as alibis. The witnesses were giving him impressions, not true descriptions, and impressions were as individual as breasts…

God. Where had that come from? Trevor pulled himself upright, took another swig of his beer. How long had it been? Weeks coming up on months, months coming up on more like a year?

He found himself envying the man who sat at the end of the bar, a man who had clearly taken advantage of a lonely, frightened girl who he had no intention of marrying, no intention of saving. The rules of Mayfair didn't apply in this part of town. Of course the impressions of the people he and Davy had interviewed were just that, impressions. The poverty and the filth of the East End acted as drugs, transporting the citizens of Whitechapel into a sort of collective stupor. A sense of timelessness, drunkenness, women walking aimlessly back and forth in search of something that did not exist in this mean part of the city, men who worked and ate and slept at odd hours. The people here wore no watches. They read no papers, kept no appointments, accepted no invitations to dine. If you stopped the average person in the street and asked the wretch the date or the month would they even be able to answer? Would there be any reason why they should? And yet these are the people, Trevor thought, draining his second beer, whose recollections are the foundation of our case.

Trevor shut his eyes. The stories buzzed around him. Was the bar usually this crowded on a Tuesday? But no, it was

Wednesday now, wasn't it? Tuesday had slid into Wednesday just as Tuesday always does, and Trevor listened to Lucy chattering on. A pretty girl, a normal girl, a girl who had committed no greater sin than believing the man who bedded her, a girl who with a single stroke of bad luck might find herself on the streets someday, as desperate as Dark Annie. Trevor let the alcohol settle over him like a blanket and listened to their voices. Not just the girl and her useless lover, but the man in the back, roaring that it must be Victoria's grandson. "'e's sick in the 'ead, you, know? Why they only let 'im out at night, so 'e won't be seen in public."

"I think 'e's that doctor from Russia," said another. "The Jew. Said in the papers these women were cut on like in surgery. Clean cuts and all."

"You know 'e's had some dealings with Old Maudy," a third voice, female, ventured. "Maybe they're working together. She 'ates all of us. Wears men's clothing, too."

Trevor pulled out his journal and made another note on Maud Minford. He kept hearing her name, but he hadn't visited her yet. John had seemed so certain she couldn't have the skills to do the deed, yet everyone had been unanimous in their condemnation of her cruelty. He closed his journal and replaced it in his breast pocket.

"Evening, Sir." A young girl – fifteen? sixteen? – slid onto the stool beside him. "Or should I say morning?"

"Morning it is," he said. "Don't you have some place you should be? Someone who's expecting you home?"

"No, Sir" she said, with a simplicity that reminded him, oddly, of Davy. "Nowhere to be. No one at home. And you, Sir?"

"Nowhere to be" Trevor confirmed, draining the last of his beer. "And no one waiting for me either. So you guessed right, love." It had been ten months, four days, and twenty hours. Afterwards, perhaps he would be able to sleep.

CHAPTER TWENTY
October 5, 1888
9:14 AM

Rain was peppering in sharp, hard drops as Trevor and Davy stepped from the coach on Atlantic Street. The two men pulled their collars up about them and held their hats tightly with one hand as they ran to a nearby canopy for shelter. Davy had written down directions they'd gotten from a witness the night before and he fumbled for the note in his pocket. Just the mention of Mad Maudy had put fear in the girl's face, even though Trevor had assured her that she was not in trouble.

"Start at the Bullwick Tavern and halfway down the third block, you'll find an alley. Follow it back to the water and then go a little further. There'll be a wooden shack with a chimney." Davy read.

"Follow it to the water and then go farther? It sounds as if her house is floating down the bloody Thames itself," Trevor said, but if the girl had been a mite uncooperative, her directions were as good as gold. Within minutes Davy and Trevor found themselves at the end of the aptly-named Atlantic Street, a broken down thoroughfare which butted the waterfront and reeked of rotten fish. The two men held their scarves over their noses as they walked toward the water and a lone crude building with smoke escaping from its chimney. Hard to imagine a young debutante picking her way through the muck to such a hovel, no matter how desperate she might be. Trevor approached the front door and knocked soundly.

"Go away, 'tis too early in the day!" a rough voice exploded from inside.

"Are you Maud Minford? I wish to speak with you," Trevor shouted, for the wind along the channel was fierce.

"You know me, do I know thee?"

"I'm detective Trevor Welles of Scotland Yard. May I have a few minutes with you?"

"Scotland Yard, is that what you say? What do you want with ole' Maudy?"

"Only to ask you some questions, Miss Minford."

Trevor and Davy took a step back as they heard a latch unlock and the door slowly widened to reveal a single squinting eye.

"I heard your voice and now I see you. I didn't hear the voices of two."

"This is Officer Davy Madley," Trevor said, although he felt ridiculous shouting into a crack. "We are both from Scotland Yard and we need a little of your time. May we come in?"

Finally, the door swung all the way open and there stood before them a huge woman several inches taller than Trevor and towering as much as a foot over Davy. Her head was flat and as round as a wooden bucket and her thin gray hair was cropped short. Nor had John Harrowman exaggerated about the amount of facial hair she sported. Her hands and arms looked strong and powerful, the fingers stubby, and her voice was deep.

"Come in if you must, but the likes of you I do not trust."

"Thank you, Miss Minford," said Trevor, as he and Davy entered. The house smelled, if possible, worse than the waterfront. Maud went back to her fireplace and stirred something cooking in a pot. A broken loaf of bread lay on the table.

"Tis time you two removed your masks. What are these questions you must ask?"

"Miss Minford, I understand you are midwife to some of the local women? Is that true?" asked Trevor, a bit unnerved by the woman's damned rhyming.

"That be my trade for which I am paid."

190

"I understand you perform another service for these ladies, if needed."

Maud jerked her shoulders, but made no comment.

"I'm not here to pass judgment on you, Miss Minford," Trevor went on. "And I don't particularly care what you do for a living. We have come to ask questions about your whereabouts on a certain evening."

"It's evil deeds that plant bad seeds."

"Why must you continue to speak in these silly poems?" Davy muttered.

"Is it a crime that I speak in rhyme?"

"Let her be, Davy. Where were you on the evening of September thirtieth?"

"In my home. I did not roam."

"Can anyone attest to that?" She gave him a scathing look and shook her head. "How do you feel about your clients, Maud?"

"I'm just a gardener with a hoe. I have no friend and no foe."

"These women that come to you for your special services. Do you wish them pain and feel they deserve it? Trying to teach them a lesson, are you?"

"They all come crying, help me Maudy, get me back to being naughty."

"We've heard, Maud, that some of these women die after being in your care."

"Some of them bleed, when I pluck their weed. Some of them never recover, when they take too soon a lover. I do them all the same. I take no blame."

Davy abruptly leaned across the sloping wooden table, surprising Trevor with his forcefulness. "I have trouble believing you don't recall where you were on September 30," he said. "It's a famous night, isn't it? Every paper in London screaming the next day about the double murders, and it's all anyone in any bar in London has talked about since. Yet you tell us you don't remember the evening."

This direct assault seemed to rattle the woman a bit. She walked over to her stove and poked a long bent spoon into her stew, stirring awkwardly. "You ask me fast, now let me think. I probably sat somewhere to drink."

"Your stew smells very good, Maud," Trevor said smoothly. "I bet you bake your own bread, too. May I try a piece?"

Davy all but rolled his eyes. He knew Trevor was just checking to see the creature's dominant hand, but he could hardly believe his boss was willing to eat anything in this filthy room.

"Could you cut me a piece, Maud?" Trevor repeated.

"Cut your own, or do you now sit on the throne?"

"I do not wish to remove my gloves, dear lady. Could you please cut me a slice?"

Maudy jabbed the spoon back down in the stew and sternly walked to the table. She grabbed a long knife, sliced off a piece of bread with her right hand, and slammed it down in front of him.

"Are you here for a crime or just here to waste my time?"

"We're finished."

Trevor pushed away from the table with Maudy still giving him a miserable stare. Davy opened the door and both of the men thanked her, in the automatic manner of the Yard, before heading back up the alley to Atlantic Street. Once out of sight of the shack, Trevor began spitting out the bread.

"I was beginning to think your stomach was made of iron," Davy laughed as he watched him shuddering and wiping.

Trevor laughed too, finally removing the last few crumbs from his lips. "She was certainly large enough to be the Ripper

192

and perhaps even had a motive. It's clear she hates her patients or clients or whatever you care to call them. But her skill with cutlery was quite sloppy, don't you think?"

"Her riddles had me almost insane."

"Did they rattle your brain? Gad, she has me doing it. The rhyming business is interesting, especially when you consider that the message slipped beneath my office door was set out like a poem. But could such an outlandish creature have strolled into Scotland Yard unnoticed?"

"Dressed as a man she could."

"Perhaps. But there's still the fact she appears to be right handed and lacks basic medical skill. I don't feel she's our Jack, but we'll still keep an eye on her, repellant as that task might be."

The dock front was jammed with activity, for apparently several boats had just come into the harbor and the men were streaming onto land. Itching for fresh food, fresh women, or just the chance to stretch their legs. They stumbled unevenly down the sidewalks, as if the land beneath their feet was swaying, and hooted back and forth to each other. You can feel their wild energy, Trevor thought, what it's like for them to walk free after being cooped up on their ships. They'll be back at sea within days or sometimes even hours, so whatever pleasures they manage to soak up in the moment will have to last them for weeks. It was easy to see how such explosive energy could very quickly come to violence.

About a block up, they passed a sailor wearing a dark pea coat, a felt hat, and a red neckerchief tied around his neck which reminded Trevor of the red fiber he still carried in his journal. He casually mentioned this to Davy and they followed the man to the breakfront where they passed another man with the same type of red scarf. And then another. Soon, he and Davy had passed dozens of sailors, all in the same dress.

"It's like a bloody nightmare, isn't it, Sir? There must be a hundred of those scarves right here."

"Yes," said Trevor, laughing despite himself. "No wonder the doctor thought I was daft. Trevor and his fibers. So this is what we come down to. Mad Maudy claims to have no memory of the evening in question, but in this part of town, where alcohol runs in the street like rainwater, hardly anyone seems to have memories. Most of them have alibis, yes, more than you can shake a stick at, but considering the alibis were provided by people just as memory-deficient and alcohol-saturated as themselves, what good are they?"

"So all these interviews, all three hundred of them, all these days....it all was useless?"

"Nothing's useless. But the interviews are the old way, Eatwell's method, and the deeper we go into this mess the more I see that my first impulse was the right one. This case won't be solved through interviews, through trying to trick someone into using their left hand or their right hand, and it sure as hell won't be solved by going up and down a row of barstools, listening to a group of drunken sailors swear their mate was right beside them on the night in question. This case will be solved by forensics. I always knew it. I just didn't have the faith to push it through in the beginning. We need hard physical evidence."

"But not the neck scarves, eh Sir?"

Trevor laughed. "Not the bloody neck scarves. Come on, boy, let's head back for the Yard. I've got a better plan now."

CHAPTER TWENTY-ONE
1:20 PM

"So we can have use of the mortuary?"

"Certainly," Phillips said. "Take the front table, but I don't understand precisely what you plan to do with the space."

"It's the beginning of my forensics laboratory," Trevor said. "Davy's off sending a wire to Paris requesting copies of their latest procedure papers and I intend to try to reproduce their experiments here. Eatwell doesn't have to know –"

Phillips waved his hand. "And he shan't. Would you like to take a final look at Stride? She's going in the ground tomorrow."

Just part of the job, Trevor thought, walking resolutely toward the small room at the back of the mortuary where the mortuary assistants were beginning the embalming process. The body lay on the table, wrapped in its muslin shroud but Trevor noted that burial clothes were draped over the camera tripod. Presumably after her blood was drained and the embalming fluid was pumped into the woman's veins she would be dressed, lowered into her coffin, and photographed.

"Stride is coming along smoothly enough, but Eddowes took us half the morning," Phillips said, coming up behind him, a cup in his shaky hand. "Even after we stitched her up tight, her wounds were so numerous and profound that the embalming fluid continued to leak. She went into the box rather wet, I'm afraid. Would you like tea?"

Any number of graceless jokes sprang to Trevor's lips, but he bit them back. Detectives thrived on dark humor, and he considered their sarcasm and perversity a defense against the horrors of the street, and thus necessary to their calling. Upstairs, the Yard was a bit of a boy's club, and, if unchecked, the boisterous spirit among the bobbies could lead to disrespect bordering on the edge of desecration. Trevor made it a point not to think of what had happened to one girl, by the looks of her likely no more than fifteen, whose naked and violated body had been found on the outskirts of London last Christmas morning - and who then had the additional misfortune of traveling to the morgue by means of a paddy wagon full of coppers angry over having drawn a holiday shift. Inspectors turned a blind eye to certain matters. The policy of releasing minor offenders "at the discretion of the arresting officer" had led to thieves bribing their way out of jail with the very goods they had just stolen, or prostitutes who, with a few minutes on their knees before a bobby, found their way back to the streets almost immediately.

And so it was an imperfect system, one created and maintained by imperfect men. Trevor did not consider the police force especially corrupt or particularly blameworthy and instead viewed this myriad of small lapses as the natural resort of a group of men left entirely too much on their own. Men deprived of female company quickly became fearsome creatures, and Trevor believed you could argue that civilization was in fact the invention of women, or at least the invention of the men who wanted to please them. If it were not for the ladies, Trevor often proclaimed, especially after a few beers, humanity would doubtlessly still be roaming the forests in animal skins.

But here, here in this small brightly lit room far below the surface of Scotland Yard, things were different. The atmosphere was as hushed and decorous as a classroom – no, Trevor decided, as he seated himself in the lone wooden chair in the corner. No, it was more like a chapel. The young assistant named Severin treated the long thin body of the woman beneath the shroud with a palpable dignity, careful to cover the parts not necessary to his work, lifting and lowering each limb with a gentle touch. He had slipped needles into various veins at her ankles, throat, wrists, and somewhere between the strips of cloth draped about her torso while the even-younger lad, whose name Trevor could not recall, was moving from one spot to another, checking the tubes. The blood was flowing out of her, flowing fast, and since this was the one that the Ripper didn't have his fair time with, there was plenty left to give. Severin and the assistant circled around the table in a ritualistic manner that reminded Trevor of a priest and altar boy.

Could he work in this room? Or would the very solemnity drive him mad? He would have to remember to tell Davy there could be no laughing down here, deep in this inner sanctum, no tobacco or belching or scratching, no whistling or passing of gas. The tubes running from the woman's body were changing from red to pink and her slender white feet, poking from beneath the shroud, glowed like marble. Severin removed the needle from her ankle and pulled the sheet over that part of her body too, hiding her soles from the insolent eyes of men. Something in his manner made Trevor ashamed of himself.

The insertion of the embalming fluid seemed to go well enough, although it did require a towel to be tightly tied around the woman's throat to make sure that everything that was flowing in did not just as swiftly flow back out. Severin asked if they needed photographs and Phillips said "Not now. When she's dressed." Glancing back at Trevor he added, "I thought it would be prudent to record the full extent of the wounds exhibited by Eddowes." Trevor nodded automatically, although it took him a moment to understand the doctor's meaning. They must have photographed the Eddowes woman's naked form. Trevor guessed she lay in the other coffin in the room, the one that had already been nailed shut.

Once the fluid was in, Severin began unrolling the cloths that bound the body. An arm tumbled free. It was strange - an

197

abrupt, spontaneous gesture, as if the woman had moved of her own accord, and Trevor abruptly stood, wavering uncertainly on his own feet. It seemed vulgar to remain to see them bare her and dress her and the complete silence of the room was beginning to unnerve him. The clank of the hypodermic needle against the steel tray sounded as loud as a scream. Phillips approached the table, glancing over at him again.

"What exactly did you need?"

"Hair samples. A scrape of skin and fingernail cuttings."

Phillips did not ask him what he planned to do with these things, which was lucky since Trevor could not have answered. He had read that the French police used samples from the victims as well as the suspects, so he wished to have them at the ready.

"From both women?" Phillips asked.

Trevor nodded, although he knew that his request meant prying the nails from the coffin in the corner and revealing what he could only assume was the horrifying visage of Catherine Eddowes. Her hollow-eyed face had visited his dreams for two nights as it was, but considering what Phillips and his assistants went through on a daily basis, he supposed he could muster up the courage to pull a strand of hair and clip the woman's fingernails.

"I'll get them," Severin said quietly. Was it just Trevor's imagination, or had the younger man looked at him with sympathy? *I haven't fooled them at all*, Trevor thought. *This is a fine business, for the chief coordinator of the Ripper case to sway on his feet at the sign of a woman's bare arm, for the man in charge to show such weakness in the presence of subordinates.*

"Excellent," he said briskly. "Hair, skin cells, fingernails, and if you'll fold them in paper and mark them with each victim's name, I'll be in my lab."

It was a rather grand statement, since his lab consisted of a bare wooden table, and Trevor turned back into the main mortuary filled with doubt. As he heard the unmistakable groan of nails being pulled from a pine coffin he sat down in a chair and stared straight ahead at the empty chalkboard. Ah, but wouldn't this be the ultimate joke? If a man moved heaven and earth to get a forensics lab, only to find he didn't have the stomach for the job?

CHAPTER TWENTY-TWO
October 9
8: 17 AM

The sun was rising brightly over Mayfair, unusual for an October morning in London. Gage had opened the draperies early to allow the rays to heat the house before Geraldine and the girls awakened for the day. He had returned from his errands with a box of fresh baked tarts and an armful of newspapers. At nine, Gerry descended the stairs still in her bedclothes and robe, as she enjoyed doing on certain lazy days such as this. A clear day seemed to cheer up almost everyone, she noted, for even Gage wore a smile as he greeted her at the bottom of the stairs.

"Morning, Madame. Tea, tarts, and newspapers in the parlor as you wished."

"Thank you, Gage. I see your walk agreed with you."

"Yes, Madame," answered Gage, again with the corners of his mouth curling up. "Seems we have the start of a lovely day."

He disappeared into the kitchen and, musing that if they lived in Tahiti, Gage would be absolutely mirthful, Gerry poured herself a cup of tea and nestled herself into her favorite chair. She picked up a copy of the London Times and glanced over the headlines before serving herself the plumpest apricot tart.

"Good morning, Aunt Gerry," Leanna said, entering the parlor dressed in her robe and bedclothes also. "Have you seen Emma this morning?"

No sooner had she asked the question, when Emma entered from the kitchen, fully clothed, but as cheery as all the others. She took a plate and the closest newspaper and sat down herself. The women were in the habit of scouring the morning news for a mention of the Ripper or a quote from Trevor. For the last few days, however, the story seemed to have died down a bit and Leanna tossed aside the Star with a sigh. "Most of the accounts are just being repeated."

"Listen to this," Geraldine said, waving her own paper. "'The police still do not know who he or she is and seem to be as baffled as the public.' Imagine that. 'He or she'. Do you think there really is a chance the Ripper is female?"

"Oh, I doubt it," Leanna said. "More likely just some reporter trying to get a new column out of the same tired old information. Raising the possibility of Jill the Ripper is just another way to sell issues, nothing more."

"Whatever they're doing, it's working, for people never tire of violence and gore," Geraldine said piously, managing to ignore the fact that she purchased more papers than anyone. Leanna shot Emma a conspiratorial smile which went unnoticed, for Emma was intent on a letter to an editor of the Times concerning anti-vivisection, and a familiar sounding phrase had caught her eye.

"Gerry! Gerry! They've printed it. The Herman Strong letter. It's here. And it's on the editorial page, too," Emma cried, jumping to her feet and showing the section to Geraldine.

"Herman Strong?" asked Leanna. "Who's he?"

"Let me see! Let me see!" exclaimed Aunt Gerry, snatching the paper from Emma's hand and spreading it across her plate. Emma and Leanna gathered around her and read along with her, Geraldine's face slowly filling with glee.

"Marvelous," she sighed. "They printed every line."

"Herman Strong?" Leanna asked again. "Who is he?"

"I'm Herman Strong," Gerry said. "I send all my letters to editors under a male pseudonym, so they'll print the blasted things. For years, I sent them with my own signature only to be rejected. Then one day while I was at a newspaper office arguing with an editor, a funny thing happened. They were in

202

the process of removing me from the premises when a very polite clerk whispered that I should sign a man's name to my letters and they would have a better chance of making the edition. So I did and at last I'm in print," she explained with an ever-widening grin. "Her-man Strong. Do you get it, darling? I'm the 'her' who is as 'strong' as any 'man'."

"Um, very clever, but I can't believe you'd…"

"Oh, I'm not happy to have to play these silly games, but it's a case of the message being more important than the messenger. If an editor believes a man wrote a letter against vivisection, he deems it a worthy topic for public debate, and in the end that's all that matters. People rename emotions, darling, when men have them. What they once called 'hysterics' becomes 'compassion.'" Gerry squinted down at the paper. "Scientific experimentation on live animals! It's absolutely repellant! I understand that even the Queen is against it."

Leanna slumped back in her chair. So many things were bothering her lately. When Tom had visited, his ease in Gerry's home had made it quite clear that he had traveled to London numerous times during his first year of school. The aunt who had been only a shadowy presence to Leanna, had been a friend to him. The city she had only glimpsed on rare occasions, had been his holiday playground. And, although she had considered her younger brother her closest confidant, it was clear he had kept many things from her. Mostly the fact that he enjoyed – merely because he was male – a richer, fuller, more exciting life.

Why had her family not taken her to London more often? During her years growing up in the country, she had rarely questioned the small scope of her daily activities but now she was renaming things herself and what she had once called simplicity was beginning to seem more like monotony. Her grandfather she could understand, for Leonard hated the bustle of the city and probably would never have ventured there himself if it hadn't been for the museums and galleries. But why hadn't her mother realized how much a jaunt to London would thrill a young girl?

Leanna's mind drifted back to her first week in London, an afternoon when she and Emma had been out looking at dresses. When the shopkeeper had noticed Leanna's interest in the wine-colored silk, he had slipped over to her side. But when she had asked him the price, he had only laughed and said not to worry. The bill would not be enough to drive her husband or her father to despair.

"I don't have a husband – or a father," she had said. "But I do have money and I'm asking how much of it you'd expect in exchange for this dress."

A hush had fallen over the already-hushed shop and the man had literally backed away from her, as if she had suddenly sprouted horns. Emma had merely looked up from the gloves she was admiring and said "The price, Sir?" and the man had said promptly, "Seven pounds."

At the time Leanna had been unable to understand where she had gone wrong. She and Emma were the same age. Leanna's mourning clothes did not indicate she was a woman of means and Emma's cultured voice did not indicate that she was a servant. So how had the man so swiftly placed them in their respective categories, decided that Emma was someone capable of discussing money while Leanna was not? She had tried to talk to Emma about it on the way home but Emma had been no help. Leanna had shaken the bundle which held her new dress – Emma had been able to talk the shopkeeper down to six pounds – and asked "Why wouldn't he tell me the price?"

"He could see you were a lady," Emma had said shortly. "Ladies may shop, in the sense that they select, but they don't haggle on the price and they don't pay."

"But how could he possibly know that – "

"That I wasn't a lady?" Emma had jerked her chin so violently that Leanna had fallen silent. "Shopkeepers always know these things, Leanna. They can smell money from two blocks away."

So I have money, but I can't just go out and spend it, Leanna thought. Someone else has to spend it on my behalf. I can't feel coins in my palm, I can't vote, or think for myself, or kiss a man, or row the Thames. And the worst part of all is that I never knew all the things I couldn't do until a few weeks ago. I've been deliberately held back from my own life. Preserved, like one of Grandfather's specimens. But for what? To what great end did they all plan to use me?

"Emma, this is cause for celebration," Geraldine said, pulling Leanna's thoughts back to the present. "Will you assist me in selecting my clothes for the day? I wish to take a walk, perhaps call on Tess and then Fleanders. Won't he paw the ground when he hears of this?"

"Today calls for the peacock silk," Emma said, following Gerry out of the room. Leanna sat alone in the parlor. How unfair it was, when a woman as intelligent and educated as Aunt Gerry cannot be taken seriously enough that her opinion can be printed in a simple newspaper, she thought, reaching for a second roll. She remembered John's words about his clinic, that nothing was fair, and the tart tasted a bit sour in her mouth.

Grandfather lied to me, she thought grimly. Trying to teach me and Tom that the world has a natural order, that everything's for a reason and it can all be understood, even mastered, if we put our minds to it. A big wretched lie. Our lives are all a matter of circumstances of birth, mere accidents of chance. Leanna set the tart aside on the nearest table and walked to the window, gazing out at the manicured gardens on each side of the street, the neat brickwork, the symmetry of the houses. This was a lie too. The whole street was a lie, an implication that the people who lived there deserved to live there, that they were kept safe within these gardens and gates for a reason, that they were somehow by birth entitled to this pretty, pleasant life. But, Leanna thought, what have I done to deserve any of this? A different spin of the wheel and I could be one of those women walking the streets of the East End.

Men were so pragmatic. Trevor and John and Tom all of them saying that it didn't matter how things are done as long as they're done. But, still, it was shocking to learn that even Aunt Gerry was willing to obscure her identity in order to serve a higher purpose.

"Evidently I'm the one who's wrong," Leanna said aloud. But she didn't really think so.

1:20 PM

"So, Neddy, you can see why we're a bit desperate," Cecil Bainbridge said, settling back awkwardly in the spindle chair. "The best legal minds that promises can buy have all insisted Grandfather's will is unbreakable. We're left to find another way 'round."

Edmund Solmes pursed his lips. "You could play on your sister's sympathies. I'm sure if you both went to her, asked for a hundred pounds apiece or so…"

"A hundred pounds!" Cecil exploded. "Scarcely a drop in the bucket to what I need, and when that's gone I shall have to go back and beg and wheedle for a hundred more and then a bit more. It's endless, Neddy, just as it was when Grandfather was alive, only more degrading this time because 'tis my baby sister who is clutching the pursestrings. Try to understand my position…"

"It's actually your position, isn't it?" Solmes said to William. "You're the eldest, the one deprived of his natural expectations."

William shrugged his beefy shoulders. "Unlike my brother, I've come to terms with the situation. In fact, I've recently made a decision. I plan to study the science of estate management."

"Estate...management?" Cecil said, his tone as incredulous as if William had announced plans to become a priest.

"It's honest work and it will allow me to remain at Rosemoral," William said. His tone was calm and steady but he couldn't quite bring himself to meet Cecil's eyes. "Leanna will need help to keep the property productive and it isn't as if I don't know the land. Truly, Cecil, there's no shame in taking up a profession. You could consider it as well. "

"Please! Can you really imagine me toiling as a tradesman or soldier or even - no offense intended, Neddy - a barrister? Taking lessons, rising at dawn, holding a schedule..."

"The will allows for it," William said stubbornly. "If you went to Tom and professed some sort of interest he would be bound to release funds for tuition and then you could - "

"Neither one of you understands the true enormity of my needs," Cecil said, bending forward to drop his pale face into well-manicured hands. "It isn't merely that I've lost what I had..."

The silence in the room grew uncomfortable and William and Edmund Solmes exchanged a pointed glance. The man must dye his hair with shoe polish, William thought, for no one could have such a weathered face and still maintain that shock of ebony hair. And his hands...they tremble with the palsy when one gets quite close to him. Cecil is a fool, fawning over this dandy, promising him their sister. Calling him Neddy, indeed, as if they were schoolboys! Precisely how old was the fellow, anyway?

"I think we do understand you, Cecil," Solmes finally said. "You've wagered not only against funds in pocket but against future earnings, that's the trouble, isn't it?"

"Strange time to hear a lecture from you, Neddy."

"And I take it Miss Wentworth is out of the picture? There's no means of escape in her?"

Cecil flushed. "You're aware she will no longer receive me."

"So," Solmes said. "All roads lead back to Rosemoral and the estate that is housed there."

"Really, Cecil," William said. "This is one time I can't say I feel that sorry for you. The will allows you income, you had Hannah all but hooked, and as Mr. Solmes said, if you had played it smart, gone to Leanna every now and again for a bit of cash..."

"In dribs and drabs," Cecil said morosely. "I can't live like that. I have my pride!"

William turned away in disgust, his vision falling on the moth-eaten tapestries suspended from the ceiling. This office, he reflected, was much like its owner, with a thin veneer of gloss applied over a crumbling core. The sort of place which impresses the eye at first glance and then upon reflection begins to disappoint in innumerable small ways. Not like Rosemoral, William thought. The surface may not be as glamorous, but there is substance and quality underneath. Although he would never confess this to Cecil, William rather liked the idea of estate management. He could see himself living out his years at Rosemoral with a plump little wife, his herb garden, a litter of children and an annuity promptly paid each month...

"Is this really enough for you?" Cecil asked, as if William's thoughts were an open book. "Begging Tom for money so you can go to school to learn how to be a farmer, for God's sake. Being in Leanna's employ! I can't believe you'd even consider it."

"I am considering it," William said. "And the more I consider it, the more I think being the estate manager wouldn't be so different from being the master of Rosemoral. It would enable me to go through with the plans I've made. The back acreage is being wasted. We could bring in sheep…"

"Sheep," Cecil said bitterly. "How appropriate."

William felt as if he were seeing his brother for the first time. When they'd been boys, people had often mistaken Cecil for the elder of the two. William had the brawn but Cecil had been the one gifted with the quick mind, the glib turn of phrase, the ability to converse with adults when he was still in short pants. Why did I envy him, William wondered. Why have I spent my entire life trying to win his approval?

"Yes, sheep," he said again, more firmly. "I think Leanna and Tom will both see my reasoning. And I want to bring in an ostentation of peacocks."

Cecil and Solmes merely stared at him.

"That's what you call a group of peacocks," William said, nodding as if the decision was already made. "An ostentation."

Cecil fumbled for his pipe. "Have you gone mad?"

"I always have rather liked peacocks," William said, to no one in particular. "They give the lawns such a regal air."

Edmund Solmes considered this remark for perhaps two seconds, then turned his attention, and his full body, back towards Cecil. "There is, of course, the chance your sister might marry someone sympathetic to your needs. If she marries, control of the funds will pass to her husband and if he were the right sort of man he might seek to rectify the mistakes of the will."

"And give all the money back to his brothers-in-law?" Cecil asked irritably. "I bloody rather doubt it, unless she marries a dunce, and even so there is baby Tom to consider."

"As her family, as her older male relatives, you may have some influence over her choice."

"Gad, Neddy, that's quite out of our hands now. Leanna's independent. She can take up with the apple seller on the corner for all I know or care. Besides, I wouldn't put it past Leanna to remain a virgin until death just to spite us, and we all know that virgins live forever."

Solmes smiled. "Actually, if your sister should happen to predecease you - "

"What?" Cecil asked, his head jerking up.

"A small provision in the will, over around page seventy or so. If your sister dies childless the estate reverts back to her three brothers to be shared in equally. But, heavens, Cecil, wipe that hungry look from your face. The girl is barely out of her teens after all, and the last time I saw her she was a bouncy little armful of flesh, looking quite healthy and capable."

"Yes, Cecil, hush," said William, infuriated that Solmes would refer to his sister in such a familiar way. "You are truly grasping at straws. Leanna is but a girl. She doubtless has fifty full years ahead of her."

"Oh, of course, rosy and healthy and just a girl…" Cecil said slowly. "But she lives in London now, doesn't she? And London is such a dangerous place."

CHAPTER TWENTY-THREE
October 14, 1888
9:05 AM

He has found her. She is younger than the others, prettier, stronger. A better specimen by any method one might wish to employ, a more suitable target for his talents. A bright bird of Africa somehow trapped here among the common wrens.

She looks straight ahead when she walks. In her arms she holds something shocking, the most surprising thing a woman in Whitechapel might possess.

She carries books.

And - although he has not gotten close enough to see their titles, nor their authors, nor even, in this ecumenical part of the city, the language they employ – the very fact she can read is enough to set her above the others.

She is like me, he thinks. She does not belong here.

He has followed her twice, plans to follow her again.

CHAPTER TWENTY-FOUR
2:29 PM

"Sounds like a foreign language, Sir," Davy said, staring at the paper in his hands.

"That's because it is," Trevor said. "Or was. Someone in security translated it from the French, but I don't think they did a particularly admirable job." He stepped back from the worktable and wiped his hands.

There had been no murders for the past two weeks. The parade of witnesses and confessors had dwindled and even the newspapers seemed to have moved on to other subjects.

Some people around the Yard were beginning to say that perhaps they'd flushed him, that Jack had moved on to a less vigilant location – the countryside, the mainland, or even America. Let him go to America, they said. It fits. Plenty of room to absorb the madness there, mile after mile of open land to stretch his violence out to the point where it would dissolve, somehow no longer matter. But Trevor could not quite bring himself to believe it was over. He was not the sort of detective who put great stock in instinct, nor was he a betting man – but if he were either of these things, he would have laid odds that the Ripper was still very close.

No matter. No more bodies were wrapped in the morgue, that was the key thing, and the last time Eatwell had passed him in the halls the old ogre had actually smiled, as if the lack of dead whores was somehow proof of the personal capabilities of Detective Trevor Welles. The general lull had allowed Trevor the time to set up a bit of a genuine laboratory in the corner of the chief mortuary, and today he was concerned with the latest report from the Parisian police. Latest brag, was more like it.

The French were claiming they had discovered a way to create a perfect replica of a knife blade from pouring wax into a wound. Trevor had read the report twice over breakfast, then headed straight to the butcher shop to ask the man behind the counter which animal's meat bore the greatest similarity to the texture and density of human flesh. The man had regarded him with open alarm until Trevor produced his credentials from the Yard and then, within minutes, Trevor had been back on the streets bearing a sizable leg of mutton. The butcher had refused to let him pay. "Catch old Jack and we're quits, Sir," he'd said, and Trevor had nodded briskly, with a confidence he no longer felt.

He was even less sure of himself now as he stared down at the mutton. "All right Severin," he said. "Bring the knives."

The young man promptly stepped forward with his tray. It held a surgical scalpel, the tip of a bayonet rifle, and a large carving knife obtained from a slaughterhouse. Severin paused before the leg of mutton with his usual measured pace, and then picked up the carving knife. With a nod from Trevor, he slashed at the mutton, left to right, a single deft wound. Next the bayonet and a different sort of movement, more of a thrust and finally the scalpel. This he used carefully, almost artfully, making a shallow curved slice into the meatiest part of the leg, the haunch.

Trevor nodded to Davy, who began reading again, more slowly, although the instructions were simple enough, really. Severin put a palm on each side of the first wound and held it open as Trevor spooned in the wax. Davy noted the time on his pocketwatch as they moved on to the bayonet and scalpel imprints.

After precisely ninety seconds, Trevor pulled the wax from the carving knife wound. Despite his care, a piece of the wax broke off, stayed embedded in the mutton and they fared little

214

better with the other two imprints. They were left with three very different wax shapes, that much was true, at least in a general sense. But the imprints were uneven and crumbled around the edges, hardly anything you could present to a court as evidence. Trevor sat down with a sigh, not bothering to conceal the frustration in his face.

"Which one would you have guessed would leave the cleanest imprint?" he asked Severin.

"The scalpel," Severin answered. "It is sharpest and the cut it produces is the most shallow."

"Indeed," Trevor said. "And that imprint is marginally better than the others. But even it..." he looked down at the wax figures before him, and sighed again. "Can you think of any reason why it might not have worked?"

"Perhaps the thick of the wax," the young man said. His voice was evenly pitched and nearly devoid of accent but when he said certain things - "thick" rather than "thickness," for example – he betrayed his immigrant roots. People are streaming into London from all over Europe, Trevor thought. Smart, and hard-working, most of them, and some as schooled as any Brit, even if they didn't learn those lessons in the mother tongue. And yet we reduce them to maids and rubbish men and assistants, rarely asking them to use their true minds. He himself had initially dismissed Severin as useless. Now Trevor wondered what this shy young man thought of him and how he really viewed the good doctor.

"We used the same kind of wax the report called for," Davy said. "I went three places to find the brand."

Severin shook his head. "Perhaps hotter," he said. "Thinner."

"Quite right," Trevor said. "We'll try again this afternoon with the wax hotter and thinner."

"And the meat cold," said Severin.

"Indeed. We'll get the mutton colder and the wax hotter and if the imprint hardens faster that might indeed sharpen the impression. Good thinking, Severin."

Severin nodded and slipped back into the back room to finish his own tasks. Trevor waited for the curtain to close behind him before turning back to Davy. "Although if the meat needs to be chilled first, I can't imagine why they wouldn't have that sort of detail in the report. Bloody French."

"Perhaps the coppers in Paris don't have things as right as they think they do," Davy said, letting the report drop to the table with a sigh of his own. "Are they really so far ahead, Sir?"

"Yes," Trevor said, although such disloyalty to his motherland did not come easily. "They're even claiming they can tell who has touched something, like a door latch or a weapon, based on the ridges people have on their fingertips. They call it a finger print. Apparently everyone on earth has one and they're all in a slightly different pattern."

Davy stared so intently down at his hands that Trevor burst out laughing. "I know," he said, "it sounds a bit fantastical to me too. Oh, and another thing we might try this after – Come in, it isn't locked."

The door swung open revealing a bobby and a man in streetclothes who was holding a parcel and seemed in a high state of agitation. "Are you a doctor?" he asked. "Am I even in the right place? They told me to turn right at the stairs but there are so many stairs in this infernal –"

"I'm Detective Welles," Trevor said, motioning both men in. "Doctor Phillips has stepped out –"

"Then send someone to get him immediately," the man said. He seemed used to barking out orders. "I am George Lusk of the Whitechapel Vigilance Committee and we were formed to protect and prevent –"

216

"I know your organization, Mr. Lusk," Trevor said, indicating a seat but Lusk tossed his head about violently, as if the idea of sitting down was ludicrous. Davy was already moving toward the door to fetch Phillips so there was nothing for Trevor to do but observe Lusk, who looked like precisely what he was – a prosperous businessman prepared to take matters into his own hands before he would let an unchecked crime wave destroy his investments.

"Before you begin your policeman's lecture, you need to know that I'm not a Johnny-come-lately to this Ripper business," Lusk said, his tone as vigorous as if he were speaking from the pulpit. "Our committee formed on the tenth of September, long before the nastiness of the double murders. We grasped, Sir, quite at once, that this was not a singular threat that would soon fade away. And I was elected chairman during that first meeting. Since then we've taken up watch on our own – "

"I know who you are, Mr. Lusk," Trevor repeated," and I know the task your committee has undertaken." The bobbies on the streets were constantly complaining about this amateur group of sleuths who patrolled Whitechapel nightly. The police largely considered the vigilance committee more of an obstacle than an advantage, more likely to be needing help than capable of providing it, and Trevor was inclined to agree. "What I don't know is what brings you here to Scotland Yard today."

"I received a letter from the Ripper himself," Lusk said, fumbling in his coat pocket.

"Would you like to put down your parcel?" Trevor inquired mildly. Letters from the Ripper were a near-daily event at the Yard. It may be unusual for someone to send such a letter to a private citizen, but, then again, Lusk had done everything possible to attach himself to the case and had undoubtedly made his share of enemies along the way.

217

"No, I most certainly do not wish to put down my parcel," Lusk said testily, "and the reason will be quite clear when the doctor arrives. Here," he added, clumsily pulling a folded piece of paper from his pocket. "Here's the letter. He says he's sending it from hell, he does."

Trevor took the paper and read:

From hell
Mr Lusk
Sor
I send you half the Kidne I took from one women prasarved it for you tother piece I fried and ate it was very nise I may send you the bloody knif that took it out if you only wate a while longer
Signed Catch me when you Can
Mishter Lusk

"And what do you think of that?" Lusk demanded.

"I think it's quite different from the other letters we've received. The misspellings and mistakes are so outrageous that I have to wonder if they're calculated – "

"Calculated!" Lusk seemed in danger of exploding.

"As if the writer were deliberately attempting to present himself as uneducated," Trevor said, attempting to counteract the man's anger with his own calm, as if they were on a sort of emotional see-saw. "The other letters we've received have been quite literate. Proper spelling. One even spoke in a rather well-constructed rhyme. It's hard to believe all these letters were written by the same person unless he's trying to mislead us into thinking he is a very different sort of man than he is." Trevor looked up at the fuming Lusk. It would be unnerving to receive such a message, no doubt about it. But to be fair, hadn't the man brought much of this on himself? He had written to the

218

papers almost daily, demanding the police do more, offering rewards for information, holding meetings in every church and community house in the East End. He has created his own celebrity, Trevor thought. It was exciting at the start but he is beginning to see the dark side of his creation.

"There are some similarities to one of the previous letters," Trevor conceded, since Lusk seemed determined to elicit some sort of reaction. "And of course the writer has threatened to send a body part before – "

"Threatened? Why the dash do you think I'm here? He didn't threaten. I have the woman's kidney!" Lusk thrust the package forward and Trevor leapt to attention. He held his hand out and Lusk gingerly placed the small package in it, wincing at the smell.

"I am not one of your eccentrics, Detective," Lusk said, clearly pleased to at last have Trevor's full attention. "This isn't my first letter from someone claiming to be the Ripper. Most I have ignored. But this one....Perhaps I should start at the beginning. On October 4 a man showed up at the doorstep of my home, my very home, Sir, where I sleep at night with my wife and children, and said he wanted to join the committee. A common enough request, but something about this fellow gave me pause. He asked rather too many questions about the routes we took on our patrols for my taste. We chatted for a minute but he must have sensed my lack of enthusiasm for his assistance. He asked to be directed to a tobacco shop, which I did, and I never saw the man again."

"And you didn't report this?"

"We have over a hundred volunteers, Detective, all assembled in much that way. Some men offer to help and then think the better of it when darkness falls and the time for the patrol draws near. Nerves, you know? There was nothing particularly noteworthy about this man except for a feeling I had and I am not a man who indulges in intuition."

"Strange that he would ask the routes you walked, though. You must have realized what he was really asking is where you wouldn't be."

Lusk rubbed his chin. "Detective, this Ripper business has brought me into contact with any number of people, not all of them the sort I would care to invite for tea. I imagine you could say the same. There was nothing terribly noteworthy about this man and the fact he asked about the routes to me indicated he was a coward, not a killer. More interested in parading down safe streets with the armband of the vigilance committee than he was patrolling the parts of the city which might lead to less glory and real danger."

"What did he look like?"

"Medium height, perhaps 30 years of age, dark hair."

"Mustache?"

"Yes, and full beard. There have been other events, Detective. People asking about me in various taverns, letters to the paper marked to my attention. I assure you, I am not a hysteric. I do not bother the police with every small incident. But this.... The parcel today was simply laid on my doorstep and my first thought is that it was a prank. An animal kidney. They say sheep have certain anatomical similarities to humans, do they not?"

"So I've been told," Trevor said wearily.

"So I took it to my personal physician, expecting that he would agree this was a prank. No more than I deserve, you doubtless are thinking, for getting myself into this whole business. But no, my doctor claimed it to be human and – not very fresh, should we say? As if it could be more than two weeks old. But he said a Scotland Yard physician would need to confirm that it may have indeed come from that Eddowes woman..."

Trevor looked down at the letter again. "So now he's not merely a killer, but a cannibal as well. Or so he claims. I'm sorry if I treated you with disrespect, Mr. Lusk and I don't consider you a hysteric. In fact, I think you may be underestimating the danger you and your family are in. We'll have bobbies posted around your home night and day. If Doctor Phillips confirms the beliefs of your physician – and I suspect he will – then once again the situation has risen to a new level."

3:30 PM

William was not entirely displeased. Having to sell the horse and carriage was distressing, but he consoled himself with the thought he'd gotten a fair price and besides, Winter Garden was no more than a twenty-minute walk from the heart of Leeds. They could manage. Pounds tucked into his pocket, he headed toward home.

But what was indeed distressing is how poorly the family had managed their money during their first month under the auspices of the will. When William had first heard the sum of their allowances, he had assumed they would be able to continue living as they had, with a staff of three, the carriage, and the genteel, if not extravagant, comforts of Winter Garden. The will had clearly been calculated to allow that. But what William hadn't realized was the extent of Cecil's debts or, even worse, the compulsion of his gambling habits. They had been running short of funds a mere two weeks after the monies had been paid and there was no doubt Cecil had been pilfering from the leather box where Gwynette kept the cash. William had already determined that the proceeds from the sale of the horses and carriage would be hidden away somewhere else.

William was so absorbed in his thoughts that he did not notice a carriage slowing behind him and was startled when a woman called his name from the window. He turned to see Hannah Wentworth waving.

Well, this was certainly awkward. He had not seen her since that monstrous day when they had stumbled upon Cecil making busy with a serving girl behind the rosebushes. But Hannah was gesturing toward him in a friendly manner, as if that afternoon, and indeed Cecil, were the farthest things from her mind.

"Come ride," she called. "We're going the same direction, are we not?"

Only if you're going downhill, William thought, but he smiled and said "No need, Miss Hannah, but thank you." He patted his chest. "I could use the exercise." With any luck she would not ask about the carriage.

"Where's your carriage?" Hannah asked.

"Sold," William said shortly. Painful to admit, but he supposed there was no real need to keep up a pretense. Everyone in the country would soon know, if they didn't already, the severity of the family's reversed fortunes.

"Then come inside," Hannah said, so firmly that William had little choice but to obey. He climbed in and sat opposite her while she tapped her cane for the coachman to continue.

"Is that what brings you to town?" she asked, settling back into the black velvet cushions.

"That, and mailing a letter," William said. "I've sent off an application to agricultural college. Does that amuse you?"

"Why should it?"

"Then perhaps this will. I am hoping to take the training course so that I might secure a position as the estate manager of Rosemoral. To do that, I will have to convince my younger

222

sister to employ me. My grandfather named Leanna, not me, as his heir."

Hannah exhaled slowly through her pale lips, and looked out the carriage window. "Then the gossip is correct."

Poor mother, William thought. When she hears I've spilled the beans, she will never show her face in Leeds again. But he also knew that attempting to bamboozle Hannah Wentworth, of all people, was pointless and besides there was something soothing about being here with her in the carriage. "The gossip is correct," he found himself saying, "but probably incomplete. As you might imagine, Cecil is struggling to accept the reality of our new circumstances and my mother has gone almost entirely into hiding. But I don't feel the same. I would be delighted to find I had been accepted at an agricultural college. All I ever wanted, Miss Wentworth, although you may find this hard to believe, was to make Rosemoral the finest estate in the county."

"I believe you," she said calmly, still gazing out the window. "Leonard was a genius but that I've always considered his land underused."

"Quite so," said William.

"Sheep?"

"Indeed."

"Alfalfa?"

"It's all that makes sense." He looked at her profile. "But it's not just about income and production, at least not for me. The gardens of Rosemoral are lovely as they stand, but with a few simple changes, they could be grand. I plan to bring in peacocks. A whole group of them. Everyone says they're loud, but I consider them glorious."

She turned from the window and looked him squarely in the eye. "I believe they call a group of peacocks an ostentation," she said.

William smiled. "Yes, Miss Wentworth. I believe they do."

CHAPTER TWENTY-FIVE
October 17
10:20 PM

The most idiotic idiom of history, Trevor thought, must be "All's fair in love in war," for these two activities above all others seemed to be the constricted by custom. It had been over three hours since they had left Geraldine's home and he was still not certain how Leanna viewed their relationship or the evening. Emma was along too – as a chaperone? Companion? A more suitable partner for Trevor? Impossible to tell. Emma had made steady and intelligent conversation since they'd left the theater but Leanna sat in silence, her profile as cool and composed as that of a cameo, offering Trevor no clue to her thoughts.

He had come home early that evening, around six, and the post had been waiting for him. Geraldine had three tickets to *Dr. Jekyll and Mr. Hyde* and wondered if he might like to escort Leanna and Emma. Trevor had rushed into the streets like a schoolboy, dashing about until he was able to locate an urchin willing to deliver his acceptance for a shilling. Then he had run upstairs, shaved so quickly that he gave his chin two nasty nicks in the process, and squeezed himself into his one tuxedo, a simple suit he had purchased several years and at least a stone ago. The cummerbund trussed him so tightly that he feared any sudden exhalation would cause it to fly off with the force of a lethal weapon.

When he'd arrived at Mayfair, Geraldine had met him at the door and confided that the tickets, nearly impossible to come by, had been furnished by John Harrowman who had been forced to cancel yet another theatre engagement with Leanna. "She was dashed, poor dear," Geraldine confided in her usual tactless way, "and when John sent the tickets anyway, in a manner of apology, I thought she and Emma would have more fun with you along. I get to the theatre often enough..." Trevor did not particularly relish the thought of being a last minute replacement for Saint John, and it also bothered him that since they were taking the doctor's tickets and Geraldine's coach, he was contributing nothing to the evening. But his hesitancy evaporated at the sight of Leanna on the stairs in a brilliant blue silk gown which fell off her shoulders like water. If she were indeed dashed, she hid her disappointment well, for her smile was bright and her step almost sprightly as she reached out to take his arm.

Emma looked lovely as well in a pale green gown which, in another manifestation, obviously had belonged to Geraldine. Trevor was both touched and amused at the way her slender neck bore the unaccustomed weight of an enormous plumed hat – undoubtedly also courtesy of Geraldine's bureau - and the nervous way she fiddled with her gloves. So now he was seated between two attractive women, riding through the well-manicured West End in an opulent carriage, Gerry's one concession to society, and if he d had any doubts about being John's understudy, they were fading fast. Trevor had enjoyed little social intercourse at all since taking the Ripper case, and this stroke of fortune was almost too much to fathom.

"You're certainly silent, Leanna," Emma said. "What did you think of the play?"

"It was everything John said it would be," Leanna said. "Utterly riveting."

"I know what you mean," Trevor said, a little deflated that she felt the need to quote John in every sentence but determined to draw her into the conversation nonetheless. "I'll confess an appalling truth to you ladies. This is only the second time I've been to the theater and the first was a frothy little comedy of

226

manners, the kind of thing one laughs at and promptly forgets. I spent much of that evening trying to calculate the cost of the chandeliers that hung overhead. But the drama tonight was certainly more.... dramatic. I'm a bit drained."

"Stevenson is a genius," Leanna said.

"He can tell a story," Emma conceded. "But do you accept his premise, that under certain circumstances a supposedly normal man could become a monster?"

"The psychology is certainly correct," Leanna said. "My grandfather used to say that we all have a dark side, a more violent nature which is always bursting to get out."

"One can only hope that the typical transition is not quite so abrupt as Jekyll to Hyde," Emma said, with a light laugh. "Richard Mansfield has certainly earned his notoriety, has he not?"

Trevor laughed too. The actor's astounding on-stage transformation from the morally upright Dr. Jekyll to the sinister Mr. Hyde had been the talk of London for months, a performance so persuasive that some audience members had literally fainted in their seats, a man had suffered a coronary, and a woman had gone into premature labor. The Yard had received more than one letter claiming that Mansfield must indeed be the Ripper, since no man could portray evil that convincingly, night after night, without it gradually infecting his soul.

"If a Jekyll were to really become a Hyde," Emma continued, "I would imagine it would be a slower transformation, perhaps over the course of a lifetime. A series of disappointments builds up, a series of disillusionments or humiliations...."

"No, no, the harder a man tried to suppress this dark side, the more suddenly it is bound to erupt," Leanna said, equally persistent in her view. She snapped her fingers. "Like so. Wouldn't you say, Trevor?"

"Possibly," he said mildly, thinking of all the prostitutes he had interviewed in the last weeks. They had, to a woman, claimed that the gentlemen who patronized them were the roughest customers, demanding unnatural acts and often with a yen for brutality. "Give me a Limey o'er a Lord any day," one girl had claimed, "For the boys who been at sea just want a quick 'un, while it's the gentry that tells ye get to on all fours and howl."

"The trouble is, Mr. Stevenson came very close to saying all humans have this dark side," Emma said, "and I can't agree with that. The play was all but asserting that everyone in the audience was a potential Mr. Hyde."

"Or potential Ripper," Trevor added quietly.

"Oh, Trevor, I am sorry," Leanna said. "Here you try desperately to get one evening away from work and what do we do but take you to a play which professes to analyze the criminal mind."

"Don't apologize. I found it fascinating, and you know I've believed from the start that the Ripper was a gentleman. We've explored a hundred avenues and they all lead back to that."

"You're no closer to a solution?" Emma asked.

"No," Trevor sighed. "We run in hundreds of poor souls, each more crazed than the last. They all have the proximity and perhaps the temperament, but I know in my heart that none of them is our man. The real Ripper is a person who can walk any street of London without calling attention to himself. What makes him frightening is precisely the fact that he blends in so well."

"So you see, the play was quite right," Leanna said firmly. "We, all of us, have this darkness inside which struggles to get out and if it does not get out at first, it becomes even more twisted and horrid…"

"I must disagree," Emma said. "My mother, for example, was the most gentle soul. I believe she was gentle within as well as without. You can't take an evening's entertainment at the theater as any universal truth. It's more..." Emma suddenly stopped herself, surprised at her own words, for she never spoke of her mother or any of her family. Fortunately, Leanna and Trevor were too intent upon the discussion to notice her discomfiture. "The play is more of an analysis of the criminal mind than the normal one," she finished lamely, glancing at Trevor.

"But healthy people remain healthy precisely because they've found a way to get it out," Leanna went on. "Through music or sporting or letters to the editor like Aunt Gerry writes or through drinking ..."

Trevor felt a twinge of discomfort as well. The girl was perceptive for her years. He had stopped patrolling the streets on foot but had still been going to the East End nearly every night, for reasons that had nothing to do with research. It was as if the night he'd taken up with the young prostitute at the Pony Pub had opened some sort of floodgate.

"...or sex," Leanna went on.

At this, both Emma and Trevor erupted in a wild gale of laughter, Trevor's being so explosive that his cummerbund finally gave way to its fate and collapsed in his lap like a deflated balloon. Sweeping it aside in the darkness, he said, "I say, Leanna, you get more like Geraldine every day."

"Thank you," Leanna said archly.

"You're quite right to thank me, for that's the greatest tribute I'm capable of bestowing. And I do agree with you. We must find a way to get it out."

"What is this 'it' that we all must get out?" Emma asked, wiping tears from her eyes with one of her enormous plumes, "Are we speaking of evil? The hidden self? The evil hidden self? And, pray tell, why must we get it out? We'll have streets full of Rippers."

"There are times" said Leanna, slightly miffed by the giggles, "when I don't think either of you take me seriously at all. The 'it' is our darker nature, the animal part of our psyche, and if we manage to find a way to vent these emotions - however that may be, and I'm not saying I know - we do not become Rippers. That's quite my whole point. Trevor knows what I mean."

"She means that when a gentleman blows, he blows harder than anyone," Trevor said, still chuckling. "And I have the corpses to back up her theories. Unfortunately, my superiors are loath to admit she could be right. Now, if only Robert Louis Stevenson was a member of Scotland Yard..."

"But truly, what news of the investigation?" Emma asked. "No deaths and no new suspects doesn't mean no news. You've been holding out on us."

"I agree," Leanna said. "And the only reason we associate with you at all is for news of the Ripper case. So come, Detective Welles. Spill your grisly secrets."

Normally Trevor would have been tempted to tell them of the events of two days ago, but he, Phillips, Davy, and Lusk had decided not to publicize the arrival of a human kidney. Almost certainly a human kidney that had once resided inside the body of Catherine Eddowes. Public panic appeared to be abating, but news like this would stir it up fresh. Nor, he suspected, would the girls enjoy details of his visit to Mad Maudy. His new pursuit seemed the safest topic for discussion.

"I spent the day in my forensics lab," Trevor said. "Which sounds terribly important, but which is actually a mortuary table that Doctor Phillips has been kind enough to turn over to my use. I'll spare you ladies of the details of my experiments, all of which failed. But apparently the French police have come up with a method whereby they pour wax into a wound and the resulting imprint tells them what kind of weapon was used. Not just something vague like 'a knife with a five-inch blade,' but they come away with a complete impression of the murder weapon. Which would be marvelous to know because Phillips makes statements such as 'like a surgeon's scalpel,' which is just enough information to drive a detective mad. Was it a scalpel or not? Is the man a surgeon or isn't he? But the French must be using a certain kind of wax because I was practicing on a leg of mutton and it wasn't working at all. Not that women are mutton," he hastily added, but Leanna and Emma were hardly offended.

"It seems you would need to study the methodology first hand," Emma said. "Reading something like that from a paper –"

"I know," Trevor sighed. "Not to mention it had probably been badly translated from the original French."

"Perhaps I could – "

"My grandfather did something similar," Leanna said abruptly, cutting Emma off and twisting completely toward Trevor in her seat. "He was interested in identifying animals by the bite marks they made and he used....it wasn't clay but I don't think it was wax either. Something that he heated and poured, I do remember that much."

"Really?" Trevor said, surprised. "What was he hoping to learn?"

"I'm not entirely sure. Maybe Tom could tell you. But I know that he gathered the method from a local taxidermist."

"A taxidermist?" Trevor sat back, mulling this over.

"Well it fits, does it not? They're always reconstructing animals, even in cases where parts are missing. If they can concoct an entire jaw from a fossilized bite mark, couldn't you reconstruct a knife blade from the imprint of a wound?"

"Possibly. That's certainly the idea. But the problem seems to be finding material subtle enough to fill the wound but strong enough to be extricated without breaking or crumbling. I need to figure what this material is, precisely what temperature is most conductive to a clean imprint, and I need to do it quickly."

"There haven't been any killings for a while," Emma pointed out.

"No, there haven't."

"So, perhaps your Jack has stopped."

"I rather doubt it. We're still getting the letters."

"But if he stops," Emma went on, "that is a victory, in a way. It means you've frightened him off and forced him to move on to a new location."

"It's a victory in the sense there are no more dead bodies," Trevor conceded, gazing out into the nimbus of a streetlight. He had often told Davy he did not care who captured the Ripper or how he was caught, but did he really mean it? "However, having the Ripper simply move along would not be a victory for justice."

"But justice is sometimes an impossible goal, is it not?" Emma persisted. "An absence of injustice may the best you can hope for."

"Quite right," Trevor admitted, for she was.

"I don't understand that line of thinking at all," Leanna said. "Trevor wants a resolution, not a mere ending. He wants to hold the Ripper in the palm of his hand, to know he's the one who has stopped him."

"I'm sure that's what he wants," Emma said. "But what Trevor wants and what ends up occurring may not be the same thing."

"Oh Emma, for once just stop and hear yourself," Leanna said, twisting her gloves in agitation. "I don't know why you always must be so, so...."

232

"Realistic?" Emma said. Her voice was so level that it translated into the deepest level of sarcasm. The carriage was going through a darkened part of the street and for a moment Trevor could see neither woman's face.

"Pragmatic," Leanna finally said. "Trevor would never be satisfied with knowing that he'd merely moved the Ripper on, that this killer was out there in the night wreaking his havoc in another district or another country. That wouldn't be enough, Trevor, would it? Tell her."

Trevor looked from Emma's shadowy form to that of Leanna, and then back again. He could hear both women breathing, waiting, and he sat between them in the silence. He no longer knew what was enough.

CHAPTER TWENTY-SIX
October 28, 1888
10:40 AM

"Blast it," a voice roared from the doorsill and Trevor looked up from his reports in surprise. Eatwell, his face flushed, was waving a letter in his general direction.

"Just came," he sputtered. "You'd better go home and dress."

"What is it?" Trevor asked, as Davy also rose to his feet.

"An epistle from Her Majesty, Queen Victoria," Eatwell said, flinching with each word. "She wishes an audience with the chief detective of the Ripper case at Buckingham Palace, one this afternoon."

"Blimey," Davy exploded, as Trevor gazed down at the letter.

"Yes, blimey sums it up," said Eatwell. "I've served the Yard for thirty-five years and I've no more than glimpsed Her Majesty through the window of her coach. But our grand Detective Welles is summoned for a private audience."

"Yes Sir," Trevor said, stomach churning, for he had no more than glimpsed the Queen from a carriage window himself.

"What a job this is," Davy said, nearly in rapture. "From Mad Maudy to the Queen."

11:50 AM

Leanna rechecked the window for the tenth time and nervously pressed her gown with her hands. This, she was sure, would be a meeting of great significance. She had seen John Harrowman on four different social occasions and each time he had been attentive company. But each time they had also been surrounded by a swarm of people and the morning he had taken her out in his carriage, a day which seemed eons ago now, remained the only time he had touched her.

Leanna didn't know what to make of him. In some ways his attitudes were like that of a suitor, but in other ways he remained maddeningly formal and correct, once even deliberately avoiding a chance to bid her goodbye on the private side porch in favor of a more public exit via the front entrance. His words were right, but they seemed to be spoken in the wrong tone of voice, as if John were an unskilled actor in a parish play, sure of his lines but unable to convey the emotions behind them. All her novels were no help, for they generally had heroes who spoke gruffly to the heroine but whose eyes betrayed an inner fire, not a man like John who told her she was lovely but who always seemed to be looking past her, into the next room.

Today, however, was going to be special. Leanna's fevered plans and a few strokes of luck had seen to that. Knowing John generally started his rounds in early afternoon, she had invited him for lunch beforehand, carefully choosing a day when she knew Aunt Gerry would be distributing blankets at the veteran's home. Emma had been the tough one. Things had been terse and uncomfortable between them since the night they'd gone to the theater. Leanna could kick herself for turning Trevor's rare chance to recreate into an awkward evening, but she had the sense that there was some greater debate going on between Emma and herself, a dialogue that had little to do with Jekyll, Hyde, or even the Ripper. Emma seemed determined to teach her something, but Leanna was tired of learning lessons. If her future was going to be any different from the narrow world society had prescribed for her, it was time to take matters into her own lands.

This morning, Emma had ultimately decided to go with Geraldine on her mission, and Leanna had rushed to the kitchen, where she flattered Gage so shamelessly about the stuffed chops he had made the week before that he had vowed to serve them to her again that very night. The chops required any number of rare ingredients so Gage would be walking from market to market all afternoon. She and John would have the parlor to themselves.

Once she finally had seen Geraldine, Emma, and Gage off on their respective errands, Leanna had sprung into action. She had managed to get some of the chicken Gage had served the night before into a warming pan with potatoes and carrots and had galloped up the stairs to change into her silk afternoon dress. She was not particularly adept at putting up her own hair, no more than she was at cooking, and she could only hope John would be so enchanted with her presence that he would overlook any imperfections. Leanna whirled around before the mirror, trying to make sure she had managed to get the back buttons in the right buttonholes. This is the first time I've ever been in a house alone, she thought. Always someone with me – a relative or governess or schoolmate. This is the first time I could sing or scream or run about naked with no one to tell.

Could she get used to it? Could this be a full life? Leanna went to the window again, and peered down into the empty street. An hour alone – such a dizzying experience, as wild an excursion in its own way as Aunt Gerry's trek to India – and then, even more amazingly, she would be entertaining John Harrowman all by herself.

Leanna's mouth twisted at the thought of an unmarried woman and man left together in a house, even for an hour in the middle of the day. Such an idea would have her mother and the other country ladies in a paroxysm of horror and Leanna suspected such a visit would not be considered proper in

London either. But she didn't care. Today, surely, John would declare himself in some manner or another and if he didn't, she would have to admit that he likely wasn't going to. An unnerving thought, that she may emerge from the parlor in a matter of hours with her hopes utterly dashed, but Leanna had lived with uncertainty ever since the night of the dinner party, and she was prepared to endure even the sharpest disappointment rather than to go on much longer in this dreadful state of Not Knowing. Leanna strained toward the window. John had told her he would be by at noon and it was still five minutes until the clock struck that hour, but perhaps he would be early. She closed her eyes and prayed to whichever small ineffectual god protects the hearts of women that he would be.

12:40 PM

In the cleanest carriage Scotland Yard had to offer, and in his best suit, Trevor jostled his way through the gates of Buckingham Palace. Despite the grandeur of the facade, the palace was a somewhat forbidding looking structure, for, at the insistence of the Queen, all of the curtains and tapestries were pulled down in mourning for the death of her husband Albert over twenty-five years earlier. The morbidity exhibited by Victoria, who had dressed in black each day of the last two decades, seemed excessive even to Trevor, who had adored the Prince Consort as a boy, and who could still remember the day when, in the school chapel, he had heard Albert was dead.

But if she had ended her social life with the death of her husband, the Queen was still more than interested in affairs of state, as his own summons proved. Trevor was whisked in and taken through several enormous halls in which his footsteps echoed and his quiet cough resounded as a roar. To his relief he was finally seated in a much smaller study, a rather cozy little nook in fact, with a blazing fire and footstools scattered about, as if this were the room in which the royal family actually lounged. The man who had shown him there disappeared with no offer of tea or of even taking his wrap, and Trevor unclasped his cape and stood uncertainly in the middle of the room.

He did not have to wait long.

The doorknob turned and in walked a short, round woman with large blue eyes and a surprisingly youthful expression. Trevor, who had expected the Queen would be announced - with a flaring of trumpets, perhaps - was so startled by this sudden appearance that he dropped his cape to the floor. He bowed, then bowed again, and when he dared to look up the Queen was right before him, extending one chubby hand for a kiss. "Detective Welles, we believe," she said. It was custom that no one spoke to the Queen until she had addressed them first. Eatwell had warned him of this much at least, and Trevor was grateful to her for taking the initiative.

"Your Majesty," he croaked, bowing again, quite stupidly. When he met her eyes, the Queen was smiling in a bemused, private way.

"We must sit," she said, nodding toward a circle of chairs. "We hope you will pardon the informality, but this is where we meet the Prime Minister and other government servants such as yourself. A private place can be had even in a cavernous home, can it not?" Her voice was clear, bell-like, beautiful to the ear. Trevor followed her to the chairs, where she sat down, propped her small feet on the nearest footstool, and, with an impatient sweep of her hand, indicated he should do the same.

"We are sure that you are busy so we won't take much of your time," the Queen said. Trevor grinned idiotically, but Victoria was looking straight ahead as if posing for a portrait.

239

"We are outraged by the killings and even more so by the gleeful way the matter has been handled by the press. The mania appears to have faded a bit of late and we're sure you are the one to thank for that. But we are also certain that you are aware of the potential for riots, for hysteria, if this matter is not definitively closed."

"Yes, Your Majesty. Certain facts have been kept private."

"As they should be." The Queen now leaned back in her chair and appraised Trevor with a measured gaze. "What we find alarming when we read the reports and we do, of course, read the reports, is that there appears to be so little physical evidence. It would seem the murderer's clothes must be saturated with blood and must be kept somewhere. And the East End is so close to the dock. Have the cattleboats and passenger boats been examined? Has any investigation been made as to the number of single men occupying rooms to themselves? Is there sufficient surveillance at night?"

Trevor exhaled sharply. The last thing he had expected to hear was an actual query about the details of the case. And she was right on the money with her questions too, as astute as a trained detective and, heaven knows, more practical than most of them.

"I too am alarmed by the fact no bloody clothes have been found. It seems incomprehensible that a man covered with blood, as this fiend must be by the time he finished his work, could simply stroll the streets without attracting someone's attention, so we can only assume he has either found a way to dispose of those clothes when his work is finished or that he is of an profession where blood on his clothing might be expected."

"Such as a butcher?"

"Such as, Ma'am, yes." Trevor gulped for air. "It has been a lengthy chore to examine the men living by themselves in the East End, but we have attempted to do this and our efforts have

240

yielded us a long list of potential suspects. Thanks to your own speech in Parliament, Your Majesty, the Yard has adequate funds to place twice as many bobbies on the East End nightshift as we would ordinarily have."

"And the docks? Could there be a way he is escaping by water?"

"Always a possibility given the location of Whitechapel, but no, I do not really think that is the case. We have put intensive surveillance all about the harbor and it's come down to nothing. I am beginning to think our Ripper is not a resident of the East End." The Queen merely looked at Trevor with an expectant expression. "My feeling, Your Majesty," he continued, "is that we are dealing with a gentleman, someone who lives in the residential districts of the West Side."

Trevor sat back. There. He had said it and he would undoubtedly be tossed from the palace at once.

"Why do you say this?" Her voice revealed nothing.

"The skill of the work for one thing and the fact that gentlemen sometimes do…"

"Have reason to visit Whitechapel?"

Trevor nodded, a little uncertainly. Victoria was known for her intolerance of improprieties and here he had waltzed through the gates of Windsor and as much as told her that he thought the Ripper was a gentryman with a taste for whores. He would probably not only be thrown from the palace, he would probably be removed from the case. "I apologize, Your Majesty, for the bold and tactless manner…"

"Nonsense, this is an unpleasant matter and cannot be discussed with pleasant words. We appreciate your frankness, Detective, and we must confess it is not only our own curiosity which has led to this discussion. The true reason we called you here today was to see how we might help in your efforts."

Trevor looked at Victoria, astounded. "Forensically, Your Majesty..."

"We are not familiar with that term."

"Ah, my apologies, there is no reason why Your Majesty should be. I am convinced this case will only be solved through evidential police work, which is forensics. Through fibers left on the body, the manner in which the incisions were made, bloodstains and other physical evidence..."

"We understand. Because of the enormous number of potential suspects you need some scientific way to eliminate a portion of them. To interview and monitor every man in London is an impossibility."

By God, she really did understand. Trevor nodded quickly. "There are techniques widely used by the Paris police, techniques we are not familiar with..."

The Queen's lips twitched. "You are suggesting the French are more informed than the English?"

"Only in this very small area, Your Majesty."

The lips twitched again, this time, Trevor was relieved to see, into the beginning of a smile. "Perhaps a man from Scotland Yard could go to France and study these techniques, then return and teach them to our coroners and detectives."

"I for one would be delighted..."

She lifted her chin. "No, Detective, we cannot spare you from your present duties. Is there another you might suggest?"

Trevor only hesitated for a moment. "Rayley Abrams. He's a very quick study."

The Queen nodded. "I shall remember the name, mention it to Sir Warren and Abrams will be in Paris within the month. Is there anything else?"

"Scotland Yard will need a true forensic laboratory before long, Your Majesty, a place set aside specifically to examine physical evidence and to impress upon the men the importance of following exact procedure. One of the reasons we are so hampered in our efforts is that the bodies of the first two victims were washed and moved before they could be examined."

"But we are sure your superiors have reprimanded those men for their carelessness."

Trevor hesitated.

The Queen nodded. "Ah. So your superiors are part of the problem. We shall issue a proclamation that in the matter of the Whitechapel murders ultimate consideration should be given to proper forensic procedure." She used the newly- learned word with pleasure, as a child might. "We assume you will be able to write a paper explaining what these procedures are to be."

"Yes, Your Majesty."

"Then we will guarantee a copy of this paper will be in the hands of each inspector within twenty-four hours. Go home and begin it immediately."

He could have fallen on the floor and kissed her feet. "This is far more than I had dared hope for, Your Majesty."

"You are dismissed," Victoria said abruptly.

Trevor rose, bowed, collected his things and began backing toward the door. The Queen was gazing into the fire.

"Detective?"

"Your Majesty?"

"I understand my grandson is one of your suspects."

Trevor stood stunned, both by the boldness of the inquiry and the fact she had for once dropped the use of the royal "we". Finally he found his voice. "All of London is our suspect, Ma'am. But your grandson's alibi proved impeccable, did it not?"

The queen managed a sound somewhere between a cough and a laugh. "Quite a clever answer, Detective, our guess is that you will go far in life. You are dismissed," she said again and Trevor fled.

1:10 PM

Leanna watched with ill-concealed impatience while John finished the last of his chicken and folded the blue napkin back to its original design. "This has been a lovely lunch," he said, smiling at her.

"Yes, lovely. Have you noticed anything unusual about it?"

"The mint sauce for the chicken? Quite daring. Was that your idea?"

"You know I'm not speaking of the mint sauce," Leanna fairly howled in exasperation, for it was impossible to tell when John was joking and when he was not. "We're alone, quite utterly alone, and please don't tell me you haven't noticed."

"I've noticed of course, but thought it would be ungentlemanly to comment on the fact and thus cause you distress."

"And thus cause me distress? Honestly, John, sometimes you can be as thick as plank. I have plotted all morning to get everyone out of the house."

"Is there something you wanted to discuss?"

Leanna nervously fiddled with the lace of her gown. Of course there was something she wanted to discuss, but there was no way a lady could ask a gentleman to declare his intentions. Strange that she had planned how to get him alone, but been unable to script the conversation to follow. She looked at John hopelessly.

"Are you upset with me?" John asked. "Because of the cancelled theater dates? I know no apology can suffice…"

"Your apologies have all sufficed. It's just that you seem so casual about our courtship. Is this even a courtship? Is that the right word? I don't know where I stand."

His eyes were so dark it was impossible to distinguish pupil from iris and Leanna noticed he was nervously pulling at the buttons on his waistcoat as if attempting to mirror her own bodice fiddling. "I explained to you, Leanna, when we first met, that I am not in a position to inherit from my family."

"Meaning what?" Leanna asked, anxiety now becoming an acute pain in her chest, for she knew what was to follow.

"Meaning that I must restrain any feelings toward you until that point in time where I am capable of pressing for a serious courtship. I have a practice to establish, a clinic to build, and to declare my intentions to you before I am in a position to offer…"

"You're saying you won't be able to court anyone for years! Money isn't all that matters. My family – "

"Your family is wealthy, is that what you're about to say? That doesn't make things better, it makes them worse. It only means the gulf between us is all the wider. Do you plan to take me home to the country, to the family estate? Do you think your mother and brothers would be delighted to welcome their precious Leanna and her penniless suitor?"

"You're hardly penniless, John. You have a thriving practice. And that wasn't what I was about to say about my family at all. If you only knew how things really stand…."

He turned from her, resting his chin on his knuckles so that she could only see his profile. "I wouldn't ask you anything until I was in the position to give you the world. It wouldn't be gentlemanly."

"Oh, dash that word 'gentlemanly' from the language. More pain has been given to more girls by men who were trying to be gentlemanly…I don't want the world, John. When have I suggested that I expect you to give me the world?"

"How old are you, Leanna?"

She swallowed, knowing that the answer would be used against her. "Twenty."

"I am thirty-two. When you are my age, you will see what I mean and you'll thank me for not promising what I cannot deliver."

"If you're saying that you think your whole career must be established before you marry, that's foolish," Leanna said, carelessly reaching across the table to grasp his arm. "I understand life better than you think I do and besides, I know wealthy people. So does Aunt Geraldine. I could help you with your work." My God, she was close to begging. She forced herself to release his wrist, sit up straight again and control her voice. He was still unwilling to meet her eyes and suddenly her desperation gave way to anger.

"But that isn't it, is it? You're only using your work and your lack of money to shield me from the real truth. You don't have to choke back passion for my sake because there isn't any passion. It's easy to restrain an emotion you don't feel, isn't it John? And to receive a reputation for saintliness in the bargain..."

"You know nothing!" he suddenly roared, sending the silver flying and causing Leanna's to jerk back her hand. "You don't know me at all, don't know what I think! How dare you tell me what is and isn't hard to bear? Thank you for the lunch, Leanna, but I'm leaving."

Leanna could barely see him rise through her tears. "I only wanted you to touch me, once, just so I would know that you cared."

"You think that when a man touches a woman it's proof of his love?" John rasped, his face splotched with anger and his hands unsteady. "By God, but you are young and stupid. And you think you can help me in my work! That is quite the joke, Leanna."

246

"Then go. You've insulted me enough."

"No, I haven't, you've insulted yourself. You may not like this, probably won't, but there are certain social truths you must learn to accept. There are women men may freely touch and there are those whom they may not. You fall into the latter group and why you find that insulting, I can't begin to guess."

"Oh, spare me your analysis," Leanna said, her own composure returning a bit. "What you really mean is that women are like curios in a shop. Some are laid out and marked quite clearly and affordable to anyone who ventures in. Others are on a high shelf and if you must ask the price that in itself is a sign you cannot afford to buy. To obtain one of those curios you have to enter into lengthy negotiation with the shopkeeper who keeps telling you how special and unique each one is. All you're saying, John, is that I am on a high shelf. In your heart you believe that, one way or another, all women are for sale and the only problem between the two of us is that you can't afford me yet."

"If that is the way you see our relationship, then there is nothing more to discuss," John said. "I'd ask Gage for my coat, but as you point out every ten minutes, Gage isn't here." He looked at her, his expression flat. "You're quite spoiled and I can't believe I ever took you so seriously."

"Kiss me."

"What?"

"Kiss me. I know you want to."

He stood up, looking down at her, and a new emotion came into his face. Sadness. "You're playing games and I can't say I fully blame you. You're young, and I may be your first suitor. You want to turn me into one of the men in your books. Restraint may be foolish in fiction, but not in real life, Leanna. No, I won't kiss you. I'm not a toy."

"Neither am I, John. I want some sign that you really do care. Evidently I am expected to wait…"

"No one is asking you to wait. Do as you please."

"I want to wait," Leanna said, vowing not to break into sobs for a second time. "Just give me a reason to believe…"

"If you need proof of my feelings then you don't know me. No, I won't kiss you. I won't touch you at all."

Leanna took a big gulp. "Why not?"

"Because I intend to marry you."

Leanna sank back into her chair, breathless and tearless, and John pulled on his coat and left the room without a backward glance. The oaken door onto Kingsly Place slammed shut with an angry crack, but Leanna did not flinch at the sound. A minute passed, measured by the dull thuds of the mantle clock, then another. Still Leanna did not move and she waited for some feeling to come. Despair? Triumph? Relief? Frustration? But no emotion rose from the solid surface of her numbness and finally, with surprising steadiness, she stood and began to collect the dishes on a platter to take to the kitchen. She gazed down at the scattered silver and linens under John's chair. A great war had evidently been fought here, but Leanna was not sure if she had won or lost.

CHAPTER TWENTY-SEVEN
October 29
4:15 PM

"I don't know how to thank you, Welles."

"Then don't. If I can't go to Paris myself, you're clearly the man for the job." Trevor looked back as he held the door for Abrams. "And there is something you can do in compensation. I'm on my way to meet Madley and Phillips for an overview of the case. Come with me. We've been through this all so often, and we can use a pair of fresh eyes."

Abrams looked about, nervous as a naughty schoolboy. "Eatwell insisted —"

"Bother Eatwell. I plan to use your brain as much as I can while it's still in London. In a matter of days you'll be sailing to France, on direct order of Her Majesty, and even Eatwell's jurisdiction doesn't reach that far. Come on, man. We go through the notes every week, for all the good it's given us."

Abrams nodded and followed Trevor deeper into the belly of Scotland Yard, down each level until they ended up in the mortuary where Phillips and Davy were already waiting. If they were surprised to see Abrams coming through the door with Trevor, neither made a sign. The four men sat down around the table and Trevor pulled out his notebook.

"I thought we'd see if Abrams brings any new thoughts to the discussion," he said. "Davy, would you like to begin?"

"Three hundred thirteen people interviewed so far," Davy said promptly. "Eighty- one of them detained, most on the grounds of a prior arrest for violence with a woman, particularly a prostitute. Most of the men are untrained, illiterate, over half of them foreign-born. Which is, of course, quite a different profile from how we originally viewed our killer." Davy looked at Abrams. "The ships bring more men in and out every day and we could continue to interview them until the turn of the century. But I don't think we'll hear anything new."

He's different from the boy I met a few weeks ago, Abram thought. All that lad could do was stammer "Yes, Sir" and "No, Sir," and the bobby before me now isn't afraid to express an opinion, even in the midst of superiors.

"Sounds like you've found three hundred and thirteen Micha Banasiks," Abrams said. "Have you interviewed any people who aren't illiterate and foreign-born?"

Davy nodded. "Of course, Sir. An actor who is apparently too good at his craft, a writer of children's books who likes to play word games similar to those in the letters, several doctors, even a woman or two. Either interviewed them or indirectly sought alibis, just as you did for the Duke of Clarence."

"The Queen's grandson?" Phillips said with surprise. "Even I hadn't heard that part. Whatever for?"

"Granted, he has no medical skills," said Trevor. "And, for that matter, no apparent skills of any sort. But he is known to be a frequent patron of the brothels in the East End."

"It's quite a jump from saying he visits whores to saying that he kills them," Phillips said sharply. His use of the word "whore" surprised Abrams. In all they had been through, he had never heard the doctor refer to the women of Whitechapel as anything but patients or victims. But Welles and Davy laughed easily.

"Quite right," Welles said. "He may be a fool or a reprobate, but the man has alibis to spare."

"Other than that, we don't have much more than we had when you worked the case," Davy said, turning back to Abrams. "It's most likely a man with some medical training who is ambidextrous. "

"Not a slaughterhouse worker?" Abrams asked, just to confirm.

Phillips shook his head. "I'm afraid the last two killings ruled that out completely. The work on Eddowes...Well, you saw. Too complete."

"We received a kidney courtesy of George Lusk, the man who leads the Whitechapel Vigilance Committee," Trevor said.

"So the newspapers got that part right?" Abrams said.

"Unfortunately yes," Trevor said. "That was one thing we were hoping to keep under our hats but Mister Lusk seems to have an unquenchable thirst for public attention. We considered him a suspect, briefly, because he always seemed to be close to the trouble, but he has excellent alibis as well."

"But he did provide the kidney," Phillips said. "Which is human, of a size that would suggest from a woman, and in the right state of decomposition to have been removed about the time Eddowes was killed. An expert job of removal, especially under the circumstances of haste and darkness, and it was then I knew beyond question that we weren't dealing with a dockworker or a barber or a butcher."

"So why are you still interviewing men from the East End?" Abrams looked around at the three solemn faces before him. "I'm sorry if it's a rude question, but it seems to me you've eliminated the very sort of man you'd find there as a suspect."

"Some of the men in the East End started life higher," Davy said. "You've got to remember, Sir, not everyone is like you and Detective Welles. I mean no disrespect, but –"

"He's fumbling around trying to find a polite way to say that not all men are ambitious climbers like us, Abrams," Trevor said with a mirthless laugh. "Not all men rise above their born station."

Davy looked down at the table. "Just the opposite for some, Sir, that's my point. A man who was once educated or professional…. he could fall in status, take a step back in his prospects. Due to a taste for alcohol or for certain type of woman or even because he emigrated from some lesser country and then he'd be dead bitter, wouldn't he, Sir? That's why I'm still interviewing men from the East End."

"I disagree with Davy," Trevor said amiably. "I think we're looking for a West End gent who goes to the East End, does his deeds, and then leaves."

"How?" Abrams asked skeptically. "Does he walk up to the fountain on Merchant Street covered in blood and casually hail a carriage?"

Trevor winced. "Quite right. That's the part I haven't figured."

"Show Detective Abrams the pictures and the letters," Davy prompted.

"Ah, the damned letters," Trevor said, reaching for another file. "More than a dozen in total and I would venture most of them are hoaxes. The question is, which ones? Some are quite polite and measured, one a wild rant supposedly sent from hell, two are in rhyme….hard to picture them all being written by the same man."

Abrams flipped through the letters, his eyes scanning a phrase here and there. "An educated man could pretend to be ignorant," he said. "He could deliberately misspell words and use incorrect grammar in an attempt to throw us off the scent." Abrams reddened as he noted he's used the word "us" instead of "you." Despite the plum of the Paris assignment, he had not fully come to terms with the humiliation of being removed from the case, and his hands almost trembled with the excitement of actually touching the Ripper letters. "But an ignorant man or a person with limited knowledge of English couldn't write any better than they knew how, no matter how hard they tried."

"Which is precisely why I don't think they were all written by the same person," Trevor said. "Now, for the pictures."

Abrams paused for a moment before flipping the file open, his fingertips resting lightly on the cloth covering. Photographs disturbed him, for reasons that he could not say. When Scotland Yard had insisted each of their detectives submit his image to the black box, Abrams had found that his heart was pounding as he waited in line for his turn. I'm as bad as those savages who fear the camera will steal their souls, he thought, and the final product – the visage of a homely, bespectacled man, whose left eye tended to drift ever so slightly toward his nose – had not pleased him. Abrams considered the recent mania for photographing the dead even more macabre, although in the case of murder victims he supposed there was an argument to be made for the practice.

With a soft exhalation, Abrams opened the folder. The first picture was of Martha Tabram, proof that Welles had not fully given up on the notion of including her in the list of victims. Her face was turned slightly to the left, mouth slack, as if she had been caught in the act of snoring. Mary Nichols had been photographed from an odd angle, as if whoever had taken the picture had stood at her feet and gazed up at her. Next came Anne Chapman, her head also lolling to the side, and Elizabeth Stride, the only one of the group whose photograph evidenced the oft-quoted claim that the dead looked at peace. He supposed it was because the Ripper didn't have much time with her. Sad to consider that this were likely the only pictures ever taken of these five women, the only way in which they would ever be remembered.

Catherine Eddowes would be the worst. He knew it and he paused again, pretending to study the face of Elizabeth Stride but really dreading the image which lay between it. He did not glance up, afraid he might see pity in the eyes of the other men who sat around the table. Finally, Abrams put aside the Stride picture and braced himself for the brutalized body of Eddowes.

"My assistant closed the wounds," Phillips said, almost apologetically, and indeed Abrams could see a neat series of stitches holding the lower half of the woman's face to the upper. The man had clearly taken care in his task, and it was, he supposed, better than gazing down into the gaping slashes the woman had borne on the night they found her. But the absent ears, flattened nose, and sutured mouth combined to make her look subhuman, a cast aside toy. The other victims had only had their faces photographed as they lay clothed in their coffins, but Eddowes had been photographed on the mortuary slab, completely naked, a Y-shaped incision beginning at her shoulders and running the entire length of her torso. With her scarred, nippleless breasts and her abdomen gathered into the loose folds of a woman who had clearly borne children, she looked far more vulnerable than the others, the perfect example of the female form fallen to ruin.

"Took him two hours," Phillips said vaguely. "Not just to stitch the face, of course, but the whole body."

Abrams could think of no response. For some reason he could not stop staring at the woman's hands, which lay curled and empty at her sides.

"The most difficult to behold," Trevor said quietly.

"Yes," Abrams said, letting the file fall closed again. "Because she's the one we could have prevented." His voice, he was relieved to hear, was steady. "I suppose you felt the need to photograph....the full extent of her mutilations."

"We didn't do it as a gentleman's pleasure, Abrams, I assure you," Phillips said drily.

"This file is completely closed by the Yard, Sir," Davy said. "Pictures won't be released to the public for....what did they say, Sir?"

254

"A hundred years," Trevor said. "By then the answers will be so obvious that the detectives of 1988 will hold their sides and laugh at us. Consider us barbarians." He pulled the file back and stacked it with the others. "Learn everything you can, Abrams, from the most logical methodologies the French have developed to the most ludicrous, because such is the future of forensics."

"I will. But I'm sorry I haven't been more help to you today."

Trevor shrugged. "It's all right. According to Eatwell, these photographs and letters don't belong in suspect files, but rather in my final report. He's convinced that it's over. Five weeks without a murder."

"Five weeks, three days," Davy said.

"Five weeks, three days," Trevor repeated. "And Eatwell says that's reason enough to consider it all behind us."

Abrams nodded. "But I take it five weeks and three days is not enough time to persuade you gentlemen that we're in the clear." He sat for a moment in silence. "You still have to wonder, though, don't you? I realize Jack doesn't operate under the same rules of logic as the rest of us but still....you have to wonder."

"Abrams has a novelist's turn of mind," Trevor said by means of explanation to Davy and Phillips. "He once told me the Ripper had a certain appeal for him, if you can feature that."

"I feel it as well, Sir," Davy said, to Trevor's great surprise. "Can't stop thinking of him, can I, even on the nights when it's not my duty, even when I'm home with my mum and dad. I'll catch myself staring at something and wondering what old Jack might be looking at, what it seems like to him."

"Curiosity is natural," Phillips said. "Inevitable, really."

"Dear God," Trevor said. "It sounds as if you all are professing sympathy for the man. I would think when you look at those pictures, of that final savaged body - "

Abrams held up a palm, shaking his head with a chuckle. "Calm yourself, Welles. No one's excusing him. But it's the eternal mystery, is it not, why evil overrides one heart and not the next? Are you honestly telling us that Jack's never made his way into your dreams? That you've never wondered what happened to the bastard to make him what he is?"

"Each man has his story, does he not, Sirs?" Davy said.

Abrams nodded. "He certainly does. Come on, Welles, stop staring down at that table. Come out for a drink."

"Thank you for invitation," Trevor said stiffly. "But I'll be working late. And no, to answer your question, I've never wondered after Jack's reasons for there are none, at least none that the rational mind can bear. Some people manage to endure the most wretched losses with their sanity intact while others...others crack at the slightest provocation. It hardly falls within the description of my job to wonder why."

"Indeed," said Abrams, pushing to his feet. "Come Davy, the beer's on my tab tonight. Will you join us, doctor? Invite the boys in your lab?" As the men scattered, gathering scarves and gloves, Abrams put a hand on Trevor's shoulder and gave it an awkward pat. "We'll be at the Copper Dome if you change your mind."

"Pointless to speculate on his reasons" Trevor said. "A man like me will never understand a man like him."

Abrams shrugged. "You're the one who's always saying his success hinges on the fact he blends in."

"Looks like us, maybe. Doesn't think like us."

"Welles," Abrams said, picking up his coat. "I think thou dost protest too much."

256

CHAPTER TWENTY-EIGHT
Winter, 1884

It had all begun simply enough. He was a medical student. They called him promising. Enough so that he had been invited to dine in the home of one of his professors. It was a rare honor, and he had found himself seated beside the professor's daughter.

He had saved his wages all summer just to purchase a single proper jacket for university. So of course he was wearing it that evening. He'd paid a barber for a shave, a trim of his mustache, the scent of sandalwood that was rubbed into his neck. He knew these dinners must be tiresome for the girl, having to feign endless interest in conversations with her father's pet students. But she had smiled at him. Laughed at his jokes. And then, near the end of the meal, when they were waiting for the cheese to be served, she had, very briefly, put her hand on his arm.

A woman's hand on a man's arm. These things are the miracles of our lives, the small everyday miracles that might be the result of mere chance or might be something more - an indication of fate, the promise of something better. He was only twenty, new to the city, friendless and poor, so of course he would see his introduction to Katrina as providence. He had never known a woman who read books, who played the spinet, whose hands were soft and free of cuts or burns. The fact she would accept his clumsy efforts at conversation, the way she favored him with a smile...Most telling of all, the fact her father invited him back to dine the next Sunday. Who but an infidel could refute that this must all be the workings of a benevolent God?

The other students teased him. They choked on their jealousy. They had never seen Katrina, so they did not understand the full extent to which fortune had smiled on him, but they certainly did notice that the professor began to take a special interest in this young man so recently come from the country. The professor chose him for the demonstrations and was not so rushed or impatient when he answered his questions. So of course the young man could not help but dream. What would his career be like under the auspices of such a father-in-law? What would his marriage be like in the bed of a woman like Katrina? Imagining the answer to the first question made him arrogant, unpopular among his peers. Imagining the second drove him deep into the slums of the city.

He wasn't the only medical student to visit the brothels. Of course not. They were as randy a bunch as any other men their age, and the profession they'd chosen required lengthy study and apprenticeship, meaning that it would be years before any of them could take a wife. Whores were as much a part of university life as books, and whenever his footsteps would turn toward the shadowed side of the city, he felt no guilt. He had a favorite among the girls, and he considered the fact that she bore a slight resemblance to Katrina to be a type of fidelity. Someday there would be a wife and a medical practice, a home with music and guests, perhaps even an appointment to the university seat the professor would vacate with his eventual retirement. Until then there was Wednesday afternoons with this thin blonde girl, who wore a Star of David around her neck but called herself by the ludicrous name of Collette. When he had asked her why, she had answered "It sounds French." The pseudonym should have been a sign. It should have shown him that she too dreamt of something finer. But the young man's ambition was so all-encompassing that it blinded him to ambition in anyone else.

And so he had been stunned on the morning he had opened the door of his rented room to find Collette - dressed and standing, two conditions in which he had rarely seen her –

weeping loudly and proclaiming him to be the father of her unborn child.

There were probably dozens of men who could claim this dubious honor, but the girl was insistent. She had counted. It was him. The very fact she had managed to track him down there, in his rooming house, was frightening enough and he knew he had been imprudently talkative in the rest periods between bouts on her bed. Bragging had become habituated behavior in him by this point, as natural as breathing, and he had told the girl all about his favored status at the university, how he had been invited to assist in any number of surgical demonstrations while the other students had been able to do no more than watch. Kidneys were his specialty. He could get one out in eight minutes, utterly intact. The girl nodded. She had either been impressed or was pretending to be.

Now he grabbed the doorframe, almost buckling from the shock of what she was saying. She had been stealthy and persistent, just as his father had warned him the Jews so often were. Had put together certain things better than he would have guessed. If she had been able to follow him to where he lived, would she be willing to follow him to the university?

He asked her what she wanted.

Marriage.

He laughed.

He laughed, but his arrogance was fading fast. She held the cards, he realized, and he himself had dealt them to her, one Wednesday afternoon at a time.

The girl stood in his doorway, waiting.

Of course he would not marry her. That was out of the question. His future wife would play the spinet and host soirees; she would not be a retired whore. And no, no, don't even bother to ask. He did not have enough money to support a child on the side.

The one thing he did have to offer her was his surgical skill.

Had he done this particular procedure? Of course not. It was scarcely on the curriculum. But it was simple enough in theory and there was no other way.

Naturally, this was not what the girl had hoped to hear. She wept. She clung to his shoulders. He took her hands and led her into the room, asked her to sit on the bed. He apologized for the laughter and said it was just the spasmodic result of his surprise, an explanation she seemed to accept. He promised future visits, a marriage someday, yes, of course, when he was out of school and could support her in the manner she deserved.

Did she believe him? Did she see a home, a family, the cozy comfort of being a doctor's wife? Hard to say, but after a long conversation punctuated with kisses and tears, Collette had agreed that this particular child should not be born.

Church bells were ringing on the morning that he met her. It had to be a Sunday, the only time of the week when he could be absolutely sure no one else would be in the laboratory wing of the university. He had consulted the books and figured the steps he must take, the implements he would need. At first he had thought about trying to remove the surgical tools from the school but they were valuable and carefully accounted for at the end of every lab, so he ultimately decided it would be easier to get the girl in than to get the knives out. He was relieved to see she had celebrated the dawn with a good bit of vodka since he had no way of predicting how painful the procedure would be. She followed him unsteadily but without question through the dark halls of the university and then into the large silver laboratory.

"Tell me something," he asked. "What is your real name?"

She didn't answer. The fear, the vodka, the strangeness of the place. They had all rendered her mute and she did not even look at his face. The laboratory was bright with sunlight. She let him help her to the table where, only two days before, he had assisted in the dissection of a heart.

If a man was gifted enough to navigate the chambers of the human heart, he figured, it should be a simple enough matter to make your way in and out of a uterus, surely the most primitive of organs. No more than a muscular sack, a cove with a single outlet to the sea. He would never understand where it went wrong, what vessel he had managed to nick or why there was so much blood. He didn't panic at first. Who could say how much bleeding might be normal in a task such as this one? The fetus had not been the problem. It had slipped out as easily as a pit is spooned from an apricot. He let the mass of material drop in a bucket and the girl had turned her head with the sound. The trouble started later, when he began to scrape the walls of her womb. This should have been the sweeping up part of the procedure, the simple part. But the blood was continuing to flow and the girl was squirming now, crying out in fear and pain. He dropped the scapula and went in with his hand.

Three walls were fine, clean, whole.

On the fourth, his finger found the tear. Slipped right through the membrane, and in that moment he knew that his whole life was turning, that everything he was and had ever hoped to be was slipping away. What now? Stitches? He couldn't hold her open and sew at once, not to mention the impossible mess of the bleeding, or the fact the girl was fighting him, trying to pull her knees to her chest, trying to knock back his hands.

He began to have the sense that he was leaving his own body. That he was floating somewhere high above the room, looking down at the figures below him, watching the blood spread like an overturned bucket of paint, a glass of wine, watching it cover the table and begin to drip upon the floor. The girl screamed – loud, too loud, and although there was likely no one else in the building on a Sunday morning, it was impossible to be sure. He tried to shush her, to contain her, and when this proved impossible, he pulled his hand from her womb and punched her face with his bloody fist until at last she felt silent.

He had asked the professor, days before, where the school got the organs they used in dissection, where they had obtained that particular human heart. The class had been concluded for the day and they'd been standing at the big silver sink, washing up. He could still see it, the perfect beads of water on the hairs of the professor's arm as he had explained that most the cadavers were indigents, whores, or criminals, people without families to claim them. This heart had been small. It had probably been taken from a female. And then the professor had suggested he make surgery his specialty, had said that he had a gift for the knife.

But what would the professor say if he could see this scene now, see him frantically trying to suture the hole he had ripped in this girl's uterus, unable to stop the flow of blood, unable to see his way though it to the site of the damage? There would be no degree. No university post, no pretty wife with her pretty voice, no money, no position, no respect. He would be disgraced, jailed, excommunicated, sent to the work houses. His father would know. His landlady, the professor, the other students. Katrina. Katrina would know it all, would see that he was just a boy from a small town who worked in the fields, who trapped pelts in order to buy a single good coat. Society knows what to do with the people who have never had hope. They know where to house them, what to feed them, even how to make use of their bodies when they die. But what becomes of the people who had hope and lost it? The young man knew he would have to be far away before the next morning when his classmates would return, when the professor would push open this door and see this sight. Would find this bounty of healthy young organs for the edification of his future medical students.

The girl was no longer crying. She was lying very still. He stepped back from the table, unable to take his eyes off her, fumbling with his left hand for a chair. How much blood could one woman hold? It was eternal. Blood without end, amen. She was so quiet now. Her chest was still rising and falling but there was no sound with the breathing.

He found the chair with his hand and lowered himself into it. He knew he should be running, running now, but he was unable to move.

So this is how it ends, he thought.

She had been his first. This was not a strange thing. Country boys who came to the city were often virgins, but what disturbed him most, oddly, was that he had never known her name.

He sat for a long time. He watched as her life flowed slowly out, taking his life along with it.

He knew he should flee and yet he did not. Instead he left the girl's body on the examination table, and went to Katrina's house. What did he expect? Was there some part of his mind that thought she might escape with him.....but no, only a fool would have thought that, and he had never been a fool. Perhaps he believed that her father would help him, that when the professor saw how much his daughter loved.....no. Not that either. Perhaps he had only wanted to say goodbye, to see the grief in her eyes when he told her some pretty lie. Maybe that

that his father was ill and he must travel home for a week or two.

She would forget him in time. He would never forget her.

He didn't knock on the door but instead waited in the garden. She had so many dogs that he had never been sure of the exact number, but one or another of the little fluffs was always needing to go into the yard to lift a leg against a bush. He stood in the edge of the poplars for nearly an hour waiting and was at last rewarded with the sight of her drifting like a cloud across the lawn.

She smiled, surprised. Walked toward him, the yapping dogs all around her, with a hand extended as if she planned to pull him from his hiding place into the light. He did not wish to reveal himself totally in case someone else was with her, but he held out a hand too, beckoning her toward the woods, and that's when she saw the blood on the cuff of his sleeve.

He was, after all, a medical student. There were dozens of plausible reasons why he might have a smear of blood on a white cuff, but Katrina's mind went to none of those reasons and he was mute, incapable of directing her there. Perhaps he emitted the stink of shame, perhaps his face was frozen in a mask of guilt. Something must have given him away, because the girl stopped in her tracks and frowned.

"What have you done?"

Her voice was stern. Contemptuous. She had no way of knowing. A girl of her class probably didn't even know it was possible to do the thing he had just done. But she looked in his face and had seen somehow, in that instant, that he had fallen, that he had made some large and ghastly mistake, the sort that would remove him from his rightful place at her father's dinner table. He thrust his hand into his pocket, felt his fingers curl around the handle of the scalpel he had hidden there.

She frowned, repeated the words. "What have you done?"

Only then did he run.

How many days had it taken him to get to London, or should the question be how many weeks? His shock and confusion were so profound he lost his senses, hopped on trains that were going the wrong direction, spent hours unto days in deep, dreamless sleep in haystacks along the way. He did not know where he would go once he finally reached the city or what he would do next.

He only knew that two women, each in her own separate way, had ruined him.

Now, almost three years later, there are ways in which he remains a mystery to himself. The monstrous injustices of the world have always tormented him and yet he has never been able to stop himself from admiring those who stand above him on the ladder. He does know that he is following this particular girl because she somehow reminds him of Katrina. The same fair coloring, serene expression, the confidence with which she moves.

A man might prepare his whole life for a profession. He trains himself from boyhood into the kind of character that will allow him to escape poverty and hopelessness. Builds himself up through a thousand small steps, taken year after painful year, only to see his whole world come tumbling down on a woman's whim. For women know how to make you want something you had never knew you wanted, and then, just when you dare to hope you might gain it, they know how to take it away. They are the apple-eaters, the dark angels, a mere afterthought of God, and whether they lay a gloved hand on your arm at a dinner party or spread their dirty legs for you in an alley, he knew that it was all the same.

The woman does not notice that he is following. Her stride is long and her chin is high. You can see at a glance that she bows for no man, that she is the one who does the choosing.

And despite it all, he has never been able to abandon hope that his betters will someday notice him. Will someday accept him as one of their own.

It is the failing of his lifetime.

CHAPTER TWENTY-NINE
November 9, 1888
5:32 AM

Trevor had taken a sleeping powder and it took several rounds of pounding on the door of his flat before he was up and, although a bit dream-drunk, purposefully heading toward the door. He noted the time on the mantle clock. Something must be dreadfully amiss.

He did not recognize the young bobby standing on his stoop by name but he recognized well enough the expression on the boy's face. "Come, Sir," was nearly all the lad could manage to get out. "A carriage, Sir." Dressing by the light of his single candle, Trevor scrambled into his suit and yesterday's shirt and emerged from his door within five minutes, unshaven and disheveled. As he swept past the young officer and into the carriage, there was little need for conversation. The driver headed for Whitechapel.

Mercifully, due to the hour, there was no gathering crowd in front of the small, rattletrap house where they stopped. Only a few officers, most in plainclothes. Trevor spotted Davy and Abrams and he relaxed a bit, knowing that no matter what the morning would bring, there was at least competent help close at hand.

"The body's inside and the door is barred, Sir," Davy said, advancing toward Trevor as he alighted from the carriage. "We're lucky to have even found this one, but a bobby saw blood on the door frame while making rounds about an hour ago. See, Sir." Davy lifted his lantern and gestured toward the door. The bobby's eyes had been sharp indeed to catch this small smear of blood in the darkness, and Trevor nodded, then put on his gloves and began to look around for something to break down the door.

"There's a pick-axe in the wagon, Welles," Abrams said in a low voice, bringing his face close to Trevor's. "But I've looked through the window and it's my advice that you have a shot of brandy before we proceed." Trevor glanced at him with some surprise, for Abrams had earned his first citation on a child-murder case and was not a man to go to nerves easily. "Don't be a fool, Welles," Abrams said, noticing his hesitation. "Have a drink first. The girl will wait."

Shrugging, Trevor accepted the offered brandy and threw it down in one gulp, as Davy and Abrams also drank, a shot Trevor suspected was their second of the morning, or possibly the third. Then they all stood back while the same bobby who had fetched him broke in the flimsy door with two big throws of the axe. Trevor, lantern aloft, led the way into the house.

His eyes scanned the room for a body and it took him a long slow look before he realized there was no body. A woman was literally scattered about the room in pieces. Trevor raised his lantern higher and, nearly screaming out as his eye caught his own fleeting image in a broad glass, brought the light back to the mirror. "Look there, a rope," he said with some confusion, for the Ripper had never strangled a victim or left behind a weapon of any sort before. He stepped closer to the mirror, and saw that he was not gazing at a rope at all, but rather at a long length of human intestines, neatly washed and draped along the top of the mirror.

"Oh, God, oh God, Sweet Mary," Davy moaned from a far corner for it had been his misfortune to find the girl's face, stretched across a bedside table like a discarded mask. The skin had been neatly peeled from the skull, which was nowhere in sight, with cleanly sliced eyeholes and the mouth opening curved upward in a mocking mile. How long would it take to skin a woman, Trevor wondered? Beside the face lay the woman's heart, cleaned and dried and resting just above her forehead.

The three men worked the rest of the room swiftly, without speaking. They located one leg, but never the other, and several bodily organs they could not readily identify. What tortures this woman had gone through they tried not to consider, knowing that if they stopped for even a second to view the scene in human terms, their nerve and objectivity would shatter and they would be unable to go on. Abrams found her amputated breasts lying on a table as if they were plates, with knives and forks laid out around them.

Dr. Phillips had arrived and stood patiently in the doorway until they had finished, the sky behind his shoulders brightening somewhat as he waited. He clasped Trevor's hands silently as the men left the room so he and Severin could gather the pieces. Trevor was relieved to see the examination was proceeding in an orderly fashion; evidently his paper on proper procedure had done some good, for the area was well roped off and guarded.

"Care for some tea and rolls, Sir?" one of the bobbies questioned cheerfully, as Trevor, Abrams and Davy made their way into the street. "If you'd fancy a bit of breakfast while the doctors work, I could dash to the bakery on…"

Abrams let out a shout of punchy laughter and Trevor said "Gad, boy, we may never eat again after witnessing such a sight. But I'm sure you meant well, so don't worry about it."

The three of them walked mutely up and down the alleyway, not talking and indeed trying not to think while they waited. Trevor, who had gone blessedly numb with shock, noted it was nearly twenty minutes before Phillips emerged, with Severin and a bobby behind him carrying one of the regulation pauper's coffins which the city provided.

"Frightful butchery," Phillips muttered. "But a well-done job, Welles, mind you of that. To dissect and skin an adult human body must have taken him half the night, and working by firelight as he did…"

"Firelight!" Trevor exclaimed. "Of course, you're right. Perhaps he tore his clothes carrying wood or something, for if worked on her all night he must surely had to have kept a fire going for hours on end. May we reenter the room, doctor?"

"I'm finished," Phillps said. For the record, the skull is missing, one leg and both kidneys. How he managed to walk the streets with such a collection of souvenirs, I shall leave to you to decide."

Trevor found the little room even more depressing by daylight than it had been in the darkness. The furnishings consisted of one small cot, a rocking chair, a chest, and a table. The only surprising piece was a bookcase and when he wandered over, he was even more startled by the titles he found there. Authors whom he must confess he had not read since his days in school, his own taste running more to travelogues and adventures. But here was a prostitute evidently quite capable of reading Milton.

"Interesting," Abrams said from where he was sorting through items on the table. "And potentially very helpful. She seemed to keep records, and in a very neat hand, I might add. No names, but addresses and notes. Her clients, I'd presume? Regulars or men she might have viewed as having the means to lift her out of this hovel? But the killer was so through in his desecration of the room. He must have seen these papers. Why would he leave them behind?"

"The door was barred, Sir. How did he leave at all?" Davy asked. Abrams pointed toward a high window, ajar and leading to the alley.

"He'd have to be rather spry to climb through that," Davy said. "'Specially carrying what he had to carry."

"Mad Maudy has her alibi at last," Trevor said.

A bureau stood in one corner of the room, and when Trevor opened it he found no clothes, but several pairs of shoes, lined up in an orderly fashion and surprisingly clean. The dead girl had dainty feet. Dainty feet, neat handwriting, and a knowledge of Milton.

"Trevor," Davy said, dropping the formality of titles in his excitement. "It's just as you suggested. Evidently the Ripper ran through the girl's firewood soon enough and he began burning her clothes to give himself enough light to perform his work. See, here, looks like the remains of women's clothes."

"That explains the empty bureau," Abrams said, bending to assist Davy as they began to retrieve pieces of cloth from the grate with a poker. "But look at the size of that skirt there. It's nearly intact and it's enormous. Was the murdered girl stocky?"

"Hard to tell from the pieces what size she was," Davy said. "I could ask some of the people outside. Surely some of them knew her and a right good crowd is gathering now."

"Do that," Trevor said. "But judging from her shoes I'd say she was a tiny thing and this skirt could fit me." To illustrate his point he stood, holding the brown cloth skirt to his waist. Abrams grimaced in wry amusement at the sight of Trevor solemnly modeling the frock, but Davy immediately caught his meaning.

"You're saying that a man may have dressed as a woman to gain entry, then after the killings he could have burned his disguise and left in men's clothes. Quite a notion, Sir."

"But not without holes," Abrams objected. "First of all, there are women that stout, your friend Mad Maudy for one."

"She wouldn't have burned her own clothes," Davy protested. "And there's no way she could have climbed through that high window, no way at all."

"Point taken," Abrams agreed. "We've wondered all along why blood-stained clothes were never found and this may be the answer. If the killer were clever enough to dress in two layers and then shuck and burn the top layer after the murder was performed..."

"It is possible," Trevor admitted, carefully folding the skirt to take back with him to Scotland Yard. "A man who dresses as a woman, a woman who dresses as a man...no wonder the working girls are terrified and don't know whom to trust. Look there, Abrams," he added, pointing toward the bookcase. "She was rather the scholar, was she not?"

"Ah," said Abrams, peering down at the titles. "It would seem that if the killer was so desperate for light he or she or it would have burned the papers on the table and then these books, but evidently our Ripper has a respect of literature." Abrams flipped open one of the books and read from the flysheet. "'To my daughters Mary and Emma Kelly, from your loving father, John.' Quite touching, isn't it? She must have had family who cared for her once. By God, whatever is wrong, Welles, you look like death."

"I know a girl named Emma Kelly," Trevor mused.

"Who's Emma Kelly?" Davy asked, wrinkling his brow. "Was she one of the girls we interviewed? There were so many."

"No, no, this girl is not a prostitute. She lives in Mayfair where she is the companion of Geraldine Bainbridge. I've shown you the place."

"I hardly think the two could be connected," Rayley said, trying to be reassuring for Trevor was now paler than he had been all morning. "Kelly is a common surname and for one sister to end up in Mayfair and the other in Whitechapel..."

272

"Yes," said Trevor, trying to steady himself. "And my Emma always said she had no family."

"So there," Abrams said, moving back to the table. "But, there was something about....oh, dear."

"What?" said Davy, for Trevor appeared to be lost in thought.

"These papers. Records, I presumed. But see this one, it reads 34 Kingsly Place. That's a Mayfair address, isn't it, Welles?"

"Dear God, that's where Gerry lives! The girl was Emma's sister!"

Trevor sank to the narrow bed, unmindful of the bloodstains and suddenly too weak to stand. "Easy man," said Abrams, dropping the paper and moving to his side. "There's more brandy out in the wagon, Madley. Pour him a big one."

"I'm a failure," said Trevor. "I have utterly failed in my mission. Don't you see? Don't you?"

"Come now, Welles, there were at least four killings before you were even put on the case. Probably more, we both know that, "Abrams said. "You can't hold yourself responsible for every crime in the East End."

"But I can't even protect the families of people I know!" Trevor sprung to his feet, wrested his notebook from his jacket pocket, and waved it in from of Abram's face. "Do you wish to see a joke, Detective? Then feast your eyes on this. It is my portable forensic laboratory, holding all manner the nonsense which I've collected for nothing. For nothing! No wonder the Ripper laughs at me! Unraveling red fibers! Plucking hairs from corpses and pouring wax into a leg of mutton! Delivering papers on procedure to bobbies who are half-asleep! What was the purpose? I'm interviewing whores while he becomes more audacious every day! Here's for all the good my fibers have done me." To Davy's horror, Trevor opened the notebook and began to shake all the bits of paper and painfully-assembled evidence onto Mary Kelly's dirt floor. Davy lunged for Trevor, but Abrams got there first, wrapping his thin arms around Trevor's torso, holding him still until the convulsions and shouting ceased. Davy knelt and hastily scooped up the contents of Trevor's notebook, cramming them back inside, and staring up at his superior with terrified eyes.

"There, get his evidence then get the damn brandy," Abrams barked, for it was taking all his strength to contain Trevor. "We'll take him back to the Yard and he'll be right as rain in an hour or so. The strain has just been too much." Davy nodded, heading toward the door. "And, lad," Abrams called after him. "No one is ever to know of this."

CHAPTER THIRTY
2:50 PM

Davy spent the rest of the day along the docks. Despite the ghastly images of the morning, his mind kept going back to the more mundane issue of the dates on which the murders had occurred. The first four – five if Trevor was correct about Martha Tabrum – had occurred in rapid succession. There had even been the sense of acceleration, of a killer becoming either bolder or more desperate, a man whose appetite for violence was growing with each subsequent crime. And then, over five weeks of silence. Had the Ripper spent that time lying in wait? Mocking them? Lulling them into a false sense of security so that this last killing would strike with the force of lightning on a sunny day?

Or….was the killer simply forced to wait five weeks?

Forced….perhaps because he was not in London?

Davy had gone from one dockmaster to another, trying to find a record of a ship that had been at sea for five weeks. Granted, this would not explain the arrival of the kidney in mid-October, and this was a troubling piece of the puzzle. But perhaps the killer could have packed up the kidney and arranged to have it delivered at a set date while he was at sea, and that would have been clever, would it not?

Or perhaps…..Jack had been on a shorter run, two weeks or so. He had returned to London, sent the kidney and sailed again. Davy wished he had someone to discuss it all with but Trevor, Phillips, and Abrams had returned to Scotland Yard and Trevor's outburst at the crime scene had frightened Davy more than the severed breasts and strands of intestines. What would happen to the investigation if its chief coordinator became too rattled to do his duties, with Abrams bound for Paris and

Phillips so feeble it had taken both of his assistants to lift him into his coach? Davy decided he must shoulder more of the responsibility before Trevor lost his mind completely.

Davy turned from the waterfront and began making his way back toward Whitechapel. The streets were quiet and deserted – not surprising, perhaps, in light of the fact the afternoon papers were full of news of the Kelly killing. He had walked several blocks before it occurred to him that he had passed not a single woman on his route. It was as if they had all faded from sight, as if London had become a town with nothing but wordless, hurrying men.

Davy stopped for a beer and spread the papers across the bar to study as he drank. Nine vessels had been at sea for the dates that supported his theory, but the problem wasn't identifying the ships, it was obtaining a record of the men who had been aboard. The vessels running in and out of the East End docks were primarily fishing boats and cargo ships, angling for a quick profit and with their captains none too choosy about who came aboard. Some of them claimed to have set crews but sailors were an unpredictable lot, prone to drunkenness and whoring on their shore leaves. If a captain found himself with a light crew, as was not uncommon, he might stroll the dock area, hiring extra hands at random. The official list of who was aboard any certain ship on any set day was undoubtedly riddled with inaccuracies. Still, it was a place to start.

"Shall I set you up again?" asked the barkeeper from halfway down the long counter.

"No thank you," answered Davy. "I best be back to work."

The streets were dark for mid-afternoon and the rain had given way to heavy mist. Davy pulled up his collar and decided to return to Mary Kelly's house to see if they might have overlooked some small detail. Unlikely, for Abrams and Trevor had gone over the hovel literally on hands and knees, but he had to do something to pass the afternoon, for he dreaded the moment he must return to Scotland Yard.

He took several shortcuts through the East End alleys and soon found himself facing Mary Kelly's front door. Davy stared at the outside for a few moments and decided not to enter just yet but rather to investigate the alleyways in the area.

He selected one at random. Although the bobbies had combed the trash that morning, Davy still looked behind the barrels and crates for anything that seemed out of place. He had searched one side for about a hundred yards and was just about to round the corner to the right when he stopped suddenly and threw himself against the wall. Before him was a slender, dark man peering into Mary Kelly's front window.

The man did not knock on the door, but rather stood staring through the glass, his black cape thrown about him and a felt hat obscuring his face. Could the Ripper have returned to admire his handiwork? Such a stratagem would be bold indeed, but Trevor had repeatedly warned him that the Ripper worked by unusual methods, and applying normal principles or reason to him would be fruitless. The man stepped back and looked at the numbers on the front of the building, as if to assure himself he was at the correct address.

Then the man looked up and down the street and started off into the mist. Davy gave him a minute to get underway and then turned out of the alley, nearly colliding with a tall figure buttoned near to bursting into a tweed jacket. "Scuse," he muttered, his chest brushing against that of the stranger and he looked up to find his eyes locked with those of Mad Maudy.

"Scuse me, ma'am," he said, diverting his face from the blast of stale breath that emitted from her scowl, but she appeared to not remember him, to scarcely register his presence. She too was watching Mary Kelly's door. Should he stay, observe her reasons for coming to this address, or follow the stranger? Davy hastily decided in favor of the latter and left Maude in the muddy street, her gaze fixated on the scene of the crime.

Davy tried to keep as close to the man as possible without making him aware he was being followed, but the stranger moved swiftly, turning on every corner, and Davy almost lost him twice. He tailed him for nearly a half-hour, out of the East End, across several wide parks which made unobtrusive following especially difficult, and finally to the middle-class neighborhood of Brixton. The stranger crossed the street and walked along a row of identical brownstones, eventually turning at one to climb the steps and disappear through the door.

Davy sought shelter beneath a tree and waited for about ten minutes, wondering when or if the man would leave again. Eventually a rickety Hansom cab halted across the street and the driver leaned over to let out his fare. Davy watched the rider mount the steps to his home before approaching the driver.

"Need a ride, Sir?" asked the driver.

"No," answered Davy. "But could you kindly tell me who occupies the house across the street?"

"That be the home of Doctor John Harrowman."

"Ah," said Davy, spreading his palms. "Then I am quite lost. Thank you for your help." He stepped back quickly so he would not be splashed as the cab pulled off and returned to the tree which offered inadequate refuge from the returning rain. Perhaps better to go back to the Yard and tell Trevor and Abrams what he'd found.

But just as forty minutes had passed, Davy heard a door shut and saw the dark figure descending the stairs from the Harrowman house. Davy's heart warmed with excitement, then nearly lurched as the doctor abruptly turned and started in his own direction. Instead of passing him, however, the man hailed a cab, gave some directions to the driver and rolled off, leaving Davy alone in the street.

278

Frantically, Davy looked about to see if another cab was available, but the street was empty. So he ran behind the doctor's Hansom and grabbed hold of the leather belt used to tie down luggage. Giving it a yank, he was able to climb onto the small lip where excess bags were stored. The driver looked back in indignation but Davy tossed him a coin, which seemed to sate the man, who clearly had no objection to gaining two fares for one trip.

The rain worsened. Davy held tightly to the leather strap, drawing his boots beneath him as the cab gained speed and weaved its way through the streets. He cursed as the dirty water splashed up on his already soaked clothing and pulled his cap over his face as best he could without losing his grip. Finally the driver began to slow, so Davy jumped from his perch and stumbled until he could shorten his stride.

He stopped to gather his breath and watched the cab come to a halt in front of a handsome house in Mayfair. John Harrowman paid his fare, ran up the steps, and rang the front bell, disappearing from view almost immediately. Davy did not have to ask who lived in this particular house, for Trevor had taken him by Geraldine Bainbridge's home before. Wet and exhausted, already beginning to cough, he turned and began the long walk back to Scotland Yard.

CHAPTER THIRTY-ONE
4:20 PM

The note is delivered to his place of work. The ultimate insult.

But there is no mistaking it is meant for him. His name is on the envelope. Badly printed from an unschooled hand. His last name misspelled, as it has been before.

He rips it open.

A crude message. Another ridiculous attempt at rhyme. His eye scans the page, fixates on one line.

I saw you.

The words go through him like a blade. Stop his breath in his throat, could almost stop his heart.

He has been seen.

He wants to scream, but there are others around him. The stupid and the weak, perhaps, but still capable of observing his discomfiture. They might ask about the note, might even draw conclusions he does not wish them to draw. He struggles to regain control over his functions. He inhales slowly. Exhales even more slowly.

The wolf has found him again.

CHAPTER THIRTY-TWO
4:30 PM

Cecil read the newspaper story of the Kelly murder a third time, the thumping in his chest growing stronger with each paragraph. The dirty dishes lay untouched on the table and he picked up the crystal bell at his right and rang it with great vigor.

"Save your efforts, darling," his mother said crisply, as she entered the dining room. "Fanny saw it fit to leave us this afternoon when she overheard your brother telling Cook we'll have to suspend wages."

"Who served tea?" Cecil asked with some surprise. It had been awaiting him when he returned from his highly unsatisfactory afternoon of poker.

"I did," Gywnette admitted, sinking into one of the faded Queen Anne chairs.

"Mother! Things surely can't be as bad as that."

"I'm afraid they are. Cook is the only one who is left now and I daresay her presence is more from a misguided sense of loyalty than anything else." Gwynette's lips were thin and tight. "She's of the old school, believes that servants are members of the family but I'm afraid the younger girls…"

"Expect to be paid."

"Indeed."

"Who shall do the linens? Attend to our wardrobes? Fetch the water and the firewood, for God's sake, and manage the carriage?"

"The horse and carriage were sold last week."

Cecil winced. "Ah yes."

"The annuities come in again on the twentieth of the month," Gwynette said in a matter-of-fact tone. "Perhaps at that time we can find some temporary help, at least a girl to do the laundry."

"The twentieth! That's over a week away!"

"I know what the date is, Cecil. We didn't seem to do very well with our money management this month, did we?"

"It's inhumane to expect us to maintain a household on the miserly amount the will allows." Cecil lit his pipe and prepared to expound further but Gwynette suddenly turned to the side table.

"Did you see the latest letter from Leanna?"

"No. Nor do I care to."

"She seems quite concerned about us. This is the second letter this week. Have you made any effort to correspond with her, Cecil? Or with Tom?"

"I've been busy…"

"Indeed. Well, you might peruse the letter. She gives a rather droll description of Geraldine and the servants she employs. There's some sort of genetic freak named Gage from what I understand, and a maid named Emma who seems to have made quite an impression upon your sister…"

"Good Lord, Mother, what does Leanna's London gossip have to do with our present situation?"

"She talks a good bit about the Ripper…"

"Really? What does she say?"

Gwynette looked at him in a reflective fashion. "So that intrigues you, does it? Your father had a morbid turn of mind as well. If you're interested, the letter is here on the tea table. I suppose I have dishes to wash."

Gwynette walked slowly out, Cecil's plates teetering on a tray, and the room fell silent. Cecil had seen Leanna's letter himself that morning for he made it a habit to rise early enough to be the first member of the family to intercept the post. It would never do for either his mother or his brother to see how many letters were arriving from Pinkernerry's, the local lending institution, or how many notices had accumulated from the bank. Writing checks on his mother's account had been simple enough, for Cecil had a clever hand and could simulate Gwynette's signature nearly as well as his own. Borrowing against Winter Garden proved a much trickier matter. The deed was in William's name and Cecil supposed he had Edmund Solmes to thank for pulling a bit of wool there, but if William ever found out…

Cecil sighed. His hard-won funds had not lasted very long at the track or the card table, for he was undeniably having a run of black luck. Why couldn't the others see that banker's interest was but a mere shilling compared to what a man could earn in a good day of wagers? He was trying to lift them all out of penury but his mother and William seemed willing to accept their new station with nary a protest.

It was not easy to be the only one in the family with any ambition.

Cecil carefully extracted a paper from the inner pocket of his waistcoat. It was Pinkernerry's "final notice," their third "final notice" to be precise, meaning that he had been frightened silly by the first two for no reason at all. But a fourth final notice? It seemed too much to hope for. Cecil placed the letter back in his pocket, along with the hastily-ripped news account of Mary Kelly's killing. The article was intriguing because this victim had been young and lovely, the artist's sketch showing a serene smile which might have belonged to a gentlewoman. The Ripper appeared to be changing his style.

After a moment of reflection, Cecil added Leanna's most recent letter to his pocket as well. He checked his pocket watch and noted that, with the carriage gone and the family reduced to foot travel, he didn't want to be late for his meeting with Solmes at the track. The ponies waited for no man.

4:35 PM

Hearing the front bell ring, Leanna went to the door and opened it. "John," she gasped, almost stumbling forward as she wrapped her arms around his neck. "It's awful." Her eyes were red and swollen with weeping.

"There, darling," said John, reaching toward her. "I had no idea you would still be so upset, but I had to return, had to. Couldn't bear the way I left you. I want to explain myself."

"You have to go to Emma."

"Emma? What's wrong with Emma?"

"You don't know? You haven't seen the papers?"

"Leanna, whatever do you mean?"

"The Ripper -"

"Yes, I read that. Another victim, a girl I knew myself, a former patient. But what does that have to do with Emma?"

"Mary Kelly was her sister."

John rocked back on his heels. "Dear God, it can't be."

Leanna wiped her eyes and sat down on a footstool. "None of us, not even Aunt Gerry, knew she had a sister. Evidently she couldn't bring herself to admit..." Leanna straightened her shoulders. "But she must have loved her, John. This girl was all the family Emma had in this world and she's distraught."

"Take me to her," John said quietly, his shock evaporating and his doctor's manner returning. "I was on my way to do rounds, so I have my bag."

Leanna led John up the flights of stairs to the third floor, where, in the hall, Geraldine and Gage were pleading with little success for Emma to open the door. Gerry too had been weeping, and Gage was making ineffectual jabs at the bolt with a butter knife.

"Oh, John, can you do something?" wailed Geraldine who suddenly looked every one of her seventy years. "The poor girl is in pieces."

Nudging Gage aside, John rapped lightly on the door. "Emma, this is John Harrowman. I just want to talk to you, dear. Please." The response was thundering silence. Leanna bit her lip.

John glanced at Gerry. "Is there another key?"

"Oh, I've taken leave of my senses," Gerry muttered. "Extra keys, of course. Gage, go to my room. On my dresser there is a jewelry box. In the bottom drawer there are some spare keys. Bring all of them."

Gage hurried as fast as his feeble body could carry him and soon returned with about half a dozen keys in his hand. John tried them in sequence and with the fourth the lock sprang free. Geraldine started to rush in, but John stopped her at the door.

"Leave me alone with her. I know about these matters," he said in a tone that made the others freeze in their tracks. He shut the door behind him and removed his hat and cape, draping them both over a chair and walking to the bed, where Emma lay sobbing. He sat down beside her and gently put his arms around her and let her cry, holding her in silence until she seemed to calm. He helped her lie back upon the bed, and stood gazing down at her face, so bloated with tears that he would not have recognized her had he passed her on the street. She looked back at him trustingly.

"Emma, I'm going to give you something to help you rest. I know you've been through a lot, but you must be strong. Losing someone dear is a terrible thing, I know for I've lost loved ones. But I knew your sister, Emma. She was intelligent and strong as well as beautiful. You can be proud of her."

Emma considered this in silence but at least the dreadful wracking sobs had left her. John pulled the sheets and blankets up, then went to the door and asked Gage to collect his black satchel from the entry. Leanna and Gerry looked at him beseechingly, but he shook his head.

"No visitors yet."

John returned to the bed and held Emma's hand until Gage came in with the bag. He filled a syringe with morphine and injected it into Emma's arm.

"I want you to sleep now, Emma," said John, brushing her forehead with his hand, knowing that within minutes she would have no choice in the matter. "You're among friends here." He waited at her side for a few more minutes until her chest began to rise and fall with the deep, profound breaths of a drugged sleep.

John found Geraldine and Leanna downstairs in the parlor, sitting as still as two stone statues. "She'll rest," he said. "And when she wakes she'll seem a bit confused. Just give her some hot soup and tea and keep her relaxed. I'll stop in again to check on her."

"And I'm going to send a message to Cambridge," he went on, when there was no response to his directions. "Under the circumstances, perhaps Tom could stay a fortnight or so until things are better."

"I want Tom," Leanna wailed, like a child.

"Of course you do, darling, and you shall have him," John said.

"You've been an invaluable help already and we're not so rattled as we seem." Geraldine attempted to sit up straighter, to reassure him with a smile. "If I'd known Emma had a sister, I would have…"

"Spare yourself, Geraldine, for there was nothing any of us could have done for Mary Kelly," John said. "Now that I stop and think of it, she was very much like Emma. Always seemed out of place, if you know what I mean." He looked from Geraldine to Leanna. "I have my patients," he said helplessly.

"Of course," Gerry said. "Tess told me you were up all of last night with her daughter. Twins, I take it. She's over the moon."

John nodded. "A long labor and Margory is quite depleted. I was headed there when I got your note. But she's young and will recover and yes, Tess is now the proud grandmother of two fine boys."

"Birth and death," Geraldine said quietly, patting Leanna's hand. "They keep flinging themselves at us, do they not?"

4: 46 PM

"We've got a new suspect, Sirs," Davy said, shaking the rain off his coat and hanging it on a post in the corner.

"Just what we need," Trevor said blearily. He and Abrams had spent most of the day in the mortuary with Doctor Phillips, attempting to reassemble the pieces of Mary Kelly's body and determine precisely what had been done to her, how, and in what order.

"But I think this one is rather likely," Davy said. "I got the notion that the five week gap between killings might indicate our man was a sailor, who'd been at sea for the month of October, so I spent the morning at the docks getting duty rosters..."

"Clever," Abrams said, with a little surprise.

"But that wasn't what led me, Sir, it was later. I went back by the Kelly house and first of all I see Mad Maudy just standing in the street. Watching a man who was paying her absolutely no mind, who was standing on his tiptoes looking right through the window. The coppers weren't stopping him because he was dressed as a gentleman, not acting guilty, you know, but as if he had every right to be there. And I thought yes, that's just how he does it, by seeming so prosperous and respectable that no one questions his movements. And he had a bag with him too, the right size for a medical bag, so I followed him." Davy stopped to take a deep breath and Abrams slid a cup of water toward him, which he eagerly drank. Funny how one could be soaked to the skin and still thirsty, he thought.

"Go on, man," Trevor said, and if they had not all been so preoccupied they might have noted this was the first time Trevor had addressed Davy as "man" and not "boy."

Followed him across town to Brixton," Davy continued, wiping his mouth with his sleeve. "Asked a passing cabbie whose house it was and he said a doctor, John Harrowman."

"Harrowman?" Abrams said. "I've heard the name. Fancies himself a white knight of the slums, always raising monies for a clinic. Goes everywhere on his missions, even the Jewish part of town."

"I haven't just heard of him, I know him," Trevor said with a sigh. "Nice try, Mabrey, but he isn't our man."

"Hear me out, Sir," Davy said, for once not backing down from Trevor's tendency to make broad declarations. "He left the house in Brixton, called another cab, and took it to Kingsly Street."

But Trevor was still shaking his head. "Harrowman is a friend of the lady of the house, Geraldine Bainbridge," he said. "In fact, that's where I met him." He proceeded with the whole story, his exhaustion making him careless and inclined toward more detail than he might otherwise be, while Abrams and Davy sat without questions. He described the dinner party, the chess game, the canceled outing to the play, and although he did not specifically mention the part Leanna had played in all these events, her crucial role in the drama escaped neither of his listeners.

When Trevor finished, Abrams and Davy exchanged a long glance, in which it was mutually agreed that the news might be better accepted if it came from Abrams.

"Welles," Abrams said in a slow deliberate voice. "I'm afraid you've made rather a classic mistake. We are all of us aware of our tendency to suspect people we don't like. Someone makes us angry, shows disrespect, or perhaps something in their appearance or speech reminds us of a former foe. And thus in a manner that we do not directly acknowledge to ourselves, this disliked person can rise higher in our minds as a suspect. We know this impulse is wrong, of course, and as men of the law we fight against it."

"Of course we do," Trevor said. "What's your point?"

"Only that the opposite impulse can be just as deadly. You have found yourself in competition with John Harrowman for the attentions of a young lady. Apart from this, you bear the man no ill will. You might even admire him, feel a kinship. Because he's like you in a way, is he not? Struggling to be taken seriously in his work, struggling to bring change to an antiquated system." Abrams took off his spectacles, blew on the lenses. "We've all known men like Harrowman, men who have all the traits women find irresistible - from his cultured voice to his height to his passion for justice. Hell, when you got to the part about his perfectly groomed mustache, even I began to hate him a little."

"In school we called them lady-slayers," Davy piped up.

"Quite," said Abrams. He put his glasses back on and looked sympathetically at Trevor. "So you sit faced opposite a paragon who will mostly likely win the battle for the Bainbridge girl's heart. You know it. He knows it. Here is where it gets tricky. He will have the girl you want, so you dislike him. But you know you should not suspect him merely because you dislike him, so you do the exact opposite. You exonerate him because you dislike him. You have bent over backwards so far in your attempts to be fair to a rival that you have managed fall quite forward, to blind yourself to the obvious. That this John Harrowman is a composite of everything we've been looking for. Tall, mustached, well-dressed, medical knowledge, access to the East End, someone the women there know and trust."

"I assure, you he isn't – "

"You said you played chess with him. Is he by any chance left-handed?"

Trevor shut his eyes. "He seems to use both hands with equal ease. But I think –"

"Think what?" Abrams snapped, now at the end of his patience. "That because you met a man at a dinner party in a fashionable part of town, this means he isn't capable of murder? By God, Welles, if any man on the force ventured such a theory, you'd call for his head on a platter and rightfully so. You've got to the face the fact that this man is not only a suspect, but is in a house full of ladies this very moment, ladies you claim as friends."

"I can't imagine –"

"That he would attack respectable women in broad daylight?" Abrams sat back in his chair and exhaled. "Nor can I. He's probably a true split of character, capable of waltzing one type of woman across the floor of a ballroom and slicing open another an hour later. So Dr. Jekyll is undoubtedly the one taking tea in Mayfair this afternoon. But we can't know where Mr. Hyde might venture later, can we?"

"Yes, Sirs, we do," Davy said. "I took the liberty. Know it isn't my place, Sirs, but I grabbed a couple of coppers off the corner of Kingsley. Told one of them to keep a watch on the

Bainbridge house and the other to follow Harrowman when he left. Didn't want to presume, but –"

"Good man," Abrams said quietly. "You've earned your pay today, Davy, haven't you?"

"Should we bring him in, Sir? Ask for his alibi?"

"Let me handle that," Abrams said. "I suspect we'll gain more by having him followed."

Trevor opened his eyes. He felt sick, disoriented, as in boyhood when he had tumbled off a sled or fallen from a tree. Abrams was right. Of course he was. There were so many logical reasons to have interrogated John Harrowman and he had somehow failed to see them. And now the very man he'd been too stupid to suspect was at this moment with Leanna, Emma, and Gerry. It had been hard to hear Abrams berating him for his blindness but that was nothing compared to the shame he felt now, looking into Davy Mabrey's face.

"Davy," Trevor said quietly. "Thank you. I have made many mistakes in this investigation but the one thing I will never regret is choosing you. Find the assignation sergeant and tell him I want round-the-clock surveillance of the Bainbridge house and a tail on John Harrowman. As of now, we will treat him like any other suspect."

CHAPTER THIRTY-THREE
November 10
5:50 PM

Cecil Bainbridge stood outside the Pony Pub that and watched people crowd their way into the small establishment. Tonight was a special celebration, for not only was it the wake for Mary Kelly, but the owner had promised free food and beer. They would drink till dawn, damn the Ripper, and take the morrow on the morrow.

With a deep breath, Cecil pushed open the door. After the events of the last twenty-four hours, God knows he was as ripe as anyone for a drink.

The night before, when he had entered Neddy's box at the track, two strangers had been waiting. Bill collectors, as it turned out, hired and sent there by Cecil's own dear friends, and Neddy had even bragged that it had been a kindness to trap him with a social invitation. "The alternative, old chap," he'd said, slapping Cecil's shoulder as if this were all some sort of grand joke, "would have been to send them to your home and I would not insult your mother in such a way."

Was he supposed to thank them for confronting him there at the track, with the townspeople gaping on, rather than in the privacy of his own home? They knew he had no way of settling his bills on the spot, but Neddy had explained – while Cecil's so-called friends stood silently in the background – that his mother had been seen in her diamond and opal brooch on the unfortunate afternoon of the Wentworth hunt. An admirable piece, was it not? Selling it would not bring enough to settle all his accounts, but it would be a start.

The brooch was the last fine thing they had. The final remains of a love match gone hopelessly awry, and the one item

Gwynette had refused to sell. She would do without the carriage and walk to town if she must. She would fire the staff and wash her own stockings, but she would not release her grip on the diamond and opal brooch.

"I'll get it for you," Cecil had said, although he wasn't sure how. "I'll have it at your office, Neddy, 10 am tomorrow." And then the man had shown the audacity to offer Cecil a glass of champagne, to urge him to take a seat.

Cecil had walked home alone that night, stumbling in the darkness. At one point a carriage passed and – rather than be spied in his pitiable state – he had hidden behind a tree. He supposed he could get the brooch while his mother slept, but what good would it do to deliver their only valuable object into the graceless hands of Edmund Solmes? Within weeks, the notes would all be due again, this time with nothing to keep the creditors at bay. He'd come to a new low, he had, and as he walked Cecil talked aloud to himself, constructing a plan. It was audacious and risky, but he could think of nothing else. The brooch was the last solid place on which to stand while he built a new life.

When Cecil had arrived back in Winter Garden, his mother, William, and the cook were all asleep, just as expected. He packed his satchel in the darkness. It was not difficult to slip shoeless into his mother's bedroom, nor to find the brooch in the top drawer of her vanity. What proved more challenging was laying his hands on some actual cash. The account box was empty except for a few shillings. Whatever had William done with the proceeds from selling the carriage?

Try the obvious, Cecil had thought, and he had moved next into William's room. He was almost to the bureau when he caught sight of William's jacket, hanging over one of the posts of the bed and Cecil had smiled to himself in the darkness. There were benefits to having a witless brother. Cecil slipped a hand into one pocket and then the other while William gently snored.

From there it had been simple enough to walk to the station, to sleep on the bench outside. To catch the earliest train to London and to find some cheap and nondescript inn where he might stash his bundle and lay his head for an afternoon nap. What was happening at home did not concern him. When he did not arrive at Neddy's office at ten, he could presume the man had sent his unpleasant minions to Winter Garden where William and Gwynette could quite honestly proclaim to have neither any knowledge of Cecil's whereabouts nor those of the diamond and opal brooch.

And this, he thought as he claimed a barstool, was the last place anyone would expect to find him. He looked nervously about but luckily the singing and drinking had already begun and his awkwardness went unnoticed. Cecil accepted a beer, slumped forward and began to listen to the stories about Mary. There were some tears, for Mary had been truly liked by many in the East End. Cecil hoisted his mug to every stranger, honoring a woman he had never met. Accepting the buss of a weeping girl in ripped black satin who obviously mistook him for a former client, he tilted his head toward the two men sitting behind him, who were deep in conversation.

"Mary 'ad family, you know?" sputtered a small sandy-haired man who had pulled a cap over his eyes in a concession to mourning. "Wealthy one's, they were. Lived up on Mayfair. She used to walk up there at times to check on 'em. I went with 'er once, I did. I 'ate the sons-of-bitches. Mary 'ad a sweet 'eart, she did. Always a smile for 'ol Georgy." With tears in his eyes, he drank down half the pint and signaled for another.

"Mary 'ad fam'ly in Mayfair?" His friend did not openly challenge Georgy's story but his tone was skeptical.

"That she did. A sister. Emma was 'er name. Mary worried 'bout 'er all the time. And 'er in that fancy house and Mary on the street. Sickens me to think."

So Mary indeed was the sister of the girl Leanna had befriended, just as he had expected and hoped. And he was not the only one who knew this. His mind spinning with a hundred small adjustments to his plan, he turned toward the men. "Someone ought to get even with that Mayfair bitch," Cecil said. "Teach that Emma Kelly a lesson."

Georgy nodded so vigorously he nearly slipped off his stool, but his more sober friend's face was still full of doubt. "Like what?" he asked. "What could the likes of us do to a lady who had found 'er way to Mayfair?"

Georgy gulped down his remaining ale and slammed down his mug in disgust on the table top. "Dunno, but 'e's right, the man is. Mary deserves better."

Cecil smiled at Georgy, who would clearly prove useful before this affair was done. "Well, Sir, it looks like you're about ready for another pint." He passed his own mug toward Georgy and signaled to the barkeep for a replacement.

"Sir? I'm no sir," answered Georgy, looking up at Cecil. "But I am thirsty. Thanks, mate." He grabbed the mug and swallowed almost half in the first gulp. "Don't think I seen ye before, mate."

"I'm not from London, but I knew Mary from a long time ago. Damn that Ripper, she was such a sweet girl."

"I know, Mary and me was close. I'll miss her more 'an anyone in this room."

"And to think she was living so poor but had family in Mayfair," Cecil reminded him. Essential to keep the man on track. The friend, with some eye rolling, stood and departed in search of livelier conversation and Cecil slid smoothly onto the stool the man vacated. "Undoubtedly Mary's heart was bigger

298

than their whole house. What did you say the sister's name was, Emma? And you know where she is?"

"Not 'ere, that's for sure," Georgy said, looking about wildly. "Safe on 'er cushion, takin 'er tea, too fine to give poor Mary the time of day. I'd like to fix 'er fancy bottom."

"Family is family," Cecil said sanctimoniously, as Georgy drained his glass. "Mary might be alive today if Emma had helped her. But what could we do?"

"I be thinking," Georgy promised, foamy spittle in both corners of his mouth.

"And I'll help you. You know, I think we should put a real scare in them. Let them feel terror the way Mary did," Cecil said. "What about this? We could send a letter to Mayfair. Tell them Mary had a baby and we'd been caring for the tot since her death. We'd tell them they should have the baby since they're blood family, but for our trouble we'd want a hundred pounds. We'd have them meet us down here. Then we'd hire someone to rob them and rough them up a bit. We could split the money and buy sweet Mary a proper tombstone. That would be getting even. Wouldn't you say?"

"I like the idea, rough 'em up a mite," said Georgy, his face lightening, then falling. "But 'ey didn't care for Mary, so why should 'ey care for 'er baby?"

Funny time for the dolt to begin getting logical, Cecil thought. He'd been relieved to note that up to this point Georgy had asked no questions about his accent or his clothes.

"Because it's a baby. Everyone cares about a baby. Anyhow, it's worth a try. For Mary's sake. If it doesn't, I mean, if it don't work we'll think of something else. You can't turn your nose up to fifty pounds each, can you?"

"Fifty pounds could buy 'ol Georgy a proper holiday."

"First we have to find someone who we can hire to do the robbing and roughing up. Do you know anyone, Georgy? This is my first trip to London. I haven't a friend."

"Lemme think."

"Someone big and scary looking."

"Know just the brute," Georgy said, rising unsteadily to his feet and waving down a passing man. "Hey chap," he said, "Whassa name of that ugly Pole from the slaughterhouse?"

The man turned to consider both Georgy and Cecil. Cecil felt his confidence erode a bit, since it was clear this fellow was completely sober, perhaps the only person in the bar who could claim that distinction. When he had looked at Cecil, he had clearly noted the gilded buttons on his jacket and the cleanliness of his hands.

"You want Micha," he said.

"Micha, that's the one," Georgy said. "'e'd put the fear in the devil himself."

"'True," the man said slowly, still gazing at Cecil. "Micha will do anything."

Cecil felt a strange chill, although he couldn't have said precisely why. His plan was coming together with lightning speed, as if ordained by the angels themselves, and yet there was something about this fellow that made it clear he was not deceived by Cecil in the least. He had stretched out the word "an-y-thing" with a strange sort of emphasis. Of course, he seemed foreign, with that dark skin and the ridiculous girth of his mustache, quite possibly a Pole himself, so perhaps he was simply over-enunciating a word that was not common to him. Cecil feigned interest in his beer and the man slipped away into the crowd.

Georgy was pounding the table in delight. "Micha, yeah, 'e's as big as Gibral'eer. And mean enough to murder 'is own mum for ten pounds."

"How do we find this fellow?"

"Leave it to 'ol Georgy."

"Good. Then I'll draft a letter and have it sent to the Mayfair home. Could you show me where it is?"

"I'll take ye in the morning. Mary will 'ave a beautiful tombstone to lay at 'er 'ead."

And Leanna will jump at this bait like no other, Cecil thought, quite pleased with himself. A do-gooder like his little sister wouldn't let a maid venture to Whitechapel alone, and venture for a helpless baby they surely would. Cecil sat back and smiled at Georgy. Life was so much easier when you were surrounded with idiots.

CHAPTER THIRTY-FOUR
November 11, 1888
4:40 PM

Trevor watched the mortuary assistants lower the torso
inside the regulation coffin. The girl's clothing had all been
burned so they had wrapped her in the same mummy-like white
muslin the coroners used to bind wounds. One leg had never
been found and the other had been reserved for research.

"Should we put in the face?" Trevor asked hopelessly,
thinking of the neatly-trimmed oval of skin he had found on the
bedside table.

"There's nothing to be gained by keeping it," Phillips said.
"But since we're bereft of a skull...."

"Perhaps this, Sir?" Severin said, holding up a wooden head
and neck. "I knew she was going in the box today and I fetched
it from a hatmaker."

"Good thinking," Phillips said, and they stepped back as the
man laid the wooden head at the top of the torso and deftly
draped the leathery skin of a woman's face across it. Trevor bit
his lip to hold back a bark of hysterical laughter. This was the
point in the process where they normally photographed the
dead, but in this case no one suggested they do so.

Everyone said that Mary Kelly had been beautiful. The
newspapers had paid for a sketch artist to reproduce her features
from the memories of friends. It was this image of a pretty,
smiling girl that Trevor tried to focus on as Severin lowered the
coffin lid for a final time. Presumably Geraldine, with her
ample funds and even more ample tendency for guilt, would
replace this pauper's box with a handsome coffin and Trevor did
not envy the unsuspecting Mayfair undertaker who would pull

out the nails and open the lid to find what was waiting for him inside.

Of course he would have to talk to Emma eventually. It was wrong of him not to have gone to Kingsly Street already, but he hoped his work would serve, as it always had in the past, as a readily accepted excuse for social laxity. For he knew that Emma, when he did finally see her, would demand the same assurances that family members always sought in these circumstances – she would want to be told that her sister didn't suffer and that Scotland Yard would catch the killer. Trevor could offer no comfort on either score. He had kept Mary's books. After a suitable time he would bring them to Emma and hope that was enough.

This morning he arrived at his lab early, and went into the back storage area where the left leg of Mary Kelly was waiting, packed in ice. He had kept this part of the body specifically because of a long slash wound that ran diagonally above the ankle, as if the killer had considered peeling back the skin there or perhaps severing the foot. Either way, the wound was deep and clean, the first real sample Trevor possessed of the Ripper's handiwork since he'd begun to read up on the French blade identification methods. He had melted wax over the little laboratory flame at one end of the table and now he pushed aside the sheet to take a closer look at the leg, to make sure it was free from any stray fibers or hairs.

"Detective Welles? Do you mind if I come in?"

Trevor automatically dropped the white cloth back over the leg, as if protecting its owner from public scandal, and looked up to see Thomas Bainbridge standing in the hall outside his office. "Tom," he said with surprise, "I was just thinking I wanted to talk to you. Come in, have a seat, and please, call me Trevor."

Tom plopped his lanky form into the nearest chair. "So this is Scotland Yard, eh?" he asked, glancing around the dim, small room. "I must say it's exciting to be here."

"Oh, the Ritz, to be sure. How are things at Geraldine's?"

Tom made a pained face. "Emma is adrift on a sea of tranquilizers, while Leanna is hovering outside in the hall. Aunt Gerry is distressed she couldn't have done something for Mary while she lived, although of course it would have been impossible for even Aunt Gerry to rescue a person she did not know existed."

"It doesn't appear the girl wanted to be rescued," Trevor said. "Evidently she liked her way of life well enough."

Tom indicated the cloth on the table. "Might I ask what you're working on?"

Trevor hesitated for a second, but the boy was a medical student, after all. "Very well," he said, and pulled back the sheet.

Tom stood slowly. "Is that what I think it is? Or rather, I suppose I should say, did it come from the body of – "

"I'm afraid so, and it's precisely why I wanted to talk to you. I recently had a conversation with your sister and we discussed a new methodology the French have to identify weapons. The report says they're using wax but I'm having no luck getting a clean imprint. Leanna seemed to remember your grandfather once make impressions from animal bites."

Tom nodded. "He did, but it was plaster, not wax."

"Leanna said he learned the technique from a taxidermist."

"Really? I thought it was a dentist. Either way, he adapted it. I wish I could tell you how. She and I were children at the time...."

"Did he keep notes on his experiments?"

"Indeed, copious ones." Tom looked at Trevor curiously. "Are you asking for my help?"

"Only unofficially. See this slash above the ankle. If we could find out what sort of weapon...."

"If I can help at all, I'm in," Tom said with enthusiasm. So much, in fact, that he seemed to realize his reaction may have been a bit too eager under the circumstances, for he lowered his voice to the point of a whisper. "I'll have our solicitor collect the journals from Rosemoral and send them here by courier. Grandfather was quite systematic in his studies, so if there's anything helpful there at all, we shall have it by the end of the week."

Trevor smiled at the young man. "Excellent, but that's not the only reason I'm glad you're in Mayfair. I hope the ladies can bring themselves to understand why I haven't called to offer my condolences. During the last few days I've been forced to face things..."

"Don't be absurd, Trevor," Tom broke in. "No one expected you to leave your work at a time like this and Emma did rouse herself long enough to admire the flowers you sent. Yellow roses were Mary's favorite, by chance, and Emma commented on it."

"I noticed that her bedclothes had yellow roses when I was in her room," Trevor said, trying not to think back too clearly upon that place. "How did you hear of the tragedy?"

"John Harrowman wired me on the very day the body was found. Leanna said he was a rock, a true rock, the only one who could get through to Emma at all."

Trevor frowned. "John Harrowman wired for you?"

"Yes, he's visiting at this very moment, which is why I stepped out for a bit."

"Tom, I suppose there's something else I must tell you. Coming to the lab during the day would be most helpful, but I'd prefer it if you stay close to home at night. We have coppers on surveillance, but there's no substitute for a man inside the house. John Harrowman is a suspect."

"You're joking," Tom said slowly.

"Do you think I would joke about this? He's a skilled surgeon that frequents the East End, he knew at least some of the victims, he's ambidextrous... "

"Those facts could apply to other men!" Tom cried. Trevor raised his hand.

"Hear me out. Two days ago, the day of the killing, my assistant was watching the Kelly house. He spotted a well-dressed man poking about, a man who loosely fit the description two prostitutes gave us after the night of the double murders. Davy followed the man to an address that turned out to be Harrowman's , then on to Geraldine's."

"I know why he was there, he told me himself," Tom said, his voice rising in anger. "Mary Kelly was one of his patients. When he learned she was the one who had been killed he went to her home as a kind of tribute, to pay respects. That was before he knew she was Emma's sister, of course. And certainly you can place him in close conjunction with the women of the East End, his profession explains that. I won't hear any more against him."

"I don't blame you for being upset. I've had trouble accepting it myself."

Tom's eyes narrowed. "I know what this is about. The evening we were together playing charades you couldn't keep your eyes off Leanna. I saw it, we all did. Teased her about it later. But it's just as plain that she's smitten for John, which is why you've concocted this ridiculous case against him."

"I don't hate John, no matter what you think..."

"Do you have real evidence? Enough to arrest him?"

Trevor sat back with a sigh. "No."

"I didn't think so. And you expect me to be the one to give it to you, by identifying that this wound was made from a surgical knife. As if he's the only man in London who might possess such a thing."

"You don't have to like it, Tom. I don't like it myself. I've got the best detective I know out on the streets right now working to determine John's whereabouts during the five dates in question. And no doubt he will establish a perfect alibi and I will most humbly beg your pardon for this whole conversation. But in the meantime, humor me and stay close to the ladies."

"I'll stay close to them, you know I will. You don't have to fabricate stories about John Harrowman to press me into my duty."

Before Trevor could reply, the door swung open and Davy entered. "Sorry, Sir, didn't know you had a guest."

"This is Thomas Bainbridge, Davy, nephew to my friend Geraldine and a medical student at Cambridge. He has come to volunteer his services on the case. Tom, Davy Madley, my assistant."

His face still flushed, Tom rose to shake Davy's hand.

"What's that?" Trevor asked, indicating a small white box Davy was carrying.

"Just came, Sir," Davy replied, glancing meaningfully at Tom. "Another message from the Ripper and a pretty grisly one at that."

"Let's hear it," Trevor said.

"Let's see it, is a bit more like it, Sir," Davy said, gingerly setting the box before Trevor.

Trevor unknotted the twine and pulled back a bit of paper to reveal, to his disgust, another human kidney, this one undoubtedly from Mary Kelly. "Oh Christ," breathed Tom. Trevor reached below the paper for the crumpled note.

"'HERE'S A FINE KIDNEY. I ATE THE OTHER ONE. IT WAS DELICIOUS! –JACK'"

"Kidneys seem to be his favorite, right Sir?" asked Davy who was rapidly becoming immune to horror.

Tom gripped the top of Trevor's desk, his face pale. "So you honestly think John Harrowman is capable of cannibalism?" he asked incredulously. "How can you believe for a second that you are not dealing with a total lunatic, a madman devoid of any human feeling?" Tom stepped back, his eyes never leaving Trevor's face. "And yet you expect me to help build your case? That shall never happen! I admire him, Detective, just as I once admired you." With this Tom spun and fairly ran from the room, his heavy boots clattering down the hallway. Trevor gazed after him pensively.

"You told him, Sir?" Davy asked with surprise. "Told him I followed Harrowman?"

"He's in the house where Harrowman visits and in the perfect position to observe and report, so yes, I told him," Trevor said grimly. "But evidently I misjudged his ability to handle the information."

"And should I try to ascertain his whereabouts, Sir?" Davy spoke with grave formality, which was marred only by the fact he mispronounced "ascertain" by putting the emphasis on the second syllable. Otherwise, the statement sounded precisely like something Abrams would say. Trevor supposed it would make sense, that the boy would choose to imitate the man who seemed polished and unflappable rather than the one who swayed and cursed and roared, but on another level he felt a pang of remorse. He was not doing an especially good job of maintaining his professional dignity and his underlings seemed to realize that. Trevor glanced around. There was virtually no privacy in the lab and Severin had been cleaning up loudly during his argument with Tom, washing his tubes and trays with such uncharacteristic clatter that he were probably just struggling not to overhear the fight. Who could guess what the mortuary assistant truly thought of him and Tom's words had stung too, that phrase "just as I once admired you." Perhaps it wasn't Trevor's job to mentor the younger men in his life, but it was still sobering to be reminded he was failing so spectacularly in the role.

"Abrams is working on alibis for Harrowman," he gently reminded Davy.

"Not Harrowman, Sir. Tom Bainbridge. He's a medical student, didn't you say?"

"Tom? But he's –" Trevor caught himself before he could make the same mistake twice, could claim that the fact he'd met a man socially eliminated him as a suspect. "He wasn't in London for the murders," he amended.

"Wasn't staying at his aunt's house, isn't that what you mean, Sir?"

"Yes, I suppose it is." Now the bobbies were schooling him. Davy was right. Not spending the night at Geraldine's was hardly proof the Bainbridge boy hadn't been in London. Trains ran between Paddington and Cambridge on the hour. "All right, ascertain his whereabouts" – Trevor took care to enunciate the word correctly – "and report back to me."

The boy nodded and left, and Trevor signaled to Severin to come and fetch this latest kidney. He could scarcely feature Tom as a serious suspect, but neither could he picture John in that role, and his instincts, he must admit, were proving no more valuable than a confession from Hoppy Darby. Friendship wasn't an alibi and neither was education nor breeding nor a Mayfair address. He had been struggling to teach these lessons to others and it was perhaps time he learned them himself.   In the future there would be no feelings in this room, only facts.

Trevor sighed as he pulled back the cloth to once again reveal the lonely leg of Mary Kelly.   Sometimes he hated being a modern man.

CHAPTER THIRTY-FIVE
5:40 PM

The second note is more direct. She wants money.

Part of him is relieved. He has lain awake the last two nights wondering at her intent. Did she plan to reveal him to the authorities? Set herself up as some sort of heroine, the woman who single-handedly learned the identity of Jack the Ripper? But of course not, he'd tried to console himself, as he tossed among the sheets of his narrow bed. If she planned to go to Scotland Yard she would have already been there. She certainly would not have alerted him to her identity, placed herself in the sights of his rifle.

Of course she wants money. That is all her kind can think to want.

He has written back, arranged to meet her in this bar. It is early and the place nearly empty, as he knew it would be. He notes her arrival by the mirror that hangs behind the whisky bottles. The jagged crack down its center distorts the woman's image, makes her look, if possible, even larger and more malformed than she is. Their paths have crossed before in Whitechapel, many times, and after a quick scan of the room, she walks toward him without hesitation. Where he prides himself on invisibility she is somewhat a legend in these parts. Strange in appearance, stranger still in behavior and while she always seems to be present, hovering on the periphery of the drunkenness and whoring, few have ever caught her in the act of conversation.

Nor does she talk now. Simply hefts herself to the stool beside his. They both stare straight ahead, as if fascinated by the familiar sight of the stacked beer steins and rows of gummy glasses. He puts the knotted handkerchief on the bar and she places her broad palm over it. She has not asked for much, but he suspects she will ask again. And yet again and again and indeed this is a problem, something he must address in the very near future. He is amazed by her boldness, at the fact she would attempt to blackmail a man she knows to be capable of murder. Does she believe that her size offers her protection? Her reputation for violence? Her own reputed skill with a knife?

Most likely she had been startled to see him leaving Mary Kelly's house, to realize with the publication of the next day paper's precisely what it was she had witnessed. Undoubtedly her plan of blackmail is in its infancy, evolving just as his is. She merely wants money now, but she may want something more later.

He gulps his beer, ashamed that she has rattled him. Normally the Kelly girl would have been enough, would have sated him for weeks. Still plenty of juice left in that memory, still plenty of souvenirs to fondle and consider. The days after a kill were normally the sweetest and most tranquil of his life. But this new complication has agitated him, has shattered his sense of well being. He gives a quick, furtive glance toward Maud. His knife is small, designed more for precision than depth, and this woman is well insulated, armored in muscle, swathed in layers of fat. Could he penetrate her, even if she wished? A stab to the torso would fall short of any vital organs and approaching her from the front could invoke hand-to-hand combat, a fight he may not win. Even a throat slice from behind would be tricky. She is taller than most men.

She shoves the handkerchief into her pocket. Grunts. Whether the sound was an attempt at communication or merely an indication of how hard it was to move her bulky arse from the bar stool, he cannot say. He has paid her this first time because she startled him, came at him before he could formulate a plan. But he will not be threatened again and again. He will not walk the streets expecting to see her beady, pig-like eyes at every turn.

Something will have to be done about Maud Milford.

CHAPTER THIRTY-SIX
5:10 PM

Even though he considered Trevor's accusations ludicrous, Tom still found himself running as he made his way back to Mayfair. He arrived to find the house not only in order, but almost a parody of tranquil domesticity, with a fire crackling in the hearth, Emma's yellow roses on the table, and the smell of baking bread wafting in from the kitchen.

No danger here. Absolutely none. Trevor Welles was a fool and Tom had been just as much of one for letting himself become swept up in the man's wild theories. Tom's hands were shaking as he made his way to Geraldine's liquor cabinet and poured a large brandy. It had been cold and dank outside like only November in London can be and Tom had not buttoned his coat or knotted his scarf in his hasty departure from Scotland Yard. He pulled an armchair near the fire, wrapping himself in a shawl Geraldine had left on her footstool, and began to drink with a steady determination.

He would send for his grandfather's old medical journals, yes he would. He would find a way to gain access to the type of knives John used in his surgical practice and he would assist Trevor in his wound studies at Scotland Yard. Because Tom had no doubt, absolutely none, that any information brought to light there would exonerate John Harrowman. He personally would discover the sort of irrefutable scientific evidence that no one could deny. Tom drained his glass, poured another, and closed his eyes as he thought of his grandfather. Leonard had always said that science was his religion, a statement he would follow with a soft little laugh, so that anyone who chose not to believe such a radical statement could say "But of course he was joking." Leonard knew the opinions held by his neighbors, and accepted that they would consider his atheism a personal assault. He didn't fear their censure, but neither did he wish to distress them. He was gentlemanly enough to couch even his deepest beliefs inside a chuckle.

But Tom had certainly known that his grandfather wasn't joking. Science was not only his profession, but the basis on which he lived his life. Leonard had taught both of his younger grandchildren to hold scientific truth in high esteem, even when that truth was neither convenient nor reassuring. Tom had been happy to hear that his sister had fallen in love with a doctor, partly because he understood how much this sort of match would have pleased their grandfather. For the first time he was also willing to concede that perhaps Cecil had a point when he said Tom's desire to flatter Leonard had driven him to attend medical school.

Tom gulped again, then poured again. The brandy had at first burned him, then warmed him, and now once more was burning. He pushed off Geraldine's shawl and reached down to unbuckle his boots. Not an easy task. He groaned and leaned back in the chair, one boot off and the other still on. Wasn't there a child's nursery rhyme about a man in just such a state? God knows, that was what his older brothers had always said, that Tom had known the route to Leonard's heart ran through the medical schools of Cambridge, that his studies were nothing more than a way to win their grandfather's approval, and ultimately his patronage.

And perhaps they were right, at least about what his motives might have been at the start. A boy doesn't know what he wants to be, so he follows in the steps of the man he most admires. Nothing criminal in that, is there? But during his time at Cambridge Tom had gradually developed, if not Leonard's all-consuming passion, at least a deeper respect for science and the character of the men who worshipped at this particular shrine.

318

John Harrowman was a man who had devoted his life to helping the wretches of the earth and it seemed that in accusing John, Trevor had been accusing Tom himself, and Leonard, and the brotherhood of doctors. Tom splashed the last of the brandy into his tilted glass. Damn the man. A shudder ran through him and Tom pulled the shawl more tightly. Cold, then hot, then cold again.

I'll send for grandfather's notebooks this very day, Tom thought. But first I'll take a nap.

The clock was striking five as Leanna entered the sitting room, and with one glance she knew Tom was drunk. Not the giggly, early-drinking type of intoxication either, but rather the cold-limbed still-bodied type of stupor that is the result of a relentless, almost medicinal type of drinking. She had seen first her father and then her brother Cecil in this same position many times and now she looked down on Tom with poorly-concealed exasperation. He had been called on to act as man of the house and a mere twelve hours after his arrival he was incapable of defending them from a gnat. Leanna pulled the pillow from behind his head, and waited for his eyes to flutter open.

"Do you want tea?"

Tom shuddered.

"You should have food."

"Brandy. I'm chilled to the bone," he said thickly.

"Brandy is the last thing you need," Leanna said irritably. "What will Aunt Gerry say when she sees you like this?"

"Doubt she'll care."

He was probably right on that one, but Leanna was not prepared to concede the point. "I thought you were going to see Trevor Welles."

"I did."

"And then came home and finished a bottle."

Tom threw back the shawl as he was hit with a heat wave which produced small prickles of perspiration all along his flushed face. "Damn it, Leanna, this has all been a bit much to take in."

"So sorry you've suffered. Emma hasn't left her room all day, not that you asked." Leanna exhaled slowly, suddenly aware of how much she sounded like her mother when her tongue grew sharp. For the first time in her life she was beginning to understand how hard it must have been for Gwynette to put her husband to bed night after night, year after year. "Aunt Gerry and I are going out," she said, her tone more civil. "A friend of hers has just become a grandmother and we're going to see the babies." She shook her head before Tom could object. "Gage is coming with us," she said. "And we'll be back early. The better question is whether or not you're fit to stand guard over Emma. She's had something to eat and will probably sleep away the evening, but I hate the thought of her calling for something and you being too drunk to answer."

"I'm fine," Tom said, standing up to illustrate his point. "I'll have a bit of tea and toast and be even more completely fine by the time you leave. But isn't Emma sleeping a lot? I have the impression she's been sedated for three days in a row and that may not be prudent."

"John seems to feel it's best."

"But she has to confront what's happened at some point, doesn't she? What did he give her, do you know?"

"Morphine."

Three days on morphine? That seemed excessive, and Tom felt a return of the same nameless unease that had stuck him while walking home from Scotland Yard. "Morphine is serious business, Leanna," he said. "The longer the drugs are in her system the harder it will be for her to shake off the effects."

"Of course, John said as much, but he was also afraid she was a danger to herself. He said he'd never seen grief that violent on anyone."

"What was she doing?"

Leanna looked at him. "Crying, of course."

"Seems a natural enough reaction under the circumstances. Why would he think that made her a danger to herself?"

"I'm sure I don't know," Leanna said in exasperation. "You can discuss it with John tomorrow. Until then just promise me you'll stay alert."

"I'm fine," Tom said, starting his wobbly progress toward the kitchen. "A bit of toast and tea and I'll be the best sentry in London."

6:10 PM

With Gerry, Leanna, and Gage gone and food in his stomach, Tom pulled his anatomy book from his satchel and returned to the fire. Thanks to his nap, he had never gotten his wire off to Galloway, but he could do that tomorrow and in the meantime, perhaps he could find some useful information about scalpels in the chapter on surgery. He balanced the heavy book in his lap and hunched over it like an invalid.

Despite his brave talk in front of Leanna, Tom was still somewhat under the effects of the brandy and after only a page or two he found himself drowsy again. He sat very still and listened, but there was not a sound from upstairs and he finally decided that a small splash of brandy might ease the pressure in his head. The first bottle was gone but Geraldine was an excellent hostess, always prepared for an unexpected guest, and

Tom suspected she kept a well-stocked bar. He pushed himself to his feet and headed back toward the liquor cabinet.

7:25 PM

Tom awoke with a start and struggled to sit up, his head throbbing and his eyes painfully slow to adjust to the murky darkness. How much time had passed? An hour? Two? He was dimly aware of a presence in the room and turned to look behind his chair. No one there, and no one in the far corner. Just as he was willing to concede the drink had made his imagination take over his senses, he saw Emma at the writing desk, dressed in a white flowing robe with her hair down. She looked like a ghostly bride and Tom nearly let loose an involuntary cry.

Emma sat still, gazing at him with a serious and unblinking expression. She had apparently begun to roam the house as the drugs gradually loosened their grip on her nervous system; Tom had observed the same effect on patients and he knew it was imperative he get her back upstairs before she stumbled and managed to really hurt herself. The only trouble was, he was none too steady on his own feet and now that his eyes could make out the mantle clock he could see it was nearly seven-thirty. The rest of the household would be back soon and would see how utterly he'd shirked his duty. He couldn't bear another lecture from Leanna.

"Emma dear," he ventured, in what he hoped was a pleasant tone of voice, for his head roared with the effort of speech and his tongue felt like cotton. "You should be up in your bed. May I help you?" She made no sign of having heard him, her eyes still unnervingly fixed. "Emma," he tried again wincing

322

with the effort of pushing his body away from the chair and stretching it to its full height. "You should be upstairs."

"No," she said. "I'm tired of that room."

"Then sit here," he said, knowing it was best not to argue with someone whose system was withdrawing from powerful doses of morphine. "Sit here in the armchair, and we'll talk, you and I. Perhaps," he added heroically, for the thought of entering the kitchen was comparable to the idea of scaling Everest, "I could get you something to eat."

"No," she said again, her small chin jutting and her arms folded corpse-like around her chest.

Think of her, not yourself, Tom's fevered brain implored. She's a patient and this is a test of your skills. A doctor must function even when tired. Even when sick himself. Yes, even when drunk on his feet.

Tom walked toward the small form, one hand outstretched. "You worry me sitting here alone, Emma."

"I'm not alone. You're here."

"I suppose I am, in a way," he admitted. "So shall we talk?"

"No! I'm talked out. Leanna thought I should talk and Doctor John and Geraldine and even Gage brought up my tea this afternoon and said 'Let it out, Miss Emma, tell Gage about your burden.' I've talked all I intend to talk."

"Very well, so that wasn't a good idea. You won't talk, you won't eat or sleep. What will you do?"

She looked at him with piercing blue eyes. "I want you to hold me."

He was a bit taken aback, wondering for a minute if he had managed to hear her correctly. But she had been through an unimaginable blow, so perhaps a bit of old-fashioned comfort was in order. Would a good doctor agree to such a request? Would John? Tom glanced at the clock. The main thing was to get her back upstairs before Leanna returned.

"Of course," he said. "But we should go upstairs. This room is so gloomy, don't you think?"

She frowned, tilted her head a bit questioningly. Perhaps she's coming round, Tom thought, because she's caught me in my little lie. Everyone knew the parlor was the warmest and most pleasant room in Gerry's house. But she allowed him to take both of her hands in his and lead her to the stairs. They ascended them like a train, with his arms around her waist, standing behind her on the step below and steadily, gently pushing. Just getting to the first landing in this ridiculous position was a struggle, but when he released her for a second, she swayed so wildly he was afraid she'd spill down the stairs.

"Better carry you," he said, and she did not resist.

He flexed his knees and scooped her up. She was a small girl so lifting her did not disturb his fragile balance as much as he feared it would. "There, there," he said, or something very like it, the sort of thing he imagined a real doctor would say. Her gown was thin, nearly wispy, and he had the uneasy thought that in better light the white muslin would be totally transparent. He cradled her gingerly, taking care not to let too much flesh touch flesh, but his efforts at restraint were pointless for, with a tremulous sigh, Emma suddenly sagged against him, her whole torso sinking into his and her head rolling back on his shoulder. It was an alarmingly good fit.

And precisely what would John do now, Tom wondered, his heart involuntarily beating a bit faster. Ironically his first thought upon leaving Trevor's office had been to seek solace in the arms of one of the Whitechapel girls. A mad impulse under the circumstances, and yet he had stood in the street outside of Scotland Yard and debated what direction to go, east or west. He'd wondered if the bars were full or empty and he'd imagined just this – that frightened bodies were clinging to other frightened bodies all over London. Anxiety and despair were stimulants in their own right, as apt to make people seek company as any other emotions. But his feet had turned west, home to Mayfair, with the familiar old ache so enormous in his chest that it had taken almost two bottles of brandy to quiet it.

Now here was Emma, Emma whom he had always liked. No... cherished, really cherished, in a way, which was all the more reason he should wrest her arms from around his neck and leave her alone in her room. He nudged open the door with his foot, carried her to the tousled bed. She murmured something indistinct, let her head fall back a bit further and their eyes met, both misting and slow to focus, and before Tom could muster another thought he was kissing her, falling over her with a mixture of relief and grief he could not begin to understand. Who was to comfort whom? Tom could hear, as from far away, the sound of someone crying, and when he pulled away just enough to gaze at Emma's face he found it damp and salty. He was so overcome with tenderness that he utterly failed to notice the tears were his own.

CHAPTER THIRTY-SEVEN
November 12
7:05 AM

Leanna was up early the next morning. Tiptoeing into the hall, she saw that both Emma and Gerry's doors were still closed and, at the top of the stairs, Gage's was likewise sealed. Tom's was slightly ajar, as she'd noticed with approval the night before. He had gone to bed before they'd returned from Tess's house, which was not terribly surprising considering the condition he'd been in when she left, but at least he'd shown enough responsibility to keep his door cracked so he could hear Emma if she called.

No telling what shape he'd be in this morning, Leanna thought. Her father had required a strange potion to bring him back from the brink of a bender. Raw eggs shaken up with Worchester sauce, if she recalled correctly. She crept quietly to Tom's door and knocked.

The door swung open, revealing a disheveled bed. Leanna frowned. The household had gone to bits without Emma's guidance, and for the last few mornings everyone had made their own bed. None of them had the experience to be really up to the task, but Tom's efforts had been especially inept. The only laughter the household had heard in days was the gentle chuckle she and Tom had shared when he'd invited her into his room the morning before to show off his housekeeping skills.

The bed looked exactly the same now as it had then. There were two possible explanations. Tom had either risen before anyone else, once again made his bed badly and departed on an early errand, or....he hadn't slept in the bed at all.

Leanna felt a growing sense of alarm. When they had come in the night before they had found the empty glass on the parlor table, the open medical book, the small plate with the crusts of toast. Leanna had carried the glass and plate to the kitchen, a little ashamed that she had been so snappish with her brother earlier. He'd come the moment she asked him, had he not? He had spent weeks fighting for her, had he not? A drunken afternoon was not exactly unheard of in a man of his age. As she had wiped the dishes and put them away she had vowed to be kinder to him in the morning,

But here it was morning and there was no Tom to be kind to. Was it possible he could have slipped out in the night? Would he really have been so completely irresponsible as to leave Emma alone?

Emma. Now Leanna's dread was growing. What if something had happened to Emma? Running lightly, still reluctant to frighten Aunt Gerry if it turned out all was well, Leanna ascended the stairs two at a time and, without knocking, threw open Emma's door, where she was greeted with the sight of Tom and Emma sprawled across the bed as if they'd both been dropped there, naked, from a great height.

"Mother of God," she exhaled, sinking back against the doorframe and involuntarily averting her eyes. The sight of the human body did not upset Leanna unduly; she had seen enough of Leonard Bainbridge's anatomy books and models to know how it was constructed. But this particular scene was so without modesty or indeed, even consciousness, that she was momentarily ashamed.

It's just Tom and Emma, she said to herself, partly to give herself courage, partly because in the dim recesses of her mind she recognized the ludicrousness of the situation. She had to have them up and dressed before Gerry and Gage awakened, so she gamely ventured toward her brother and dropped a nearby pillow over his hips.

"Tom," she said sharply, bending low and shaking him. "Tom, I don't care how badly you feel, you simply must get up." He remained immobile, his arm a dead weight when she tried to lift it.

Perhaps she would have better luck with Emma, who at least, in the worst case, she could probably lift. "Emma," she said pleadingly, crawling over Tom in an undignified manner and slapping Emma smartly on the face. "Emma, do you hear me?" She was rewarded with a slight stirring. Spying a water glass on the bedside table, Leanna picked it up and splashed it in Emma's face. To her great relief, Emma's eyes began to blink.

"Darling," Leanna said, helping the girl sit up. "Try to focus. Do you know where you are?"

Emma shook sleep from her eyes and pulled herself into an Indian position. Her eyes grazed across Tom, then to the overturned hassock at the foot of her bed and finally to her muslin gown, discarded in a corner and - not too surprisingly, Leanna noticed - smeared with a faint trace of blood.

"Oh my God," she said, nearly sinking down again, but Leanna caught her behind the shoulders.

"You're going to have to put your gown on help me get Tom back to his room."

"What....?"

"You don't remember?"

Emma looked vaguely around the room and then at Leanna. "I remember."

"Perhaps it's not what it looks like?"

"It's just what it looks like."

"I'm sure Aunt Gerry would under –"

"No," Emma cried out, with such ferocity and such clarity that Leanna jerked back. "We must get him back to his room. What time is it?"

"Just past seven," Leanna said.

"Gage will be up any minute," Emma said, and the girls sprung into action, Leanna moving quickly to gather up the strewn articles of Tom's clothing and Emma behind her, far less steady on her feet but just as systematic. She pulled on her gown and, grabbing Tom's shirt, began to push one of his hands through the sleeve.

Leanna shook her head. "No time for that," she said. "My mother always said it's impossible to dress a drunk. If we can just get him through the door of his room it won't matter that he wakes up naked." She piled Tom's clothes on his chest and took his hands in hers. "The top half of a body is the heaviest," she said. "If I can carry this end, can you carry the other?"

"I suppose," Emma said, too surprised by Leanna's rapid-fire barrage of information to argue. She grabbed one of Tom's ankles in each hand and with the deep exhalation of a dockworker, started to pull him off the bed. When his body came to the edge of the mattress and dropped the girls nearly lost their grips but they readjusted their hand holds and managed to lug him to the door.

Leanna opened the door and peeked out. Gage's room was directly opposite Emma's and she could only hope that the thud caused by Tom's fall to the floor had not been audible in Gage's room or, far worse, awakened Gerry sleeping below. But Gage's door remained shut and Leanna turned back to face Emma.

With a nod, Leanna reached down again for her brother's hands and Emma took up the feet. They moved awkwardly out the bedroom door and toward the stairs. Leanna started down first but it was immediately apparent that if she preceded Emma, Tom's head would hit each step during their descent. Which served him right, as far as she was concerned, but Emma had immediately frozen and indicated through a jerk of her chin that they should switch positions, allowing her to go first. Leanna leaned against the railing to let Emma pass her, which Emma could only do by pulling Tom's legs around her waist and bringing her pelvis up against his own. Leanna shut her eyes and tried to persuade herself that she would laugh about this someday. That someday she would be an old lady and the memory of this morning would be amusing indeed. But for now all she could do was press into the railing, looking first up at Gage's closed door and then down at Gerry's, praying that neither would open while Emma inched her way around her. The clothes piled on Tom's chest fell off during the transfer of positions, but there was nothing to be done about that. Both girls simply looked down at his nude body with dismay and Leanna kicked the garments aside. Then, with Emma moving backward and Leanna forward, they managed to turn on the landing and make it down the final flight of stairs. Leanna's arms felt like they were breaking by the time they reached Tom's door and dragged him through. The bed was impossibly high so they abandoned him on the rug. Emma sprinted out, presumably to fetch his clothes from the stairwell and Leanna stood gazing down at her brother.

"If you ever gain consciousness," she said aloud. "I'm going to kill you."

"I suppose you think I'm dreadful," Emma said, entering with the clothes which, after a second of thought, she dropped back on top of Tom.

"No," Leanna said. "I don't know what I think, but I know it isn't that. He never should have – "

"Tom was blameless. Truly. I seduced him. Come on, they can't find us here."

They returned to the door, looked both ways and slipped out, both going down the stairs toward the kitchen. Leanna was trying to figure out what the word 'seduced' meant. The only thing that made sense was that Emma was saying that she was the one who had initiated something. I'll look it up later,

Leanna thought. She couldn't admit to Emma she had never heard the word.

"Emma," she did say, turning into the kitchen. "Why are you even awake?"

Emma used both hands to lift the tea kettle. "I stopped taking the medication yesterday. John used the injection needle the first two days but then he started leaving powder for me to mix in my tea. And I mixed a little less than he said and then a little less again."

Leanna stared at her. "You don't trust him?"

"Of course I do. It's just I know he would have let me sleep forever and a woman has to wake up eventually, wouldn't you say?"

There were a thousand things Leanna wanted to ask Emma. This odd morning, she thought, it's made us closer friends than we've ever been, but where do I begin? Her sister, my brother, the morphine, the Ripper, or the fact that she has done a seduce and I don't even know what that means? Women have to wake up eventually but girls...girls can apparently doze forever. Emma was waiting, tea kettle in hand.

"Are you hungry?" she asked.

"Yes," said Leanna. "But you should sit down. The strangest thing has happened in the last four days. You won't believe it and you'll take it as undeniable proof that we truly have come to the end of one world and the start of another."

"Really?" Emma said, and little hiccup slid through her lips. "Please tell me."

Leanna moved toward the stove. "I've learned how to fry an egg."

8:20 AM

They were a subdued party at the breakfast table. It was the first time Emma had joined them for a meal in days and both Gerry and Gage were very careful with her. Gerry was even whispering. For weeks the breakfast routine had included a pile of the daily papers but of course they were now verboten, and in their absence the conversation lagged. If it were not for the sounds of Emma's fork scraping against her plate as she ate with the slow and steady pace of a convalescent, there would have been times when the room was completely silent.

Tom entered at some point, wrapped tightly in his dark blue bathrobe. If he had been surprised to awaken on the floor, utterly naked, with his clothes tossed across his chest, his face didn't show it. He smiled at Emma and Leanna and told Gage he would only take toast.

Emma smiled back, but fleetingly, and her gaze soon returned to her eggs. Geraldine, who had never been able to bear prolonged silence, began some rambling story about the newborn twins while Leanna, glancing from her brother to Emma in what she hoped was a nonchalant manner, struggled to evaluate the situation. Unless Tom was a consummate actor, which she knew he was not, he had no memory beyond passing out in front of the fire and awakening in his own room. And Emma was doing absolutely nothing to jostle his recollections. In fact, she was completely playing the part of a woman straight from her sickbed, a patient still trying to shake off the last effects of morphine.

He doesn't remember, Leanna thought. And she doesn't want him to.

Earlier that morning, when Leanna had found Emma and Tom in bed together she had said that Geraldine would understand. And Emma of all people must have known that

Leanna was right, that Geraldine's big heart would have expanded around the idea of Emma reaching for Tom in a dark hour, of him tumbling into the temptation. It had never been Geraldine's disapproval Emma feared, Leanna saw that now. Emma had simply not wanted Tom to know of their night together.

But why? Leanna frowned down into her tea, trying to sort it all out as Aunt Gerry droned on, Emma ate steadily, and Tom accepted a plate of dry toast from Gage. If she had given herself to John Harrowman only to find that the next morning he did not remember the event she would have been crushed, but Emma seemed almost to have designed the evening this way. She is already slipping it back into some secret pocket of her mind, Leanna thought. She's tucking it away to pull out and reexamine at a later time, some evening when she's lonely, some morning when she needs a bit of private comfort.

It suddenly occurred to Leanna that Emma might love Tom, that she could have loved him for months. It was a painful thought.

So, if this was true, why would Emma do a seduce when Tom was barely conscious? Perhaps it was a matter of class, just one more thing that the circumstances of her birth doomed Leanna to never understand. Emma was a schoolteacher's daughter, had lived for years under the protection of Gerry's roof, and had most likely been, if the red smear on her gown was true indication, a virgin. Yet she had chosen to surrender that virginity in a situation that would not lead to love and marriage, would not even lead to a shared memory between herself and the man.

Her quest for John had certainly suffered some setbacks but at least their union was in the realm of social possibility and Leanna couldn't imagine what it would feel like to love a man you knew you would never have. Would you try to tamp down

334

the emotion? Scold yourself for going outside your station? Divert your desire onto the corner greengrocer or some more likely target? Or would you find a way to get at least a little of what you craved, to pull a few tattered pieces of satisfaction though the iron bars of the class system? Leanna remembered once, a Christmas back at Rosemoral, when she had looked up from the blessing at the holiday table and seen the servants clustered in the hallway, waiting for the signal to enter with their dishes. They had evidently been standing with their platters and tureens for some time, for the village parson tended to overpray, especially whenever he found himself dining in the homes of the wealthy. Leanna had opened her eyes in the middle of his prayer and looked around at the scene – the holly and red roses spilling down the center of the table, the gleaming silver, the frosted panes, and the servants waiting in the wings, their own heads bowed as well. She had happened to see one of the girls – had her name been Agnes? Abigail? - run her index finger swiftly along the rim of a platter and lift it to her lips for a quick taste. Leanna had clamped her eyes shut quickly, as if she had been the guilty one. It was much the same feeling she'd had when she stumbled across Emma and Tom this morning, the sense she was seeing something she had no right to see. She didn't blame the serving girl. There was such bounty all around her and yes, she would have access to the remains later, after the family had spooned though the dish and eaten all the good parts. But who could blame her for wanting just a little taste now, when the food was so lovely and hot and those who considered themselves better than her were all pretending to pray?

And perhaps this was just what Emma had done on the previous evening. Taken a bit of something she wanted while the family's attentions were devoted elsewhere. Considering it like that, Leanna thought, it makes a kind of brutal sense.

"….two fine boys, both plump and healthy," Geraldine said, finishing her story with such a note of triumph you would think she'd given birth to the twins herself.

"When were they born?" Tom asked.

"Friday nignt," Leanna answered, with a calculated glance at Emma. She did not have to add "The night Mary was murdered," for Tom understood her meaning at once.

"How did the mother fare?" he asked mildly.

"Oh, a long labor to be sure," Geraldine said. "But Tess praised John Harrowman to the skies. She said he arrived at her daughter's bedside at nightfall and was still there at dawn….."

There, Tom thought triumphantly. Let the envious Detective Welles put that in his pipe. John Harrowman spent the entire evening of the Kelly murder attending the delivery of a prosperous Mayfair matron. And I bet there's a way to prove that the murder weapon wasn't even a surgical knife. Tom was beginning to feel a little better, with a slow glow of energy and optimism rising in his chest. God knows he had drunk too much the night before, and there was no telling how he'd gotten himself upstairs, but the toast was helping and through the windows the sun was coming out. It showed promise of a cold and clear day, perfect for the task at hand, and even if he had not slept long, Tom had the sense he had slept well. Fragments of dreams had been coming back to him all morning. Odd dreams, but very pleasant.

CHAPTER THIRTY-EIGHT
9:30 AM

He has decided to flatter her. There are few of us immune to flattery, or to the ambition hidden beneath its husk. Even those who live in a dung heap dream of occupying a higher peak within the heap.

And so perhaps an abortionist fancies herself a medical practitioner, might welcome the chance to commune with a colleague.

He composes a note to her, taking care with the prose. Hoping that, as is so often the case, she can read better than she can write. He has been to the ironmonger, so he is prepared.

The note says that he has studied as a doctor, as she undoubtedly knows. That he sees the financial possibilities in her line of work. That perhaps it would be better if they put aside their differences in order to consider how they might help one another. She has her skills – how it pains him to write this sentence, how it gnaws at his gut – and he has his unique social position, one which brings him into contact with all manner of society including women who might have need of such her unique services. But unlike the Whitechapel wretches with their shillings and farthings, these women are prepared to pay in pounds and sterling.

He need go no further. She is a business woman, greedy to the core. She will see the advantages of such a union. He tells her that he has found a first client already and suggests a place where the three of them might meet. The girl in question is of good family. In a spot of trouble, true, but not willing to show her face in the Pony Pub. They must meet in a more secluded place. But the money will be good, he assures her. Far more than she could ever hope to get shaking the pockets of a working man like him.

He hopes she will believe him. That some combination of vanity and greed will overrun her senses. Convince her to drop all common sense and join league with the devil himself.

CHAPTER THIRTY-NINE
9:50 AM

Smoke billowed from Rayley Abrams' pipe as he stood on the dock and watched the other passengers walking up the gangway to the channelboat. The cargo was still being loaded and he hoped he had time to get through a full bowl before he boarded the ship. As pleased as he was by this opportunity to study in Paris, he did not relish the idea of crossing to France. He had taken to sea several times in his life, but had never enjoyed much luck with his stomach.

"We thought we might not catch you before you boarded," said Trevor, coming up from behind and slapping his shoulder. He seemed in unusually high spirits, almost as if he were taking the trip himself.

Abrams removed his pipe. "I still feel as though I'm deserting you."

"Nonsense. You'll be of much greater aid to us after you have learned all you can from the French. Ah, the ocean air," Trevor added, puffing out his chest. "Nothing quite like it, is there?"

"Nothing," Abrams said dryly.

"Calais is but three hours as the crow flies," Davy said, looking at the man's pale face with sympathy. They were all fellows now, since the morning at Mary Kelly's house. Odd that something so perverse could make men better friends, but Davy was beginning to suspect that the grimmer the case, the greater the sense of camaraderie.

Abrams sighed, for the ship's steward had positioned himself at the top of the plank and given a quick blast of his whistle for last call. "I'd better be off. You two catch old Jack while I'm gone," he said. Davy reached into his pocket and pulled out a bag.

"Here, Detective. Peppermint candy to smooth your insides. The Channel can kick up pretty good this time of year."

"Thank you, Davy. I hope I don't need to use them."

"And remember to keep your mind on the science and not the ladies. The French women are like no others," shouted Trevor, who had never been to Paris, as he waved at Abrams' retreating back.

The gangplank was now hauled onto the ship and the dock keepers untied the heavy ropes that lashed the boat to the pier. Abrams was on his way.

Trevor turned to Davy, shrugged, and the two men started back down the long pier.

"Sorry it isn't you that's going, Sir?"

"Glad it's someone. He'll do the job. Perhaps not in time for this particular madman, but on the morrow there shall be others."

"Tomorrow and tomorrow and tomorrow," Davy said, "Creeps in this steady pace from day to day."

Trevor looked at him quizzically.

"Shakespeare, Sir. My mum quotes him while she does the laundry."

Trevor laughed as the two men came to the end of the pier and stepped back into the cobblestones. "Ah, Davy," he said. "You're full of surprises."

10: 10 AM

Cecil asked the driver to pull over and let him out before getting much closer to Whitechapel. He was meeting with Georgy that morning on Commercial Street, where the

340

slaughterhouses were located, and he certainly did not want the little man to know he was wealthy enough to hire coaches. Wealthy, he supposed was a relative term since between the train, the inn, and this coach, he had made a surprisingly large dint in the money he had found in William's pocket. But he figured his coffers would be replenished soon enough.

Cecil rounded a corner and, to his relief, saw Georgy resting on a barrel on the opposite side of the street.

"Morning, Guv'ner," Georgy greeted him. "Found 'ol Micha."

"Good work. I knew I could count on you."

"Tis Mary who can count on me, no offense to you, mate. Right this way." The two set off toward the water. "You send the letter?"

"It will be delivered within the hour. You're going to have to make a few stops before the Pony Pub. They're ladies, and I thought they might be more likely to meet you if I chose a tea room in a more middle-class part of town."

"Me? You wanna be there?"

"It's my damn pale eyes, Georgy, you know they make me too easy to pick out of a line," Cecil said. "But you have that nice common face, you know? Hard to describe in case the coppers get nosy."

"And two of 'em? Mary just had one sister, dinna she?"

"Society ladies never go anywhere without a companion," Cecil said, thinking he was certainly betting heavily that Leanna's guilt would compel her to come along. "Now here's the plan. When you meet them you'll say the baby is in a different place, a different part of town. By then we have them hooked and I have no doubt they'll follow to another bar, and then another, and finally back to the Pony Pub. Sometimes you have to do these things in stages, Georgy, give the fish a bit of slack line before you pull it in. Micha and I will be waiting. I want to make absolutely sure he knows who his victims are. Micha follows them out and does his job, then we have the money and they have a lesson they won't soon forget."

Georgy's brow puckered. "It's a fancy plan."

"The letter couldn't invite them into the bowels of Whitechapel," Cecil said, failing to hold back an exasperated sigh. "I know ladies like this. We can lure them to a tea room easily enough, but they would never set out alone for an establishment like the Pony Pub, no matter how persuasive the letter."

Georgy sighed too. "'ope this works."

"Trust me, everything will be fine."

Cecil would smell the slaughterhouses before he could see them. He made Georgy stop while he covered his nose with a handkerchief, but the stench seemed to have no effect on the smaller man, who pushed a door open and motioned for Cecil to follow.

This, Cecil reflected, must be what the waiting room for hell looks like. Blood was everywhere and they passed ten or so young boys who were completely covered in it. Sides of beef and pork hung from the rafters, dripping. The butchers, whose heads jerked up at their arrival, were cutting the carcasses into pieces and loading them on carts to be sold to shops all over the city. Every man in the building looked capable of doing the job Cecil had in mind, and half the boys as well.

When they reached the back of the slaughterhouse Cecil saw a huge man with his arm around the neck of a struggling cow. As Cecil watched with a fascinated horror, the man twisted the cow's head and it popped with a sound that rang through the crowded, noisy room. Cecil staggered a bit, and Georgy and the other workers laughed. They had seen the same reaction many times from people first witnessing Micha's specialty. As Georgy approached, the giant let loose of the now-limp cow, which fell to the floor with a thunderous thud.

"'ello, Micha. 'ow are you this morning?"

The giant grunted something back at Georgy.

"I wanna you to meet a friend of mine and Mary Kelly's. This is..." a puzzled look came across Georgy's face. "Excuse me Guv'ner, but I don't think you've ever told me your name."

"Nice to meet you," Cecil called out, nodding toward the bloodied giant and praying it would not be necessary come closer, or, God forbid, to shake hands. After a moment's pause, during which Micha looked him over with impudence, it became apparent this would be the case.

"Well there, Micha," Georgy spoke up, still anxious to play the proper host. "We came wonderin' if we might have a word outside. We'd like to 'ire ye for some work."

Micha mumbled something to a worker and started for the door, grabbing a remnant of raw meat from a butcher block as he passed. He popped it in his mouth like a candy and Georgy grinned, knowing this was all mostly for show. Cecil shuddered and scurried after them, his feet sticking to the cement floor with each step.

In the alleyway, Micha stopped and turned toward them with his bloody mouth. "What you want?"

"Remember sweet Mary Kelly? Murdered by Jack a few days back?" asked Georgy. The man nodded thoughtfully. "Well she 'ad wealthy family in Mayfair who snubbed 'er for years. Dinna even come to 'er wake. We wanna show them a thing or two. We'll set a trap to pull 'em down to Whitechapel tonight and we want you to rough them up a bit and steal their purses. There'd be ten pounds in it for you. Can you 'elp us?"

"They?"

"Two people," Cecil said. "But both ladies."

"Twenty."

"Twenty pounds?" Georgy said, genuinely shocked. "You think we be royalty, do you?"

"Twenty's fine," Cecil said, for his brief observation of Micha had convinced him the man was perfectly suited to carry out his whole plan, not just the aspects understood by Georgy. He dug into a pocket and extracted a handful of silver. "Here's ten as a show of good faith. The rest tonight, when you meet me at the Pony Pub at seven. You know the place."

Micha took the coins, turned his massive frame, and started into the building.

Cecil was left to stare after him. "That's it? Is he even going to do it?"

"Don't think so, Guv'ner. Better go in and get yer money back." Georgy burst into laughter at the panicked expression that came over Cecil's face. "'ad you going there, mate, sure but I did. Yeah, Micha will be there. But where we gonna get the other ten pounds, that's what ole Georgy needs to know."

"Leave that to me," Cecil said. They both turned and headed back toward the smokestacks of Commercial Street.

10:14 AM

Tom sent two telegrams that morning. One was to Galloway, requesting the prompt delivery of his grandfather's medical journals. The other was to Cambridge, this one asking for a leave of absence for the remainder of the school year. From an academic standpoint, the term had been a lost cause. His grandfather's funeral, the ensuing legal problems, now the murder of Emma's sister....Tom had decided his place for the next few months was here in London. Who could concentrate on craniums when his whole world was falling apart?

344

Trevor's accusations about John Harrowman weren't true, the delivery of the twins was proof of that. But Tom was further determined to prove that Trevor was wrong about the Ripper being a medical man and he believed he knew just how to do this. He didn't have a surgical scalpel himself – he was at least four classes away from the point where he could do dissections. But Tom knew where to find one.

11:15 PM

"Thirty?" Cecil said, his voice gone soft and low in disbelief as the pawnbroker lifted his mother's diamond and opal brooch to the light. "Look again, man, because you're mistaken. The weight of the center diamond alone –"

"Would fetch a much higher price if you cared to take the piece to a pawnbroker in a different part of town," the man said agreeably. "But something tells me you don't want to do that." He gently placed the brooch on the square of black velvet he had spread across the table and gave Cecil a little smirk. "Thirty's fair enough when you consider that it's thirty with no questions asked."

He thinks I stole it, Cecil thought with disgust. Thinks I'm some sort of highway bandit or, more likely, a grave robber. Why else would a man waltz into a pawn shop in the saddest alley of the East End with a handful of diamonds? Cecil turned to look at Georgy, pacing outside the pawnshop window. He had obviously been curious about the purpose of this particular mission and had wanted to follow Cecil inside the shop. But Cecil had insisted he stand guard outside and something in the word "guard" had appealed to the man's ego.

"It's a ludicrous offer," Cecil said, turning back to the pawnbroker with as much dignity as he could muster. Ever since the trip to the slaughterhouse his clothing had assumed a peculiar smell. The smell of poverty, he supposed, but poverty smelled much differently in the city than it did back in Leeds. There the farmers carried the faint odor of earth and sun and sweat on their clothes. Not so unpleasant really, nothing like the smoky stink of the city. How quickly he had fallen into the gutter. Thirty-two hours out of Winter Garden and here he stood, as rank and malodorous as any man in London.

"A ludicrous amount," he repeated. "And an offer I would not normally accept. I will be back for the piece within the week, you understand."

"It will most likely still be here," said the pawnbroker, still as pleasant as if they were taking a stroll in the park. All the advantages were on his side and he knew it. "Not much call for such jewelry in this part of town. Thirty now.....and fifty to take it back next week."

"Barbaric," Cecil said. "No wonder they warn against your kind in the Bible. Keep it safe, you hear me? And I want a receipt. Because if you think you're keeping jewels of this value for a mere thirty pounds, you're a madman."

The pawnbroker pulled a small ledger pad from a drawer. He filled out the amount and pushed the receipt toward Cecil. "Can you write your name?"

"Of course I can write my name. Dear God," Cecil said. He hesitated a moment, then signed with a flourish. "My father bought this brooch for my mother in Italy, you know. Florence. They were on their honeymoon." And for the first time since childhood, he felt the urge to weep.

11:15 AM

Tom had never followed anyone in his life but he flattered himself that he must have a natural gift for subterfuge, for John

346

had not appeared to notice him at all. He'd had very little trouble locating him in Whitechapel, in the quiet alleys where the pubs were sleepy in the morning. Tom envied the ease with which John moved among the people there, how relaxed he seemed in conversation with the working girls.

John had steered a couple of the women into a pub, making a great show of holding the door for them, as if they were ladies. Tom gave them a few minutes to settle and then pulled down his hat and walked by the window, glancing through the glass as he passed. John must have ordered the women bowls of stew because he was simply sitting opposite them at a table, watching them eat. This should, Tom thought, occupy him at least for an hour, and the important thing was that John didn't appear have his medical bag with him.

Ten minutes later a coachman dropped Tom a few blocks from Brixton and he walked the remaining distance. He'd gotten the address from Geraldine earlier that morning, on the excuse he planned to call on John and borrow a textbook. The neighborhood was neither as fashionable as Mayfair nor as squalid as Whitechapel and seemed nearly deserted. This is where the tradespeople live, Tom thought, the rising working class, probably not yet able to afford servants and conveniently gone to work during the day. Tom found the house number – a brownstone in a row of others just like it – and rang the doorbell, on the off chance John employed a housekeeper. But, just as he'd suspected, no one answered. He slipped around to the back and used a drainpipe to climb as far as the top of the porch. From there it was a bit more frightening to inch his way across the sharply-pitched roof to the windows, but luck was with him. The second one he looked in was John's bedroom and he could see a study located beyond. Presumably the man's medical bag would be in one of these rooms.

The house was in a bit of a shambles, Tom noticed, as he used the blade of his pocketknife to chip away a layer of paint around the window. The bed was unmade, with clothing draped over the chairs and books stacked on every table in the room. Even the small garden below him looked poorly tended and dispirited. Apparently this was what he had to look forward to as a bachelor doctor, a mess of a home and meals in a pub with whores. Tom was prepared to break a pane of glass if necessary, but once he had cracked through the heavy layer of paint it had proven simple enough to wrench the window open. Whatever fears troubled John Harrowman, robbery was not among them. Glancing around to confirm no neighbor was watching, Tom crawled inside.

Medical bags were big, heavy, and awkwardly shaped, so John's shouldn't be hard to find. But it wasn't in the study, where newspapers and academic journals were scattered about the floor, along with, Tom noted with some amusement, the latest copy of a pornographic quarterly, The Pearl, which lay atop the heap. He supposed Trevor and the men of the Yard might view such a magazine as evidence of a perverse twist of mind, prigs that they were, but Tom had left the same issue back in his dormitory in Cambridge. Good to know that even Saint John - the kind of man who would invite a woman into a pub because he wanted to feed her - had all the normal impulses.

Tom moved back into the bedroom and did a quick scan. Still no bag, but his eye fell on a hamper in the corner. He pulled up the lid and found that almost every item of clothing inside bore traces of blood. Doctors certainly had occasion to be splattered with blood but this, Tom was forced to admit, seemed excessive. The clothing in the bottom of the hamper was crusted with the color of old bricks, but the items near the top were – for these, splattered was not the word. One shirt was

348

soaked. Without knowing fully why, Tom pulled it out to take with him. A professor at university had lectured on a new technique known as blood typing and Tom wished he had paid more attention. The lecture had been about how you could infuse blood from one body into another, an idea radical enough in itself, but someone in the class had also raised a hand to ask if it might be possible to test blood and ascertain who it had come from. Why had he not listened better?

At the other corner of the bedroom, there was a large armoire, a handsome old piece that hinted of inheritance. The sort of family heirlooms, Tom noted dryly, offered to third and fourth sons. He opened the creaky doors and was immediately rewarded with the sight of the medical bag, which John had tossed on top of his shoes in a haphazard manner. Tom pulled it open and studied the array of knives tucked into side pockets. You'd need a rather big one if you planned to slice deep and the wound on the leg Trevor had certainly looked deep enough. The trouble was that if he pulled a knife from this neat formation, sequenced large to small across a felt panel, John would immediately notice its absence. The man might be a sloven of the worst sort in his rooms – luckily Leanna would be able to employ armies of maids to clean up after any husband she chose - but John was also a typical doctor, neat and systematic with the contents of his medical bag. Tom pulled out one of the larger knives and tossed it across the room so that it landed noiselessly on the bloodied shirt. Perhaps if he put something else in the felt slot, it might not be immediately evident to John that a knife was missing. He looked around the room until he found a pen on the desk about the same length as the knife and slipped it into the felt holder. It hardly looked like a knife and, in fact, now that he considered it more carefully, the substituted pen was clear evidence that someone had deliberately removed the knife. Perhaps if the slot was left empty, John would simply conclude he had left the knife somewhere.

No. No, that was no good either. Doctors weren't in the habit of leaving their medical knives lying about. Tom rocked back on his haunches, suddenly unsure why he was in this room or what he hoped to accomplish. If John was a serious suspect in the Ripper case, he would undoubtedly be made aware of this fact soon enough, so Tom couldn't say why he was going to such lengths to disguise the fact someone had been in this room. And there was also something about being here, in the normally private world of another man's bedchamber, that was making Tom uncomfortably aware of how little he knew John. There was the man he'd watched earlier who laughed and slapped a whore on the rump. Then the same man had held the door open for her, all but bowed as she passed. Bought her a bowl of stew, sat and watched to ensure she ate it, like a father might stand guard over a sickly child. Hard to reconcile all that with the weedy garden, the sloppily-painted windowsills, the sad tumble of this room. Not to mention a hamper full of bloody clothes, large stacks of medical books, an expensive armoire, a collection of knives, and pornography. Any of these things were simple enough to explain on their own, but brought together they created images Tom could not quite reconcile into a single picture.

Could Trevor have been right?

I don't know John, Tom thought again. I defended him on the basis of his profession, his public manners, the fact my sister seems to fancy him. I've come here certain I would find evidence to exonerate him and what I've gathered might just as easily be his downfall. Tom slowly looked around the bedroom, trying to memorize the details for future reference, but profoundly sorry that he had ever come. Who among us, he thought, could survive this sort of scrutiny? Who among us

350

would like to have every bit of paint chipped away, every drawer opened, every paper read aloud?

And just then, from downstairs, Tom heard the unmistakable sound of a key turning in a lock.

CHAPTER FORTY
11:50 AM

After breakfast, Emma had insisted on getting back to her daily duties, and although the girl was still a bit shaky on her feet, Geraldine let her have her way. Activity and the solace of a routine were probably the best things for her, at least now that her mind had cleared. Gerry could hardly see the wisdom of packing the girl back up to her room and leaving her there alone to mull over the events of the last few days.

But now, even though it had been her idea, Emma was staring down at her own bed and wondering if she were truly up to the tasks of housekeeping. She had done such a poor job of making the bed that the wrinkled sheets were visible through the dainty pink coverlet, like veins extending throughout a woman's hand. She tried to smooth the wrinkles out, but abandoned the project after a few feeble tries and finally ended up lying down altogether. Perhaps she should rest a bit and then go to the market. Since she had not been managing the cupboards, the kitchen had fallen into such disarray that they had actually run out of tea at breakfast. Emma closed her eyes.

Downstairs, Gage heard four loud bangs on the front door, only to open it and see not a soul. Granted, Gage had never been fleet of foot but it still struck him as odd that whoever had rapped was totally out of sight, not visible even when he went out on the stoop and looked first one way and then the other. Just as he was going in, he noticed a piece of paper lying at the doorstep, folded, sealed and with the words 'Mistress Emma' printed on the front in a neat hand.

"Who was pounding so on the door, Gage?" asked Geraldine from the top of the stairs.

"No one, Madame. Only this note lying on the door step. It has Emma's name ."

"That's queer."

Gage climbed the stairs to the landing and handed her the note. "It says 'Mistress,'" he pointed out.

"I can see that," Geraldine said, turning it over in her palm. "Do you suppose it is some sort of cruel joke, a prank set in motion by someone who realized Mary was her sister?"

"Shouldn't she see it anyways, Miss?"

"I suppose so," said Geraldine, slowly. She walked up the stairs to Emma's room and saw that the girl was napping. So she propped the letter on the bedside table and gathered up a few items of rumpled clothing from a chair. How long had it been since anyone had done the laundry, Gerry wondered, descending the stairs to the kitchen where, with a great deal of splashing, Leanna was washing dishes.

"We have truly sunk to a new low, haven't we?" Leanna said, noting her aunt's expression. "But I'm not sure how much we can expect from Emma. I think we must face facts, contact that home for the unmarried mothers and have them send a girl over for a day or two. Perhaps one not too close to delivery. The stairs are atrociously dusty."

"Something else," Gerry said, nodding but not really listening. "A letter just came for Emma."

"A letter? Who would write Emma?"

"My thoughts exactly. Whole family deceased, at least as far as we know. But she kept her council about Mary and perhaps there are others out there too." Gerry dropped the armful of clothing to the table. "You're right about getting some help. The cupboard's bare, the banisters are laced in dust, and we'll all be naked by the end of the week unless someone does the laundry." Gerry sighed. "And poor Emma is asleep again, stretched out like some princess who needs a kiss to awaken her.

354

But where is that prince going to come from? It occurred to me as I saw her there on her bed that I've been very unfair to the girl. She's young, as young as you are, but what are her prospects cooped up in this house with me and Gage? You've heard her speak. What shop lad would be brave enough to pay her court, and yet, on the other side, what gentleman would notice her in that little white apron? She's in a social nether land, neither servant nor peer. Lost between the classes and I'm the one who's put her there."

Leanna turned from the sink, wiping her hands on her apron. "I thought you didn't believe in class."

"I believe in a pretty young girl having someone to marry." Geraldine looked up to the ceiling, as if she could somehow see Emma sleeping far above them. "If she stays in this house, she'll die a virgin and that isn't a fate that suits everyone, is it darling?"

"Um," said Leanna, biting her lip as she untied the apron. "I didn't know you believed in marriage, either."

"Don't be ridiculous, Leanna. We're talking about Emma's life, not mine." Gerry's face softened with a sudden thought. "This letter. Perhaps she does have a secret friend. A beau."

"I take it you didn't peek."

"It was sealed with wax," Gerry said, glancing again at the ceiling.

"The only person I know who still uses sealing wax is my brother Cecil," Leanna said, idly sorting through the pile of Emma's clothes on the table. "And he considers himself quite a swell with the ladies."

"Well there you have it," Gerry said. "She's received a note from a man, perhaps a lover from her past or someone who knows her only slightly but is stepping forward now to offer his condolences. Emma's a healthy, normal, lovely woman and I've been foolish not to realize that young men would notice her. Sometimes we don't see the things right under our nose."

"Hmmm…" Leanna said, staring down at a delicate lace collar in her hands while her thoughts rushed back to the image of Emma and Tom tangled in the sheets. She had always imagined that an act such as that would change a woman in an immediate and visible way, and yet Emma had been simply herself at breakfast. A bit quieter than usual, but seemingly without stain or guilt. It was obvious that Emma had been born into a home of quality but that at some point, through circumstances the girl would not confess, her life had cracked and fallen apart. And now Gerry was quite right - Emma existed in a sort of undefined and as yet unsettled moral territory, on a social strata which was neither servant nor equal. At what point had she decided that the rules of society no longer applied to her? When had she realized that the form of her previous life was so fractured that it was not worth preserving, that she was better off walking away from the ruins of her girlhood and starting anew?

I don't know Emma, Leanna thought, and then the gaze of her memory fell on the image of her brother's bare back. Perhaps I don't really know Tom either, or anyone at all.

"It's possible, is it not?" Gerry persisted. "That Emma has a beau?"

"I suppose," Leanna said, running a fingertip along the bodice of Emma's dress. The cloth was coarser to the touch than material used for her clothes. Is that how the shopkeepers could so unerringly discern a lady of means from a paid companion, a sort of genteel servant, by the texture of the cloth in her dress? Leanna held the dress up and to her and said "I've never noticed this before, which I suppose makes me sound very foolish, but look….a servant's dress is designed with the buttons in front because she must do it up herself. A lady's buttons are in the back because someone else fastens them for her. It's one way you can tell, isn't it? Part of the costume."

"I've never been a student of fashion, Leanna," Gerry said, sinking into one of the kitchen chairs with an inelegant thud. "And I don't know why you're talking about buttons when I feel as if the whole world has gone loose in its axis. That letter for Emma....it could bring good news, or just another fresh horror and I don't know if I should have taken it to her or not."

"You did what you had to do," Leanna said. "And the only thing any of us knows for certain is that this household can't go on much longer without tea."

11:50 AM

At the sound of the front door pushing open, Tom sprang into action. Coming in from errands, he figured, could be noisy business. The clanging of the keys, the scraping of the door, the disposal of the coats and wraps. Tom calculated he had perhaps forty seconds before John was through the foyer and silence would descend on the house once again. No time to worry about whether or not he should remove the pen from the medical bag. Just time enough to close it and place it back, hoping John would not notice the armoire door left gaping open in the general dissemble of the room. Dragging his feet slowly across the rug instead of stepping – a trick he'd learned from his days playing hide and seek with Leanna among the creaky floorboards of Rosemoral – Tom made it to the window where he bent and tied the sleeves of the bloodied shirt into a little sack with the knife buried inside. Thank God for the briskness of the day. John would have to remove his gloves, hat, scarf, and coat which gave Tom exactly enough time to step through the still-open window and out onto the roof. He pushed the window closed as quietly as he could, dropped the bundled shirt off the roof, then scrambled down the drainpipe after it. He dropped the last few feet, rolling an ankle as he landed, twisting it so badly that he had to bite his tongue to keep from crying out.

All the yards were connected so Tom picked his way through them until he came to the end of the building. He was panting, nearly breathless, as much with fear and pain as with the exertion of climbing down from the roof. He stopped for a moment, leaning against the side of the last brownstone. A glance around the side of the building confirmed just what he feared. Trevor had indeed placed surveillance on John, for a man, evidently a plainclothes policeman, was standing on the corner with a newspaper, glancing periodically at the house.

What a brilliant mess, thought Tom. The whole city is on alert for the Ripper so how am I supposed to stroll past a policeman carrying a bloody shirt and a six-inch knife? He could think of only one thing to do. He dropped the bundle, pulled off his jacket and finally, shuddering with cold, his shirt.

It was, to put it mildly, an uncomfortable experience to pull a piece of clothing still moist with God-knows-whose blood onto his body and John's shirt was entirely too large for him, the cuffs dangling past his fingertips and the shirttail hanging almost to his knees. But rolling up cuffs and stuffing in shirttails was simple enough and his coat, just as he'd prayed it would, covered the entire mess. He slipped the knife into his inner pocket and left his own shirt to billow across some stranger's tiny yard. Then, taking a deep breath, Tom stepped into the street. Almost immediately, he winced. Now that the frenzied energy of his escape had begun to dissipate, it was increasingly evident he had landed much too hard on his ankle when he'd dropped from the drainpipe. Wonderful. Just fine. Now he had not only a knife and bloody clothes, but also a limp. If only I'd thought to bring an eyepatch, Tom thought, the effect would be complete.

358

He tried to console himself that he had gotten the things he'd come for, but he was no longer certain as to what end those items would be used. Not to mention that in the upper rooms of the house he was passing just now, John was undoubtedly realizing his possessions had been ransacked and, just as undoubtedly, was finding enormous piles of proof that Tom Bainbridge was the man who had done so. Worst of all, any evidence associated with the shirt or the knife was being contaminated by their exposure to his own body, more so with each step he took, and thus in all probability would be deemed useless by Scotland Yard.

It's official, Tom thought, nodding to the bored policeman on the corner as he hobbled past. I am the worst detective who has ever lived.

11:55 AM

Leanna had enjoyed considerably more success with her own foray into espionage and was walking up the steps of Geraldine's house with tea in hand and a smug smile on her face. No one had seemed to notice the fact that Emma's dress revealed the ankles of the taller Leanna. She had walked eight blocks to find a grocer who would not know her and the man had treated her with a brusque directness that had thrilled Leanna because it had proven her theory. Men did not really look at women, they merely took note of the costume and setting and adjusted their behavior accordingly.

The outing would have been a total triumph had her gaze not fallen on one of the newspapers in the shop. The three days since the Kelly killing had done nothing to dampen the public's obsession with the case and Leanna's eyes had darted over the cover of the paper, coming to rest on words like "dismemberment" and "evisceration." Emma must never see these papers, even if it meant keeping her confined to Gerry's house for a fortnight. To accept your sister's death was one thing. To read a five-page account gleefully documenting every horrid detail was something else.

As she turned the key and stepped into the house, Leanna was startled to find Emma herself was waiting in the vestry, ready to pounce upon her before she was fully through the door. "Listen," Emma said, her voice rapturous. "Listen to this!" Leanna seated herself on the divan in the parlor, the package of tea still in her lap, while Emma began to read:

Dear Mistress Emma,

I am sorry about the loss of your sister, Mary. She was a dear friend and greatly missed by many. The reason I am contacting you is that your sister has a child, which we have been keeping since her death. We are a poor family and the extra mouth has been a burden. The baby is a girl and is as sweet as Mary. We call her Sarah, after you and Mary's beloved mother, and you being the child's only relative, we think it right you should have her. We only ask to be repaid for what it has cost to keep her up. I feel one hundred pounds would be fair. Please meet me tonight at the Three Sisters tea house on Hanover Street. Six o'clock. Take a table and when I am sure no one has followed, I will sit down and we will talk. NO POLICE. Don't forget, bring the one hundred pounds with you. If you do not come, we will sell the baby to someone going to America and you'll never see her.

A Friend of Mary's

"Can you believe it? Mary had a child!"

"Emma, are you sure such a thing is even possible? Wouldn't John have known about a baby? He was her doctor, and he hasn't mentioned a thing to us about a child. This sounds very odd. I mean, to sell a baby for a hundred pounds. What kind of people could do such a thing?"

"Poor people, that's who. I don't care about the money. I've saved much more than that. It's my sister's baby, Leanna, the only blood I have left in the world. I have no other choice."

"They didn't even sign their name, Emma. Can we trust anyone who's willing to sell a baby? And the tone of the letter changes so fast. It starts out sweetly, then becomes a bald threat in the end. I think we should show this to John. Or Trevor. Let's send a note to Trevor and have him accompany us."

"No! You heard what they said. No police. They'll sell her away and I'll never see her. I'll go by myself if I must. Hanover Street is safe enough and I'll be home by eight. Geraldine will – " Emma looked around wildly. "What will Geraldine do?"

"Dote on little Sarah as if she were her own granddaughter. Do you even need to ask? But she will also lock us in our rooms and throw away the key if she hears anything of this plan." Leanna sat back on the couch and studied Emma's face, which was more animated than it had been since the day she met her. Was this baby really the child of Mary Kelly? In the final analysis, did it really matter? "But someone has to go with us, and I refuse to yield the point. Perhaps you're right, Trevor's profession wouldn't allow him to stand by and watch us purchase a human being like a tin of tea. But John could come along. Or even Tom."

"We can't take that chance, Leanna. If the person who wrote this letter looks in the window and sees a man at our table, he might bolt and take Sarah with him. Even allowing you to come is risky enough, although I don't think a woman would scare him off quite so—" For the first time, Emma paused long enough to really look at Leanna. "Why are you wearing my dress?"

"An experiment," Leanna said. "And one rather apt to our mission tonight. All right, Aunt Emma, you'll have you way. At least to a point. As you say, Hanover Street is safe enough and there will be plenty of people about at the hour. We will dress simply, very much so. I doubt that any displays of privilege will work in our favor. And I'm sending notes to both John and Tom telling them where we'll be. Not why we're going there, since we can only hope that baby Sarah proves winsome enough that anyone who sees her will cease to worry about exactly how she came to live in Mayfair."

"If she's like her mother, she will be able to charm the birds from the sky," Emma said softly. "Mary was beautiful."

"I know," Leanna said, just as softly. "And none of us can help what happened to her. But we can see that her daughter has everything the world can offer. Come. Gerry keeps bags of clothing to be donated to the poor in the attic. Let's choose some proper outfits, let me write my notes, and we shall plot our path to Hanover Street. Anything the baby needs for now we can get from the unwed mother home. Lord knows they should loan us a few nappies and a nurse in exchange for all that Aunt Gerry has done for them." Her mind rolling, Leanna cocked her head. "And at least let me provide the a hundred pounds. You were lying when you said you've saved that much, weren't you?"

Emma ducked her head. "I'll pay you back in time, I promise."

"Don't be silly," Leanna told her. "You get the clothes and baby supplies, I'll go to my bank and find a messenger boy." Emma nodded and sprinted up the stairs.

362

So I spent the morning dragging my naked brother about and now I'm off to buy a baby, Leanna thought. Life in Leeds was never like this. She picked up the letter from the table and read it again, slowly. The author had a lovely turn of hand and the paper was heavy, hardly the sort of stationery a poor family would have at the ready. Very little there to support the writer's claim he had known Mary Kelly, save from the use of her mother's name, but there was no stopping Emma from this mission and the more Leanna thought about it the more merit Leanna could see in the plan.

For, after all, how many times has salvation come in the form of a baby? Whether or not the child in question was truly Mary Kelly's, the very thought of becoming an aunt was already returning Emma to life and who knows, it might shake the rest of the household from their dreadful doldrums as well. Leanna imagined Gerry proudly pushing the pram through Hyde Park alongside of Tess and her twins, announcing to everyone that she had taken on a young ward. Folly, yes. But sometimes folly saves. Leanna had already decided to hire three message boys – one for Tom, one for John, and one for Trevor. Hanover Street was a respectable area and the hour was early, and Emma was probably right about their safety. But in times like this, a girl couldn't be too careful.

CHAPTER FORTY-ONE
5: 38 PM

Trevor was finishing up his paperwork and debating taking a break for a pint or perhaps even a decent supper. His cheerfulness that morning on the dock had all been for show, calculated to ease Abrams's guilt at leaving. Trevor had spent the day going through the crew rosters Davy had obtained from the dockmasters, checking to see if any of the men aboard had a history of medical training. A long shot, but perhaps worth taking.

"The work is never finished," a voice said gently. "You just have to find those points where you can put it down and walk away for a bit of rest."

"I know," Trevor said, looking up at the creased and kindly face of Phillips. "I'm just about ready to step out for dinner. Shall you join me?"

"Wife waiting at home," Phillips said, surprising Trevor, who hadn't known the doctor was married. The nature of the Yard meant that men might bond into a quick brotherhood behind these walls, but not necessarily that they were friends on the outside. In fact, quite the opposite. Most of the people in criminology were nearly fanatical about keeping their private lives separate from their professions. Still, it was hard to picture Phillips with a wife.

"Do you need assistance, Sir?" Severin asked, emerging from the backroom, with his shirt sleeves rolled up, wiping his hands on a towel.

Phillips snorted softly. "I believe I can make my way up the stairs and into a carriage without a nursemaid, thank you." He walked out a bit more briskly than his usual pace, as if to illustrate his capabilities, and as they listened to the fading sounds of the doctor's cane tapping up the stone staircase, Severin's shoulders sagged.

"You were quite right to ask," Trevor told him. "His decline over these last weeks has been noteworthy. It's just hard for a man like Phillips to admit he needs help."

Severin nodded and turned back toward the sink.

"And you should be finishing up as well, shouldn't you?" Trevor added. "The good doctor is quite right. The chores will all wait for the morrow and there's a point where we all simply must walk away from them."

The young man gave him a small smile. "Hard for me to leave work undone, Sir."

"Indeed. Then consider it an order. I shall order you to do what I cannot manage myself." Trevor leaned back in his chair and watched Severin take a final swipe at the counter with a rag. He reminded Trevor of Davy, whose own methodical work ethic had produced these very ship rosters spread out before him, and Trevor reflected that, difficult as it might be, the older men on the force were going to have to start entrusting the younger men with more significant responsibilities. Trevor shook his head ruefully. Davy and Tom and now Severin. They were the true modern men, were they not? The ones who would carry England into its bold new future.

"Are you going home to a wife as well?" Trevor asked, as Severin pulled on his cape. He meant the question almost as a joke, but Severin flushed.

"Hope to be soon, Sir," he said quietly.

"Ah, then. Bully. It's a fine thing to have a special girl."

Severin nodded and then asked, almost as an afterthought, "And for you, Sir?"

"No," Trevor said shortly. "No one." Clearly fearful that he had managed to offend two superiors within five minutes, Severin scuttled out the door, leaving Trevor to stare down at

366

the ship rosters. No one special and no one waiting. He may as well give the crew lists one more look.

5:42 PM

"How do I look?" Leanna asked, turning in a slow circle before Emma.

Emma considered for a moment. "Respectable. But not especially prosperous."

"Perfect," Leanna said, bending to pick up the clothes scattered about the room and stuff them back into the bags designated for the workhouse. "That was precisely the effect I was going for."

"And how do I look?" Emma asked, turning herself.

"Just the same. Respectable but not prosperous."

"Ah, but that's how I always look."

Leanna laughed uncertainly. Since the shock of Mary's death and her long stint on medication, Emma's behavior had been uncharacteristically erratic, and it was hard to tell when she was joking.

"We certainly had a lot of dresses to choose from," she said, attempting to iron her skirt with her hands, as she often did when nervous. "Where does Aunt Gerry obtain all these garments anyway?"

"Her friends bring clothing from their maids," Emma said "which in turn is passed along to women not fortunate enough to be maids. I suppose there's rather a protocol to how the clothing descends through its various owners. Women who are respectable and prosperous, followed by women who are respectable but not prosperous and then, finally, those poor creatures who are neither."

"Oh yes," Leanna said, rather breathlessly. "Quite right."

Emma bent to tie a shoe. She seemed to take her time, then finally she stood and straightened, looking directly into Leanna's face. "In other words," she said. You to me and then on to Mary and last of all women like Annie Chapman and Cathy Eddowes. That's the order in which it all descends."

5:59 PM

Trevor was thinking he should truly finish for the night when Tom Bainbridge showed up at his door, looking exhausted and a little guilty. Trevor waved him inside and watched in surprise as the boy took off his shirt to reveal a bloodstained chest and, grimacing, fished a surgical scalpel from the inner pocket of his coat.

"I'm afraid I've been a fool," Tom said. "These items came from the home of John Harrowman."

"Harrowman gave them to you?" Trevor asked, frowning in confusion. The boy didn't seem to be hurt, so why was he covered in blood?

Tom violently shook his head and collapsed into a chair. "I broke into his home while he was out for luncheon," he said. "Bungled it all, I'm afraid, but I did come away with this shirt, which was damp when I started out, and this knife ..."

"Whyever did you take his shirt? You must realize that any blood that was still damp couldn't possibly belong to Mary Kelly."

"But the blood itself....There are tests to be run, are there not?"

"Perhaps. But we'd only need a trace of it and that is....rather a large shirt and rather a lot of blood, is it not?" As Tom moved into the light, Trevor absorbed the full impact of his costume and couldn't resist a chuckle. "In the future you and I must discuss the meaning of the word 'sample' and the various non-surgical ways in which a man might use a knife."

"I don't know why you're laughing," Tom said, with as much dignity as he could muster under the circumstances for the full force of his ridiculousness was hitting him as well. "I'll admit that the more time that passes the more I'm unsure what I hoped to gain in bringing you this shirt, much less this shirt in its horrible entirety. But I must tell you that there were certain elements in John Harrowman's room that make me think you were right about calling him a suspect."

"What sort of elements?"

As Tom gave a brief recount of his morning's adventures, Trevor began to shake his head.

"The presence of knives and bloodied clothes are explained away by his profession," Trevor said. "And as for the fact his private quarters were in shambles and you found a smutty book....I'm afraid if we used that as criteria, every bachelor in London would be behind bars before morning, with me, and perhaps even you, among them. No, we need more than that, especially now that it appears Harrowman has somewhat of an alibi."

Tom looked at him blearily. "How the deuce does a man have 'somewhat of an alibi.'"

"This was Abram's last task before he sat sail for Paris," Trevor said, opening his notebook. "Learned that Harrowman spent most of the night at the bedside of a Mayfair woman in labor. The daughter of your aunt's friend Tess, in fact, named Margory Cuthberson. You may have met her."

Tom shook his head. "Most of the night?"

"Twins, a long birth, and when the lady became fatigued, apparently Harrowman offered her a respite with chloroform. And while she rested, so did the rest of the house, including him." Trevor shrugged. "Therein lies the 'somewhat.' This rest period gives us a small window of opportunity, perhaps two hours, in which Harrowman could have conceivably left the Cuthberson home."

"Time frame?"

"Very early morning. Which, yes, I'm well aware coincides with the Kelly killing. It's conceivable he could have crossed town in a coach, done the deed, and returned to Mayfair in time to deliver the twins. But it's far-fetched, Tom, and would have required either a bizarre set of coincidences or absolute genius to ensure he'd find a victim at precisely the right time, could calculate how long it would take to butcher her and how long the family he was using as an alibi would continue to slumber. Plus the thoroughness of the work on Kelly....Phillips think it would have taken the better part of a night."

"For a man Phillips's age perhaps. You've seen John. A man at the height of his powers might have done it all far faster."

"Possible," Trevor said. "But to my mind still unlikely. I say, you've gone from his biggest defender to his first accuser rather fast, haven't you?"

Tom's ankle was throbbing and he eased it onto the chair beside him. "The bit about the chloroform is rather convenient."

"Whyever would you say that? It's standard use in childbed for the women who can afford the cost of such oblivion. The Queen herself accepted it for her later births, did she not? And made the doctor who administered it to her a knight or a duke or something of the sort?"

Tom nodded. "A baron, I believe. Yes of course, the chloroform can be explained away too, just as everything else. But his proclivity for drugging women may be a factor in all this, don't you see? John has prescribed large doses of morphine for Emma in the last few days. I know what you're thinking, that it's natural to do so for a girl who's had such a severe shock, but Emma has been quite disoriented." Tom drew a deep breath, struggled for a way to explain the next part. "I have the sense that last night I was trying to help her. That I carried her, had to assist her in the most profound way."

"What do you mean you have the sense? Did you carry her or didn't you?"

"My own memory has been a little-"

"You're suggesting he drugged you as well?"

"No, no I did that task for him. I was rattled when I left here yesterday and I'm afraid I may have had a bit too much brandy. So granted, I'm hardly the best witness to Emma's behavior over the last twenty-four hours but I will say that based on Leanna's descriptions, John is being quite cavalier with her medication. Apparently he's decided that the cost of oblivion isn't too high."

"Perhaps he just doesn't like to see a woman suffer," Trevor said quietly, although he was also busily scribbling down everything Tom had told him. "Can't bear the sight of it myself, to be honest. If I had a means for relieving their pain, I might act just the same."

"Consider the pattern. That's what Grandfather always taught me and Leanna, that the beginning of all science is just this, the recognition of a pattern. Doctors have access to knives, which you've realized was significant from the start, but they have knowledge of drugs too, do they not? It's possible a physician might use them not just to relieve suffering, but for his own darker purposes. Selecting victims. Providing alibis."

Trevor frowned. "How is Emma today?"

"Much clearer. Really almost her normal self."

"And you?"

"Better too."

"But where have you been all afternoon? You said you went to Harrowman's home at luncheon but it's dark outside. So for the last four or five hours have you-"

To Tom's relief, Trevor's inquiries were cut short by the arrival of Davy, bearing a letter.

"This came special, Sir."

"Another confession? Another kidney? Put it with the others."

Davy shook his head. "You'll want to see this one. It's from Miss Bainbridge."

"Why the devil would Gerry send a message here?"

"Not that Miss Bainbridge, Sir. This is from the other one. The girl. Leanna."

6:21 PM

Cecil walked into the Pony Pub and took a moment to survey his surroundings. It appeared things were coming together well. Georgy had been dispatched to meet the girls in Hanover Street and Micha was already here in the pub, earlier than could be expected considering the man was a Neanderthal, probably no more capable of reading a clock than he was of quoting Plato. Micha had taken residence at the bar and, with a sigh, Cecil joined him. He would have preferred to conduct this particular piece of business in privacy but privacy, he was beginning to understand, was as rare a commodity in Whitechapel as a diamond and opal brooch. Besides, the hour was early and pub yet uncrowded. It was unlikely anyone would take note of their conversation.

Cecil slid onto the barstool beside Micha and gave him a companionable nod. "Beer for both of us," he said to the barmaid, a pretty little thing who giggled at every word that was said to her. Cecil waited until his beer had descended a few inches in the glass and then turned to Micha.

"You were offered a certain amount for a certain task," he said. "But you can add ten more pounds very easily." Micha did not answer, which Cecil took as an invitation to continue. "Two girls will appear, just as planned," he said, keeping his voice low and his focus straight ahead. "Your prey is the blonde one, rather tall. Blonde, you know. Means she has yellow hair. She'll be dressed as a lady. My life would be easier if this girl didn't exist. Do you catch my meaning?"

"What I do with other?"

Cecil shrugged. "Makes no difference to me. Have your way with the chit if you fancy her, and consider it a bonus. Not the blonde." Cecil could not have explained why this mattered to him, in light of all that was about to happen, but he turned to the huge man for the first time, staring into his face to impress the point. "She won't be sullied and she needn't suffer. Needn't see it coming." Cecil took a deep drag from his glass, shuddered as the sting of the five-pence pint washed across his tongue. "She should go fast, like the cow. Can you manage?"

Micha nodded, but the phrase "ten more pounds" was all he'd heard. Whatever came next was just details, and details were the sort of things rich men could afford, of no interest to a working class bloke like Micha. Who could tell yellow hair from any other kind, in the dark? Thirty pounds, that's what mattered. More than a month's worth of wages at the slaughterhouse, paid up prompt for a moment of sport. Wasn't this the damndest country, Micha thought, one where a man could be paid so well for doing what came naturally, and as he looked up his happy glance fell on one of his kinsman.

"Tell me," he said, "I am here all the night, am I not?"

He was speaking to the well-dressed man Cecil had seen the first night, the man who had, in fact, told Cecil how to find Micha. "Here all the night," the man said, raising a pint from the end of the bar. "Both of us, eh, Lucy?"

"Drinking all night, the both of you," the girl said.

So this is how they establish an alibi, Cecil thought. Each claims that the other was in the Pony Pub, and all the while any number of villainies are being perpetrated in the streets beyond.

Despite his vow to remain unobtrusive, to keep his scarf pulled high and his hat pulled low, Cecil found himself staring at this other man, the one with the mustache.

He's like me, Cecil thought, the notion coming on him abruptly, with the bitterness of cheap beer. We're men who once knew greater means, men who thought their lives were destined for different ends, but we've fallen on hard times, haven't we? The man's coat, while worn and dirty, had a certain quality. An elegance in the cut and Cecil had always prided himself that he could recognize elegance, even when it was tattered and concealed, just like this, in the tawdry streets of Whitechapel. He raised his beer in tribute and, after a moment's pause, the man raised his back.

6:25 PM

John emerged from an alleyway just off Toddle Street, carrying his black bag at his side, and, walking swiftly, began to make his way toward the waterfront. This area was better lit than most of Whitechapel and as John passed under a street lamp, someone called his name. She had been searching the streets for him for twenty minutes, had sent a note to his house, and she was shaking with relief at the sight of his tall form silhouetted in the fog. He turned at the sound of her voice and she tumbled into his arms in relief. They conferred, very briefly, and then linked arms and started walking away from the water.

6:25 PM

"Well, o'course I wouldna bring a baby here." The little man's tone was offended, as if to suggest while it might be morally permissible to sell a child, only a beast would put one in a pram and push it to a tea house. "The baby should be with me wife, natural enough, that's where we be headed."

"Then why did you ask us to meet you here?" Leanna asked through gritted teeth. Everything about the situation smelled wrong but Emma only seemed bewildered. She sat across from Leanna, gripping her cup so tightly that it seemed the porcelain might crack at any minute.

"Ladies like you might not likely meet old Georgy 'less the place was posh, am I right?" The man had probably scrubbed up as well as he could, Leanna thought, but he still stood out in a neighborhood tea room, surrounded by gossiping women and the occasional husband treating his wife to a piece of pear tart. Georgy kneaded his hands nervously and looked from Leanna to Emma. "Money here, baby when ye follow," he said.

"There's isn't a baby at all, is there?" Leanna said coldly.

But Georgy, thanks to Cecil's planning, was prepared for just such an inquiry. They had found a blonde child toddling about in an alley and offered her sister – this child herself no more than seven – a shilling to let them cut a lock of the baby's hair. Even children did not ask questions in the East End. The older girl had promptly lifted the baby up, slapping its rump when it squirmed, and Georgy had made a quick tug with his pocketknife across a single curl. The result was this lock of hair, so soft, wispy and light that it clearly came from the head of a child, which he solemnly unwrapped from a handkerchief and presented to the girls.

The effect on Emma was just what Cecil had predicted. A soft exhalation, the rise of tears, an almost involuntary reaching for the hair. But Leanna's eyes remained narrow and suspicious. "We only agreed to meet you in a public place," she said. "That holds, so you had better find a way to summon your wife. And there will be no money exchanged until the child is in our arms."

And wasn't she the duchess, Georgy thought. Micha would have a good time bringing her rump down to the street. The other girl was clearly more trusting, and as Emma raised the lock of hair to her face and brushed it against her cheek, Georgy knew he had her thoroughly hooked. Let Miss High and Mighty try to set the rules, let her squawk like a peahen, no matter. The other one, the sweet one who was Mary's sister....it was clear she would follow wherever he led.

6:45 PM

"Don't worry, Sir," Davy said, as the Scotland Yard carriage made its way down Hanover Street. "The area's crawling with bobbies and Miss Bainbridge has her guard up, else she wouldn't have sent the note."

"True enough," Trevor said tersely. He had been tapping his cane against the door the entire trip, a sound that had driven Tom almost to the point of screaming. "But they're walking into a trap."

"There's no way Mary had a baby?" Tom asked.

Trevor shook his head. "In the past four days I've interviewed everyone who ever knew the girl and there wasn't so much as a peep about a child. It's a play for money, that much is clear. I only hope that money is all they're after."

Tom was struggling to control his breathing. "What else would they be after?"

"Emma is Mary Kelly's sister. That fact alone might make her a trophy, at least in the eyes of some."

Davy leapt out before the carriage had rolled to a complete stop in front of the Three Sisters. Tom and Trevor sat in strained silence for several minutes until he reappeared.

"They were here, Sir, the owner remembered. Came and went. Sat at a table with a little man with dirty clothes, the lady said. And then Miss Bainbridge...." Here Davy stopped and climbed back into the carriage, shaking off water. It wasn't raining, but the fog had closed in fast. "Miss Bainbridge was the one to pay the fare, Sir, and she left this with her money."

He handed Trevor what looked to be the standard sort of bill a server leaves on a café table. The party had ordered three cups of tea, and when Trevor turned it over he saw that Leanna had scribbled a few words on the back. How she had managed to do so undetected, he could not imagine, and her scrawl was nearly illegible. But it was enough to tell Trevor that they, like the women, had been misdirected. He rapped on the side of the carriage again with his cane and yelled "Merchant Street, immediately" to the driver. Then he sat back and looked into Davy and Tom's worried faces.

"It's bad," he said. "I think he's trying to lure them to Whitechapel."

"They wouldn't go to Whitechapel," Tom said. It was such a preposterous notion that it almost made him feel better. "A baby is the perfect bait, no doubt about it, but neither of them are fools."

"They're being led there in stages," Trevor said, running a palm across his face, for he had begun to sweat. "Keep an eye,

Davy. Tall blonde woman, shorter one with red hair, tiny dirty man." Mabrey nodded and leaned out the window of the carriage, while Trevor turned back to Tom. "The first stop is perfectly respectable, a tea room full of ladies. Then he pulls them in a little deeper. Leanna's note says they are now going to 'a public place,' which scarcely points an arrow, but which I suspect means a pub. There are ghettos that skirt up right to the edge of Whitechapel, like the Jewish area Abrams used to work. Simple shops and homes, but the streets are clean and well-lighted enough that Leanna and Emma might follow him without question. From there they are dangerously close to the East End. A five minute walk - "

"Doesn't this carriage go any faster?" Tom said, yanking at the sleeves of his shirt. He'd shucked the bloody one he'd stolen from John back at the Yard in favor of a substitute provided by Davy. In the haste of their departure he had not asked who the garment belonged to or why it might have been so readily available in the mortuary. The sleeves were short for Tom, but at least the shirt was clean, and Tom tried not to think hard about its origins.

"We're making good time," Trevor said. "They're almost certainly on foot, which is why Davy is hanging out the window, making sure we don't pass them. But I suspect this little man is leading them through a lot of twists and turns, trying to disorient them so they lose their sense of where they are and how long they've traveled. We'll beat them to Whitechapel, that much is sure. When we get there, we'll tell every copper we see who we're looking for and the three of us will split up. Or at least Davy and I will take different routes and you can stand watch. I forgot about your ankle."

"The ankle's fine," Tom said. "I won't slow you up."

Trevor looked into Tom's ashen face and gave what he hoped was a reassuring nod. "And eventually we will find them, especially if he takes them to a pub, as he most certainly plans to do. The man we're looking for knew Mary Kelly, which means he most likely is from the same neighborhood."

"And that's the good luck in this," Davy said over his shoulder. "We've spent the last four days retracing Mary Kelly's steps so we know exactly where she'd go to find clients, the routes she used to get there. It isn't as if we're looking in every pub in the East End, Sir. We know where to start." His eyes turned back to the street. "There's a limited number of people who could have sent that note, isn't that true? The first one, the letter to Miss Emma about the baby, I mean."

"Quite right," Trevor said. "Emma was private, Mary evidently less so. Even the people living in the same house with Emma were unaware she had a sister but Mary must have confided in someone."

"I scarcely see how that narrows the field," Tom said. It seemed the carriage was moving so slowly he was tempted to jump out and run on foot. "Could be any working girl she'd befriended. Or any regular client."

"It narrows the field because it means that for once we can toss out the notion of a hoax, a completely random person from the streets," Trevor said. "Remember what Leanna said in the letter she sent to Scotland Yard. The person who contacted them claimed the baby was named Sarah, after Emma and Mary's mother. So it was someone close enough to Mary to know that she had a sister, where that sister lived, and even their mother's name."

"Someone who knew Emma would be able to get a hundred pounds," Davy added. "That's a lot of money for a maid, so why would they ask it?"

"Perhaps they knew of Geraldine's generosity, her penchant for sad causes," Trevor mused. "Or perhaps whoever wrote the letter didn't understand that Emma was a maid. They could have seen a Mayfair address as evidence she had married well, had immediate access to funds."

A sudden dreadful thought flitted across Tom's mind. "Are we even certain Emma is the target?" he asked. "Leanna is the one with money."

Trevor pursed his lips thoughtfully. "She comes from an established family...."

"It's not just that," Tom blurted out. "Our grandfather left her Rosemoral, the whole bloody estate, and that makes her.....what did you call it? If someone knew she was an heiress, that would make her as much a trophy as Emma, would it not?"

What it made her was the ideal candidate for a kidnapping, but Trevor did not share this particular thought with Tom. "How many people are aware of the terms of your grandfather's will?"

"No one but family. And a handful of barristers back in Leeds."

"And the letter was sent to Miss Emma, not Miss Bainbridge," Davy reminded them. "Whoever wrote it couldn't have known Miss Bainbridge would come with her."

"Right again, Davy," Trevor said. "Emma was Mary's sister so we should start there, with the most obvious and direct connection. The lure of the baby was designed to tempt Emma. There's no reason to think Leanna's wealth is even a factor."

"She's so trusting," Tom said. "Too trusting for her own good."

"She was suspicious enough to send us notes," Trevor said. "Leanna's clever. Smart enough to know they shouldn't follow the man to the second location."

Tom shook his head. "I was speaking of Emma."

380

7:10 PM

Mary Kelly had solicited the majority of her clients from three pubs: The Cornwall, the Pony, and the Prince of Wales. Trevor's plan was to circulate through the area between the three, informing any copper he saw along the way of the situation and providing a description of the people they sought. All they knew about the man was the tea shop owner's vague claim he was small and dirty, and Whitechapel was home to any number of men who fit that description. As for the women, Trevor hoped that the mere fact they would be well-dressed and neatly groomed would be enough to draw the eye in this part of town. He sent Davy on a wider loop of the area, since he still believed that the man was most likely leading Emma and Leanna into the East End via one of the immigrant neighborhoods to the west.

Despite Tom's promise that his ankle was fine, it was immediately clear that he'd be unable to keep up the pace. Trevor led him to the nearest of the three likely pubs, the Prince of Wales, and deposited him at a table near the door with instructions to keep an eye on anyone who entered. His demotion from amateur detective to watchdog rankled Tom, but he knew that Trevor was right. He was a liability on the streets. He had begun to suspect the ankle was broken, although he didn't share this with Trevor for fear he'd be sent home altogether. He propped it on the chair across from him and stared anxiously out into the street where Trevor had stopped to talk to a bobby. Word of mouth spread quickly among the men on their beats, Trevor had assured him, and there were more coppers on duty in the East End now than in any time in memory. By the time the women arrived via their long and most likely circuitous route from Hanover Street, half of Whitechapel would be expecting them.

Although his lost afternoon in some nameless bar had put him a little off his alcohol, Tom ordered a beer. He figured that drinking, or at least pretending to drink, was the best way to fit in with the swarm of regulars in the Prince of Wales. But the beer had scarcely arrived when Tom saw John Harrowman pass in the street. He was arm in arm with a woman and they were walking so fast as to be almost running.

Tom limped to the door of the pub and stared after the pair. Looked up and down the street but, damn it all, there wasn't a copper in sight. After a second or two of internal debate, Tom stepped into the street.

CHAPTER FORTY-TWO
7:35 PM

They had walked with Georgy for over an hour, making several stops, only to end up here, in the last place on earth they should be. Leanna knew she had been foolish to ever leave the Three Sisters, but Emma had been so determined that Leanna was forced to choose between going deeper into this ridiculous scheme or leaving Emma on her own. This was the last stop, the man had promised, and he'd left them in a little bar called the Pony Pub, where they sat waiting for him to return with Mary's baby.

No. Not exactly. Emma may have been waiting for a man to return with a baby, but Leanna knew better. This entire evening had not only been a dangerous and fruitless quest for a child who'd never existed, but it might also be the event that snapped Emma's sanity. It broke Leanna's heart to see her sitting there so calmly at their table, smiling, humming a little, stroking the lock of golden hair. Emma had not noticed that they were being pulled into the fringes of the East End. She had not noticed the dozens of bobbies they had passed on the way here or how the men's eyes had slid past them without interest, just two more raggedy women in the night. Leanna was not entirely afraid, not yet. The streets were well lit and full of people and she had no doubt they would find their way back to Mayfair. What she feared is what Emma would do when it finally dawned on her that Georgy was not coming back.

Leanna's mind was churning with possibilities. The thing that made no sense was that Georgy had not yet demanded their money. A hundred pounds was a fortune to anyone in this neighborhood, incentive enough to drive them to any level of depravity, and yet Georgy had escorted them into the Pony Pub, helped them find seats, and left. The pounds were still in a blue silk pouch Leanna had tied beneath her skirt and it had slapped her thigh with every step she had taken, from Mayfair to Hanover to Petticoat to hell. They had fallen into some sort of plan, that was clear enough, but if the scheme hadn't been about money, what was the motive?

It was her fault entirely, Leanna thought, as she sat rubbing her temples vigorously. She should never have come, never have let Emma come, and then she'd compounded her folly by sending notes to John, Tom, and Trevor, telling them they would be at Hanover Street when they were in fact here, wherever here was, in this dingy little bar with its sticky tables and smoky air. She thought of the three letters she had written, tossing them to the winds of fate, hoping that at least one would find its mark, and had a brief vision of Tom, Trevor, and John all converging on the Three Sisters only to learn she and Emma were gone. It's a tale of missed letters and messages gone awry, she thought. Rather like Romeo and Juliet.

And we all know how well that ended.

"Emma," she said gently. "He's been gone for quite some time."

Emma nodded.

"We must go back to Gerry's house, you see that, don't you, darling?"

"Not without Sarah," Emma said. "He'll bring her in a moment."

"No. No, I don't think so."

Emma looked at her with confusion bordering on anger, as if Leanna was the one who had duped her. "Leave if you must," she said. "But I will wait here for Sarah."

"I don't believe that Sarah exists. You know this too, Emma, I can see it in your face."

"He's gone to get her now."

384

"I think he's simply gone. He was a very bad man, darling, a very mean one. He lied."

They sat for a moment and then Emma made a slow half-nod, her lips slightly parted. She might not want to know the truth, but on some deep level, she still did.

"What do we do now?" she asked.

"We find a cab," Leanna said with relief. "And we go home."

7:40 PM

Cecil had noticed, of course, when Emma and Leanna had entered the pub and the sight of his little sister, here in the flesh, had unnerved him. He pulled his scarf over his mouth and sank in his chair, but Leanna seemed oblivious to her surroundings. For the last twenty minutes, ever since Georgy had run out the door – practically skipping, the fool – she had been solely preoccupied with watching Emma's face.

So when Leanna suddenly stood, Cecil jumped. She walked right towards him, and Cecil twisted in his seat, his heart thumping. She was no further than an arm's length away as she leaned across the bar and said to the half-wit girl behind it "Excuse me, miss?"

The politeness of the address confused Lucy. She stared at Leanna but did not answer.

"Do you know where we might secure a cab and driver?"

"A cab and driver?" Lucy seemed as surprised as if Leanna had requested a coterie of elephants. Cabs for hire did not visit Whitechapel. They stopped at the fountain near the mouth of Merchant Street and from there anyone seeking to transact business in this district must make the rest of his way on foot, a fact well-known to the West End gentlemen who visited on a regular basis. The fact would have been known to Leanna too, if she'd paid any attention on her way in, Cecil thought, but his sister did not seem to have fully grasped the reality of her present situation. She seemed to think her shabby clothes, gathered from God knows what improbable source, provided an effective disguise, while the truth was that everything about her – the posture, the accent, the clear skin and even white teeth – revealed her to be an outsider. Whores who try to put on airs give themselves away with a thousand small mistakes, Cecil knew this. But before this moment he had never understood that it worked the same in reverse, that it was just as easy to lose one's balance stooping as it was while climbing. A woman like Leanna could not help but be a lady, even here among the trash of the Pony Pub.

"Yes, a Hansom cab," Leanna repeated. "Or perhaps a carriage. Any form of transport. Is there a lad who can summon one?"

My God, Cecil thought, she's so utterly out of her element that she doesn't even realize that she's out of her element. I didn't have to pawn mother's brooch to be free of her. If I'd left the girl to her own devices she probably would have managed to fall into the Thames and drown.

"There are always cabs for hire at the waterfront, Miss."

The lie was outrageous. If no sane cabbie would venture into Whitechapel, he would be even less willing to go down to the waterfront, the worst part of the worst part of town, where the sailors spilled from their ships fueled with pent-up desperation, ready to erupt at the slightest provocation. Only the oldest, ugliest, and most hopeless of women walked the waterfront. The crime rate there made the rest of the East End look like Eden.

But the tone of voice had been what Leanna was accustomed to – low, measured, and polite. She turned toward the man at the end of the bar with a radiant smile of gratitude.

"Not such a bad walk either, Miss. Lighted streets, enough people, a straight five minute path down to the docks. Isn't that so, Lucy?"

"A straight path," Lucy parroted. She was obviously trained to agree with anything he said, and Cecil wondered if the bruises up and down the girl's arms were put there courtesy of this well-dressed, soft-spoken man. In a room full of idiots, Cecil reflected, Lucy was queen. She had been sniveling that she was afraid of the Ripper all evening, with short pauses to agree to provide an alibi for every thug in Christendom, and it did not seem to have occurred to her there might be any contradiction in these two activities.

But the man had been clever to draw Lucy into the conversation, because the corroboration of a woman seemed to sweep away whatever doubts Leanna may have had. She smiled again, turned and made her way back to table where Emma was weeping.

"Smart to send to docks," Micha said. Like Cecil, he had observed the exchange in a shrouded silence, but the minute Leanna moved out of earshot he had stood up. "Dead end, yes?"

Quite right, Cecil thought. A dock is the ultimate dead end street. In the black-specked mirror behind the wall he could see Leanna pulling Emma to her feet and the two of them making their way out the door. The girls would not only be in the most dangerous part of town, but cornered. Micha laughed and pulled on his coat, pausing behind Cecil to make a single slashing motion with his hand, drawing his imaginary knife around Cecil's throat in a gesture that eerily mimicked that morning when they had all been collected around the family breakfast table, reading their newspapers. Tom had made just such a motion on Leanna, slipping behind her, his arm around the waist, brandishing his finger as a weapon and they had all sat in the comfort of their sunny breakfast room and laughed.

How long ago had that been? No more than a few weeks, but it seemed to Cecil as if these events had occurred in another lifetime. He gazed into the cracked mirror behind the bar and watched as Micha stepped into the streets and turned in the direction of the docks.

7:48 PM

Tom was not making good time on his wounded ankle and had nearly lost track of John twice. The figure of the man and the woman had faded almost to grayness within the fog and the two of them kept turning. This was the nature of the streets around the waterfront – they grew more winding, less linear or predictable and what seemed to be a busy thoroughfare sometimes trickled down to an alley. It seemed as if the entire neighborhood had been cruelly designed to deceive outsiders, as interwoven and illogical as a web.

A woman brushed against him. Later he would realize it was an attempt to catch his attention, to draw him into an alley or a bed, to initiate a transaction that would end with his money in her pocket, his seed between her legs. But at the time, he instinctively stepped aside to allow her passage, murmuring an apology as if he had been the one who'd jostled her. It all took no more than a few seconds, but when Tom looked back up John was out of sight.

7:48 PM

The girl had been polite, as ladies always pretend to be, but something in her voice has brought it all back. The memory of his fall from grace, the beginning of the long slow descent of his life. She had asked for a cab. She had tossed her head. He could imagine her on that bright lawn, looking down at his

388

hands, seeing the blood there and asking – in that cool, superior voice - "What have you done?"

The ladies. How they lift you up and how they set you down.

He shakes his head, tries to clear the jumble of memories, to concentrate. The whores, yes, of course the whores must be punished, but their crimes are miniscule compared to the ones who called themselves ladies, the ones who looked down their small white noses, the ones who could fully see you no matter how cleverly you hid, the ones who knew at a glance all the bad things you had done. Mary Kelly, walking with her books. Everyone said she was kind, all those fools sobbing over her at the pub, but once he had spoken to her in the street and she had literally drawn back from him, as if she too could see the blood on his sleeve. Like Katrina with her yapping dogs, like this girl who had stood at the bar of a broken down pub and calmly requested transport. They could see it, they could see him, every one. Whenever they came near he heard the old question. Whathaveyoudone,whathaveyoudone, whathaveyoudone.

He checks his pocket watch. He has told the beast to meet him at half past eight, and he wishes to arrive first. To have the chance to prepare himself, to prepare the space.

He slips off his barstool, heads towards the door. He has not bothered to pay for his beer. But then again, he never does.

7:50 PM

No more than a minute later, Trevor Welles was entering the Pony Pub and approaching the barmaid. He knew this place and he even knew this girl. He had spoken with her several times since the night of the double murders, eventually revealing himself as a detective. She seemed to remember, for she greeted him with enthusiasm. Some people liked to be

389

interviewed by the authorities, Trevor had noticed. It was a strange thing, for having the police come to your door in most neighborhoods was social disaster. But in the East End, it seemed to give one a certain status among her peers.

He described Emma and Leanna to the girl and she said, yes, they'd been there. No more than minutes before. She glanced around for confirmation, but all the men who had been seated nearby seemed to have scattered too.

Trevor felt like pounding the bar in frustration. The girl said they had entered with a man called Georgy but had left alone. She was sure of this. She nodded emphatically as she spoke.

Trevor could only hope the fact they'd left alone meant the funds had exchanged hands and this Georgy was done with his game. Most of the bobbies were congregated along Merchant Street, so if the women were seeking transport, as they almost certainly were, someone would undoubtedly intercept them.

Trevor turned to go. He was almost to the door when the girl called after him.

"Oh, Sir, one other thing. They're headed to the waterfront."

7:59 PM

Leanna had long since given up on consoling Emma. Instead she linked arms with the girl, concentrating on keeping her upright and mobile, and trying to take note of the sign posts they passed. She didn't know what the man at the bar considered a five-minute walk but they had been on the streets for nearly twenty, with no waterfront in sight. This was a disaster. No one could blame Emma, who had been in a stupor for days. It was Leanna who should have seen the truth. That the man at the bar had been a bad man too, possibly in consort with Georgy, equally intent on misleading them. Leanna shuddered at the sight of the mean houses with rags stuffed in the shattered windowpanes, at the pinched, yellow look the women all wore beneath their garish makeup, at the mingled smell of sweat, urine, and wet wool which seemed to steam from everyone they passed, choking her and occasionally making bile rise up in her throat.

Yet Mary Kelly had lived in these streets and John and Trevor walked them every day. Even Aunt Gerry, and those society matrons Leanna sometimes dismissed as foolish, came to Whitechapel regularly to dispense food and clothing. Why was she the only one too cowardly to look into the face of need, the one who was made literally sick by the stink of poverty?

"We've got to keep moving," she said, tugging at Emma, who had paused on a corner. The street lamps were a comfort as they passed below them at certain intervals on each block, not only because they allowed her to read the signposts, but also the faces of the people. It was like walking between waves of darkness and light. As the girls would leave the glow of one lamp, Emma seemed to strain forward to the next, but Leanna was in the pattern of looking back at the light behind them as a way of marking time and distance.

When they came to the darkest part of the seventh block, she glanced behind her and saw a faint shadow moving under the street light they had just passed. Leanna continued to look back, but did not tell Emma. There had been men pressed all around them earlier, too many to note, but now the crowd had thinned out and each figure took on a different sort of significance.

"Emma, I'm not sure we're going the right direction. We've been walking for nearly twenty minutes, so if the man in the bar was right, we should have been at the dock a long time ago. I think we've gotten ourselves turned. We should ask someone."

"No," Emma said. "Not anyone here. They know who we are."

Leanna looked over her shoulder. The shadowy figure was still there... but then again, there was a shadowy figure coming towards her from the other direction as well, and two more passing on the opposite side of the street. The fog reduced everyone to the same amorphous grey shape, she thought, trying to push her panic down. Perhaps the fact that the mist seemed to be getting thicker did indeed mean they were close to the water. Besides, the Ripper had taken his victims to dark alleys and rooms with doors that locked. He had never attacked a woman early in the evening on a major street, no matter how badly lit it might be, and while she and Emma might be lost and vulnerable, at least there were two of them. "What do you mean they know who we are? Georgy knew your name but he —"

Emma shook her head. "The costumes aren't working," she said. "The people in the bar knew we were rich, at least that you were, and if we speak to anyone, even to ask directions, our voices will just confirm what our clothes suggest. We don't belong here."

"All right," Leanna said hollowly. "Keep your hood pulled tight. Perhaps our safety depends on our ability to blend in."

8:08 PM

Tom attempted to run the next few blocks, paused to read a street sign and realized, to his utter frustration, that he had traveled in a circle. John and the woman must have taken a side street. He turned back, retracing his steps. Up to Hadley, back to Toddle, and then, without warning, Tom heard a sound. It was muffled and hard to pinpoint in location, but the nature of sound was irrefutable. A woman was screaming.

His breath was coming in ragged gasps and Tom was forced to stop for a minute, to lean against a wall. There. The sound again. Muffled but persistent. A long low wail and Tom went in search of the source, praying that whoever was making it had the courage and the faith to keep calling.

8:12 PM

Alcohol made the world very clear.

Cecil knew that not everyone would agree with this theory. Conventional wisdom, of course, would have declared that the seven beers he had gulped out of nerves at the Pony Pub might have impaired his ability to judge what was going on around him. But Cecil knew better. From the first time he had partaken – breaking into his father's liquor cabinet at the age of twelve – Cecil had understood that alcohol was a type of religion, capable of guiding a man to insights he would never obtain with his workaday mind. There are levels of reality, he'd thought, as he'd heard his sister sign her death warrant with a well-spoken phrase, as he felt the butcher Micha drag a calloused finger across his neck in a mimic of the Ripper's blade. As he watched that smug, barrel-chested detective lean over the bar and ask Lucy if she'd seen the girls from Mayfair.

There are levels of reality, beginning with the simple shiny world of sensation where people like Georgy and Lucy and Micha dwelt, where coins might strike the palm or they might not, where there was sometimes the solace of food or sex or a warm place to sleep, but more likely hunger, loneliness, and chill. The pains and pleasures of animals – hardly enough to engage a man like himself. And then there is the level of thought, wherein lay the good detective and Cecil's worthy siblings and the people who waltzed and plotted at the

Wentworth balls. The people who live within this strata believe it to be the highest.

Only a select few have experienced the next realm, that abstract band of infinite possibility that hums above the surface of everyday life. Cecil knew he needed alcohol to take him there, just as priests require Jesus to take them to God, and there is no shame in such dependence on an intermediary. He sat at the bar with his empty mugs spread out around him, watching colors grow brighter and edges grow sharper, and after the detective left the Pony Pub, Cecil had risen shakily to his feet. His sister had been sent to the water. The brute Micha had been sent after her and the detective after him and somewhere in this grand parade was the man whose soft voice had sent Leanna to the waterfront, a man Cecil understood to be a fellow acolyte, a student of the fringes. He had left the pub too, sometime after Micha and before the detective, but Cecil was not sure why.

He threw money on the bar. He did not count the amount. Money always became inconsequential when he was in this particular state of grace. Counting money was nothing more than an attempt to measure the immeasurable. The coins he tossed were meant to pay for him and Georgy and Micha and anyone else within earshot of the tinkling sound, because Cecil would be a rich man by sunrise, surely so. He could not say why he felt this sudden urge to enter the streets. Leanna was doomed whether he stayed or whether he left, but Cecil felt compelled to follow her, propelled perhaps by the alcohol or perhaps by adrenaline, the last chemical throb of his fear.

Or maybe it was just by a betting man's desire to see the game played out. Neddy used to laugh at him about it. They would go to the tracks and lay their bets and even if Cecil had a willing girl on one arm and a bottle of champagne in the other, he still could not resist rising whenever he heard the sound of a starting trumpet. Neddy couldn't understand why Cecil stood at the railing. He always said that the horses would either run or they would not. The winners were determined by the gods, Neddy would call after him, they were chosen long before a lad like you was even born. Cecil knew Neddy was right, but he had stood watching every race he'd ever bet on, and now, as the clock of a faraway church struck the quarter-hour, he cast coins across a counter and turned toward the street.

CHAPTER FORTY-THREE
8:12 PM

She has come early to the alley. She turns toward him slowly, and he thinks, somewhat irrelevantly, that her bulk actually gives her a sort of strange elegance, since it makes it impossible for her to do anything quickly. Her face registers surprise that he is alone and then anger, most probably at an anger at herself for ever believing that he was bringing her a client, ever thinking he would wish to erase his debt with the promise of fresh business.

This is what happens when you strike a bargain with the man who calls himself Jack the Ripper. He stands before you in a dark alley with a gun. A cheap gun, purchased just this morning from an ironmonger, clumsy and unsteady in his hand.

But at this range, it will do.

8:12 PM

The woman's voice had come from a room in the back of a boarding house. Tom looked both directions, hoping against hope to see one of the bobbies Trevor had promised would be patrolling the area, but once again there was no one in sight, nor were there lights in any of the other windows of the house. Tom stood in the alleyway and debated what to do next. Stillness had settled, making him wonder if his nerves were getting the better of him and he'd imagined the whole thing. Then a fresh scream pierced the silence and, without thought, Tom was back in motion, ducking around the corner of the house and straining on tiptoe to see inside.

One look was enough to tell the story. John's back was to Tom, but it was unmistakably him, bending over a woman, wrenching apart her bare legs while she struggled and screamed. Tom flung himself against the wooden door of the hovel, and fairly bounced off, landing back in the yard with a thud and a scream of his own. He rolled over in the grass, bent double in pain and frustration and then the door jerked open, revealing the tall angry form of John Harrowman, shouting "What the hell is going on here?"

It occurred to Tom that he should have done a better job of thinking things out. John was upright and armed, he was flat and defenseless. He made a sound which was intended as a roar of outrage but came out more like the beginning of a sob.

John peered into the dark yard and frowned. "Is it Tom Bainbridge? Why on earth are you here?" He didn't sound like a maniac, merely confused, and then the woman Tom had seen him with earlier appeared at the door, fully dressed and apparently fine except for the worry that creased her brow.

"Doctor?" she said. "I think she's fainted."

"Probably for the best," John said, turning back into the room. He shot one final glance at Tom. "You say you want to be a doctor, do you? Very well, I could use a hand. Have you ever seen a breech birth?"

8:16 PM

As they got nearer the lights of the waterfront, Leanna's spirits lifted a bit. Emma had slowed to the point where she was virtually dragging her, but at least they appeared to have lost the figure in the lamplight. "We have to keep moving, Emma," she said. "We can rest when we get home to Mayfair. And let's cross to the others side of the street for a while."

"I'm exhausted. I need to stop and get something to eat."

398

"Something to eat? Are you mad? We aren't returning from the theatre with Trevor. Come on, see the lights? We have to be close to the waterfront and we'll find a cab there."

"We passed a pub just back," Emma said. "I must rest, just for a moment."

"We can't," Leanna said, turning back to give the girl a tug. It was at that moment that she saw the man.

The man or was it simply a man? Was it the same one who had followed them earlier? This one seemed taller, thinner than the first, with a long-loped gait. No, not the same man. The first one had been heavier and he had stayed on the opposite side of the street, but this man was right behind them, and growing closer with each step.

"Emma," Leanna said, struggling to keep her voice from cracking. "I think we're being followed."

"Followed? What?" Emma stopped in her tracks and turned around. "I see no one."

"Come," said Leanna, yanking her sharply

But Emma stood stubbornly, facing back. She was about to tell Leanna she was the one who was mad when she saw him. He was nearly a full block behind them, just passing under a street lamp, his shadow moving like a blade of darkness through the circle of the light. There was a moment when she might have seen his face, but then he stepped out of the bright circle, and ceased to exist.

There was no other movement, just darkness as smooth and vast as an ocean and Emma stared at the next streetlight along the block, waiting for someone to cross beneath it. No one did.

"Is he there?" Leanna asked desperately.

Emma shook her head. "I'm not sure."

8:17 PM

Going down one of the main throughfares would have
assured that he passed more bobbies along the way and perhaps
even, depending upon how steadily they were moving, overtaken
the girls. But the back streets were faster and, debating even as
he ran, Trevor decided to take the most direct route to the
water. His anxiety increased with each block. How could he,
not to mention half of Scotland Yard, have missed them? Was
he utterly wrong about the reason Emma and Leanna had been
lured to Whitechapel? Tom's blurted confession that his sister
was an heiress had stunned Trevor, made him realize that he
could have once again misread the situation, that Leanna might
indeed the intended target.

He screamed her name. Then Emma's. No answer,
although there were other noises coming from the alleys.
Moans, grunts, giggles, the raw sounds of sex and of life's
neverending needs. The Ripper comes and goes, but London
continues.

The street he'd chosen was considerate enough to slope
downhill but it lacked streetlights and Trevor stumbled over the
irregular cobblestones, his feet sliding in the ruts and muck.
The wind roared through these narrow venues, as loud as water
in a river, and once he thought he heard a woman cry out. A
sound that could indicate pleasure or pain and how similar the
cries are, he thought, how indistinguishable in the dark. "Are
you there?" he shouted, waving his light torch, but he saw no
one. "Leanna?" he screamed, trying to push down fear and keep
his voice low enough to carry. "Emma? Can you hear me?"

The dim glow of the waterfront drew him onward. The
downhill slope, the river, the place where all the threads would
be drawn together. And just then he heard the last thing he
expected. The sound of a pistol.

400

8:17 PM

Death by gunshot would not ordinarily be his first choice. It is eruptive, imprecise, and noisy but perhaps, upon reflection, the creature before him deserves no better. She has threatened him and tried – what's the English phrase? Yes, she has tried to turn the tables, and a price must be paid for such impunity.

He looks at the heap of clothing before him and reflects that it hardly looks human. No one will ever connect this one to him. A different sort of method, a different type of victim. The death of a woman no one liked. They will all say she deserved it, and they will give her not a moment's thought.

Nonetheless, he uses his scarf to wipe the gun. He remembers what Trevor said, that the French had means of reading the patterns that swirled about the ends of a man's fingertips. There might be a chance, however slight, that someone could connect this gun to him, so he cleans it carefully before tossing it on the body of Maud Milford.

He pulls his knife from his pocket, almost by habit. But he feels not the slightest urge to approach her body, no curiosity about what lies beneath her clothes or beneath her skin. His heart rate is normal. His breath is regular and there is no film of sweat upon his brow. His mind is already somewhere else.

On the Sunday morning he fled Warsaw he had the clothes on his back and the knife in his pocket, the same knife he is holding now. It had taken him three weeks to get to London. He had huddled in cattle cars, earned his passage across the channel by scrubbing decks. Luckily, he had studied some English at the University and he worked hard to eradicate his accent.

His first job had been for an undertaker, a position he accepted because it included a room in the back where he could sleep. He found the dead bodies to be soothing company in the evenings after everyone else had left. He spoke to them sometimes, first in Polish and then in English, until he was afraid he was going mad. In time he found his way to the Pony Pub and it was there that he overheard a copper saying the Yard needed coroners. He had not recognized the word in English so he had asked the barmaid what it means. She'd turned to him, all giggles and smiles, and said "But it's a doctor for dead people, isn't it?"

Phillips, with his shaky hands, had been amazed at how fast he could drain a body. Was amazed at how neatly he could suture a wound, how unperturbed the young man was by the endless gore of the Scotland Yard mortuary. And so he became a doctor of the dead.

He hadn't been meant to overhear that bit about the fingerprints, but nor did they bother to keep secrets from him. Over the last few months, he had learned many things and filed them away in his mind, information to be used at some future point. They considered themselves men of science and thus without prejudice, but the first time he'd been introduced to Trevor Welles the man stumbled over his last name, as all the English seemed to do. Despite the round of hearty handshakes that followed, it was clear he'd been discounted in their eyes. Had been put in a certain category, lumped with the Michas and Lucys, the ones who could not understand, who never would.

Trevor had mispronounced his name, had shaken his hand, and from that point on had behaved as if Severin Klosowski were deaf.

Tom had warred within himself as he followed John into the shabby room. He felt he should explain that Leanna and Emma might be in danger... but then again, Trevor had undoubtedly intercepted the girls by now and was transporting them home to Mayfair while this woman writhing on the bed was most clearly in need of assistance. So he had pushed up his sleeves and worked beside John and within minutes the two of them managed to maneuver the child feet first into the world. They left the baby and mother in the care of the other woman, who had turned out to be her sister, and stepped back into the misty night.

"Come with me," Tom said. "We need to walk and I'll tell you where we're going on the way."

"You're limping," John said. "Why?"

Tom told John an abbreviated version of the story and when he got to the part about Leanna and Emma, John jerked to attention. "My God, you're just now telling me this?"

"They're undoubtedly home as we speak, sleeping in their beds. I just want to go back to the pub and see if I can find Trevor or Mabrey, explain to them why I disappeared."

"You shouldn't be on that ankle."

"It doesn't hurt as bad as my shoulder, to be truthful. I think I dislocated it trying to break down the door."

"Do you want to ride on my back?"

Tom looked at him, surprised and offended. "Of course not."

8:22 PM

"Emma," Leanna said breathlessly "What's that smell? It's fish, is it not? Dead and rotting fish, thank God, and it may as well be roses. That means we're getting close."

8:22 PM

It would seem impossible to lose a man as large as Micha, but Cecil had managed to do just that. He had followed his lumbering shape for several blocks and then lost sight of him. Leanna and Emma were trodding along as steadily as lambs to the slaughter, but the man he'd paid to slaughter them seemed to have disappeared. Cecil could only assume he'd elected to take another street and lie in wait for them down by the waterfront. At least that's what he hoped. For all he knew the man had taken his coins and was drinking Polish champagne in a bar somewhere.

But just as Cecil had stepped into one of those infernal streetlights, something unexpected had happened. The girls stopped and the Kelly chit had turned on her heel and faced him. The sight of her staring up the street so directly and boldly startled Cecil and he had stood frozen in the circular light beneath the lamppost like an actor on a stage. If it had been Leanna who had whirled about to look, she doubtless would have recognized him, and then what would he have done?

He was following far too closely. Best to slip into an alley for a second and let them get a bit farther down the street.

Cecil had no sooner stepped into the shadows before he realized he was not alone. A man was standing there. Ah, the man from the bar, the one with the mustache. The one who was dillying and probably beating the barmaid, the one who stayed sober while everyone around him drank, the one who had

404

so obligingly sent Leanna to the waterfront and to her doom. Now this was a strange coincidence. Why was this man lurking in an alleyway, and not Micha? Was he supposed to greet the fellow?

"Hello," he said. "Fancy finding you here. Name's Severin, isn't it?"

And then Cecil saw the knife.

CHAPTER FORTY-FIVE
8:23 PM

"I'm not sure where he went," Emma said. "Perhaps our nerves have gone so bad we've imagined every man in the street is following us."

"I know," Leanna says. "And listen to those foghorns. We must have come full circle because we truly are near the docks."

"Thank God," Emma said. "When we find the cab we —"

But as they turned the final corner they came face to face with a man. Strange, Leanna thought, but it seems as if he's waiting for us. Emma's mind went even more into the sort of slow-motion abstraction that often accompanies shock and makes it feel dreamlike. Or perhaps she was turning pages in one of her father's old storybooks. A bear was before them. He was standing with his weight equally on each foot and in a bit of a crouch, the paunch of his belly thrust forward.

The bear smiled.

And then he lunged.

Leanna tried to cry out but, before she could make a sound, the man's arm swooped down, as swift and mechanical as a sickle, and lifted her straight up by the base of her throat. She gasped for air as she felt herself being pushed skyward until, when she struggled to open her eyes, she found herself staring down into his grinning face. Her feet kicked and dangled below her, as ineffectual as ship sails on a windless day. Emma, snapped free from her shock, let out a shrill scream and pounded at the back of the man. The sound echoed through the streets, and, although no one came to help, someone must have lit a light in one of the rooms overlooking the waterway for a pale yellow glow began to diffuse the darkness, allowing Emma to see. Leanna had stopped kicking and swung about like a rag doll, her feet grazing the rough boards of the dock.

She's dead, Emma thought. He's broken her neck. Using all her strength she leapt on the man's back and threw both of her arms around his face, gouging her fingers into his eyes and biting the fleshy overhang at the base of his skull. She was not strong enough to pull him down, but the pain in his eyes and neck had the desired effect. He released Leanna to the ground and staggered blindly while Emma crossed her hands, grabbed her own wrists, and simply dropped. The dead weight of her body hanging behind him made the big man sway and she kicked as hard as she could. She was screaming, screaming for every pain she'd ever suffered, every loss, every fear. Her voice echoed up and down the waterfront.

This time Trevor heard her. He had been pacing the docks since he'd arrived minutes before and now he began running toward the sound of her voice, blowing his police whistle in short hard blasts. Other coppers in the area picked up the signal and began to blow their whistles too, converging on the pier. Davy Mabrey, coming from the west, was among them.

Micha had regained his balance but, since Emma was hanging down the back of his body, he was unable to reach her. He whirled sharply, a move that nearly sent her spinning off of him, and finally slammed his own back, and thus hers, into a piling. Emma's head hit the boards and she slid to the ground, her mouth full of blood and her vision gone cottony.

It was as if she was looking down at herself, as if this was all happening to someone else, a substitute Emma, another person. It would be easy to give into it and just sink from this time and place. Easy to release her grasp on this sad life and fall into some bigger, brighter world. Emma let her head roll back. She had sat at her mother's bed at the end, had seen the startled look that had come across the woman's features with her last earthly exhalation. Emma had always wondered what this final revelation had been, but now she knew. Had Mary seen this? Had her father or her brother?

It is easier to die than to live. That is the great surprise.

8:25 PM

Severin drew the blade of the knife lightly across his own palm.

"You did not know?" He said it as a question but meant it as a statement. "Did not know I was one they are looking for? Looking for a very long time."

Cecil inched back, knocking over a trash can, his boots slipping over the piles of fish bones and slimy fruit. He wanted to tell the man he didn't see him, that he would never tell anyone they had been here, but his voice seemed to have left him. He could do no more than shake his head.

Severin stepped toward him slowly. "And now at last I am caught," he said. "What are we to do about this?"

And then, like the vengeance of angels, a crescendo of police whistles began to rise up all around them. Not one or two but a dozen, coming from all directions. Severin's dark eyes flickered and he hesitated. Just long enough to allow Cecil to turn.

8:25 PM

"What's that sound?" Tom said. "It's coming from the water."

"Get there when you can," John said. He bent to slide Tom from his back and then he began to run.

8:26 PM

The three figures before him were images from a nightmare. The giant at the mouth of the dock was Micha - the man Abrams had served up to him on a platter and that he had been fool enough to release. Micha had thrown Emma's limp form to the pavement as casually as a man shucks a coat. Even as Trevor ran down the dock with his whistle screaming, Micha did not pause at the sound or hesitate in his task. He left Emma and turned toward Leanna, who was struggling to sit up.

Trevor dropped the whistle from his lips and began to simply roar the same word over and over again. The darkness around him had a new name. Jack. Jack. Jack.

The big man moved with an almost leisurely grace, stooping over Leanna, lifting a shank of her hair, which glowed snow-white in the streetlight, pulling back his hand....but Trevor saw that Emma had somehow gotten to her feet, was running at the man, throwing her small body against his, and in just that moment Leanna also managed to get her knees beneath her, to push up from the dock like a diver from a board. The collective movement of their bodies disturbed the man's equilibrium. Just for a moment, but it was enough. They weaved and staggered, six arms about each other, in a bizarre triangular dance, and they were moving down the mouth of the pier, over the water. The man's arm rose, there was a flash of silver in the sky, and then Leanna was slung to his right, toward the dock, and Emma to his left, toward the pier. Trevor was running, pulling off his coat, screaming, and at last someone seemed to hear him. Emma turned, stumbling, and her eyes locked with Trevor's for a split second, just as she made one final grab at the giant's arm, just as she was starting to fall.

Leanna was slowly regaining her breath. She rolled to her back, looked up at the sky. Her throat ached, her vision was

410

blurred, and all there seemed to be in the world was the noise of the whistles, sharp and insistent, and beneath them, another sound. She heard the splash of a body falling into water, then another, and finally, a few seconds later, a third.

CHAPTER FORTY-SIX
8:34 PM

Thanks to shouted orders of Davy Mabrey, nearly every bobby in the East End was on hand to fish Micha Banasik out of the Thames. Emma's final lunge had managed to knock him off balance and the two had gone tumbling into the water below the pier. Trevor dove in a few seconds later and reached Emma just as she was breaking the surface. He had pulled her to the stones where Davy had gone scrambling down the bank to help them both back to land.

John had found Leanna sprawled on the dock, the back of her hair blackened with blood and for a horrible moment he thought she was dead. But then he heard her cough. "Don't try to talk," he said, bending over her, straining to see the marks on her throat in the shadows. "Lie still," he whispered. "I'm here. We all are."

Trevor stumbled up with Emma in his arms and simply said "Doctor?"

"She's alive," John said. "We need a coach." He unclasped his cape and gave it to Trevor to wrap around Emma while Davy sprinted off in search of the Scotland Yard carriage.

Tom, who had not only been limping but who had been further delayed by slamming right into a man with a mustache who'd come fairly flying out of an alley, finally stumbled up as well. At the sight of the two girls lying side by side on the dock, he burst into deep racking sobs.

"They're all right," John said hoarsely, for he felt like weeping himself. "Leanna's got some nasty bruising and we don't want Emma to get hypothermia. We need to get them to Geraldine's as fast as possible. You too, Welles. You're drenched straight through."

But Trevor had turned away, was staring toward the bobbies collected around Micha.

"The carriage is just here, Sir," Davy said quietly.

"Tell the doctor," Trevor said, just as quietly. Within minutes John had Emma, Leanna, and Tom loaded in and the coach rumbled off in the direction of Mayfair.

Micha was equally battered and wet but not so well-attended. He coughed and sputtered while it took three men to get his dead weight lifted into the back of the wagon. As it rolled away, a shout of glee went up among the bobbies. They would all someday tell their grandchildren of the night they single-handedly collared Jack the Ripper.

Trevor and Davy were standing off to the side.

"Not the man we expected him to be, is he Sir?" Davy said.

"No," Trevor answered shortly. He was beginning to feel the cold.

"Not the man at all," Davy confirmed, and Trevor shook his head. They had caught a brute to be sure, but he knew in his heart the clumsy beast inside the wagon wasn't the Ripper. He had known it while he was falling through the air, heading towards the knife-cold water of the Thames, had known with a kind of finality that had felt like his heart being cut from his chest.

He turned. People were trying to talk to him. More than one of the men offered to buy him a beer. Reporters were arriving, flashing their cameras and shouting questions. He couldn't see, couldn't think. Would they not all face away and leave him alone? But he did note that the police had roped off the area, that they were holding the press back while they combed the pier for fibers and hairs, chips of mortar, the remnants of the struggle. His legacy to the Yard. That's something, he thought. Maybe it's enough.

"An ending, but not a conclusion," he said aloud.

"Beg your pardon, Sir?"

"Nothing. Get me my pipe."

Davy nodded and went back to where Trevor's coat lay. The detective must've known they would end up in the water, Davy thought, else why would he have pulled off his coat while he was running? He extracted Trevor's battered notebook from a pocket and gazed at it for a moment, sadly. Then he went to the next pocket and found the pipe and tobacco. Returning to the shadows, he handed both to his boss, then waited to give him his coat. But Welles was already walking back toward the pier.

Poor Leanna and Emma, he thought, they had been on foot for an hour but had managed to get, in all their circling, no more than ten blocks from where they had started. "We've never gone as far as we think," Trevor informed a gull, who gazed at him meditatively, then took flight. Trevor sat down on the pilings and lit his pipe, surprised that his hands did not shake in the effort. Inhaling deeply, he looked out at the water, which, deceptive in the moonlight, was almost lovely. He exhaled, and the puff of smoke escaped into the fog.

Tom's frantic pounding brought Gage to the door with Geraldine right behind him. They watched in shock as the girls they assumed were dining out were carried in by John one at a time. Geraldine helped Emma get changed into dry bedclothes while John, with the unsteady assistance of Gage, rinsed the blood from Leanna's scalp and stitched up her cut. The bruising around her neck would take longer to heal. Then he went downstairs to see to Tom, whom he suspected was the most badly injured of all.

The boy had collapsed on the couch. It was almost impossible for him to believe that this just this morning he had awakened naked on the floor with a hangover and that so many strange things could have happened in the course of a single day. He had broken into a house, stolen a knife, sprained his ankle, walked through London in a bloody shirt, gone on a bender, ridden in an official Scotland Yard carriage, dislocated his shoulder, witnessed his first birth, and nearly lost his sister to Jack the Ripper. Now that he was safely back within the confines of his aunt's home the adrenaline had abruptly left his body and he could not seem to stop trembling. John, who was nearly as exhausted as Tom, wrapped his ankle and popped the boy's shoulder back into its socket. The pain was great enough to make him cry out and afterwards the two men sat on the couch, side by side, staring into the fire.

"Did you talk to them?" Tom asked.

"Offered them something to help them sleep," John said. "But they both said no."

He does like it when women go to sleep, Tom thought. He is indeed quick to offer the needle. But he had seen John's face as he eased the infant from her mother's body, the deep and unfeigned relief when he heard her first cry, and that had told Tom everything he needed to know about John's character. When the women had babbled in the carriage, all that they could speak off was Trevor. How he had appeared like some sort of vengeful god, Leanna said, swooping down unexpectedly through the air, but Emma thought his arrival was more like a warrior on horseback or perhaps, no, perhaps more like a locomotive, swift and powerful. He had been heroic, certainly, on that they could agree. Leanna kept repeating "He saved our lives" in a mechanical fashion while Emma had been so distracted that she'd lain beneath John's cloak and allowed him to cut her wet clothes completely off her body.

John had worked steadily, moving back and forth between the two girls, offering what medical care he could in the darkness of the coach, and he had not spoken during the entire ride. Tom considered the man's profile for a moment and then looked back into the fire. It was too early to predict how things would play out.

Geraldine came down the steps reporting that both the girls were asleep. She dropped into the chair opposite the couch and said "John, I don't know what we'd do without you."

John smiled wanly. "I hope you never have to find out."

"Please stay the night." Geraldine said. "I wish I could offer you the guest room, but - I forgot to tell you Tom, in the thrash of getting the girls upstairs, but your brother is here. He just showed up unexpectedly saying he had news."

Tom's heart sank. "Why did you let him in?"

Geraldine looked surprised. "He's my nephew, of course."

"But Cecil won't rest until he –"

"No, not Cecil. Of course not. Cecil's dreadful. It's William."

A little better, but still confusing. "What the devil is William doing in London?"

Geraldine shrugged. "He said he was exhausted and would be turning in early. Should I wake him?"

"Yes," Tom said. "And bring Gage in too. I only want to tell this story once."

10:10 PM

They all poured brandies and settled in. When Tom described the contents of the letter that had been sent to Emma, Geraldine closed her eyes and wept softly. William had sat through the tale with both feet on the floor and both hands at his side, Gage paced, and when Tom got to the part about stealing the bloody shirt from John's hassock they all actually laughed a little.

"At the time I didn't know how much blood there was in childbirth," Tom said. "Now I do."

But as he had tried to explain how they'd all wound up at the waterfront, the story grew so complicated that Tom hobbled over to fetch the pieces of the chest set so that he might demonstrate the sequence on the tabletop. He used the queens for Emma and Leanna, the bishop for John, the knight for Trevor, a rook for Davy and a pawn for himself. He would never be able to explain why the Ripper was represented by the king, but they all bent forward in concentration as he went through his tableau. When he finished with the scene of the bobbies fishing the big brute out of the water, he flicked the king to its side and said "Checkmate."

Geraldine leaned back in her chair, shaking her head. "When I picture those poor girls walking the streets of Whitechapel…."

Tom looked at his older brother. "You must think you've come into absolute insanity. Aunt Geraldine said you had news?"

"Oh that," said William. "It hardly matches your story for drama, in fact it doesn't seem worth mentioning in the light of all this." He looked at John. "My sister will fully recover, won't she?"

"Up and about in a day or two," John said.

Something in him has shifted, Tom thought. The anger has gone. He hasn't come to London to rant and rave, to fight the will, or to try and drag Leanna back to Rosemoral. He's thinking of something other than himself now.

"Tell us, William, really," Tom said. "Why are you here?"

William shifted his large frame uncomfortably in the chair. "Well, it's the damnest thing," he said. "But Cecil has disappeared."

CHAPTER FORTY-EIGHT
November 13
7: 20 AM

The man asks the woman to marry him.

It doesn't happen exactly as she'd dreamed.... but then, what does? He is not on one knee, but instead bending over her on the bed. He may not speak of love, but he does promise to take her away and that's all she ever wanted, really. She wants this man to be here with her, holding her hand, talking of a different place, where they can live a simple life and forget everything that has happened to them in London.

So Lucy says yes.

Severin had endured a very bad night. He sat until daybreak on top of a rum keg and for the first time in recent memory, he was frightened. The man from the bar, the tall dandy who threw around his money and rolled his pale eyes in disdain, had stood no more than two feet away, staring at the knife in Severin's hand. Drunk as he was, he had understood at once what he was seeing.

The man had glanced at the form of Maudy, had swayed on his feet a bit, and had then looked back at Severin. It was a strange moment, a sense of seeing oneself in a carnival mirror. Each had sensed from the start how much they were alike. Of course, Severin would never let himself go to drink in such appalling fashion and he didn't know what manner of unsavory business this dandy was up to, but he knew they shared a certain way of looking on the world.

He genuinely regretted that he would have to kill him. Severin had never killed a man.

But when the air had suddenly split with sound and an avalanche of bobbies had come rolling toward the waterfront, the dandy had bolted. He ran into the street and when Severin tried to follow, he found himself caught in a swarm of rushing men. They rumbled past him, nearly knocking him off his feet, and the shrillness of their whistles was unendurable, like a woman's scream. The one thing Severin despised above all else was the sound of a woman screaming.

He let himself be carried down to the docks with the wave of the crowd and he stood back while they dragged Micha from the water. Tied his hands and threw him into the back of a wagon, and when the thud of Micha's great weight hit the floorboards, Severin had felt it deep in his own gut. Because last night was the very first time it occurred to him that someday he too would be caught. There were so many coppers when you saw them like that all together, swarming around with their clubs and lanterns, so many that you knew no man could escape forever, no matter how clever he might be.

Severin had stepped back from the crowd and focused on the figure in the middle of it all, Trevor Welles.

He had, of course, watched Welles for weeks. Setting up his ridiculous laboratory at the Yard, reading his reports from France, giving lectures to anyone who would listen, and imagining himself the great detective. The fat fool had even come into the Pony Pub to interview Lucy and had somehow failed to notice Severin sitting at the end of bar. So much for his self-proclaimed powers of observation. Severin had eavesdropped on Trevor throughout that whole night, as sickened by the man's hypocrisy as by his arrogance. As it turns out, the hero of Scotland Yard likes his young whores just as much as the next man.

It had been such a game to mislead them. Sometimes when he was alone in the mortuary, Severin had interfered with Trevor's experiments, poking a fork into one of the wounds on Mary Kelly's leg, replacing the human hairs in his notebook with a few he'd plucked from a passing Whitechapel dog.

Pulling an enormous skirt off a clothesline to burn in Mary Kelly's fireplace, sending them kidneys plucked from bodies in the next room, scribbling messages about Jewes just to fuck with that prissy Raylay Abrams. Stirring a bit of arsenic into Phillips' tea - not enough to kill him, just enough to hasten the shakes. Watching them all search so earnestly for a scalpel that was – here's the great joke – all the while within an arm's reach. He had even left a button from a bobby's coat on the roof of the Kelly house but they hadn't found it, had they? How that would have set them spinning.

He had listened to every meeting, every conference, and at times it had taken the sum total of his substantial self-control to keep from laughing in their faces.

Yes, it had been easy to disregard and mock Welles for weeks but something in his manner last night had pulled Severin up short. Welles knew Micha was not the Ripper. He knew the minute they pulled him from the water and plopped him on the dock that Scotland Yard had caught a whale, but not a shark. Severin had watched as the detective's shoulders sank with disappointment. Just a little, but enough that Severin had understood that Welles was not deceived.

This was going to be a problem.

The police had gotten very close last night. They had touched him, had jostled him, had shoved him and shouted "Step aside, damn you." Much worse, there was a man out there somewhere who knew his name and had seen his face. Severin had walked back and forth among the crowd at the waterfront and when he had not found the man, he had stationed himself on his rum keg and watched each figure that passed. But the drunk dandy with the pale blue eyes had eluded his grasp.

And when the sun finally rose, Severin had known it was over.

So he had walked back to the rooming house where Lucy slept, had crawled through her window as he had so many times before, slipped into her narrow bed beside her. She had awakened with a start, almost crying out in her surprise, but he cupped his hand around her mouth.

Beneath his palm he can feel her muffled cry turn into a smile. She loves him. God knows why, but she does, and at long last her devotion might prove useful.

"You were right all along," he tells her. "There was dreadful business in the streets last night and this is no city for decent people like us."

Under his palm, she nods.

"I could learn to like the country life," he says, removing his hand. "So yes, we'll get married and we will go to your sister in Jersey."

She laughs softly. "You don't listen," she says. "Men never do. My sister isn't in Jersey, she's in New Jersey."

He frowns.

"New Jersey," she repeats. "In America. You'll still go, won't you? You'll take me that far away?"

"Oh yes indeed," he says quietly, slipping his hand beneath her flimsy bedgown. "America is even better."

7:34 AM

The household in Mayfair had managed to sleep a few hours but with the rising of the sun most of them were up too. Trays had been prepared for the girls and William had insisted on carrying up Leanna's. What passed between the two siblings, he did not divulge, but Tom thought William seemed lighter as he came downstairs, relieved and full of appetite. Despite his own aches and pains Tom was ravenous too and the brothers sat together at the breakfast table with Geraldine. William did not seem surprised when Gage emerged from the kitchen with his own plate. Instead he slid his chair a little to make more room for the man, and began to tell them all his plans for getting a degree in estate management.

"Will you release the funds for the tuition?" William asked Tom, his mouth crammed full of toast and jam.

"With great pleasure," Tom said. "Leanna will be thrilled when you tell her."

William smiled shyly. "She was. She said it would be a great load off her mind and I have the impression she doesn't see herself returning to Rosemoral to live. Is something keeping her in London?"

As if on cue, there was a rap at the back door and John Harrowman entered.

"Take a plate, John," Geraldine directed. If the household had been casual before, Tom reflected, this Ripper business had turned them into absolute bohemians.

"No time," John said briskly. "I wanted to check on the girls and then I need to see Mrs. Byrd, the woman Tom helped me deliver last night."

"Dear Lord," said Geraldine. "Do doctors ever sleep?"

John grinned, grabbed a roll from a serving plate, and kissed her on the cheek. "Not often," he said, and then turned toward the stairs.

"He's a saint," Geraldine said.

"And I think he's going to be our brother-in-law," Tom said to William, who gazed thoughtfully toward the staircase. "Now, what's this business about Cecil?"

"Do Gage and I need to give you privacy?" Geraldine asked, but William shook his head and took a gulp of tea.

"The time for pretending is long past us," he said and then proceeded to tell them of Cecil's last disastrous night at the tracks, the missing pounds from his pocket, the notable absence of Gwynette's opal and diamond brooch.

Tom groaned. "Where do you think he's headed?"

William turned up his broad palms. "I could only think he came here, to beg funds from Leanna, but now I'm at a loss."

Another rap at the back door, this time Trevor Welles. He looked as if he had slept no more than John, but he had at least changed out of his wet clothes.

"Trevor," Geraldine said. "Get a plate."

"No time," Trevor said briskly. "I just came by to check on Leanna and Emma."

"John's up with them now," Tom said. "This is our eldest brother, William."

Trevor extended a hand, surprise on his face. "I'm not sure I knew there were two older brothers."

"Congratulations, darling," Geraldine said. "It came at a high price, but we have our Ripper at last."

"Afraid not," Trevor said, sitting down with a sigh. "Maybe I will take a few sausages," he said, as William slid the platter toward him. "What we have is one Micha Banasik, a hired killer who, thank God, is not very skilled at his craft."

"Hired?" Geraldine said with a gasp. "So this wasn't a random crime? Are you saying he was after Emma?"

"Leanna was his target. Just as you said last night, Tom, someone who knew she had money." Trevor looked pointedly at Tom and then William, but did not elaborate, and they both seemed to understand there was something he wished to discuss with them later, truly in private. "So no, Geraldine, we don't have our Ripper. Not yet. But I think we came very close."

"Close enough to scare him off?" Tom asked.

426

"That's exactly what Davy Mabrey thinks, that Jack may move on somewhere of his own accord. I envy you younger men your optimism, and who knows, perhaps you're right. But here's the thing. Whether the Ripper is in London or not, I fear he has opened up some sort of door that others will now walk though. He will always be with us in some form or another, just as Jesus said about the poor."

"The criminal of the future," Tom said.

"Precisely. A modern man. Death for the sake of death and this is uncharted territory for the Yard, a sort of new world order." Trevor thoughtfully chewed his sausages. "So yes, the next time I fall into my bed, which may be months from now, I will take a moment to send up a prayer asking God to please let young Tom and young Davy be right. That we have frightened Jack off and that we have – if not a conclusion, at least an ending. And if that ending is not entirely happy, it is at least one we can all live with precisely because we all lived." He looked at Geraldine. "Emma and Leanna are better today, I trust?"

"They both took breakfast."

"Good. I will give them my best before I go."

"Trevor, what would we do without you?" Geraldine said.

"Gad, Auntie, that's precisely what you said to John last night," Tom said, as Trevor left the room. "You're quite the coquette, are you not? Going from one man to another, declaring you can't live without any of them. Oh, and there's an equally good chance he might be our brother-in-law," he said to William, who turned again to look up the stairs.

"They both seem all right," William said.

"But it's true," Geraldine went on, setting down her teacup with a clatter. "We don't have a practical skill among us and Trevor and John have held us up during this whole appalling mess."

"I beg your pardon," William said, smiling. "But very soon I shall have any number of practical skills."

"Well she's right enough about me," Tom said, smiling too. "I was a detective for precisely one day and managed to sprain my ankle, dislocate my shoulder, and be knocked to my arse by a stampeding mob."

"It's lucky that we're rich," Geraldine said, with a sigh. "Come, Gage, I'll help you clean up in the kitchen. Don't look at me like that. You heard Trevor. There's a new world order."

7:45 AM

Trevor met John on the stairway, coming down. The two men looked at each other for a moment and then John dropped his bag and sat down on one of the steps.

"Congratulations," he said. "Your path is clear. All she could talk about is where Trevor could be, when Trevor is coming, how profusely she must thank Trevor."

Trevor shook his head. "It's not like that."

"Isn't it? What chance do I have now?" John Harrowman was staring up at him, mixed feelings evident on his face. "You've saved her life, for which I am abundantly grateful...."

"In the line of duty."

"Perhaps, but in the process you've become the dashing hero."

"If I saved her, I saved her for you, as you must surely be aware."

"You don't intend to court her?"

"No. I don't think I ever really did," said Trevor, realizing as he said it that it was true.

John awkwardly pushed to his feet. "I suppose you think I'm an ingrate, speaking like this after you've done so much."

"What I think is that you're exhausted and suffering from delayed shock, as are we all. No apologies are necessary. We simply go forward. You'll see to your patients and I'll see to my criminals, which we both have in endless supply."

John nodded uncertainly and walked down the stairs and out the front door. Trevor finished climbing the stairs and stood first in Emma's doorway, then Leanna's, speaking to each of them in turn. Leanna's voice was raspy and he waved her silent when she tried to thank him, and Emma had been nearly asleep, so Trevor kept the visits brief. There was nothing left to say to Leanna, not really, and the things he needed to tell Emma would wait for another day. He dallied just long enough to give John time to leave the house and to make sure Geraldine and Gage were busy in the kitchen, then he went down the stairs where Tom and William were still sitting at the breakfast table.

"We must talk," he said quietly.

"Indeed," said Tom. "We've been waiting. Who on earth hired that creature to kill Leanna?"

Trevor pulled up a chair across from them and fumbled for a way to begin.

"Micha's confessions are not the easiest to understand. His English is suspect under the best of circumstances and last night he was raving with rage and shaking with cold. He will stay in jail a long time on the charges of assault and attempted murder, so there's a chance we'll get more out of him at a later date. He claimed it was not his idea, which is probably true, and then he told us a tale that originally I found a bit hard to believe. But we've done some checking, and it seems his statements were accurate."

Trevor took a breath.

"Go on," Tom said, suspicions beginning to grow in him. William had still not looked up from his plate.

"Micha claimed he was hired by two men, one of them a local named Georgy. We had no trouble locating him, and this Georgy, in turn, claimed not to know the name of his co-conspirator. But he was quite sure of one thing. When the time came to pay Micha this second man had gotten the money by pawning something of value. Georgy lead us to the pawn shop first thing this morning and the owner did indeed remember the transaction. Not only are items of this quality a rarity in the East End, but his customer, he said, insisted upon a written receipt." Trevor reached into his pocket, withdrew his notebook, and pulled a folded piece of paper from the pages.

"You see the signature," he said, pushing the receipt toward the brothers. "Looks as if he started to write a 'C' and then thought the better of it and changed it to an 'E.' Do either of you know a man named Edmund Solmes?"

"Edmund Solmes is our brother Cecil's solicitor," William said, sinking back in his chair. "But I assure you, he wasn't the one to sign that receipt." Trevor nodded and William put a fist to his lips. "I knew Cecil had come to a desperate point but I swear to God I never thought – "

Trevor shook his head. "No one's suggesting that you did. I took the liberty of redeeming this item, which I believe belongs to your mother." He extracted a folded handkerchief from his other pocket and carefully unwrapped the opal and diamond brooch. The sight of it shattered the last remnants of Tom's composure.

"I can hardly believe it," he said. "Cecil is vain and lazy, yes, but to picture him as a murderer - "

"You only say that because you haven't been home these past months," William said. "His decline has been swift enough to rival a character in a Greek tragedy and I'm the one to blame

430

for not seeing where he was headed. So," he added, looking across the table at Trevor. "Cecil has almost killed our mother with worry and has now attempted to murder our sister outright. Please tell me you can find him."

"We'll certainly try. But I must warn you that, given his proximity to the docks the odds are he's already fled. Does he have a favorite place, friends on the continent? Somewhere he might try to go?"

"He likes Paris," William said bitterly.

"I have a colleague there I will contact," Trevor said. "But since finding him is, in the language of the tracks, a long shot, there's one more thing to discuss. Should we tell Leanna?"

"She thinks it was the Ripper," Tom said. "A random attack."

"It will come out soon enough that the man we caught isn't the Ripper," Trevor said. "But she still might accept it was a random attack. A robbery attempt, a scam built around the lie of Mary Kelly's child. That is what she is primed to believe and we could let her rest in that belief."

"And so we shall," William said decisively. "She doesn't need to hear this story and neither does our mother. Cecil always spoke of going abroad to seek a rich wife. America, isn't that where all the fortune hunters go? They'll accept that explanation for his absence readily enough."

Tom nodded at Trevor. "William's right. Mother and Leanna needn't know. "

"It's an infuriating image," William said. "Cecil in his deck chair, sailing for America."

"If he's sailing, he's hardly in a deck chair," Trevor said, turning the receipt back toward them. "Did you notice how much Cecil got for your precious family heirloom?"

Tom and William leaned toward the paper and then both erupted into laughter.

"Perfect," Tom said. "I bet he pissed his pants."

CHAPTER FORTY-NINE
8:20 AM

When Cecil Bainbridge awakened tangled in fishing nets, the irony was not entirely lost upon him. He fought his way free from his briny nest and forced open the top of the crate where he'd hidden the night before. The sun was blinding, so he lay back for a moment with the lid ajar, waiting until his eyes gradually adjusted and he could find his way out. The dock was filled with activity and Cecil crouched a few minutes more behind the crate, watching the people stream by. Not likely to see that Severin character again, he told himself. At least not in broad daylight. Finally Cecil stepped out and stretched, then began his cautious way along the waterfront.

There were a few forgotten coins left in his pants pocket. Perhaps enough for a plate of eggs or whatever people ate for breakfast in this godforsaken part of the city. The day may have been bright , but the wind coming off the water was brisk enough to send shudders through Cecil's body and he went into the first pub he could find and took a seat at the bar.

"G'day, Sir," the barmaid said.

"Is it?" Cecil was not only damp and dirty but cramped from hip to shoulder. It was nearly too much for a fastidious man to bear. But he was comforted to know that something about his presence still commanded respect from a serving girl.

He dug the coins from his pocket and placed them, in a neat line, on the counter before him.

"What can I get for this?"

"Toast 'n kippers?"

He nodded. His eyes stung with salt and sleep and the remains of last night's alcohol but down the bar a bit he could see an abandoned newspaper. An early edition, thin and

433

incomplete as they often were, but he leaned over and seized it. The headline said RIPPER THWARTED and beneath it was a picture of the stolid looking man he'd seen the night before in the Pony Pub and a sprig of a boy who apparently was his assistant. They stared out of the grainy photograph as if they had been startled by the flash.

Cecil grimly skimmed the article then dropped the paper with a sigh. Both Micha and Georgy had been taken into custody and were likely singing their story to Detective Welles at this very moment.

He'd failed. Leanna and Severin were both quite utterly alive and if one of them didn't manage to pull him down, the other doubtless would. He may as well finish his breakfast. He had paid everything he had in the world for it, and besides to his great surprise, it looked good. The kippers fried crispy, the bread fat and brown. Cecil bit into it with the concentration of a priest. There is a certain strange freedom that sets in when things have gotten as bad as they possibly can, he thought, a strange certainty that comes when there is only one thing left to do.

The answer was clear enough. Run. The continent, perhaps, for he had always been fond of Paris and Vienna. But those fair cities required scads of money and Cecil lacked even enough for a channel passage. He continued to steadily eat as he thought, not overly concerned with an analysis of where his plan had gone awry, for he suspected he would have more than enough hours ahead of him to replay the whole affair in his mind. Leanna was a damned lucky chit and perhaps that was all there was to it. He, in contrast, had apparently been cursed by the gods at birth.

He left his last coin in gratuity, more from habit than compassion, and the girl squealed "Come back again, Sir."

434

Not bloody likely, Cecil thought, as he pushed open the scarred door and walked back into the dizzying brightness of the waterfront. A dozen or so fishing ships were to be found in the first basin but he walked swiftly by these, his boots skidding on the dock. Three larger ships lay in the next basin and at the first one he was abruptly turned away. The second was christened the *Injured Pride* which seemed to be a favorable omen, and Cecil walked up the ramp. The captain was too busy pouring over a pad of paper with a stubby pencil to return his greeting, but a half-dozen or so young boys scurrying about stopped to give him a proper stare.

"May I ask when you're leaving, Sir?" Cecil began.

"You may ask and I may answer," the captain snorted, spitting into a cup. Then, glancing up, "The tide turns at two this afternoon. What's it to you?"

"Do you by any chance need an extra hand for the voyage?"

"You don't look experienced."

This was an undisputable observation, but Cecil knew he had to get out today, not tomorrow or the next. The captain turned and Cecil extended an arm to block his progress. "I won't pretend I've been to sea, but I'm twenty-four, in good health and I can learn."

The captain looked at him through rheumy blue eyes. "You haven't asked wages."

"I don't care. I'm seeking passage."

"You haven't asked where we be bound."

"I don't rightly care that either." Cecil hesitated. "Sir."

Surprisingly, this proved to be the proper answer, for the captain leaned against the ship railing and looked Cecil from top to bottom, his face contorting in contempt when his glance fell upon his supple leather boots. "Well, everyone is running from something," he finally allowed. "I daresay most of my crew didn't turn to the sea as a first choice of life's work."

I bet the Virgin you're right on that, Cecil thought, his eyes flitting from the rotting floorboards to the frayed rigging. The tub scarcely looked seaworthy.

"We're short-handed true enough, Cap'n," piped up one of the ragged boys who had been carrying provisions aboard. "What with poor Andy knockin' up that wench and Harry down with the misery and a six week passage ahead."

"Um," said the captain, his interest in the subject obviously fading fast. "So grab one of the crates below, and come aboard. What'd you say your name was?"

"Jack," Cecil blurted.

"Then fetch up a load and be quick on it. Today's your schooling and by tomorrow you'll be expected to be pulling your weight or you'll be food for the fishes, right enough."

"Aye, Sir," muttered Cecil. The crates had no handles and he struggled to get the first one aloft, nearly pitching it into the water in the process to the great amusement of the rest of the crew. "Where are we headed?" he gasped out to the boy beside him, the one he supposed he had to thank for his job.

The boy shrugged, wiping sweat from his face. "Argentina, mate."

CHAPTER FIFTY
December 4
11:45 AM

As the train sped through the slush and wet snow toward Rosemoral, Gerry tactfully napped so that John and Leanna were essentially alone in the back seat of the compartment, gazing out the broad window. He leaned forward and grasped both of her hands in his.

"Sometimes," he said. "I wonder if this is all happening too fast."

She shook her head. "It's hard to believe that just a few months ago I was a country girl, waiting weeks for a single ball, my whole life tied to the change of seasons. For that Leanna, almost any change was too fast. But now, I feel ready for whatever comes next."

"Will your mother approve of me?"

"I'm sure." It amused her to think that after all they had been through John still believed that he would have to ask her mother or her brothers for permission to court her. Just a few days earlier he'd received an anonymous benevolence from the country for his clinic, a donation which had surprised him, but which he believed was a delayed result from one of his fund-raising trips to parishes and garden clubs. The check had given him confidence, at least enough to accept her invitation to Rosemoral.

She pulled her wrap a little more tightly around her. "Do they have any tea in the dining car, do you suppose?"

"My guess would be yes," he said. As he made his way up the rattling aisle, Leanna leaned back, thinking of Rosemoral, where her mother waited with William and Tom and where she was sure certain pivotal decisions would be made before this visit was complete. It's a second chance for us all, Leanna thought. Our chance to be a completely different sort of family.

"Are you comfortable, Miss?"

She smiled up at the conductor, who stood in the compartment door. "Oh yes," she said. "It's such a lovely day for a journey, isn't it?"

The conductor was a bit taken back by this response and glanced out the window into the gloomy slush. "Is there anything you need, Mistress?" he repeated.

"I truly am - oh. Oh dear, you want my fare. Of course." Leanna stood, straightening her skirts with embarrassment. Perhaps at heart she still was an idiotic child. Now where was her purse? Geraldine was sleeping the sleep of the dead, slumped against a pile of their bags, and Leanna could not remember which one held the small blue pouch with her pounds. "Just a minute," she said, flustered. "I assure you the money is here somewhere."

John strode up behind the conductor and slipped a bill into this gloved hand. "Here, Sir, and keep the change in fair trade for the time we have cost you."

"Yes Sir, thank you Sir," the conductor said, beaming at Leanna as though she were the Queen. Then he left them alone and both John and Leanna began to laugh.

"You never seem to have any money."

"So you do remember the first time we met."

"Oh course. I saw you fumbling about in your bag and thought 'Now here's a girl who needs my help.' And there is nothing on earth so irresistible to a man as a girl who needs his help." He leaned over and kissed her roughly on the cheek. "Why are you smiling like that?"

"Sit down, John," Leanna said. "There's something we need to discuss."

12: 15 PM

"Trevor," Emma said with surprise, opening the door a bit wider. "You just missed them. They took the 11 o'clock train."

"I know," Trevor said. He stood on the stoop to remove his coat, which was half crusted over with the first snow of winter. "I actually dropped by to visit you."

"And caught me lazing, I'm afraid," she laughed as he stepped in. "It's so rare to have the house to myself. Or almost to myself, for Gage is quiet as the proverbial mouse." She looked at Trevor more seriously. "So you deliberately missed the chance to say goodbye?"

"My God, are my feelings that plain on my face?"

Emma smiled. "Yes, yes they are."

"Very well then, my dear detective of the heart, I'll confess to you that it will be difficult at first if they do indeed return from the countryside engaged, but I can't very well say it's unexpected, can I? Things always end as they should. People end up partnered as they should. None among us can fight his fate."

Emma could think of nothing to add to this. "I was just about to have a bit of lunch. Would you join me?"

"Thought you'd never ask," said Trevor, following her into the cozy parlor and seating himself on the huge armchair Gerry normally secured. The parlor was warmed by a roaring fire and he propped up his feet and was seized almost at once with the feelings of peace and homecoming which engulfed his senses whenever he entered this particular house. Odd, he had always thought it was Geraldine who radiated the comfort and security, but she was miles away. It must have been Emma all along who had made this house a home. The knowledge surprised him, but it was not displeasing.

Emma returned within minutes, carrying a tray of fruit, cold meats and cheese. "I hear congratulations are in order. Another Ripper has confessed, according to the morning papers."

"Yes, we're up to thirty-seven at last count. This one was a bit dramatic, by any standards. A public hanging, yesterday, of a man who had gleefully admitted to poisoning his mistress. He's up on the scaffolding and just as the trap door opens, he yells 'I am Jack the...' That's it, the neck is broken, the crowd is in hysterics. They like to watch them go down but this was a bit more of the excitement than anyone bargained for."

"Could there be any truth to it?" Emma asked, slicing a bit of cheese and popping it in her mouth.

"No, he was in America when the first three murders were committed. Just a ploy to get his name in the history books, I gather. Poor sots. Some of their confessions are quite convincing."

"And what of the others? The one whose friends committed him to the asylum? Or the man who threw himself into the river?"

Trevor's face changed, grew somber and dark. "Both legitimate possibilities and growing more plausible each day that passes without a murder. If a man commits suicide, or is quietly put away, and then the killings stop we will probably conclude, by default, that our Ripper has been caught."

"Or was simply scared off, which has the same effect." Emma said, speaking with surprising detachment of the man who had murdered her sister. "But either way, the case stays open for all eternity, just as Madame Renata predicted it would on the evening of the dinner party. Could that have been just four months ago? It seems more like a lifetime."

"I owe you an apology," Trevor said. "I never came to see you after Mary died."

She shrugged. "You blamed yourself."

440

They sat for a moment, concentrating on their food. Finally, Emma spoke again.

"But life goes on, does it not? The heart doesn't really break at all."

"Do you think he will be enough for her?"

It was an abrupt shift of topic, but she knew his meaning at once. "I don't know. He sees things rather simply."

"And perhaps in time it might become tedious to find yourself married to a saint?"

"Well, if he isn't enough on his own, she won't rest until she makes him so. We women are like that, Detective Welles. Men are our careers. We read things into them, we convince ourselves that our devotion in and of itself is enough to lift them to a higher level. Leanna will convert John into whatever sort of man she needs him to be."

"It is your gender's highest accomplishment."

"Really? I would have said it's our greatest failing." Emma turned her chin toward Trevor. "Do you mind if I ask you a very personal question?"

He snorted. "I think you've earned the right."

"What bothers you more, losing the Ripper or losing Leanna?"

"Now don't laugh…"

"I seriously doubt that I shall."

"…but I think they were somewhat bound together in my mind. Get the killer, get the girl, as if I were a character in a penny dreadful. Instead, it's almost as if I lost them both in the same moment."

"You learned that some things matter more to you than solving crimes."

Trevor winced. "Which makes me a bad detective."

"I don't agree."

"So Leanna goes to John, the Ripper goes into the darkness, and I am left with gratification of knowing that in the moment of decision, I opted to save a human life."

"I assume Leanna thanked you."

"Copiously." He looked at her out of the corner of his eye. "But if memory serves, the life I saved was yours."

"Only by mistake. You dove in after Leanna and came up from the water with me."

He shook his head. "I saw more than you think that night on the pier."

She was sorry she'd been so harsh. He had rescued her, no matter how or for precisely what reason, and she could not say exactly why she fought that knowledge or found it so difficult to express her gratitude. We are too much alike, Trevor and I, she thought. We can't stop wanting things we'll never have. We claim to be creatures of intellect, and yet we have both made dreadful mistakes of logic. In the moment of truth, we both follow our hearts instead of our heads, and life will pound us over and over for this frailty, the way waves repeatedly pound against rocks.

She struggled for a way to change the subject. "I understand you have the funds for your forensic laboratory."

"Yes," Trevor said, brightening. "Can you imagine? From the Queen herself, no less. Someday I may go to France as well."

"C'est merveilleux."

"You speak French?"

"You forget that my father was a schoolmaster. He taught all three of his children any number of useless skills, especially in the area of linguistics."

"It wouldn't be useless in Paris. Abrams writes that they insist on speaking French there."

"How very unreasonable of them."

442

"Those papers on forensic technique… Could you possibly have a look at them? And then… I know I'm thick and slow to learn, but even a phrase or two would help. Would you teach me?"

"Oui. Naturellement."

"We don't have to start right now," Trevor said, cramming a bit of cheese into his mouth. "Here's the thing, Emma. Rayley Abrams is already in Paris and Davy Mabrey has shown such promise… I need a physician to serve as coroner, someone who isn't a million years old like Phillips, and then I'll have it, the beginnings of my forensics team. The lad I was considering just told me he's had his fill of London and plans to decamp with his fiancé for that paradise known as New Jersey." Trevor chuckled. "Now, don't scoff, but I've been thinking of asking Tom to join us. His actions that night may have been misguided but they showed a lot of courage. Trying to kick in the door where Harrowman was delivering the baby, that sort of thing."

Emma sat silent.

Trevor frowned. "You think he's too young, don't you?"

"Young may be better. No bad habits to unlearn."

"Quite. He's a boy in many ways, but he has his qualities."

"I agree. He has his qualities."

He tilted his head to observe her face more closely. "It occurs to me my team will need a linguist."

Emma's lips turned up. "Indeed."

"Oh, I'm quite serious, especially if we train in Paris and then take cases all over the continent. That's what the Queen envisions, you know. That when there's an unsolvable crime anywhere in the world, the authorities will scratch their heads and say 'We must bring the forensics team from Scotland Yard.'"

"Complete with the schoolteacher's daughter."

"Whyever not? The Yard employs women in any number of ways when there's a task the men simply can't assume. Off the record, of course."

"You mean as spies."

"A harsh word, my dear." Trevor thoughtfully bit into a pear. "When did you begin to wear your hair down? It's lovely. How would someone say that in French?"

"You think this will help you in forensic research, to be able to tell the French women they have lovely hair?"

It was not terribly witty banter, and yet they both laughed, and in the laughter certain things began to shift between them. Emma said something in French and Trevor tried to repeat it, failing so badly that they both continued to chuckle. Gage was about to go out the front door on his way to the market but there was something in the tone of their conversation that made him freeze in his tracks. He stood very still for a moment, eavesdropping, smiling. Then he walked through the kitchen and went out another way.

Historical Note

Several of the characters in City of Darkness are based upon real historical figures. The six murders in the book are fictionalized accounts of slayings credited to Jack the Ripper, including the names, dates, and crime scene details. Although Jack the Ripper was never caught, the villain of City of Darkness was an actual man and is considered by Ripperologists – as Jack devotees are known– as one of the most likely suspects. The methodologies used by Scotland Yard, as well as their limitations, are reflective of the late Victorian period.

All members of the Scotland Yard forensics team are entirely fictional, as are the members of the Bainbridge family. Victoria, of course, is real and did indeed take a surprising degree of interest in police matters during her reign, including the specifics of the Ripper case. Although I imagined the conversation between the Queen and Trevor, the suggestions she makes to him in that scene are based on a letter Victoria sent to Scotland Yard in 1888.

Other Stories in the "City of Mystery" Series

Volume II, City of Light, follows Rayley Abrams to Paris, a city swept up in excitement over the Exposition Universelle, the World's Fair which debuted Edison's phonograph, Buffalo Bill's Wild West show, and the Eiffel Tower. But when bodies begin to wash up on the shores on the Seine and a socialite goes missing, members of the newly formed Scotland Yard forensics unit find themselves thrust in the middle of their first international mystery. City of Light is currently available on Amazon.

City of Silence, the third installment in the City of Mystery series, is set in St. Petersburg at Christmastime. The Queen's beloved granddaughter Alexandra is determined to marry the young tsarevich Nicholas, but Victoria has doubts about how well her sheltered and naïve "Alecy" will fare in the venomous court of Imperial Russia. When a young dancing instructor with ties to the royal family is found murdered in a most bizarre fashion, Trevor and the Scotland Yard forensics unit will travel to the Czar's Winter Palace to investigate. City of Silence will be available in December.

If you'd like to receive notification of further publications of the series, join the City of Mystery Facebook page or send your email address to cityofmystery@gmail.com.